DEVILISH
D'ANGELOS

ITALIAN BACHELORS
COLLECTION

July 2017

August 2017

September 2017

October 2017

November 2017

December 2017

Italian BACHELORS

CAROLE MORTIMER

MILLS & BOON

Published in Great Britain 2017
By Mills & Boon, an imprint of HarperCollins*Publishers*
1 London Bridge Street, London, SE1 9GF

ITALIAN BACHELORS: DEVILISH D'ANGELOS © 2017 Harlequin Books S.A.

A Bargain with the Enemy © 2014 Carole Mortimer
A Prize Beyond Jewels © 2014 Carole Mortimer
A D'Angelo Like No Other © 2014 Carole Mortimer

ISBN: 978-0-263-93136-5

09-1217

Our policy is to use papers that are natural, renewable and recyclable products and made from wood grown in sustainable forests.
The logging and manufacturing processes conform to the legal environmental regulations of the country of origin.

Printed and bound in Spain
by CPI, Barcelona

A BARGAIN WITH
THE ENEMY
CAROLE MORTIMER

To my six wonderful sons.
I am so proud of you all.

Carole Mortimer was born in England, the youngest of three children. She began writing in 1978, and has now written two hundred books. Carole has six sons, Matthew, Joshua, Timothy, Michael, David and Peter. She says, 'I'm happily married to Peter senior; we're best friends as well as lovers, which is probably the best recipe for a successful relationship. We live in a lovely part of England.'

PROLOGUE

'Don't worry, Mik, he'll be here.'

'Take your damned feet off the desk,' Michael snapped in reply to his brother's reassurance, not even glancing up from the papers he was currently reading in the study at Archangel's Rest, the secluded Berkshire home of the D'Angelo family. 'And I'm not worried.'

'Like hell you're not!' Rafe drawled lazily, making no effort to swing his black-booted feet down from where they rested on the front of his older brother's desk.

'I'm really not, Rafe,' Michael assured mildly.

'Do you know if—?'

'I'm sure it can't have escaped your notice that I'm trying to read!' Michael sighed his impatience as he glared across the desk. He was dressed formally, as usual, in a pale blue shirt and neatly knotted navy blue silk tie, dark waistcoat and tailored trousers, the jacket to his suit draped over the back of his leather chair.

It had always been something of a family joke that their mother had chosen to name her three sons Michael, Raphael and Gabriel to go with the surname D'Angelo, and the three brothers had certainly taken their fair share of teasing about it when they were at boarding school. Not so much now they were all in their thirties, and the three of them had been able to utilise their names by making the three Archangel auction houses and galleries in London, New York and Paris the most prestigious privately owned galleries in the world.

Their grandfather, Carlo D'Angelo, had managed to bring his wealth with him when he fled Italy and settled in England almost seventy years ago before marrying an English girl, and producing a son, Giorgio: Michael, Raphael and Gabriel's father.

Like his father before him, Giorgio had been an astute businessman, opening the first Archangel auction house and gallery in London thirty years ago, and adding to the D'Angelo wealth. When Giorgio retired ten years ago and he and his wife Ellen settled permanently in their Florida home, their three sons had turned that comfortable wealth into a veritable fortune by opening up similar Archangel galleries in New York and Paris, resulting in them now all being millionaires many times over.

'And don't call me Mik,' Michael instructed harshly as he continued to read from the file in front of him. 'You know how much I hate it.'

Of course Rafe knew that, and he considered it part of his job description as a younger brother to annoy the hell out of his older sibling!

Not that he had as many opportunities to do that nowadays with the three brothers usually at a different gallery at any one time. But they always made a point of meeting up for Christmas and each of their birthdays, and today was Michael's thirty-fifth birthday. Rafe was a year younger and Gabriel, the 'baby' of the family, another year younger at thirty-three.

'I last spoke to Gabriel a week or so ago.' Rafe made a face.

'Why the grimace?' Michael quirked a dark brow.

'No reason in particular—we all know that Gabe's

been in a bad mood for the past five years. I never understood the attraction myself.' He shrugged. 'She looked a mousy little thing to me, with just those big—'

'Rafe!' Michael cautioned in a growl.

'—grey eyes to recommend her,' Rafe completed dryly.

Michael's mouth thinned. 'I spoke to Gabriel two days ago.'

'And?' Rafe prompted impatiently when it became obvious his older brother was doing his usual clam impersonation.

Michael shrugged. 'And he said he would arrive here in time for dinner this evening.'

'Why the hell couldn't you have just told me that earlier?'

Rafe swung his booted feet impatiently down onto the carpeted floor before rising restlessly to his feet. He ran an irritated hand through the short thickness of his sable-dark hair as he paced the room, tall and leanly muscled in a fitted black T-shirt and faded denims. 'That would have been too easy, I suppose.' He paused his pacing to glower at his older brother.

'No doubt.' Michael gave the ghost of a smile, eyes dark and unreadable, also as usual.

The three brothers had similar colouring, height and build; all a couple inches over six feet tall, with the same sable-black hair. Michael kept his hair short, his eyes so dark a brown they gleamed black and unfathomable.

Rafe's hair was long enough to curl down onto his shoulders, his eyes so pale a brown they glowed a deep gold.

'Well?' he rasped impatiently as Michael added nothing to his earlier statement.

'Well, what?' His brother arched an arrogant brow as he relaxed back in his leather chair.

'How was he?'

Michael shrugged. 'As you said, as bad tempered as ever.'

Rafe grimaced. 'You two are the pot and the kettle!'

'I'm not bad tempered, Rafe, I just don't choose to suffer fools gladly.'

He raised dark brows. 'I trust I wasn't included in that sweeping statement…?'

'Hardly.' Michael relaxed slightly. 'And I prefer to think of all three of us as perhaps being just a little… intense.'

Some of Rafe's own tension eased as he gave a rueful grin in acknowledgement of the probable reason none of them had ever married. The women they met were more often than not attracted to that dangerous edge so prevalent in the D'Angelo men, as much as they were to their obvious wealth. Obviously not a basis for a relationship other than the purely—or not so purely!—physical.

'Maybe,' he conceded dryly. 'So what's in the file you've been looking at so intently since I arrived?'

'Ah.' Michael grimaced.

Rafe eyed him warily. 'Why do I have the feeling I'm not going to like this…?'

'Probably because you aren't.' His brother turned the file around and pushed it across the desk.

Rafe read the name at the top of the file. 'And who might Bryn Jones be?'

'One of the entrants for the New Artists Exhibition being held at the London gallery next month,' Michael supplied tersely.

'Damn it, *that's* the reason you knew Gabriel would be back today!' He glared at his brother. 'I'd totally forgotten that Gabriel's taking over from you in London during the organisation of the exhibition.'

'And I get to go to Paris for a while, yes,' Michael drawled with satisfaction.

'Intending to see the beautiful Lisette while you're there?' He eyed his brother knowingly.

Michael's mouth tightened. 'Who?'

The dismissive tone of his brother's voice was enough to tell Rafe that Michael's relationship with the 'beautiful Lisette' was not only over, but already forgotten. 'So what's so special about this Bryn Jones that you have a security file on him?'

Rafe knew there had to be a reason for Michael's interest in this particular artist. There had been dozens of eager applicants for the New Artists Exhibition; since Gabriel had organised the first one in Paris three months ago and it had been such a success, they had decided to go ahead and hold a similar one in London next month.

'Bryn Jones is a she,' Michael corrected dryly.

Rafe's brows rose. 'I see....'

'Somehow I doubt that,' his brother drawled dismissively. 'Maybe this picture will help....' Michael lifted the top sheet of paper to pull out a black and white photograph. 'I had Security download the image from one of the security discs at Archangel yesterday—' which explained the slightly grainy quality of the picture '—when she came into the gallery to personally deliver her portfolio to Eric Sanders.' Eric was their in-house art expert at the London gallery.

Rafe picked up the photograph so that he could take a closer look at the young woman pictured coming through the glass doors into the marbled entrance hall of the London gallery.

She was probably in her early to mid-twenties. The

black-and-white photograph made it difficult to tell her exact colouring. Her just-below-ear-length hair, in a perky flicked-up style, looked to be light in shade, her appearance businesslike in a dark jacket and knee-length skirt, with a pale blouse beneath the jacket—none of which detracted in the least from the curvaceous body beneath!

She had a hauntingly beautiful face, Rafe acknowledged as he continued to study the photograph: heart-shaped, eyes light in colour, pert little nose between high cheekbones, her lips full and poutingly sensual with a delicately pointed chin above the slenderness of her throat.

A very arresting, and slightly familiar, face.

'Why do I have the feeling that I know her?' Rafe asked, lifting his head.

'Probably because you do. We all do,' Michael added tersely. 'Try imagining her slightly more...rounded, with heavy, black-framed glasses, and long mousy-brown hair.'

'Doesn't sound like the sort of woman any of us would ever be attracted to—' Rafe broke off abruptly, his gaze narrowing sharply, suspiciously, on the black-and-white photograph in front of him.

'Oh, yes.... I forgot to mention that perhaps you should look closely at...the eyes,' Michael drawled dryly.

Rafe glanced up quickly. 'It can't be! Can it?' He studied the photograph more closely. 'Are you saying this beautiful woman is Sabryna Harper?'

'Yes,' Michael bit out crisply.

'William Harper's daughter?'

'The same.' Michael nodded grimly.

Rafe's jaw tightened as he easily recalled the uproar five years ago when William Harper had offered a supposedly previously unknown Turner for sale at their London gallery. Ordinarily the painting would have remained a secret until after authentication had been made and confirmed by the experts, but somehow its existence had been leaked to the press, sending the art world and the media into an excited frenzy as speculation about the painting's authenticity became rife.

Gabriel had been in charge of the London gallery at the time, had gone to the Harper family home several times to discuss the painting while it was being authenticated, meeting both the wife and daughter of William Harper on those occasions. This made it doubly difficult for him when he'd had to declare the painting, having undergone extensive examination by the experts they had brought in from all over the world, to be a near-perfect forgery. Worse than that, the police investigation had proved that William Harper was solely responsible for the forgery, resulting in the other man being arrested and sent to prison for his crime.

His wife and teenage daughter had been hounded by the media throughout the trial and the whole sorry story had blown up again when Harper had died in prison just four months later, after which his wife and daughter had simply disappeared.

Until now, it would seem....

Rafe eyed Michael warily. 'Are you absolutely sure it's her?'

'The file you're looking at is from the private investigator I hired after I saw her at the gallery yesterday—'

'You *spoke* to her?'

Michael shook his head. 'I was passing through the entrance hall when Eric walked by with her. As I said, I thought I recognised her, and the private investigator was able to establish that Mary Harper resumed using her maiden name just weeks after her husband's death, and her daughter's surname was changed to the same by deed poll.'

'And this Bryn Jones is really her?'

'Yes.'

'And what do you intend doing about it?'

'Doing about what?'

Rafe breathed his impatience with his brother's continued calm. 'Well, she obviously can't be one of the six new artists exhibited at Archangel next month.'

Michael raised dark brows. 'Why can't she?'

'Well, for one thing her father was put in prison for attempting to involve one of our galleries in selling a forged painting!' He eyed his brother. 'Not only that, but Gabriel went to court and helped to put him there!'

'And the sins of the father are to be passed down onto the daughter, is that it?'

'No, of course that isn't it! But—with a father like that, how do you even know the paintings in her portfolio are her own?'

'They are.' Michael nodded. 'It's all in the file. She attained a first-class arts degree. Has been trying to sell her paintings to other galleries for the past two years with very little success. I've looked at her portfolio, Rafe, and, despite what those other galleries may have thought, she's good. More than good, she's original, which is probably why the other galleries refused to take a chance on her work. Their loss is our gain. So much so that I have every intention of buying a Bryn Jones painting for my own collection.'

'She's going to be one of the final six artists?'

'Without a doubt.'

'And what about Gabriel?'

'What about him?'

'We warned him repeatedly but he refused to listen. She's the reason he's been in a bad mood for five years— how do you think he's going to feel when he realises exactly who Bryn Jones really is?' Rafe bit out exasperatedly.

'Well, I think you'll agree, she's definitely improved with age!' Michael said dryly.

There was no doubt about that. 'This is just— Damn it, Michael!'

Michael's mouth firmed. 'Bryn Jones is a very talented artist, and she deserves her chance of being exhibited at Archangel.'

'Have you even stopped to think *why* she might be doing this?' Rafe frowned. 'That she might have some ulterior motive, maybe some sort of revenge plot against us or Gabriel for what happened to her father?'

'It did occur to me, yes.' Michael nodded calmly.

'And?'

He shrugged. 'I'm willing to give her the benefit of the doubt at this stage.'

'And Gabriel?'

'Has assured me on numerous occasions that he's an adult, and certainly doesn't need his big brother interfering in his life, thank you very much!' Michael drawled dryly.

Rafe gave an exasperated shake of his head as he began pacing the study. 'You seriously don't intend to tell Gabriel who she is?'

'As I said, not at this stage,' Michael confirmed. 'Do you?'

Rafe had no idea yet what he was going to do with this information....

CHAPTER ONE

One week later...

SHE WAS ENTERING the enemy camp—again!—Bryn realised with a frown as she paused outside on the pavement to look up at the marble frontispiece of the biggest and the best of the privately owned galleries and auction houses in London, the name Archangel in large gold italics glittering in the sunlight above the wide glass entrance doors. Doors that swung open automatically as she stepped forward before walking purposefully into the high-ceilinged entrance hall.

Purposefully, because this really was the enemy camp as far as Bryn was concerned. The D'Angelos, Gabriel in particular, had been responsible for both breaking her heart and sending her father to prison five years ago....

She couldn't think of that now, couldn't allow herself to think of that now. She had to focus on the fact that the past two years of rejection from gallery after gallery were what had brought her to this desperate moment. The same two years, after leaving university with her degree, when she had believed the world was now her oyster, only to learn that the recognition she craved for her paintings was ever elusive.

Many of her friends from university had caved to the

pressure of family and stretched finances and entered advertising or teaching instead of following their real dream of painting for a living. But not Bryn. Oh, no, she had stuck doggedly to her desire to have her paintings exhibited in a London gallery, believing that one day she would be able to make her mother proud of her and erase the shame of her family's past.

Two years later she had been forced to admit defeat, not by abandoning her paintings, but by being left with no choice but to enter the New Artists competition at Archangel.

'Miss Jones?'

She turned to look enquiringly at one of the two receptionists sitting behind the elegant cream-and-rose marble desk, which was an exact match for the rest of the marbled entrance hall; several huge columns in the same marble stretched from floor to ceiling, with beautiful glass cabinets protecting the priceless artefacts and magnificent jewellery on display.

And this was only the entrance hall; Bryn knew from her previous visit to the Archangel Gallery that the six salons leading off this vast hallway all housed yet more unique and beautiful treasures, and there were many more being prepared for auction in the vast basement beneath the building.

She straightened, determined not to be intimidated— or at least not to *reveal* that she was intimidated—by her elegant surroundings, or by the cool blonde and elegant receptionist who couldn't be much older than her own twenty-three years. 'Yes, I'm Miss Jones.'

'Linda,' the other woman supplied as she stood up from behind the desk and walked across the entrance hall, the three-inch heels of her black shoes clicking on

the marble floor as she joined a hesitant Bryn still standing near the doorway.

Bryn felt distinctly underdressed in the fitted black
trousers and loose flowered silk shirt she had chosen to
wear for her second meeting with Eric Sanders, the gallery's in-house art expert. 'I have an appointment with
Mr Sanders,' she supplied softly.

Linda nodded. 'If you would care to follow me to the
lift? Mr D'Angelo left instructions for me to take you
upstairs to his office as soon as you arrived.'

Bryn instantly stiffened, her feet suddenly feeling so
leaden they appeared to have become weighted to the
marble floor. 'My appointment is with Mr Sanders.'

Linda turned with a swish of that perfectly groomed
blonde hair as she realised Bryn wasn't following her.
'Mr D'Angelo is conducting the interviews this morning.'

Bryn's tongue felt as if it were stuck to the roof of
her suddenly dry mouth. 'Mr D'Angelo?' she managed
to squeak.

The older woman nodded. 'One of the three brothers
who own this gallery.' Bryn knew exactly who the three
D'Angelo brothers were. She just had no idea which one
Linda was referring to when she said 'Mr D'Angelo'.
The haughty and cold Michael? The arrogant playboy
Raphael? Or the cruel Gabriel, who had taken her naive
heart and trampled all over it?

It didn't really matter which of the D'Angelo brothers it was; they were all arrogant and ruthless as far as
Bryn was concerned, and she wouldn't have come within
twenty feet of a single one of them if not for the fact that
she was as determined to become one of the six artists
chosen to take part in the Archangel New Artists Exhibition next month, as she was desperate.

She gave a slow shake of her head. 'I think there's

been some sort of mistake.' She frowned. 'Mr Sanders' secretary phoned me and made the appointment.'

'Because Mr D'Angelo was out of the country at the time,' Linda said, nodding.

Bryn could only stand and stare at the other woman, wondering if it was too late for her to just cut and run while she still had the chance....

Gabriel rested his elbows on his desktop as he watched the link to the security camera in the entrance hall of the gallery on his laptop.

He had recognised Bryn Jones the moment she entered the gallery, of course. Seen the way she hesitated, before her expression turned to one of confusion as Linda spoke to her, followed by total stillness as her face went completely blank, making it easy for Gabriel to guess the moment Linda had told her that her appointment this morning was now with him rather than Eric.

Bryn Jones...

Or, more accurately, Sabryna Harper.

The last time Gabriel had seen Sabryna had been five years ago, day after day across a crowded courtroom. She had glared her dislike of him with glittering but velvet-soft dove-grey eyes from behind dark-framed glasses every time she so much as glanced at him. And she had glanced at him a lot!

Sabryna Harper had only been eighteen at the time, her figure voluptuously rounded, her manner a little clumsy and self-conscious, light brown hair growing silky and straight to just below her shoulders, dark-framed glasses making her eyes appear large and vulnerable. A vulnerability and appeal that Gabriel had been inexplicably drawn to.

Her figure had slimmed down to a svelte elegance that

was shown to full advantage in a loose floral blouse and fitted trousers. The light brown hair looked as if it had been given blonde highlights, as well as being expertly cut and styled as it winged out perkily about her ears, nape and creamy, smooth brow. And she had dispensed with the dark-framed glasses, probably in favour of contact lenses. She also possessed a new self-confidence that had allowed her to walk into Archangel with purpose and determination.

The loss of weight was even more noticeable in her face; there were now slight hollows in her cheeks, revealing sculptured cheekbones either side of a pert little nose. Her mouth— Thank God Rafe had warned him about that sexy mouth. As it was, he had an arousal that would need several minutes to subside—the same minutes it would take Linda to bring Bryn Jones to his office, he hoped.

Would Gabriel have recognised this beautiful and confident young woman as the Sabryna Harper of five years ago if Rafe hadn't prewarned him of her real identity, after Michael had decided to act with his usual arrogance by remaining silent on the subject?

Oh, yes, Gabriel had no doubts he would have recognised Sabryna. Voluptuous or slender, glasses or no glasses, slightly gauche or elegantly poised, he would have known Sabryna under any guise she cared to take on.

The question was, would she betray by word or deed that she remembered him too?

Delicious, decadent, sinful, melted-chocolate brown. It was the only way to describe the colour of Gabriel D'Angelo's eyes, Bryn acknowledged with self-disgust as, Linda having delivered her to his office, she now stood in front of the marble desk looking at the man she had long considered her nemesis. The man who, with the whiplash of his arrogant and ruthless tongue, had not only helped to send her father to prison, but also succeeded in killing Sabryna Harper and necessitating that Bryn Jones rise from her ashes.

The same man that the youthful Sabryna had been beguiled by, kissed by and lost her heart to five years ago.

The same man who only weeks later had stood in a courtroom and condemned her father to prison.

The same man that Sabryna had looked at across that courtroom and known that she still wanted, despite what he was doing to her father. Just looking at him had aroused her when she should have felt nothing but hatred for him, robbing her of both breath and speech.

A reaction, a dangerous attraction, that in the years that followed Bryn had convinced herself she hadn't felt. That the emotions that had bombarded her whenever she looked at him must have been dislike, perhaps even hate, because she couldn't have still been attracted to him after what he had done to her family.

One look at him now and Bryn knew that she had been lying to herself for all these years; that Gabriel D'Angelo, despite being the one man she should never have been attracted to, never have allowed herself to be flattered by or allowed to kiss her, had then, and still now, held a dangerous fascination for her.

So much so that she could feel how his overpowering presence managed to dominate the dramatic and opulent elegance of the huge office with floor-to-ceiling windows looking out over the London skyline and original artwork adorning all of the delicate pink-silk-covered walls.

Gabriel D'Angelo…

A man who should by now—Bryn had many times

wished it so!—be balding, running to fat, with lines of dissipation etched into his overbloated and self-indulgent face.

Instead, he was still well over six feet of taut, lean muscle, all shown to advantage in a dark and tailored designer-label suit that probably cost as much as a year of Bryn's university fees! And his hair was just as thick and dark as she remembered it too, brushed casually back from his face to fall in silky ebony waves to just below the collar of his cream silk shirt.

As for his face...!

It was the face of a male model. The sort of face that women of all ages would have drooled over before buying whatever it was he was selling; a high intelligent brow above those sinful brown eyes, his nose aquiline, cheekbones high and sharply defined against light olive skin—with not a line in sight, of dissipation or otherwise! He had perfect chiselled lips—the top one fuller than the bottom—and the strong line of his jaw was exactly as Bryn remembered it: square and ruthlessly determined.

'Miss Jones.' His cultured voice, as Bryn had discovered five years ago, wasn't in the least accented, as might have been expected from his name, but was as English as her own. The same deep and husky rumble of a voice that had once caused Bryn's knees to quake, and had still done so even as she had listened to that voice condemn her father and seal his fate.

Bryn almost took a step back as Gabriel D'Angelo stood up and moved out from behind the marble desk. She managed to stand her ground as she realised he had only risen to his feet in order to hold out his hand to her in greeting. A lean and elegant hand totally in keeping with the strength Bryn could discern in every leanly muscled inch of him.

The sort of strength that she had no doubts was capable of crushing every bone in her own much smaller hand, if he chose to exert it.

Bryn gave an inward jolt as she realised he was studying her just as closely through narrowed lids, those melted chocolate-brown eyes appearing to see everything and miss nothing.

Would he recognise her as Sabryna Harper? Somehow she doubted it, given the fact that the gauche Sabryna, despite Gabriel having kissed her once, would have made very little impact on the life of a man like Gabriel D'Angelo, and there would have been so many other women in his life—and his bed!—during the past five years.

Besides which, her name was different, and she looked dramatically different: she was twenty pounds lighter, her hair was now cut short with blonde highlights, her face thinner, more angled, and she wore contact lenses rather than dark-framed glasses.

But was it possible—could Gabriel D'Angelo have recognised her, despite those changes?

Bryn moved one sweat-dampened hand surreptitiously against the thigh of her trousers before raising it with the intention of brushing it as briefly as possible against his much larger hand. A move Gabriel D'Angelo instantly circumvented as those long, lean fingers closed firmly about, and retained hold, of Bryn's—instantly renewing and deepening that jolt of electricity, the sexual awareness, as it throbbed from his hand into hers, moving the length of her arm before settling in the fullness of her breasts, causing her nipples to tingle and harden beneath her blouse.

A jolt that Gabriel D'Angelo also felt, if the tightening

of his fingers about hers and the increased narrowing of those captivating eyes, was any indication.

'We meet at last, Miss Jones,' Gabriel murmured as he deliberately continued to hold the slenderness of her hand firmly within his own.

Bryn blinked, her expression suddenly wary, those dove-grey eyes even more beautiful now that they weren't hidden behind glasses. 'I—I'm not sure what you mean.'

Gabriel wasn't completely sure what he meant either!

Rafe's advice, when the two brothers had met for dinner before he flew back to New York five days ago, had been that the easiest and best way for Gabriel to avoid any further unpleasantness with the Harper family was to simply tell Eric Sanders to take Bryn Jones off the list of possible candidates for the upcoming New Artists Exhibition.

And on a professional level Gabriel understood exactly why his brother had given him that advice; given the circumstances of his past history with her late father William Harper, it was sound, even necessary, advice.

Except...

Gabriel had a history with Bryn too. Brief, admittedly, just a stolen kiss when he had driven her home from visiting Archangel one evening, but he had hoped for more at the time, had thought of Bryn often the past five years, had wondered, speculated, what would have become of the two of them if not for the scandal that had ripped them apart.

Gabriel wasn't in the least proud of the part he had played in the events of five years ago. Not William Harper's conviction and incarceration for fraud, his death in prison just months later or the way in which his wife and teenage daughter had been hounded and harassed during the whole ordeal.

Against his brother's advice Gabriel had tried to see Sabryna, both during the trial and after her father was sent to prison, but she had turned him away every time, refusing to answer the door to him and changing her number so he couldn't call her either. Gabriel had decided to step back, to give her time, before approaching her again. And then William Harper had died in prison, putting an end to any hopes Gabriel might have had for himself and Sabryna ever having a relationship.

He had also taken an objective look, a purely professional look, over the past few days at the paintings Bryn Jones had submitted to the competition. They were really good—her still-life paintings so delicately executed it was almost possible for him to smell the rose petals falling gently down from the vase. To want to reach out and touch the ethereal beauty in a woman's eyes as she looked down at the baby she held in her arms.

Gabriel could see genuine talent in every brush stroke, the sort of rare artistic talent that would one day make Bryn Jones' paintings highly collectable, as both objects of beauty as well as a sound investment. Because of this Gabriel didn't feel he could eliminate her as a candidate for the New Artists Exhibition just to save himself from the discomfort of facing her and having her hate every breath of air he took.

He did, however, have every intention of keeping the question of Bryn Jones' own motivation for entering the competition in the forefront of any of his future dealings with her.

Gabriel released her hand abruptly before moving to retake his seat behind the desk, very aware that his earlier arousal had returned with a vengeance the moment he had touched the silky softness of Bryn's hand. 'I was referring to the fact that you're the seventh, and last, can-

didate to have been interviewed in the past two days.'
The only candidate that Gabriel was interviewing personally, but she didn't need to know that.

Her cheeks slowly paled. 'The *seventh* candidate?'

He gave a dismissive shrug. 'It's always best to have a reserve, don't you think?'

She was a *reserve*?

Bryn had been so desperate she had swallowed her pride, her dislike of all things D'Angelo, to enter their damned competition, only to be told she was a reserve?

Bryn had thought—*believed*—that being asked to come in to Archangel for another interview meant that she had been chosen as one of the final six artists for the Archangel New Artists Exhibition. And now Gabriel D'Angelo was telling her she was a reserve! Like an actor who was expected to learn all the lines and then stand in the wings of the theatre every night, in the full knowledge they might never have the chance to appear on the stage!

Had she been recognised after all? And if she had, was this Gabriel D'Angelo's idea of amusing himself, of extracting further retribution for the scandal her father had brought upon the Archangel Gallery, and the three brothers who owned it, five years ago?

'Are you quite well, Miss Jones?' A frown now creased Gabriel's brow as he stood up once again and moved round the desk. 'You've gone very pale....'

No, Bryn wasn't 'well'. In fact she was feeling far from well! So much so that she didn't even attempt to back away as Gabriel moved far too close to her. She had swallowed her pride, risked everything, the whole persona and life she had made for herself these past five years, by even bringing herself to the attention of the

D'Angelo brothers, only to now be told she wasn't good enough!

'I— Is it possible I could have a glass of water?' She raised a slightly shaking hand up to the dampness of her brow.

'Of course.' Gabriel was still frowning darkly as he strode across to the bar.

She was a reserve.

How disappointing was that?

How humiliating was that?

Damn it, she had been living in a state of nervous tension since entering the competition and this was the thanks she got at the end of all that anxiety, all that swallowed pride: to be made the reserve artist for the Exhibition!

'I've changed my mind about the water,' she snapped tautly as she straightened. 'Do you have any whisky in there?'

Gabriel turned slowly, eyes narrowing as he saw that colour had returned to Bryn Jones' cheeks, her eyes taking on a similar angry glow. A glow he easily recognised as being the same one he had felt directed at him across the courtroom. Why was Bryn suddenly so angry? They had been in the middle of a conversation about—

Ah. Gabriel had stated she was the seventh candidate being interviewed in a six-candidate competition.

Gabriel strolled back with the glass of whisky she had asked for. 'I believe there's been a misunderstanding—'

'There certainly has.' She nodded, taking the crystal glass of whisky he held out to her and drinking it down in one swallow, only to breathe in with a gasp before coughing as the fiery alcohol hit the back of her throat.

'I think you'll find that thirty-year-old single-malt whisky is meant to be sipped and savoured rather than guzzled down like lemonade at a child's birthday party,' Gabriel drawled dryly as he took the empty glass from her slightly lax fingers and placed it safely on his desk as she bent over at the waist, obviously still fighting for breath. 'Should I—?'

'Do not even think about slapping me on the back!' she warned through gritted teeth as she straightened and saw his raised hand, her cheeks now a fiery red, eyes ringed with unshed tears caused by her choking fit.

At least, Gabriel hoped they were caused by her choking fit and not from disappointment. She had obviously misunderstood his earlier comment; he had caused this woman enough heartache already in her young life. 'Would you care for that glass of water now…?'

She glared even more fiercely. 'I'll be fine,' she snapped. 'As for your offer, Mr D'Angelo—'

'Gabriel.'

She blinked long silky lashes. 'I beg your pardon?'

'I asked that you call me Gabriel,' he invited warmly.

A frown settled on her face. 'What possible reason could I have for wanting to do that?'

Gabriel eyed her mockingly; with her hair styled in that short spiky fashion, at the moment she looked very much like a bristly, indignant hedgehog! 'I thought, perhaps, in the interest of…a friendlier working relationship?'

She gave an inelegant snort. 'We have no relationship, Mr D'Angelo, friendly, working or otherwise.' She picked up her shoulder bag from where it had fallen to the floor during her choking fit. 'And, while I'm sure many artists would feel flattered to be chosen seventh out of a six-candidate competition, I'm afraid I'm not one of them.' She turned sharply on her heel and marched towards the door.

'Bryn.'

She came to an abrupt halt at hearing her name spoken in that throaty rumble through those perfectly sculptured lips. The same chiselled lips that had once kissed her, that had filled her fantasies every night for months before, during, and after her father's trial and incarceration.

Her name sounded...sensual, when spoken in that husky voice. Soft, seductive and definitely sensual. A sensuality Bryn's body instantly responded to, her breasts once again feeling fuller, the nipples firming, aching.

Bryn turned slowly, her expression wary as she acknowledged, inwardly at least, that her traitorous body still thought Gabriel D'Angelo was the most decadent, wickedly attractive man she had ever set eyes on.

And it shouldn't.

She shouldn't.

How could she possibly still feel this way when this man had been instrumental in destroying her family?

They had been five tough years for both Bryn and her mother. The two of them had remained living in London while her father was in prison, only changing their surname and moving out of London after he had died.

On top of their grief had come the ordeal of finding somewhere to live, finally moving into the cottage they had found to rent in a little Welsh village.

Then had come the difficulty of Bryn finding and getting into a university that allowed her to live at home; she hadn't wanted to leave her still-devastated mother on her own. Her mother was a trained nurse, and had found a job at a local hospital, but Bryn had had to settle for working in a local café and fitting her hours of study around her work shifts.

In amongst all that change and struggle there hadn't been a lot of time for men in Bryn's life—the odd date here and there, but never anything prolonged or intimate. Besides which, any serious involvement would have eventually necessitated that she confide her real name wasn't Bryn Jones at all, and that her father had been William Harper, something she had been loath to do.

At least Bryn had thought, until now, that was the reason she had avoided any serious involvement....

To look at Gabriel D'Angelo now, however, to hear his voice again, and realise that *he* was the reason behind her lack of interest in other men, was humiliating in the extreme.

To realise, to know, that it was this man's sensual good looks, that deep voice, that filled her senses and created a sexual tension within her without even trying.

To acknowledge that the hateful Gabriel D'Angelo, a man who had kissed her just the once, a kiss he had no doubt regretted as soon as it had happened, had been the yardstick against which Bryn had judged all other men for the past five years, was not only masochistic madness on her part, but disloyal to both her mother, and her father's memory....

CHAPTER TWO

'YOU'VE GONE PALE again,' Gabriel said, striding determinedly towards where Bryn now stood transfixed and unmoving by the closed door of his office. A dark scowl creased his brow as he saw how the colour had once again leeched from those creamily smooth cheeks. 'Perhaps you should sit down for a minute—'

'Please don't!' She stepped back and away from the hand Gabriel had raised with the intention of lightly grasping her arm, her fingers tightly clutching her bag, her eyes deep pools of dark and angry velvet-grey as she gave a determined shake of her head. 'I have to go.'

Gabriel's mouth tightened at her aversion to his even touching her. 'We haven't finished our discussion yet, Bryn—'

'Oh, it's definitely finished, Mr D'Angelo,' she assured him spiritedly. 'As I said, thank you for the—the honour, of being chosen as the seventh candidate, but I really have no interest, or time, to waste on being a runner-up.' Her eyes flashed darkly. 'And I have no idea why you would ever have thought that I—'

'You were far and away the best of the six candidates to be chosen for the exhibition, Bryn,' Gabriel bit out briskly—before she had chance to dig a bigger hole for herself by insulting him even further. 'I saved the best till last,' he added dryly.

'That I might be, so thank you for your interest, but—' She broke off her tirade to stare up at him blankly as his words finally trickled through the haze of her anger. She moistened her lips—those sexily pouting lips!— with the tip of her tongue before speaking again. 'Did you just say…?'

'I did,' Gabriel confirmed grimly.

'But earlier you said— You told me that I was the seventh person being interviewed—'

'And one of the previous six is the reserve. And happy to be so,' he added harshly.

Bryn stared up at Gabriel as the full horror of what she had just done, what she had said, was replayed back to her in stark detail. At the same time realising he was right; at no time had Gabriel said she was the seventh-place candidate, only that she was the seventh artist being interviewed.

She swallowed as the nausea washed over her, and then swallowed again, to absolutely no avail, the single-malt whisky she had 'guzzled down like lemonade at a child's birthday party' obviously at war with her empty stomach; she had been far too tense about coming back to the gallery to be able to eat any breakfast this morning. 'I think I'm going to be sick!' she gasped as she raised a hand over her mouth.

'The bathroom is this way,' Gabriel said quickly, lightly grasping her arm and pulling her towards a closed door on the opposite side of the office.

Bryn didn't fight his hold on her this time, too busy trying to control the nausea to bother resisting as he threw open the bathroom door and pushed her inside. Bathroom? It was more like something you would find in a private home, with a full glass-enclosed walk-in shower along one wall, along with the cream porcelain facilities, and had to be as big as the whole of the bed-sit in which Bryn had lived and painted this past year!

Bryn dropped her bag to the floor and ran across the room to hang her head over the toilet only just in time, as she immediately lost her battle with the nausea and was violently and disgustingly sick.

'Well, that really was a complete waste of a thirty-year-old single-malt whisky!' Gabriel commented dryly some minutes later, when it became obvious from Bryn's dry retching that she had nothing else left in her stomach to bring up.

Adding further to her humiliation Bryn realised he must have remained in the bathroom the whole time she was being physically ill. 'I'll buy you a replacement bottle,' she muttered as she flushed the toilet, and avoided so much as glancing at the dark figure looming in the doorway as she moved to the sink to turn on one of the gold taps and splash cold water onto her clammy cheeks.

'At a thousand pounds a bottle?'

Bryn's eyes were round with shock as she lowered the towel she had been patting against her cheeks, before turning to look at him as he leaned against the doorframe, arms folded across the broad width of his muscled chest.

She instantly wished she hadn't looked at him as mockery gleamed evidently in his eyes. 'Who pays that sort of money for—? You do, obviously,' she acknowledged heavily as he raised his dark brows. 'Okay, so maybe I can't afford to buy you a replacement bottle right now.'

He gave an appreciative and throaty chuckle. And instantly threw Bryn into a state of rapid, heart-thumping awareness.

It had been years since she had seen Gabriel laugh—there had been no room for humour or soft words between them once her father had been arrested!—and the transformation that laughter made to his harshly handsome face reminded her of exactly why she had fallen so hard for him all those years ago.

She had believed—hoped—that if they should ever meet by chance, she wouldn't still respond to him like this, but the warmth that now shone in his eyes, the laughter lines beside those eyes and the grooves that had appeared in his chiselled cheeks, along with the flash of straight white teeth between those sculptured and deeply sensual lips, instantly proved how wrong she had been to hope. Gabriel might be sinfully handsome when he wasn't smiling, but he became lethally so when he was!

Bryn abruptly averted her gaze to finish drying her face and hands before checking her appearance in the mirror behind the sink—dark shadows beneath tired eyes, pale cheeks, throat slender and vulnerable. A vulnerability she simply couldn't afford in this man's presence.

She took a deep, controlling breath before turning back to face Gabriel. 'I apologise for my comments earlier, Mr D'Angelo. They were both rude and premature—'

'Stop there, Bryn,' he interrupted as he straightened. 'Abject apology doesn't sit well on your defensive shoulders,' he explained as she looked at him warily.

Angry colour rushed back into her cheeks. 'You could have at least let me finish my apology before mocking me.'

He was obviously having difficulty holding back another smile as he answered her. 'As I just said, abject apology doesn't appear to come naturally to you!'

She sighed at the deserved rebuke. 'I apologise once again.' Bryn didn't even attempt to meet his mocking gaze now as she instead kept her gaze fixed on the beautiful marble floor. She might know exactly why she harboured such resentment against this man, but as she had guessed—hoped—Gabriel didn't remember her at all, and she didn't want to do or say anything that would make him do so either.

'Shall we go and finish our conversation now?' he prompted briskly. 'Or do you need to hang over my toilet for a while longer?'

Bryn gave a pained frown. 'It was the whisky on top of an empty stomach.' And the fact that she knew, as did he, that she had prejudged his words without so much as a single hesitation!

'Of course it was,' Gabriel humoured dryly as he stood aside for Bryn to precede him back into the office, only too well aware that it was her resentment towards him for past deeds that was responsible for her having jumped to the wrong conclusions. 'And it's sacrilege to drink single-malt whisky any other way but neat.'

'At that price I can see that it would be, yes,' he heard Bryn mutter derisively. A mutter he chose to ignore as he instead returned to the reason for her being there in the first place. 'As I said, you are definitely one of the six candidates to have been chosen for the New Artists Exhibition being held in the gallery next month. Shall we sit down and discuss the details?' He indicated the comfortable brown leather sofa and chairs arranged about the coffee table in front of those floor-to-ceiling picture windows.

'Of course.' She noticeably chose to sit in one of the

armchairs, rather than on the sofa, before crossing one of her knees neatly over the other and looking up at him questioningly.

Gabriel didn't join her immediately, but went to the bar instead to take a bottle of water from the refrigerator, collecting a clean glass as well, then walking back to place them both down on the coffee table in front of her before lowering his length down into the chair opposite hers.

'Thank you,' she murmured softly, taking the top off the bottle and pouring the water into the glass. She took a long, grateful swallow before speaking again. 'Mr Sanders told me some of the details last week but obviously I'm interested in knowing more...' Her tone was businesslike.

Gabriel studied her through narrowed lids as they went on to discuss the details of the exhibition more fully, Bryn writing down the details in a notebook she had taken from her bulky shoulder bag.

Five years ago this woman had still been sweetly innocent, a young woman poised on the cusp of womanhood, a combination that had both intrigued and fascinated him. The passing of those years had stripped away all that innocence, in regard to people and events, at least; Gabriel had no way of knowing whether Bryn was still physically innocent, although somehow he doubted it. Five years was a long time.

But not only had Bryn grown more beautiful during those years, she had also grown in confidence, especially where her art was concerned, and she talked on the subject with great knowledge and appreciation.

'Have you ever thought of working in a gallery like Archangel?' Gabriel prompted as their conversation drew to an end half an hour later.

Bryn looked up from placing her notebook back into her handbag. 'Sorry?'

He shrugged. 'You're obviously knowledgeable on the subject, enthusiastic and bright, and those things would make you an asset to any gallery, not just Archangel.'

Bryn frowned as she looked warily at Gabriel across the glass coffee table, not sure if she had understood him correctly. 'Are you offering me a job?' she finally prompted incredulously.

He returned her gaze unblinkingly. 'And if I was?'

'Then my answer would have to be no! Thank you,' she added belatedly as she realised she was once again being rude, a rudeness that was totally out of keeping with her expected role as one of the grateful finalists in the New Artists Exhibition.

'Why would it?'

'Why?' She gave an impatient shake of her head at his even having to ask that question. 'Because I want my paintings to hang in a gallery, to hopefully be sold in a gallery, not to work as an assistant in one!'

He shrugged. 'Do you have something against taking a job to help pay the bills until that happens?'

Bryn eyed him guardedly, only too aware that her rent was due to be paid next week and that she had other bills that had reached the red-reminder stage too. And yes, a job did help to pay the bills, but she already had a job, at yet another café, even if it didn't pay nearly well enough to cover both her monthly rent and the bills, no matter how much she tried to economise.

It was almost as if Gabriel had guessed that and was offering her charity....

She instantly chided herself; of course Gabriel D'Angelo wasn't trying to help her. He just knew, as she did, that she was more than capable of doing the job he was offering, and he had no doubt assumed she would jump at the chance to work at Archangel, based on the fact that, historically, artists were known for starving in garrets.

Bryn wasn't starving, exactly, she just didn't eat some days. And while her third-floor bedsit wasn't exactly a garret, it was barely big enough to swing the proverbial cat in, with one half of the room put aside for sleeping and cooking and the other half utilised as her studio.

'No, of course not,' she answered him lightly. 'But I already have a job—'

'At another gallery?'

Bryn frowned as she heard the sharpness in his tone. 'What does it matter where I work?'

He raised dark brows. 'It matters in this case because it would hardly be appropriate for your paintings to be displayed at Archangel when you're working for another gallery.'

Good point, Bryn acknowledged ruefully. 'Right.' She nodded. 'Well, I don't work for another gallery. But I do have a job,' she continued briskly as she bent down to retrieve her bag from the floor. 'And my next shift starts in half an hour, so—'

'Your next…shift?'

'Yes, my next shift,' Bryn confirmed abruptly, stung by the incredulity in his cultured voice. 'I work behind the counter in a well-known coffee-shop franchise.'

His brows rose. 'Latte, cappuccino, espresso and a low-calorie muffin? That sort of coffee-shop franchise?'

The previous half an hour of conversation had gone smoothly; it had even been enjoyable at times, as they'd discussed which paintings from her portfolio Bryn was going to show at the exhibition next month, the timelines and other necessary details. But that had so obviously only been a brief lull in the tension between them if Gabriel had now decided to pull his arrogant-millionaire rank on her. Bryn eyed him challengingly. 'You have something against coffee shops?'

Those sculptured lips thinned. 'I don't recall ever having been inside one.'

Of course he hadn't; people as rich as Gabriel D'Angelo frequented exclusive restaurants and fashionable bars, not high-street coffee shops.

'But I do have something against one of my artists working in one of them, yes,' he continued evenly.

She stiffened. 'One of your artists?'

'This will be your first public exhibition, I believe?' he prompted evenly.

'I've sold one or two paintings in smaller galleries in the past couple years,' she came back with defensively.

'But am I right in thinking this will be the first time that so many Bryn Jones paintings have been shown together in an official exhibition?'

'Yes…' Bryn confirmed slowly.

He nodded. 'Then in future, whether you like it or not, your name will be linked with the Archangel Gallery.'

Bryn certainly didn't like it. It had felt as if she were being forced to walk over burning-hot coals by even entering her paintings in a competition being run by the hateful D'Angelo brothers; she certainly didn't like the idea of her name being for ever linked with either them or their galleries.

She hadn't even told her mother of the desperation that had forced her to enter the competition, dreaded thinking how her mother would react if she were to ever find out Bryn was having her work shown at *this* gallery!

And maybe Bryn should have thought about that a

little more deeply before deciding to walk over those burning hot coals and enter the competition.

Gabriel could almost actually see the war being waged inside Bryn's head. The natural desire to have her artistic talent not only shown for the first time but also recognised for the talent that it was, obviously totally at war with her desire not to be in the least beholden, or associated with in the future, either the D'Angelo name or the Archangel Gallery. Yet another indication of how much she still disliked him and all he stood for. If he had needed any. Which he didn't.

'Your point being?' Bryn now prompted guardedly.

He grimaced. 'I think it would look better in the catalogue being printed and sent out to our clients before the exhibition if you weren't listed as currently working in a coffee shop.'

'Better for whom?'

Gabriel bit back his irritation with her challenging tone, having no intention of admitting that he had already known about her working in a coffee shop—and that it was him, personally, who didn't like the idea of her working there. He might never have been into such an establishment, but he had driven past them numerous times, and the thought of Bryn being run ragged in such an establishment, day after day—evening after evening—just so that she could pay her bills every month, wasn't particularly appealing.

Besides which, Gabriel also knew, from the discreet enquiries he had made about her once Rafe had told him exactly who she was, that Bryn Jones suffered a constant struggle to pay those bills. A job as an assistant at Archangel would go a long way to relieving her of that burden, at least.

A dark frown creased his brow. 'What possible reason could you have for refusing a job here if it was offered to you?'

'Let me see…' She lifted a finger to her chin in exaggerated thought. 'First, I don't want to work in a gallery. Second, I don't want to work in a gallery. And third, I don't want to work in a gallery!' Her eyes glittered determinedly.

'This gallery in particular, or just any gallery?' Gabriel questioned evenly.

'Any gallery,' Bryn answered firmly. 'Besides, couldn't it be considered as a little…incestuous, if I were to start working at Archangel now?' she forestalled Gabriel D'Angelo's next comment lightly.

'Because of your inclusion in the exhibition?'

'Exactly,' she confirmed with satisfaction.

His mouth tightened. 'And that's your final answer?'

'It is.'

He scowled darkly. 'You're very…intractable in your attitude, Miss Jones.'

'I prefer to think of it as maintaining my independence, Mr D'Angelo,' Bryn came back sharply.

'Perhaps,' he drawled as he stood up in one fluid movement, the dryness of his tone implying he thought the opposite. 'I think we've said all that needs to be said for today. I have another appointment in—' he glanced at the expensive-looking gold watch on his wrist '—ten minutes or so.' He looked at her expectantly as she remained seated.

'Oh. Right.' Bryn stood up so hastily she accidentally kicked her bag across the floor, instantly scattering the contents far and wide. 'Hells bells and blast it!' She immediately dropped to her knees on the carpeted floor, her cheeks flushing with embarrassment as she began collecting up her scattered belongings, some of which were personal in the extreme, and cramming them back into her handbag.

'I've always wondered what women kept in their handbags,' Gabriel D'Angelo drawled in amusement.

'Well, now you know!' Bryn had paused to glare up at him, and instantly became aware of how his well over six feet of lean muscle towered over her so ominously. 'And I would get this done a whole lot quicker if you were to help rather than just stand there grinning!' Like an idiot, she could have added, but didn't, because it wouldn't have been the truth.

The last thing Gabriel was, or looked like when he grinned in that way, was an idiot; devilishly rakish, devastatingly attractive—lazily, sensuously so—and maybe even boyishly mischievous, as that grin knocked years off his age, but he certainly didn't look like an idiot.

Besides which he had stopped grinning now, those chocolate-brown eyes narrowed on her in totally male assessment.

A frown creased Gabriel's brow as he looked down at Bryn on her hands and knees in front of him. It was a… provocative pose, to say the least. As the ever-increasing bulge in his trousers testified.

Bryn's cheeks were flushed, her lips slightly moist and parted and it should be illegal what those black trousers did for her heart-shaped bottom—and Gabriel's arousal—bent over like that…!

'Right,' he rasped harshly as he crouched down beside her, his gaze averted as he gathered up the notebook and pen she had been using to make notes in earlier, as well as a small bottle of hand cream and a lip salve. 'Hell's bells and blast it…?' he prompted gruffly, aware of her perfume now; nothing so anaemic as something floral for Bryn Jones, she was a mixture of spices, with an underlying hint of sensual woman.

He saw her shrug out of the corner of his eye. 'My mother has never approved of a woman swearing, so I learnt to improvise at an early age.'

Gabriel only half listened to her answer as he moved down onto his knees. The smell of those spices—cinnamon, something fruity, maybe a hint of honey and that more elusive smell of sensual woman—all served to increase his awareness of the woman beside him. 'A pot of white pepper, Bryn?' he questioned as he held it up for inspection.

'It's cheaper than pepper spray!' She snatched the pot from his hand before thrusting it back into her bag.

Gabriel sat back on his heels to look at her. 'Pepper spray?'

'I have to walk home late at night several times a week.' She dismissed his concern without looking up, missing the frown of disapproval that clouded Gabriel's face.

'From the coffee shop,' he said stiffly.

She gave him a brief glance before looking away again. 'Why does that bother you so much?'

Good question. But not one Gabriel could answer. Not without revealing that he knew exactly who she was, and the part he felt he had played in her current circumstances—something her defensive attitude told him she definitely didn't want from him.

And the past half hour in Bryn Jones' company was enough to tell him that what she claimed as independence was actually defensive pride, and that she had more than her fair share of it.

Because of the scandal involving her father five years

ago? No doubt that was a contributing factor, but Gabriel had a feeling she would have always been more than a little prickly; her feistiness was all too apparent in those flashing eyes and the stubborn tilt of her pointed chin.

'I thought you had another appointment in a few minutes?' She gave Gabriel a pointed look as he knelt unmoving beside her.

Make that a whole lot prickly! 'I was just wondering what a third party, if they should walk into my office right now, would make of the two of us being down here on the floor together like this,' Gabriel came back with deliberate and husky provocation.

'We may just find out if your next appointment arrives early!' Colour warmed her cheeks as she bent over to retrieve a lipstick from beneath the coffee table.

As that next appointment was the elderly Lord David Simmons, an avid art collector, Gabriel worried the other man might have a heart attack on the spot if he should catch so much as a glimpse of Bryn's shapely backside!

'Did I say something amusing?' Bryn sat back on her heels to look at Gabriel, who was grinning again, his dark hair having fallen rakishly over his forehead, causing Bryn's hands to curl into fists as she resisted the impulse to touch those silky dark locks.

'Private joke.' His grin faded, his eyes deepening almost to black as he continued to look at her intently.

Except Gabriel wasn't looking at all of her, Bryn realised self-consciously, just her lips. Moist and slightly parted lips that she immediately clamped shut as she rose abruptly to her feet and slung her bag over her shoulder.

Only to as quickly freeze in place as she realised, with their difference in height, that Gabriel's face was now level with her breasts.

A fact he took full advantage of as he made no effort to hide his interest in the fact that he could see Bryn's bared breasts beneath the gauzy material of her floral blouse....

CHAPTER THREE

'Mr D'Angelo…?'

'Hmm?' Gabriel couldn't look up from the mesmerising view he currently had of Bryn's breasts, full and perfect breasts, tipped by rosy areolas and plump nipples. Rapidly firming nipples that deepened in colour even as he continued to gaze at them.

'Mr D'Angelo? Gabriel!' Bryn's voice became more urgent as he failed to respond.

Gabriel ran the tip of his tongue moistly over his lips as he imagined taking those nipples into his mouth and suckling hungrily, his roused shaft instantly throbbing its approval of the idea. 'You aren't wearing a bra….'

'No. I—'

'Do you intend to wear this blouse to work today?' He scowled at the thought of Bryn's seminaked breasts being ogled by other men across the counter of a high-street coffee shop.

'We're all required to wear a black T-shirt with the franchise logo on it,' Bryn answered him dismissively. 'And will you please get up!' She grasped hold of his arm and tried to pull him to his feet.

A move that jiggled those plumped and roused breasts temptingly in front of Gabriel's heated gaze. If he just moved forward, ever so slightly, he would be able to put his mouth on them and actually taste—

'Damn it, Gabriel, someone is knocking on the door!' Bryn hissed. The urgency of her tone, as much as the words, finally broke through Gabriel's sexual haze, causing him to frown darkly as he realised exactly what he was doing. What he had been thinking of doing.

And with whom....

Bryn breathed out shakily as Gabriel finally rose abruptly to his feet, running his fingers impatiently through his hair as he shot her a scowling glance before striding across the room to wrench open the outer door.

'I'm sorry, Mr D'Angelo, I didn't realise Miss Jones was still here.' The receptionist took a wary step back as she obviously saw and recognised the aggression in Gabriel's scowling expression.

'Good to see you again, Gabriel!' The elderly man at the receptionist's side appeared less concerned as he greeted the younger man warmly before stepping into the room and giving Bryn a friendly if curious glance. 'Are you going to introduce me to your young lady?' he prompted Gabriel.

'I'm just Mr D'Angelo's previous appointment,' Bryn supplied quickly, dismissing even the suggestion of her and the arrogant Gabriel D'Angelo ever being a couple. 'And I've already taken up far too much of his time,' she added lightly as she joined them near the open doorway before turning a cool gaze on the still-frowning Gabriel.

Damn it, she was doing her best to allay the speculation she had seen in the receptionist's eyes and the curiosity in Gabriel's visitor's. The least Gabriel could do was try to reciprocate rather than continuing to scowl his irritation at the interruption!

An interruption of what? Bryn wondered....

There had been no doubting the hunger she had seen in those seductive eyes as Gabriel had looked at her breasts so appreciatively, or the flush of arousal high in those sculptured cheeks as he had begun to lean towards her. Evidence that, if they hadn't been interrupted by the knock on the door, he would have acted on that unmistakable hunger, and actually kissed her breasts? Perhaps more than kissed them?

Bryn felt her knees go weak just thinking of having those sculptured lips latching on to her aroused nipple, suckling deeply, his tongue a hot and arousing rasp—

'Bryn, this is Lord David Simmons.' Gabriel's voice was harsh as he made the introduction. 'David, this is Bryn Jones.' His tone softened to politeness. 'One of the six artists whose paintings will be appearing in the New Artists Exhibition next month.'

'Indeed?' David Simmons' warm blue eyes lit up with pleasure as he and Bryn shook hands. 'I'm very much looking forward to attending the exhibition,' he informed Bryn warmly as he retained a hold on her hand. 'I flew over to Paris two months ago to attend the New Artists Exhibition at the Archangel Gallery there, and I can assure you you're in good hands with Gabriel here. He has a definite eye for recognising new talent.'

Bryn's smile froze on her lips, not just at being told she was in good hands with Gabriel but also because she knew, only too well, that Gabriel had a definite eye for spotting a forgery too. She released her hand from David Simmons'.

'Then no doubt I'll see you again next month, Lord Simmons—'

'Please, call me David,' he invited warmly.

'Bryn,' she returned tautly, very much aware of Gabriel's brooding presence beside her. 'Now, if you will all excuse me...? I have another appointment as well.'

Gabriel knew Bryn's other 'appointment' was her shift at the coffee shop, a fact that still displeased him greatly. His bad mood was added to by the way David Simmons, a man old enough to be Bryn's grandfather, had maintained far too long a hold of her hand when introduced.

'Linda, please make an appointment for Miss Jones, before she leaves, for her to see Eric on Monday,' Gabriel instructed abruptly.

'Certainly, Mr D'Angelo,' the receptionist responded brightly.

Bryn blinked her long lashes. 'May I ask what for?'

Gabriel's mouth tightened. 'We need more personal information and photographs for the catalogue we're sending out to existing clients—as I believe we discussed earlier?'

Her cheeks coloured slightly at the rebuke, and a flash of anger illuminated her eyes. 'Obviously I must have been so overwhelmed at being told I was one of the six artists chosen for the exhibition that I didn't hear all the details that followed.'

Some of Gabriel's tension eased as he saw the continued anger in Bryn's eyes accompany her too-sweetly-made statement. It also reminded him that Bryn had actually been physically ill, rather than 'overwhelmed', once he had fully explained her inclusion in the exhibition, a nausea she had no doubt still been suffering from when the two of them had sat down together and discussed the details of what still had to be done before the exhibition.

Not to mention the distracting attention he had given her breasts a few minutes ago!

Not that Gabriel was particularly proud of that lapse;

he had recognised five years ago that she represented a danger to his self-control, and his meeting today with the older and more self-assured—even more beautiful!— Bryn Jones had shown him that danger still existed. Very much so…

Perhaps he should have taken Rafe's advice after all and stayed well away from Bryn Jones.

'Just make the appointment, Bryn,' he bit out tersely. 'I'll instruct Eric that he needs to explain those details to you again on Monday.'

She turned to give the older man a warm smile. 'It was a pleasure to meet you, Lord Simmons. Mr D'Angelo.' Her voice had noticeably cooled, and there was no smile, or mention of her feeling any of that same pleasure in meeting Gabriel.

'Pretty girl,' David Simmons remarked as the two men watched Bryn join Linda out in the hallway before closing the door firmly behind her.

'Linda?' Gabriel deliberately misunderstood the older man.

David gave him a knowing glance. 'Does Miss Jones paint as beautifully as she looks?'

'More so, if anything,' Gabriel answered truthfully; Bryn's work really was exceptional, and he had no doubt that David Simmons would recognise that talent as easily as he had, and would most likely be happy to buy one of her paintings in the exhibition next month.

'Interesting…' The older man nodded as he followed Gabriel to the seating area in front of the window.

It wasn't until much later, after his business with David had been concluded and Linda had escorted the older man down the stairs that Gabriel was able to pause and replay his meeting with Bryn from earlier.

The prickly outspokenness she had been unable to

hide had shown that she hadn't even begun to forgive him for the part he had played in her father's downfall. A defensive manner that was also an indication of the resentment she felt at having to be even slightly beholden to the D'Angelo family—clearly telling Gabriel that Bryn wouldn't have entered the New Artists competition, or the Archangel Gallery, if she hadn't considered it the very last resort. It was—

A glance across the office showed something glinting from beneath one of the armchairs. A something that, upon closer inspection, proved to be an item that he knew must have fallen out of Bryn's handbag earlier.

'And what can I get you to drink this evening— Gabriel?' The last word came out much louder than Bryn would have wished after glancing up and seeing that her next customer was Gabriel D'Angelo.

A Gabriel D'Angelo who was much more casually dressed—but no less lethally attractive—than he had been in his office earlier today; he wore a thin black cashmere sweater, the sleeves pulled up to just below his elbows—which emphasised every toned muscle and dip of those broad shoulders, chest, and the flatness of his stomach—with faded denims resting comfortably on the leanness of his hips. His overlong dark hair had also been slightly tousled by the warm evening breeze outside and fell softly, rakishly, onto his brow.

He'd claimed earlier never to have been inside a coffee shop, which posed the question of what was he doing in one now? And not just any coffee shop, but the one in which Bryn worked, because there was no way she believed his being here was just a coincidence.

She frowned slightly as she realised the people in the queue behind Gabriel were getting restless; six o'clock in the evening was one of their busiest times, when the people leaving work called in to collect a drink and something to eat on their way home, or to linger in the coffee shop while they relaxed for an hour or so with friends. It was even busier as it was a Friday evening, and the end of the working week for most people.

'What can I get for you this evening, Mr D'Angelo?' she repeated tightly.

He looked up at the board behind her. 'Black coffee?'

'Black coffee,' she repeated slowly; the coffee shop served six different brands of coffee and just as many types, as well as several flavoured teas, all of which could have milk, runny or whipped cream or several different flavoured shots, and Gabriel was asking for black coffee!

He nodded. 'If it's not too much trouble,' he drawled derisively.

'It's no trouble at all.' Bryn was aware of the keen eyes of the manager fixed beadily on the two of them as she watched Bryn ring up the sale and take Gabriel's money—unless, of course, Sally was just enjoying the chance to ogle the six feet three inches of hot, heart-poundingly attractive man standing on the other side of the counter.

Which appeared to be what all the other women in the coffee shop were doing—surreptitiously by the ones with a man of their own, the others openly eating Gabriel up with their eyes!

'If you would like to follow me,' Bryn instructed sharply as she moved farther down the crowded counter to fill his order, at the same time allowing one of the other assistants to take her place and serve the next customer. 'What are you doing here, Mr D'Angelo?' she muttered under her breath as she prepared his tray.

'Sorry?'

'I said—'

'You'll have to speak up a little, Bryn,' he drawled. 'I can't hear you with all the other noise and chatter in the room.'

She shot him an irritated frown as she raised her voice slightly. 'I asked what you're doing here.'

'Oh.' He nodded. 'You left something of yours on my office floor when you left earlier today, and I thought you might want them back.'

Bryn stilled, her breath catching in her throat, as she realised that the half a dozen or so people standing closest to them had fallen silent as they overheard his remark, their eyes wide as they obviously drew their own conclusions as to what Bryn might possibly have left on Gabriel D'Angelo's office floor....

'Did you do that on purpose?'

Gabriel looked up at Bryn a short time later as she came over to wipe and clear the table next to the one where he sat in a comfortable armchair, enjoying his mug of surprisingly good Colombian coffee. 'Did I do what on purpose?'

She frowned, her skin appearing creamier than ever against the black T-shirt she now wore in place of the gauzy blouse of earlier. 'You implied— You deliberately gave the impression a few minutes ago that I had left an item of clothing on the floor of your office earlier today!'

He raised dark brows. 'I did?'

Bryn's mouth thinned as she pretended to wipe his table. 'You know you did.'

He had, yes. Because, until she had seen him, Bryn had looked relaxed and smiling as she served customers, that smile instantly replaced by an annoyed frown the moment she'd recognised him, arousing his own feelings of irritation.

It had been a mistake for him to come here at all; he accepted that now. He should have just passed her property on to Eric Sanders to give back to her on Monday, or bagged it up and had it delivered by courier to her tomorrow rather than come here personally.

He knew he should stay well away from Bryn, that it was better for both of them if he did so; she so obviously wanted nothing to do with him outside Archangel, and he knew from their meeting how dangerous she was to his self-control.

It seemed he just hadn't been able to stop himself from coming here when the opportunity presented itself.

His jaw tightened. 'I do have something of yours that I thought you might need returning to you sooner rather than later.'

'Really?' She eyed him sceptically.

Gabriel leaned back in the leather armchair to look up at her through narrowed lids. 'You know, Bryn, I've found your attitude towards me to be…less than polite since meeting you. Surprisingly so, considering that I'm one of the owners of the gallery where your paintings are going to be exhibited. If you have a problem with me, or my gallery, then perhaps now might be a good time for you to tell me what that problem is?'

A delicate blush coloured her cheeks as she chewed on her bottom lip, her artistic ambitions obviously once again at war with the past—and present—resentment Bryn felt towards him.

It was a resentment Gabriel understood, and sympathised with, but it rankled that Bryn still so obviously held him to blame for what had happened in the past; Gabriel wasn't responsible for William Harper's attempt to sell a forged Turner to the D'Angelos. Only for showing the other man up as the charlatan he so obviously was.

Bryn had initially talked herself into entering her paintings in the New Artists competition by reassuring herself that in all likelihood she would never have to meet any of the three D'Angelo brothers personally. She now found it totally disconcerting that she had met and spoken with one of them—twice in one day!—and that that one should happen be Gabriel!

Even so, she knew she deserved Gabriel's criticism. She *was* guilty of allowing the past to influence her manner towards him, something he must consider highly disrespectful, as well as puzzling, given that he only knew her as Bryn Jones, aspiring artist, and had given no indication of recognising her as Sabryna Harper. If Gabriel ever learned the truth, it would no doubt result in that seventh, reserve artist being asked to take her place in the exhibition!

'I apologise if I've seemed less than…grateful, Mr D'Angelo,' she muttered stiffly. 'Obviously it's a privilege and an honour to be chosen as one of the new artists to display their paintings in a gallery as prestigious as Archangel—'

'As I told you earlier, Bryn, abject apology doesn't sit well on your slender shoulders,' he drawled, dark eyes gleaming with mocking humour.

Her gaze fell from his. 'In that case, I believe you said you came here this evening to return something of mine?'

'I did, yes.'

'And?' she prompted.

He glanced down at the gold watch on his wrist. 'What time do you finish this evening?'

Bryn frowned. 'In a couple hours.'

'Eight o'clock?'

'Eight-fifteen,' she corrected warily.

He nodded. 'Then I'll meet you outside at eight-fifteen.'

Bryn's brows rose. 'I don't understand.'

He shrugged those broad shoulders. 'I think it would be a good idea for the two of us to have dinner together, so that we can discuss, and hopefully dispose of, whatever your problem is with me or my gallery.'

Bryn's mouth gaped open. Had she imagined it or had Gabriel just— Had he just invited her to have dinner with him tonight?

No, of course he hadn't, Bryn answered her own question; Gabriel had made a statement, not asked a question. Because he was a man used to issuing orders and then expecting them to be obeyed? Or simply because it didn't even occur to him that Bryn—or any other woman, for that matter—would ever think of turning down a dinner invitation with the darkly attractive and eminently eligible Gabriel D'Angelo?

Bryn had a feeling that both of those things were true, but going out to dinner with him, discussing whatever her problem was with him or his gallery, was *not* an option.

Gabriel could almost see the struggle going on inside Bryn's beautiful head as she tried to find a polite way of refusing his invitation.

An invitation Gabriel knew he never should have made when he couldn't even look at Bryn without wanting her and she so obviously detested the very sight of him.

This prickly Bryn was so different from the Sabryna of five years ago, but even then Gabriel had known how much her beauty and innocence had appealed to him. He had only kissed her the once, a sweet and yet arousing kiss, a kiss that had affected him so deeply he had continued to think about her for months after her father's trial was over and she had refused to so much as see Gabriel again, and off and on in the years that followed too, as he'd found himself wondering what she was doing with her life, if she was happy.

That single meeting with her earlier today had shown him that the woman she had become, the woman she was now, had just as deep an effect on him.

So much so that being alone in his office with her, knowing he would have been able to touch her soft and creamy skin if he had just lifted his hand, and that unique spicy, womanly smell of her had invaded his senses, had resulting in his thinking of nothing else but her for the past six hours.

As for his arousal…! That had been a pounding ache for those same six hours, and even now the hardness of his shaft was pressing painfully against the restricting material of his jeans.

Which was as good a reason as any for him to get the hell as far away from Bryn Jones as was possible.

'Obviously not,' he dismissed harshly, pushing his cooling mug of coffee away from him before standing up abruptly. 'These are yours, I believe,' he rasped abruptly as he withdrew a silver metal tube from the front pocket of his jeans.

Bryn was still so shocked by Gabriel's suggestion that the two of them have dinner together this evening that it took several seconds for her to register the significance of the metal tube he held out to her. 'My reading glasses…' she finally recognised softly as she took the tube from him, glancing up at him quickly—guiltily—as she realised he really had come here this evening to return something that had obviously fallen out of her handbag earlier.

She moistened her lips with the tip of her tongue before speaking. 'It was very kind of you to return them to me so promptly and in person.'

He gave a hard, derisive smile. 'That sounded as if it actually hurt.'

'Of course it didn't.' Her cheeks had warmed at the taunt. 'And I apologise if you think my manner towards you has been...less than polite. I really am grateful for the opportunity to show my paintings at Archangel.'

'As far as you're concerned, Bryn, I *am* the Archangel Gallery,' he admonished harshly.

And quite what she was going to do about that Bryn had no idea; she only knew, having come this far, having worked so hard and for so many years towards this, it was now totally unthinkable she should be forced to withdraw her paintings from the exhibition because of the man who owned and ran the gallery! Or for Gabriel to decide her manner was so unacceptable he decided to withdraw them for her.

'I'm not sure what you mean by that, Mr D'Angelo,' she prompted uncertainly; she hadn't forgotten those few brief moments of intimacy between them in his office earlier, when she had been certain that he was going to touch or kiss her breasts. But, grateful as she was that he hadn't recognised her, if Gabriel believed for one moment that his position as owner of the Archangel Gallery gave him some sort of power over her, then—

'I'm not sure I like your implication either, Bryn!' he responded, dismissing that illusion.

Her throat moved as she swallowed before speaking. 'Maybe we could go somewhere and grab a bite this evening after all? Talk this through—'

'I can see no point in us even attempting to do that unless you're going to be completely honest with me.' Those brown eyes glittered as he looked down the length of his nose at her. 'Are you going to be honest with me, Bryn?'

Bryn's breath caught in her throat as she looked up at him sharply, searchingly. Had Gabriel realised who she was after all?

Of course he hadn't! For one thing Bryn doubted this man had ever given so much as a single thought towards William Harper's wife and daughter once her father had been sent to prison. For another, she had changed so much in the past five years, not just her name, but the way she looked and behaved too that he couldn't possibly have recognised her as the gauche teenager he had once kissed. And last, if he had known who she really was, he would never have allowed her anywhere near him or his gallery—

'Bryn, I need you to go back on the counter now.' There was an underlying edge of steel to her manager's tone as her rebuke cut across the tension between Gabriel and Bryn.

Bryn gave a guilty start as she turned to face Sally, knowing that the pointed remark was deserved; she had been talking with Gabriel D'Angelo for far too long. 'I'll be right there,' she promised lightly before turning back to Gabriel. 'Shall I meet you outside at eight-fifteen?'

For a moment Gabriel thought about refusing, about walking away from this woman and not looking back.

The plans for the exhibition were well in hand, and as such there was absolutely no reason why the two of them should even meet again before the night of that exhibition. Eric was more than capable of handling any and all future meetings with Bryn Jones.

And there were far too many reasons why Gabriel should keep his distance from her....

CHAPTER FOUR

GABRIEL WAS STILL having second, third—and fourth!—
thoughts as to the wisdom of meeting up with Bryn Jones
again this evening as he sat in his parked car waiting for
her to emerge from the coffee shop.

It didn't take too much intelligence to know what
Bryn had been thinking earlier. Or to know why she
had thought it. Gabriel's behaviour earlier hadn't exactly
been businesslike, most especially that remark about her
not wearing a bra. Especially considering the fact that
he had been down on his knees in front of her, staring
at her breasts, when he'd made it!

Which was, Gabriel had reasoned with himself, all
the more reason for him to meet with her again this evening, if only to reassure her that the two of them were to
have a business relationship in future and nothing more.

Gabriel's senses all went on full alert—making a
complete nonsense of that last sentiment—as he looked
through the smoked glass of the window beside him and
saw Bryn step out of the coffee shop at last, a short denim
jacket over top of the gauzy blouse she had worn earlier
today, a frown darkening her creamy brow as she looked
for him amongst the crush of people still milling about
on the busy pavement.

No doubt she was adding tardiness, or standing her up completely, to Gabriel's already long list of sins.

'Bryn.'

She turned in the direction of Gabriel's voice, giving a rueful grimace as she saw he had emerged from the sleek black sports car parked illegally outside the coffee shop. The smoky black windows had prevented her from seeing him seated inside. 'Mr D'Angelo,' she greeted as she hurried over to where he stood. 'I hope I haven't kept you waiting long?' she murmured politely.

'Not in the least.' He just as politely opened the passenger door of the car before standing back to allow her to get inside. 'And it's Gabriel,' he reminded her gently.

Bryn didn't move, or respond to his comment. 'Er— there's a pizza place just round the corner.'

He grimaced. 'I saw it. And trust me, Bryn, what they serve isn't real Italian pizza.'

'But—'

'The name is D'Angelo, Bryn.' He quirked dark, pointed brows.

It hadn't been part of Bryn's plans for this evening to go off somewhere in Gabriel's car with him. She had envisaged them getting a quick slice at the place round the corner, an hour or so of—hopefully—pleasant conversation, before they each went their separate ways. But, considering this was supposed to be a conciliatory meeting, it would look petty for her to refuse him now— besides which, with his Italian ancestry he probably did know more about pizza than she did!

'Fine.' She gave a bright, unconcerned smile as she moved forward to slide into the black-leather passenger seat, determined that this evening was going to go better than their previous two meetings had. Determined that she was going to act more like the fledgling-artist-grateful-to-the-art-gallery-owner-for-this-opportunity that she was supposed to be.

She had to push firmly to the back of her mind that the sleek sports car, the interior smelling richly of leather, along with a spicy, totally male smell that was pure Gabriel, was so reminiscent of that evening he had kissed her.

Gabriel closed the passenger door once Bryn had settled into the seat, before moving back to the other side of the car and resuming his seat behind the wheel. 'You didn't have any trouble after I left earlier?' he prompted as he fastened his seat belt and turned on the ignition.

'No, it was fine,' she dismissed; there was no need to tell him of the lecture she had received from Sally earlier about not spending her time talking to one of the customers, no matter how hot he was, and how there were plenty of other people who would like her job if she didn't want it. 'Where are we going exactly?' Bryn prompted interestedly as Gabriel manoeuvred the vehicle out into the evening flow of traffic.

'It's a little family-run place I know in a back street in the East End— Trust me on this, Bryn,' he drawled as he noticed her surprise.

'I'm sure it's fine. I was just— It doesn't sound like your sort of place,' she amended awkwardly.

'My sort of place being…?'

Bryn realised she was once again on shaky ground as she heard the hard challenge in Gabriel's tone; it hadn't taken long for the tension to return between them, despite her earlier promise with herself to keep the conversation light and pleasant. 'I have absolutely no idea,' she answered honestly.

'Good answer, Bryn.' Gabriel chuckled wryly, his seat

all the way back to accommodate his long legs, and appearing very relaxed as his hands moved lightly on the steering wheel of the powerful sports car.

He had nice hands, Bryn noted abstractedly. Long and artistic, and yet gracefully powerful at the same time. 'How did you become such an art expert?' she prompted interestedly. 'Do you paint yourself? Or did you inherit the galleries?'

It was clear to Gabriel that Bryn had decided to make a concerted effort to be more polite to him and to keep their conversation impersonal rather than personal, if possible. Unfortunately she had chosen the wrong subject if that was her intention.

'I wanted to paint,' he answered abruptly. 'I even took a degree in art with that intention, only to very quickly realise that I'm someone who can appreciate art rather than be good enough to participate.'

'That's...unfortunate.'

'Very.' One of the biggest disappointments of Gabriel's life was realising that his real artistic talent was for the visual rather than painting itself.

Bryn was frowning slightly as she turned sideways in her seat to look at him. 'I can't imagine not being able to express myself through my painting.'

'The art world would be all the poorer for it too,' he assured gruffly. Knowing it was true, that Bryn showed an insight in her paintings, a sense, a knowing, for what was inside her subject, even a dying rose, rather than what was only visible with the naked eye; it was the quality that made her paintings so unique.

'The art world hasn't exactly been beating a path to my door before now,' she said with a shrug.

Gabriel gave her a sideways glance. 'That's probably because the galleries you've approached with your work

before now have all been looking for chocolate-box paintings, stuff they can sell to the tourists to hang in their
sitting rooms when they get back home to remind them
of their visit to London. Your paintings are too good for
that. Archangel would have no interest in showing them
if they weren't.'

Bryn had stilled beside him. 'I don't remember mentioning what galleries I've approached in the past.'

'You didn't need to,' Gabriel dismissed lightly, having
no intention of reigniting the tension between them by
confiding that he now had a file on her at Archangel—
another file on her. Michael apparently had one too, a
security file, although Gabriel hadn't seen that one. To be
fair, they now had a professional file on all seven of the
finalists of the competition, which listed previous sales,
of which Bryn had three. But Gabriel had good reason
to know that Bryn was more sensitive than most—quite
rightly so—about sharing the personal details of her life.

'But—'

'We're here,' Gabriel announced as he saw they had
reached Antonio's; just in the nick of time too, as Bryn
seemed intent on pursuing a subject he would rather not
continue. 'Don't be misled by the exterior. Or the interior either, for that matter,' he added dryly as he parked
the car in front of the small bistro before getting out and
moving around to open Bryn's door for her. 'Antonio
makes the best Italian food in London, and none of his
customers gives a damn about the decor.'

Bryn was glad of the warning as they walked into
the brightly lit interior. There was a strong smell of gar-
lic in the air, crowded tables covered with plastic red-
and-white-checked tablecloths, artificial plants dangling
from every conceivable nook and cranny and an overly
enthusiastic Italian tenor playing over the audio system.

'Toni sings and records all his own songs,' Gabriel explained as he saw Bryn wince at a particularly off-key moment.

'Something else I'm going to have to trust you on, hmm?' she came back teasingly. Only to stiffen as she realised what she had just said. And Gabriel D'Angelo was the very last man she should ever trust. For any reason.

'Gabrielo!' A round-faced and portly man rushed across the room to greet them, standing at least a foot shorter than Gabriel as he shook the younger man's hand enthusiastically. 'We 'ave not seen you 'ere for some time.'

'That's because I've been in Paris—'

'Aha, I see what has kept you away from us, Gabri-elo.' Warm brown eyes had settled knowingly on Bryn. 'You 'ave brought your young lady to meet Mamma and me, yes?'

'No—' Bryn started to interrupt.

'I promised Bryn one of your famous pizzas with everything on, and a bottle of your best Chianti, Toni,' Gabriel interjected, cutting lightly across Bryn's denial as he took a firm hold of her elbow and squeezed warningly.

'No problem.' The older man beamed. 'You will find somewhere for you and your young lady to sit, and I will 'ave Mamma bring the wine to you.' He waddled off in the direction of the door at the back of the room marked Kitchen, stopping often to chat with one or other of his many customers.

Finding somewhere to sit wasn't as easy as it sounded; Gabriel was right, the place was heaving, despite the decor and the music. Luckily a young couple with a baby were just preparing to leave, and Bryn and Gabriel were able to grab their table before someone else did.

'This is wonderfully mad,' Bryn murmured a few

minutes later, feeling slightly bemused by all the people around them talking in loud voices, most of them in Italian, and gesticulating with their hands to emphasise a point.

Gabriel grinned. 'My mother always refers to Antonio's as "picturesque".'

Bryn looked across the table at him. 'Your mother comes here too?'

He nodded. 'My father insists on coming to eat here at least once a week whenever my parents are back in London.'

Bryn slipped off her jacket as she settled more comfortably on her chair. Talking about Gabriel's parents might not be ideal but it was certainly a safer subject than her own family. 'Where do your parents live?'

'They moved to Florida ten years ago when my father retired, and left the running of the original Archangel Gallery, which was all we had at the time, to myself and my two brothers.' Gabriel shrugged, surprising Bryn by appearing totally relaxed in his surroundings.

She smiled slightly. 'That would be Raphael and Michael.'

He grimaced. 'My mother's romantic choice of names rather than my father's.'

'And you've opened two more galleries since then, one in New York and one in Paris. With the Italian connection, why not Rome?'

'The D'Angelos have always visited Italy for pleasure, not work.' He gave one of those totally disarming smiles that made him appear several years younger and which made it all too easy for Bryn to guess exactly what sort of 'pleasure' the three D'Angelo brothers enjoyed when in Italy.

'Have you—?'

'Gabrielo!' A tall, voluptuous, dark-haired woman—no doubt Toni's wife—descended on them, placing a raffia-bottomed bottle of Chianti and two glasses down on the table before pulling a now-standing Gabriel in tightly against her overabundant bosom as she burst into a flourish of Italian.

'English, please, Maria.' Gabriel chuckled.

'You are as 'andsome as ever, I see!' She leant back to beam up at him. 'Ah, if I were only twenty years younger!' she added wistfully.

'Even if you were you would never leave Antonio.' Gabriel smiled at her warmly.

Bryn felt a bit disconcerted, both by the friendly way that Toni and Maria had greeted Gabriel, and his warm response to them in return. It was much easier for her to keep her own distance from Gabriel when she could continue to think of him as that cold and ruthless man who had sealed her father's fate. The warmth shown to him by Toni and Maria, and his own obvious and long-standing affection for both of them, revealed a completely different side to the arrogantly ruthless Gabriel D'Angelo than the one Bryn had come to expect. Especially following so quickly on the heels of those moments of intimacy between them in his office.

'Toni tells me you 'ave brought your young lady with you?' Maria eyed Bryn speculatively as she stepped away from Gabriel.

'No embarrassing Bryn, please, Maria!' Gabriel warned quickly as he slipped off his jacket and hung it on the back of his chair, wondering if it had been a wise move on his part to bring Bryn to Antonio's. The Italian couple were always asking when he intended settling down and having *bambinos*, and Bryn was the first woman he had ever brought here.

In his defence, bringing Bryn to Antonio's had been a knee-jerk reaction to her obvious belief that he was a man who thought himself far above frequenting high-street coffee shops, or little Italian bistros, instead favouring exclusive restaurants and bars. Gabriel had just forgotten to factor in the consequences of bringing a woman to Antonio's for the first time; in the past he had only ever come to the bistro with members of his family, knowing the women he usually dated wouldn't give a damn how good the food was—this little bistro simply wasn't fashionable enough or exclusive enough for their 'sophisticated' tastes.

Not that he thought Bryn unsophisticated. His sole reason for bringing her here had been to show her that he wasn't the arrogant sophisticate she so obviously believed him to be.

Nor should he think of this as being a date—

Oh, to hell with this; whatever his reason for bringing Bryn here, she was here now, and it was his own fault if he had to suffer Toni and Maria's teasing speculation. 'Maria, Bryn. Bryn, Toni's wife, Maria,' he introduced stiffly.

'None of this is what you expected, is it...?'

Bryn took a sip of the Chianti that Gabriel had poured into the two glasses, Maria having hurried off to the kitchen shortly after the introductions to see if their pizza was ready. Introductions where, Bryn had noted, Gabriel had made no effort to correct Maria's assumption as to who Bryn was—or wasn't!

And no, this disorganised and noisy bistro wasn't the sort of place Bryn would ever have imagined seeing the Gabriel D'Angelo she had met earlier at Archangel, when he had looked every inch a wealthy and arrogant D'Angelo brother in his designer-label suit and silk shirt and tie.

'I have every reason to hope the pizza will be as delicious as this Chianti,' she murmured noncommittally.

'Oh, it will be.' Gabriel nodded, dark eyes hooded as he looked across the table at her. 'But I probably should have taken you somewhere a little more…upmarket, to celebrate your inclusion in the New Artists Exhibition.'

Her brows rose. 'Then shouldn't the other five finalists, and the reserve, have been invited too?'

He gave a hard smile. 'No.'

'Oh.' Bryn could feel her cheeks warm, but wisely said nothing; she had already made one wrong assumption about Gabriel this evening, an assumption he had taken exception to, and she wasn't inclined to make another. 'Well, this is absolutely fine for me,' she continued quickly. 'I would probably have felt out of my depth somewhere overly sophisticated anyway. Dining out hasn't exactly been something I've done a lot of since— This is fine,' she repeated flatly, lowering her eyes to avoid meeting his suddenly piercing and probing gaze. She had almost—almost—said 'since my father went to prison'. A slip that could have been extremely costly to her inclusion in the exhibition.

Bryn had no doubts that it was the very informality of their surroundings that was responsible for her feeling so relaxed she had almost spoken without thinking, rather than the man seated opposite her. There was nothing about Gabriel that caused her to feel in the least relaxed—not his dangerous good looks, or her own unwelcome response to them.

'To you, Bryn.' Gabriel held up his glass in a toast, seeming unaware of her inner turmoil. 'Let's hope that the Archangel exhibition is not only a successful one but also the first of many for you.'

'I'll drink to that!' Bryn took a grateful sip of her own wine. 'Do you—? Oh, wow!' Her eyes widened as she saw Maria winding her way deftly through the other diners towards their table, holding aloft the biggest pizza Bryn had ever seen in her life. Maria placed the hot plate down in the centre of their table with the beaming instruction to 'Enjoy!' before she hurried off again.

Bryn's mouth watered as she stared down at the laden pizza, seeing pepperoni, mushrooms, onions, spinach, ham and aubergines.

'I hope you don't mind that there are no anchovies?' Gabriel shrugged ruefully. 'Toni knows that I don't like them.'

'Are you kidding? Who would ever miss them with all these other toppings?' Bryn laughed delightedly as she continued to look at the pizza.

Gabriel felt his mouth go dry as he drank in the sight of Bryn relaxed and smiling; those dove-grey eyes warm and glowing, her creamy cheeks slightly flushed, her full and sensual lips—that had no need of the lip gloss so many women wore and which Gabriel, for one, found such a turn-off—delectably plump and rosy.

And watching those tempting lips as Bryn ate the pizza was going to be nothing short of physical torture for him!

'Tuck in before it gets cold,' he encouraged gruffly. 'There are no knives and forks,' he added dryly as Bryn frowned slightly at the obvious omission of utensils from the table. 'The only way to eat pizza is with your fingers,' he explained as she looked up at him questioningly.

'Is that another Gabrielism?' she teased as she helped herself to a slice of the pizza.

'Trust me,' Gabriel murmured softly.

She stilled before raising suddenly guarded eyes. 'You keep saying that....'

Yes, he did. Because, after meeting Bryn again, after spending time with her this evening knowing that she believed he had no idea who she was, and knowing how much he still wanted her, Gabriel did want Bryn to trust him.

'I had a really good time this evening, thank you,' Bryn murmured as she and Gabriel sat together in the darkened interior of his sports car. He had parked outside the old Victorian building where she lived, only the moonlight from above illuminating the quiet residential street.

Apart from the fact that it wasn't raining, it was an end to the evening so reminiscent of the one five years ago. A memory that had remained etched in Bryn's mind.

She had been mooning about Gabriel for weeks by that time, totally infatuated with his dark good looks and confident air. After he had come to her parents' house to talk with her father a couple times, she had taken to calling in to the Archangel Gallery several times a week on the off chance she might see him again.

That evening she had hung around outside at closing time, telling herself it was because she was waiting for the rain to ease off before making a dash for the bus stop, but in reality she had been hoping to catch a glimpse of Gabriel as he left the gallery.

Her breath had caught in her throat when she'd seen him coming out of the main doors, a fiery blush on her cheeks as he'd looked up and seen her, his face going blank for several seconds before recognition had widened those chocolate-brown eyes and he'd stopped to chat with her. It had been a blushingly stilted conversation on Bryn's part, and she had been rendered completely speechless when Gabriel had asked if he could drive her home.

She had been so aware of Gabriel's proximity once they were seated in the confines of his sleek sports car, the silence between them on the drive to her home seeming heavy with possibility and causing Bryn to tremble with nervous anticipation.

She had given him a shy glance from beneath dark lashes once he'd stopped the car outside her parents' house. 'Thank you for driving me home.' She had groaned inwardly at her lack of sophistication.

'You're welcome.' His voice had been husky as he'd turned in his seat to look at her. 'Sabryna, I— Tomorrow there's going to be—' He had broken off, frowning darkly. 'Oh, to hell with it, if I'm going to burn I may as well go down in a ball of flames!' he had muttered fiercely before his head had swooped down and his lips had captured hers.

It had been the most exquisite kiss of Bryn's young life, slow and searching, but at the same time so erotically charged she had felt as if she might drown in the feelings, emotions, coursing through her body.

She had been totally dazed by those emotions as Gabriel had suddenly wrenched his mouth from hers to look down at her briefly with hot, passionate eyes before moving back and turning away.

'You should go in,' he muttered darkly. 'And try not to— Never mind,' he had bitten out abruptly as he'd turned to look at her with tortured eyes. 'I'm sorry, Sabryna.'

She had blinked. 'For kissing me?'

'No,' he had rasped harshly. 'I'll never be sorry I did that. Just— Try not to hate me too much, okay?'

At the time Bryn had believed she could never hate Gabriel, that she loved him too much to ever hate him.

The following day, that 'tomorrow' Gabriel had referred to so obliquely, her world had blown up in her face, as her father had been arrested for forgery, with Gabriel lined up as the prosecution's lead witness against him.

'I'm glad,' Gabriel murmured now in answer to her earlier comment.

Bryn came back to the present with a bump. 'I'd ask you in for coffee, but...' She trailed off with hard dismissal.

It had been a surprisingly enjoyable evening, Bryn acknowledged self-disgustedly, knowing that the past shouldn't have allowed her to enjoy an evening with the hateful Gabriel D'Angelo.

But she had....

The food had been so excellent and the decor, the crowded room and loud conversation had all become part of that enjoyment. Two glasses of wine and she had even become fond of Toni's off-key renditions of classical Italian arias!

As for the company... Gabriel had proved to be an amusing and entertaining dining companion, as they discussed their favourite artists as they ate, along with some of the funnier stories from Gabriel's years of running the Archangel Galleries with his brothers.

Bryn had felt totally relaxed in his company by the time they left the bistro, from the good food, the wine and the good company, so much so that it had seemed like the most natural thing in the world to agree to Gabriel driving her home.

Enjoyable as the evening had been though, she admittedly inwardly that she found Gabriel even more disturbing now than she had five years ago.

As Gabriel D'Angelo he was unmistakably intelligent, sinfully handsome, as well as being equally sinfully rich and powerful.

As Gabriel he was obviously intelligent and handsome, but he was also relaxed and charming, plus he had a slightly wicked sense of humour, and a warmth that had allowed him to accept, without so much as a blink, the enthusiastic kiss Maria had planted on his lips, with the plea to 'come back and see me soon', before they left the bistro earlier.

All of those things, together with those dark and mesmerising good looks, that Bryn had become so increasingly aware of as the evening progressed made her very aware that she was in danger of falling under this man's spell for the second time in her life.

'But?' Gabriel turned in his seat to prompt Bryn out of her continued silence.

She raised startled eyes. 'Sorry?'

'"I'd ask you in for coffee, but…"' he reminded her.

She smiled ruefully. 'That's a woman's polite way of saying thank you for the evening but now it's over.'

'You don't have any coffee?'

'I always have coffee.'

'Then why not invite me in?'

She blinked long lashes. 'I—well—it's late.'

'It's only eleven o'clock.' Although it was obvious to Gabriel that Bryn didn't want to invite him into her home, and he knew she was right to feel that caution, he wanted so badly for her to change her mind.

He hadn't thought it was possible, but his attraction to her had deepened in the past few hours and he was now desperate to taste and feel those plump lips that had been tormenting him all evening.

So desperate he moved to close the distance that separated them. 'Bryn—'

'Please don't!' She immediately held her hands up defensively, her eyes wide with alarm as she leaned back against the door behind her.

'Why not?' Gabriel prompted.

She ran the moistness of her tongue over her lips before answering him. 'Why ruin a perfectly good evening?'

He frowned darkly. 'My kissing you would ruin the evening?'

'Please, Gabriel—'

'But that's what I want to do, Bryn— To please you!' He closed the last of the distance between them as he pulled her gently forward into his arms before looking down at her hungrily.

'I can't!' Her eyes glittered with unshed tears, her hands still held up defensively between them, not pushing Gabriel away, but desperately trying not to touch him either. 'I can't, Gabriel,' she repeated achingly.

It was the despair in her voice, along with those unshed tears glistening in her beautiful eyes, that caused an icy chill down the length of Gabriel's spine as he stilled. 'Talk to me, Bryn,' he encouraged gruffly. 'For God's sake, talk to me!'

'I can't.' She gave another desperate shake of her head.

'I have to kiss you, damn it,' he said, wanting Bryn, but more than that wanting her to trust him.

With her body. With her emotions. With her past....

She looked up at him searchingly in the moonlight for several tense, timeless seconds, before she gave another slow and determined shake of her head. 'I really can't,' she repeated flatly.

'Not good enough, Bryn!' he rasped. 'Tell me you

don't want me to kiss you, that you don't want that as much as I do, that you haven't ached for it all evening, and I won't ask you again,' he encouraged gruffly.

Her throat moved as she swallowed convulsively. 'I can't do that either,' she acknowledged achingly, her voice carrying a desperate sob.

'You want me to make that decision for both of us, is that it?' he bit out harshly.

Bryn was no longer sure what she wanted!

Well... She was, but what she wanted—to kiss and to be kissed by Gabriel—was what she shouldn't want.

He was a D'Angelo, for goodness' sake. And no matter how charming and entertaining he had been this evening, underneath all that charm he was still the cold and ruthless Gabriel D'Angelo from all those years ago. To allow— To *want* to kiss and be kissed by that man went against every instinct of loyalty she had, as well as every shred of self-preservation she possessed.

Except... She couldn't escape the fact that the man she had met earlier today, the man she had just spent the evening with—the same man who made her pulse race and caused her body to be so achingly aware of everything about him—wasn't in the least cold or ruthless, but was instead hot and seductive. *That* man she desperately wanted and longed to kiss.

Which was utter madness, when she knew exactly how Gabriel would react if he knew who she really was.

'Please let me, Bryn.'

She couldn't breathe as she looked up at Gabriel, unable to make a move to stop him as his hands moved up to cup her cheeks and lift her face to his, feeling herself drowning, becoming totally lost in the dark and enticingly warm depths of his piercing brown eyes as his mouth slowly descended towards hers.

CHAPTER FIVE

BRYN MELTED AS Gabriel first sipped, tasted and then devoured her as he crushed her lips beneath his, hearing the low groan in his throat as her fingers became entwined in the dark hair at his nape. Her breasts were heavy and aroused as they pressed against the hardness of his chest, Gabriel having pulled her in as tightly against him as was possible in the confines of the car as he continued to kiss her with an ever-deepening hunger.

A hunger that Bryn couldn't help but feel in return, groaning low in her throat as she felt the brush of Gabriel's tongue against her bottom lip, light, questing, possessing as her lips parted and his tongue surged inside, licking and tasting, learning every nuance, every dip and curve, his hands a restless caress along the length of her spine.

Bryn broke their kiss, her slender neck arching as she felt Gabriel's hand push her blouse up, his fingers lightly caressing the bareness of her spine, her abdomen, before his hand cupped beneath the bared fullness of her breast.

The soft pad of his thumb was a light, sweeping torture across her aroused nipple, his lips a hot caress against Bryn's throat as pleasure coursed hotly through her body, heating, dampening between her thighs, as he captured her aching nipple between thumb and finger, squeezing lightly.

His ragged breath burned against her throat as his other hand moved to unfasten the buttons of her blouse, allowing his questing lips to move lower, his tongue a sweeping, hungry caress against the tops of her breasts before dipping lower as he sucked her aching, straining nipple into the moist heat of his mouth.

Bryn's head fell back against the headrest behind her, her fingers becoming entwined in the dark thickness of Gabriel's hair as she held him against her, the intense pleasure of the dual assault of Gabriel's lips and fingers against her breasts almost too much to bear.

Almost.

The pleasure was just too good, too exquisite, as it built higher, and then higher still, as Gabriel continued to draw deeply on her nipple, his tongue a moist and rasping caress against that burgeoning heat, rising higher, deeper, until she felt as if she would explode into a million pieces that could surely never be completely put back together again.

Never.

'Gabriel, you have to stop!'

Gabriel was so aroused by the taste of Bryn and the desire that had raged so deeply, so out of control between them, that it took him several moments to realise that her hands were now pushing against his chest, her face turned away from him as she struggled to free herself from his arms.

He backed off the instant he realised what she was doing; he had never forced himself on a woman in his life before and he certainly wasn't about to start now. He desired Bryn too much to ever want to do anything that she didn't want, ache for, as much as he did.

Gabriel's breathing sounded harsh in the confines of the car. 'Hell, I totally forgot where we were.' He gave a wince as he realised they were still sitting in his car parked outside the building where Bryn lived, and that although the side windows of the car were darkened glass, the windscreen certainly wasn't. 'I'm sorry, Bryn.' He ran an agitated hand restlessly through the dark thickness of his hair.

She avoided so much as looking at him as she straightened and refastened her blouse with hands that shook slightly, her face pale in the moonlight.

'Bryn?'

'Not now, Gabriel. In fact, not ever!' she insisted shakily. 'I have to go.' She turned to look out of the side window. 'I— Thank you for dinner. I enjoyed Antonio's.'

'Just not what followed?' Gabriel murmured knowingly.

Bryn gave a pained grimace. 'I'm sure you'll agree it wasn't the most sensible thing either of us has ever done—'

'Bryn, will you, for the love of God, look at me?' he rasped his frustration with the situation. 'Talk to me, damn it!'

She turned slowly, eyes huge and shadowed, her cheeks as pale as ivory in the moonlight. 'I don't know what you want me to say.'

'Don't you?'

She looked away from the intensity of his gaze. 'How about, this should never have happened?' She gave a shake of her head. 'We both know that already.'

'Do we?'

'Yes.' Bryn looked at him searchingly. 'Unless— Is this standard procedure? Did you think, expect, that I would be so grateful to be included in the exhibition at

Archangel I would—?' She broke off abruptly as she obviously saw, and recognised, the tightening of Gabriel's jaw and the anger now glittering in the darkness of his eyes.

'I'm getting a little tired of that accusation, Bryn.' He spoke softly, dangerously so. 'And no, kissing me isn't the price you're expected to pay for inclusion in the exhibition!'

She winced. 'I didn't exactly say that—'

'You didn't *exactly* have to!' Gabriel bit out harshly, wondering if he had ever been this angry in his life before. 'What the hell sort of man do you think I am? Don't answer that,' he immediately amended. He already knew what sort of man Bryn thought he was.

Gabriel had thought, believed, that after a rocky start they had managed to spend a relaxed evening together, that Bryn was starting to see beyond what happened in the past—starting to see him beyond that—and instead she now thought him capable of using his position as one of the owners of the gallery to— What an idiot, what a fool he was, to think that Bryn could ever see him as anything more than the man who had helped to put her father in prison....

'You're right, Bryn. You should go inside now,' he growled coldly. 'Before you think of something else to say to insult me.'

Bryn hesitated, continuing to look at Gabriel searchingly, unable to read anything from his suddenly closed expression. 'It wasn't my intention to insult you—'

'Then heaven help me if you ever do mean it,' he muttered disgustedly.

She moistened her lips with the tip of her tongue. 'I was— I just— Our going out to dinner earlier, what happened just now, it was a mistake.'

'Mine or yours?'

'For both of us,' she insisted firmly. 'And I think it would be better, for the sake of the exhibition, if it didn't happen again. If we keep things on a purely business footing between the two of us from now on,' she added.

'As opposed to?'

'Anything less than a business footing,' she maintained determinedly.

Gabriel gave a grim smile. 'Do you really think that's possible after what just happened?'

Bryn wasn't sure a business footing had ever been a possibility between herself and Gabriel—and she was utterly convinced of it after her response to him just now. Gabriel had only needed to kiss her, to touch her, to caress her and she had forgotten everything but him and the moment. Nothing else had mattered at that moment. Nothing.

And it had to. It must. Because she wasn't about to allow herself to suffer the heartache of falling in love with Gabriel D'Angelo.

Not again.

Gabriel took in the stubborn lifting of Bryn's chin, the determined glitter in her eyes, and knew that she meant it when she said she wanted the two of them to go back to having a business relationship only.

If not for the reason she stated.

He was thirty-three years old, had been sexually active for almost seventeen of those years, and he was experienced enough to know when a woman desired him. And, whether she liked it or not, Bryn had been looking at him all evening as if she desired him as much as he desired her, and what had happened just now had been a direct result of that mutual desire. Bryn might wish it weren't so, might believe it was insanity on her part to be attracted to Gabriel while still carrying the pain of the past, but none of that changed the fact that she *did* want him.

Whether or not she actually *liked* him was something else entirely.

And that mattered to Gabriel.

Because he not only desired Bryn, he liked her. He had liked her five years ago too, even before he had seen her unshakeable loyalty to her father, and the quiet strength she had offered her mother as the two of them had sat together in the courtroom day after day.

Just as he admired Bryn's determination since meeting her again, her tenacity to succeed so intense that she had even been willing to become involved with the Archangel Gallery, to meet with at least one of the detested D'Angelo brothers, in order to achieve the success she so desired.

Kissing and embracing Bryn while knowing she didn't return that liking was not an option for Gabriel. Not with this particular woman. 'Okay, Bryn—' he nodded tersely '—if that's how you want it, then that's how it will be from now on,' he bit out abruptly.

She blinked. 'You're saying you agree to—to just a business relationship between the two of us?'

His jaw tightened. 'I believe I just said so, yes. Do you not believe me?' he rasped as she continued to look at him warily.

Of course Bryn believed Gabriel; why shouldn't she, when he had never done anything, five years ago or now, to give her cause not to believe he always did and meant what he said?

It was just— She didn't— Damn it! Part of her was actually irritated and hurt that Gabriel had agreed so easily to the two of them resuming a business relationship. Even if it had been her suggestion.

Which was utterly ridiculous. The exhibition wasn't until next month, and she knew from the things Gabriel had told her earlier—she had heard at least some of what he had to say—that she would be expected to go to Archangel often during the next few weeks, sit for photographs and provide the contents for the blurb for the catalogue, and to oversee and approve the framing of her paintings. And it would be far better, for everyone involved, if she and Gabriel could manage to maintain at least a semblance of politeness between the two of them during that time.

Bryn knew all that.

Logically, she accepted all of that.

Illogically, she knew that the attraction she had felt towards Gabriel five years ago might have been buried, might have remained dormant for those same five years, but that it was still very much alive inside her, and had only needed for her to see him again, to be with him again, for it to be rekindled.

To rage out of control.

As she had been out of control a few minutes ago, so much so that she had been balanced on the edge of orgasm just from the touch of Gabriel's lips and hands on her body.

What made it all so much worse, so much harder to fight that desire the second time around, was knowing that Gabriel obviously returned the attraction.

An attraction he felt for Bryn Jones. A desire he felt for Bryn Jones.

Because he wouldn't have allowed Sabryna Harper within ten feet of him!

Which was why the two of them couldn't do this

again, why they had to set down the rules right now for any future meetings between them. 'That's good.' She nodded as she bent to collect her shoulder bag from the floor of the car before turning to open the door.

'Wait there,' Gabriel instructed tersely as he turned, climbed out of the car and came round to open her door for her. 'My mother taught me it's polite, and safer, to always walk a lady to her door,' he explained as Bryn looked up at him questioningly.

A courtesy that Bryn wasn't sure, with her own lack of politeness to Gabriel just now, that she deserved. 'Once again, thank you for dinner and introducing me to Antonio's. It's definitely the place for pizza,' she murmured as she searched for her keys in her bag once they were standing outside her door.

He nodded tersely. 'I'm going away on business for a few days, so I probably won't see you on Monday.' He shrugged. 'But you've already met and like Eric?'

'Yes.' Was that sudden, heavy feeling in her chest disappointment because she now knew there wasn't even a possibility of her seeing Gabriel again on Monday? If so, then she was in more emotional trouble than she had thought she was. 'Are you going anywhere interesting?' she prompted conversationally.

'Rome,' he replied.

Bryn's eyes widened as she remembered Gabriel telling her earlier that he only went to Rome for 'pleasure'.

And, having stated that she was only interested in a business relationship with him, she had absolutely no right to show the least curiosity—let alone feel that curl of jealousy in the pit of her stomach—about the reason for his going there now.

And yet she knew she did.

'Bryn?'

She forced herself to look up and smile unconcernedly as she unlocked the front door of the house before stepping inside and turning back to face him. 'Enjoy Rome.'

'I usually do,' Gabriel accepted distractedly as he looked down at her searchingly for several long seconds, before accepting there was nothing else for them to say. He turned and returned to his car, part of him wondering if he had imagined the way Bryn had gone suddenly quiet after he had mentioned going away on business, and the slight edge to her tone when she did speak. And if he hadn't imagined it, what did it mean?

Not what he hoped it did, he answered himself derisively. No, all it indicated was that Bryn was relieved, because even the possibility of the two of them meeting again on Monday had now been removed. If he thought it had been for any other reason then he was only fooling himself; Bryn had made it more than clear what she thought of him a few minutes ago. What she believed had been his reason for kissing her.

When his real reason had been because he just hadn't been able to resist any longer. Hadn't been able to fight the fact that she was the last woman on earth he should get involved with because the need, the hunger he felt to taste her was too great. And she had tasted so damned good. She might try to deny it to herself, but she had responded to those kisses and made no protest when Gabriel had touched her breasts.

He now needed this time away from her, to put some distance—literally—between himself and Bryn. And hopefully, by the time he saw her again, he would have his desire for her back under his control.

It was several hours later—several hours and half a bottle of single-malt whisky later—as he relived the evening over and over in his mind, that Gabriel remem-

bered he had told Bryn that he only ever went to Rome
for 'pleasure'.

He wondered—hoped—that might be the reason for
that edge to her tone.

'That looks amazing, Eric.' Bryn's face glowed as she
looked admiringly at the silver gilt frame that had been
put on the painting she always referred to in her mind as
Death of a Rose. It represented so much more than the
death of a single bloom, of course; it was symbolic of
any death: love, hope, dreams. And, as they had hoped,
the silver gilt frame was perfect against the misty back-
ground, the blood-red bloom weeping dew and petals
onto the base of the canvas.

Bryn had spent most of her free time at Archangel
the past four days, safe in the knowledge that Gabriel
was still away in Rome. The highlight of each day had
been the hours she spent in the cavernous basement of
the gallery with Eric choosing the frames they thought
suited to bring out the best in the ten paintings she was
to exhibit at the gallery next month. This evening was
no exception.

As far as Bryn was aware, Gabriel had spent those
same four days—and nights—in Rome, no doubt indulging his every 'pleasure'.

Bryn had kept busy while at the same time determinedly not thinking of Gabriel, the evening they had
spent together, or the ways in which he might now be
indulging his pleasure in Rome!

And she wasn't going to think about him now either.
'It's perfect!' Bryn enthused as she continued to gaze at
the painting in the silver gilt frame.

Eric nodded. 'Gabriel will have the final yay or nay,

of course, but I think he'll like what we've done so far. No doubt he'll change it if not,' he added ruefully.

Bryn's smile faded at mention of Gabriel. 'He will?'

'He has a really good eye for this stuff.' Eric shrugged.

'Better than you?'

'Much better,' Eric confirmed without rancour. 'All of the D'Angelo brothers do. They're the reason I wanted to work for the Archangel Galleries.'

Eric took the painting down off the wall where they had hung it so as best to appreciate the effect of the framing. 'Feel like going for a drink somewhere when we've finished here?' he suggested lightly as he stored the painting away safely.

'I—'

'I believe you'll find that Bryn doesn't believe in mixing business with pleasure.'

Bryn's heart stopped beating at the harsh sound of Gabriel's voice behind her. She whipped round quickly to find him standing in the doorway just feet away. And looking—

Looking more lethally attractive than when she had last seen him—if that was possible—his dark brown bespoke suit obviously designer label, his cream shirt and tie of the finest silk, his ebony hair slightly tousled in that just-got-out-of-bed style, his face tanned a deeper gold, intensifying the colour of his warm, chocolate-brown eyes.

No, his eyes weren't warm this evening. They were icy. Like a deep arctic chill.

An arctic chill that swept contemptuously over Bryn as the coldness of that gaze moved over her slowly from head to toe and then back again. Gabriel's top lip curled back derisively as he took in her casual appearance in a black short-sleeved T-shirt and black low-rider denims and a face that was completely bare of make-up. At the very least Bryn felt she looked like the penniless student she had once been—still was?—compared to Gabriel's expensive and sartorial elegance.

Bryn looked more stunningly beautiful than ever, Gabriel acknowledged irritably, her eyes glowing a warm dove-grey, her cheeks flushed with becoming colour.

At least, her eyes *had* been glowing a warm dove-grey, and there *had* been colour in her cheeks too, as she obviously enjoyed Eric's company.

Until she turned to look at Gabriel, at which point her gaze had quickly become guarded and her cheeks had paled.

His mouth tightened as he glanced across at Eric. 'If you've finished with Bryn for this evening, I need to speak with her for a few minutes.' It was a statement rather than a question, Gabriel having no intention of taking no for an answer. From either Eric or Bryn.

'Actually,' Bryn began tentatively, 'I—'

'I think it's best if we go upstairs to my office for this conversation, Bryn.' Gabriel held the door open pointedly.

Her eyes widened, her creamy throat moving as she swallowed then wet the dryness of her lips with the tip of her tongue. 'I— Yes, of course.' Her hands were gripped tightly together in front of her, knuckles showing white. 'A rain check on that drink, Eric?'

Eric gave a relaxed smile, obviously completely oblivious to the underlying tension between Gabriel and Bryn. 'No problem,' he agreed easily.

Which was perhaps as well; Gabriel had always had a healthy respect and liking for their London in-house art expert, and he would hate to ruin their working relationship by having to exert his executive power. 'Bryn?' he prompted tersely.

She grabbed her denim jacket and shoulder bag from a chair before hurrying across the room to join him, pressing her spine back against the door frame so as not to come into contact with him as she slipped out into the hallway, her expression apprehensive as she waited for Gabriel to join her.

An entirely appropriate apprehension, as it happened. 'Whisky?'

Bryn stood awkwardly in the middle of Gabriel's elegant office watching as he removed his jacket and draped it over a chair before moving to the bar in long, easy strides. They had travelled up in the lift together in complete silence. Bryn's apprehensive. Gabriel's grimly foreboding.

It didn't help that Bryn was still uncomfortably aware of how young and gauche she must appear to him, in her casual clothes and wearing no make-up, only to then chastise herself for even caring what, if anything, he might think of her appearance. Gabriel D'Angelo was one of the owners of the gallery where her paintings were to be exhibited next month, nothing more. She couldn't allow him to be any more than that.

'It's a little early in the evening for me, thanks,' she refused lightly. 'Unless you think I might need it?' she added uncertainly as she saw the hard implacability of his expression.

A hard implacability that showed her just how relaxed Gabriel had been on the previous occasions the two of them had met and spent time together....

Gabriel made no comment as he poured an inch of whisky into two crystal glasses before crossing the room and holding one out to Bryn.

The past four days had been successful ones for him as far as business went, but far less so on a personal level, as Gabriel hadn't been able to shake off thoughts and memories of Bryn. Of that last evening with her, when the desire the two of them felt for each other had raged so out of control.

As Gabriel had no doubt it would rage out of control again, despite the business-only arrangement Bryn had suggested and Gabriel had reluctantly agreed to. Gabriel had wanted this woman five years ago, and he wanted her still. A fact that had been brought painfully home to him after he had spent an evening with the beautiful Lucia while in Rome, and then politely walked her to the door of her apartment before leaving again, rather than spending the night with her as he would normally have done. He hadn't felt a shred of desire to bed the raven-haired beauty because Bryn was the woman he wanted. In his arms. In his bed. In his possession! And that was never going to happen while the events of the past were allowed to continue to lurk in the shadows between them.

'You're going to need it,' he confirmed gruffly. 'We both are,' he added with hard self-derision, taking a much-needed sip from his own whisky glass as Bryn's perfume, that heady spice and desirable woman, invaded his senses.

Her hand moved up and her fingers curled around the proffered glass, a hand that shook as she made no effort to drink any of it. 'How was Rome?'

'Beautiful, as always.' Gabriel stepped away from her to stand with his back to one of the floor-to-ceiling picture windows, needing to put space between himself and Bryn—between himself and that insidious perfume invading his senses. 'It took some persuading but I finally managed to acquire the two magnificent frescoes for the gallery that I went to look at.'

'Oh?'

His mouth twisted mockingly as he saw, and recognised, the surprise in her expression. 'I did tell you I was going away on business.'

Yes, he had, but Bryn hadn't believed him, after his previous comment. Not that it really mattered whether or not she believed him, then or now; it was none of her business what Gabriel had been doing in Rome for the past few days.

At the same time as she knew part of her wanted to know, had anguished over it during those days and nights, as to what woman, or women, Gabriel was spending his time with in Rome.

Nor did she feel in the least reassured about his mood now as she saw the grimness of his expression. 'So what was it you wanted to talk to me about?' she prompted with forced lightness.

'Sabryna Harper.'

CHAPTER SIX

'BRYN, SIT DOWN here, put your head between your knees and just breathe, damn it! Yes, that's right,' Gabriel rasped harshly, slamming his glass down on the coffee table before guiding Bryn over to an armchair to push her head down between her knees as she drew huge gasping breaths of air into her starved lungs. 'Damn it, woman, do you have something against my thirty-year-old single-malt whisky?'

Gabriel bent down to retrieve the glass from where Bryn had dropped it a minute or so ago as she'd looked in danger of passing out completely. He put the glass back on the bar and grabbed a cloth to soak up the golden puddle of whisky that had seeped into the pale carpet.

'What did you say?' He frowned as he heard her mutter something in the vicinity of her knees.

'I said,' she bit out succinctly as she raised her head to glare at him, her face deathly pale, eyes deep grey wells of anguish, 'I don't give a damn about your thirty-year-old single-malt whisky!'

'I doubt you'll feel that way when I take the price of the bottle out of the sale of your paintings,' Gabriel assured her dryly as he sat back on his heels.

'What sale?' she came back bitterly, sitting up in the chair now that the first danger of her fainting had obviously passed, her expression one of proud fragility. 'How could you do that?' she continued accusingly before he could answer. 'How could you just come out with a statement like that without—without giving me some sort of prior warning?'

Well, it hadn't taken long for her to recover from the initial shock, Gabriel appreciated ruefully. 'What sort of warning should I have given you, Bryn?' he challenged as he stood up to throw the sticky whisky-soaked cloth disgustedly down onto the bar. '"Oh, by the way, I think the two of us may have met before across a crowded courtroom"? Or, "You look a lot like Sabryna Harper, the daughter of—"? Do not collapse on me again, Bryn!' he warned harshly as her face took on a grey tinge, her chest barely moving beneath the black T-shirt as she breathed shallowly.

'I'm not about to collapse.' Instead, she stood up abruptly, taking a few seconds to steady herself before straightening determinedly, her chin held high. 'How long have you known?'

He quirked one dark brow. 'That Bryn Jones is Sabryna Harper?'

'Yes!' she hissed, jaw clenching.

Gabriel gave a dismissive shrug. 'Since the beginning.'

'Since...?' Bryn gasped, reaching down to grasp the arm of the chair as she felt herself sway again, despite her earlier claim that she wouldn't collapse again. She gave a shake of her head. 'You can't have done!'

Brown eyes looked across at her calmly. 'Why can't I?'

'Because— Well, because— Because you can't!' Her mouth firmed as she shied away from listing those reasons why. 'I would never have got this far in the competition if you had known who I was from the beginning!'

He shrugged, his shoulders wide and muscled in the cream silk shirt. 'Admittedly my brother Rafe advised against your inclusion, but I decided—'

'Your brother Raphael knows who I am too?' She stared at him in disbelief.

'You know, Bryn, we're going to get a lot further with this conversation if we work on the understanding that I invariably tell the truth. No matter what the consequences,' he added harshly.

And one of those consequences had been Bryn's father going to prison. An indisputable fact that hung between the two of them, unsaid but there nonetheless.

'It was Michael who recognised you initially,' Gabriel continued calmly. 'He saw you when you came in for an interview with Eric at the gallery that first day, and then he spoke to Rafe about it, who then told me.'

'Quite the secret little coterie of spies, aren't you?' Bryn snapped defensively, still completely thrown and befuddled by Gabriel's admission of having known who she was from that first day.

Something she was still having trouble absorbing. Because if that really was the truth, as Gabriel claimed it was, then he had chosen her as a finalist for the New Artists Exhibition knowing exactly who and what she was.

Had ogled her breasts, that first day here in his office knowing exactly who she was. Had taken her out to dinner at Antonio's knowing exactly who she was. Had kissed her later that same evening in his car knowing exactly who she was.

Which made absolutely no sense to Bryn whatsoever.

'I don't think insulting me, or my brothers, is helpful to this conversation either,' Gabriel drawled.

Gabriel had decided while he was away in Rome and thinking of her constantly that the truth couldn't remain unspoken between them once he returned to London. And if Bryn wouldn't tell him the truth, then it was up to him to do it.

Bryn so obviously disliked, perhaps even hated, Gabriel for the part he had played in her father's trial. Her desire now, her physical response to him, much as she might hate it, and him, was just as undeniable. And Gabriel couldn't see any way forward for the two of them if the truth of who Bryn really was continued to remain unspoken between them.

Of course, there was always the possibility that there was still no way forward for the two of them once they had spoken of it, but Gabriel knew they couldn't go on any longer with this lie standing between them, that the longer he allowed that omission to continue, the less chance there was that he and Bryn could ever come to any sort of understanding of each other.

'I asked you to trust me several times, Bryn, to talk to me,' he reminded huskily.

Her eyes widened. 'And this was what you meant? That I should trust you enough to tell you I'm really Sabryna Harper, William Harper's daughter?'

'Yes,' Gabriel bit out tautly.

Bryn continued to stare at him disbelievingly. 'That's the most ridiculous thing you've ever said to me!'

He gave a derisive smile. 'Nevertheless, it's the truth.'

She gave a dazed shake of her head. 'In what universe did you think that was ever going to happen?' Gabriel seriously expected her to— He had really thought that she would one day trust him enough to tell him, to confide in him. 'It was never going to happen,' she stated flatly.

He drew in a sharp breath. 'That's…unfortunate.'

'I don't see why,' she challenged scathingly. 'Luckily for you, you already have your reserve candidate for the

New Artists Exhibition, so no problem there once you've had the pleasure of kicking me off—'

'I'm not kicking you off anything, Bryn, and I resent the fact that you think it would ever be a pleasure for me to do so,' he cut in harshly, running an agitated hand through the darkness of his hair as he scowled. 'And why the hell would I do that, when you're far and away the best artist in the exhibition?'

'Why would you?' she repeated challengingly. 'I'm William Harper's daughter!' she reminded him—as if saying it repeatedly would help her to accept that Gabriel really did know, had always known, exactly who she was.

'And, as I've already stated, I knew that when you were chosen as one of the six finalists.'

Yes, he had, which again made absolutely no sense to Bryn. Her father's name was so shrouded in scandal that her mother had decided to distance them from it all by changing their last name after he had died. A scandal that had been connected to this very gallery and the D'Angelo name; she couldn't believe that Gabriel would ever want to risk the resurrection of that scandal by exhibiting the paintings of William's daughter. And certainly not intentionally.

She looked across at him guardedly, once again aware of how he owned the elegantly furnished office rather than the opulence dominating the man; Gabriel was such a force in his own right that he seemed to own the very air around him, no matter what his surroundings. Something that had been all too apparent during her father's trial—even the judge hearing the case had treated him with a deference and respect he hadn't shown to anyone else in the courtroom. Something that had no doubt added weight to the evidence Gabriel gave against her father.

Not that any weight had needed to be added; there had been no doubting her father's guilt, not only for attempting to sell a fake Turner, but for having commissioned the forgery in the first place, having paid an artist in Poland a pittance to paint the forgery and then attempting to sell it for millions of pounds to Gabriel and the Archangel Gallery.

'Bryn, even without Michael's help, I would have known who you were the first time I looked at you again….'

She looked up at Gabriel sharply. 'I don't see how when my name and appearance are so different from five years ago.'

He gave a humourless smile. 'It's unlikely I'd ever forget the young woman who glared her hatred across a courtroom at me for days on end. Those eyes alone would have given you away.'

Bryn had never forgotten him either, but for quite a different reason.

Gabriel D'Angelo had, quite simply, been the most charismatic and darkly intriguing man she had ever set eyes on. But it was more than that; *he* was more than that. Gabriel had awakened something deep inside the eighteen-year-old overweight and slightly shy Sabryna that had filled her night fantasies for weeks before her father's arrest, and months after the trial had ended.

The same fantasies that had filled all of her nights since meeting Gabriel again a week ago. The same desire that had awakened in her again, a few minutes ago in the basement, the second she had heard his voice behind her. The same desire that had caused her breath to catch in her throat when she'd turned to look at him. The same desire that raged through her even now, just from seeing how his cream silk shirt fitted so well over the broadness of his shoulders and tapered waist, the tailored brown trousers of his suit draping elegantly from his hips. This man—Gabriel—awakened that hunger inside her just by being in the same room with her.

'How is your mother, Bryn?'

She looked at him warily. 'Why are you asking?' she came back defensively.

He shrugged. 'Because I'd like to know?'

'My mother is fine. She remarried two years ago. Happily.'

'That's good.' He nodded.

'Gabriel, if this is some sort of guilt trip on your part—'

'It's not,' Gabriel cut in harshly. 'Damn it, Bryn, I have nothing—absolutely nothing—to feel guilty about. Am I sorry for the way it happened, the way your mother's and your own life were affected? Yes, I am. But your father was the guilty one, Bryn, not me. Am I sorry that he died in prison only months later? Yes, of course I am,' he rasped. 'But I didn't put him there. He put himself there by his own actions!'

Yes, he had. And part of Bryn had never forgiven her father for that.

Which was something *she* had to live with. 'You kissed me the night before my father was arrested!' she reminded accusingly.

He closed his eyes briefly before opening them again. 'I know that. And I wanted to tell you— Despite being warned by the police, and my lawyers, not to discuss the case with anyone, I almost told you that night! It almost killed me not to do so.' He gave a shake of his head.

'I don't believe you,' she breathed heavily.

'No,' he accepted heavily. 'I tried to see you, Bryn. Against the advice of my lawyers I tried to see you again, after your father was arrested, during the trial, after the trial. I tried, Bryn! I wanted to explain, to— I never wanted to hurt you, Bryn,' he assured earnestly.

'But you did it anyway.'

'I told you, I had no choice, damn it.'

Perhaps he hadn't, but that didn't stop Bryn from resenting his silence. From resenting the fact that he had kissed her that night. From resenting the fact that he had broken her heart the following day....

'I didn't want to see or speak with you again.' She gave an abrupt shake of her head. 'You had nothing to say that I wanted to hear.'

'I guessed that,' he said bleakly.

She breathed in deeply. 'So where do we go from here?'

Gabriel looked at her from beneath hooded lids. 'Where do you want us to go?'

To his bed. On top of his marble desk. On the sofa. Up against a wall! Bryn didn't care about the 'where' as long as Gabriel finished what he had started in his car last Friday evening. The desire she had felt then was nothing compared to what it was now, after days of not seeing him, not being with him.

And she hated herself for it. Hated that in spite of everything, she still felt that way, still wanted him!

She moistened her lips with the tip of her tongue. 'I need to know— Have these past few days all been some sort of sick game? An act of revenge for what my father—'

'I could ask the same of you!' he grated harshly, anger flaring in those deep brown eyes, lips thinned, a nerve pulsing in his aggressively set jaw. His body was rigid with that same tension, his hands clenched at his sides before he reached out to pick up the whisky glass he had put down earlier, drinking down the contents in one swallow. 'In fact, my brothers insist on it!'

'Then ask, damn it,' Bryn bit out shakily. He looked at her guardedly.

'Why did you do it, Bryn? Why did you enter your paintings in a competition being run by the gallery, the man, who helped put your father in prison?'

Bryn drew her breath in sharply, all the colour draining from her cheeks as the starkness of Gabriel's words hammered into her like a blow she wasn't sure she was ever going to recover from.

The truth was completely out in the open now, spoken aloud between them with no going back, and no fooling herself, allowing herself to indulge her desire for this man, by assuring herself that it was okay to do so because Gabriel had no idea who she really was. Because he did know. He had always known.

She avoided meeting that accusing gaze. 'The truth?'

That nerve pulsed in his clenched jaw. 'In the circumstances, I'll accept nothing less.'

Bryn nodded. 'I was desperate. I'm an unknown artist who wants more than anything to succeed, and the best way to do that is to be exhibited in the most prestigious private gallery in London.'

'Thank you,' he accepted derisively.

Her anger flared again at his obvious sarcasm. 'I was stating a fact, not giving a compliment!'

Gabriel knew that. Knew Bryn. Not as well as he wanted to, but he did know her as being determined, gutsy and proud. All traits he could admire. It was the beautiful and desirable that destroyed him!

'Heaven forbid you should ever do that,' he drawled, eyeing the whisky bottle longingly as he placed his empty glass down on the bar before walking away. The enigma that was Bryn might be enough to turn any man to drink, at the same time as that same man—namely Gabriel!—would be well advised to keep his wits about him whenever he was in her company.

'Yes. Well.' She turned to walk over to the long picture windows, hands thrust into the back pockets of her jeans as she stood with her back towards him, her spiky hair in silhouette. 'Believe me, nothing less would have induced me to come anywhere near your gallery or you ever again!'

Gabriel gave a wince. 'Perhaps a little less honesty on your part might be preferable after all.'

'What do you want me to do now, Gabriel?' she continued tersely. 'Quietly withdraw from the exhibition?'

'I've already said that isn't an option,' Gabriel bit out.

She turned back slowly, stance defensive, breasts thrust forward, hands in her pockets. 'Then what are my options?'

That was a good question.

Having made the decision to put an end to this pretence, Gabriel had gone over the possible scenarios of this conversation over and over again in his mind on his flight back from Rome.

There seemed to be only two possible outcomes.

Outcome one—the one that was undoubtedly the best one for Bryn—was that they would continue with the business-only relationship they had agreed upon, and she would exhibit her paintings in the gallery next month. Outcome two—the one that Gabriel disliked the most—was that Bryn would walk away now: from the gallery, the exhibition and from him.

There was a third outcome—the one that Gabriel wanted but knew was never going to happen. In that Bryn continued with the exhibition, and the two of them agreed to put the past behind them and continue from where they had left off on Friday evening!

An outcome that Gabriel knew to be pure fantasy on his part, following on from Bryn's blunt comment.

His mouth tightened. 'What's going on between you and Eric?'

She blinked, lashes long and dark around those dove-grey eyes. 'Sorry?'

Gabriel's days in Rome, persuading an elderly count to sell two small frescoes to the Archangel Gallery, had been something of an ordeal as his thoughts had constantly wandered to the problem of what to do about Bryn rather than concentrating on the task in front of him. And his flight back to England had been consumed with thoughts of the conversation he needed to have with her.

He had only called in at the gallery for a few minutes to drop off some papers in his office before going to Bryn's apartment. He had been surprised to learn from the night security that Miss Jones and Mr Sanders were still in the building. Going down to the basement and seeing Bryn there with Eric, obviously totally at ease with him, laughing with him—being invited to go out for a drink with him—had not improved Gabriel's already taciturn mood.

'If you decide to go ahead with the exhibition at Archangel, and the business-relationship rule, then that rule will apply to all employees of the gallery, not just me,' he bit out harshly.

Bryn gave a slow shake of her head. 'I don't— Are you suggesting— Do you think that Eric and I are involved? Romantically?' she added incredulously.

It had occurred to him, yes.

Eric Sanders was only a year or two older than Gabriel, and pleasant enough to look at. He was also an extremely well qualified and respected art expert, and Archangel was lucky to have him.

Even so, Gabriel knew that he wouldn't hesitate to find some way to dismiss the other man if it should turn out that he and Bryn were now 'romantically involved'.

Bryn stared at Gabriel D'Angelo in disbelief. This was the same man she had almost allowed to make love to her in his car just days ago, a lapse on her part that still made her feel hot all over every time she thought of it—and she had thought of it a lot since Friday evening!

Did Gabriel really think— Did he believe that she would have become involved with another man in the time he had been away in Rome?

'If you bothered to find out a little more personal information about your employees,' she snapped angrily, 'then you would know that Eric is engaged to a very lovely girl called Wendy, and that the two of them are getting married in three months' time!'

Gabriel nodded tersely, lids hooded over those dark brown eyes. 'As it happens, I do know that.'

Her eyes widened. 'But you still think that I— That the two of us have been— You don't think much of me, do you?'

Gabriel thought *about* this woman far too much than was comfortable. Or wise. Or conducive to a calm or logical frame of mind. Which was why he had jumped to the conclusion he had in regard to the friendly ease that obviously existed between Eric and Bryn!

None of which he was about to admit out loud to Bryn when she was this prickly and defensive. 'I'm tired and irritable and I haven't eaten yet this evening.'

Her eyes widened indignantly. 'And that's the excuse you're giving for accusing me of being involved with a man who's happily engaged to another woman?'

Gabriel gritted his teeth. It was definitely the only explanation he was willing to admit to at this moment; admitting his jealousy of the other man wasn't an option. 'It is, yes.'

She gave an impatient shake of her head. 'We seem to be veering off the relevant subject.'

He quirked mocking brows. 'My being hungry isn't relevant to you?'

'You've just dropped the equivalent of a bombshell on top of my head, by revealing that you've been aware from the beginning who I am, so no,' she snapped, 'your being hungry isn't of the least importance to me. Or the fact that you're also tired and insultingly irritable!'

He should have followed his first instinct when they had entered the privacy of his office a short time ago, Gabriel realised ruefully—which had been to strip Bryn naked, pick her up in his arms and carry her over to his desk to lay her down on the top of it, before making fierce and satisfying love to her!

That was what he *should* have done.

What he still wanted to do....

He now wanted that so badly, his erection so hard and aching against the soft material of his trousers, that the past few days might just as well not have happened.

Bryn eyed Gabriel uncertainly, her mouth suddenly dry as he began slowly stalking towards her, a determined glitter in the intensity of his dark gaze. 'Gabriel, what are you doing?' She took a step back, only to feel the cold of the window down the length of her spine as she stood flush against it.

'What I should have done the moment I saw you again,' Gabriel growled as he stood in front of her, the heat of his body not quite touching hers as his hands moved up to rest on the glass of the window on either side of her head, effectively holding her captive within the circle of his arms. His breath was a warm caress across her cheeks, those deep brown eyes holding—possessing—hers as she found it impossible to break away from the intensity of his gaze.

Bryn's heart was pounding rapidly in her chest, and she couldn't breathe, certainly couldn't have moved, even if someone had shouted 'fire'. Because the only fire that mattered to her was right here between the two of them as it blazed fiercely, heatedly, out of control.

'That might have been a bit awkward, considering that Eric was in the room at the time,' she said, attempting to lighten the tension currently sizzling between them.

'Do I look as if I care who else was in the room?'

The reckless glitter in his eyes answered with a resounding no to the question. 'You do realise that this—whatever this is—is only going to complicate an already impossible situation?'

He nodded briefly. 'And I'm currently in the mood to complicate the hell out of it!'

Bryn swallowed before running her tongue over her lips.

'Did you know you have a habit of doing that?' Gabriel murmured achingly.

'I do?' Bryn's voice was just as hushed; the whole building was so empty and quiet at this time of night, with none of the sounds from outside penetrating the thick glass behind her either, giving the impression that they were the only two people in the world. The only two that mattered at this moment.

'Mmm.' He nodded, gaze transfixed on her slightly parted lips. 'And every time you do it I want to replace your tongue with mine.'

'You do?' Bryn still couldn't move, her heart beating

even louder, faster in her chest, as a wave of heat washed
over her, plumping the lips between her thighs, causing a
fire in her belly, swelling her breasts, her nipples becoming
engorged against her T-shirt, before that heat licked
up the slenderness of her throat and coloured her cheeks.

'Mmm.' Gabriel gave another nod as he raised the
fierceness of his gaze to meet hers. 'And the way I see
it, you have two choices right now.'

She swallowed. 'Which are?'

He smiled slightly. 'One, you can take me away
from here and feed me. Two—and this is my personal
favourite—we stay here instead and indulge a very different
appetite.'

Against her better judgement, the second choice was
Bryn's personal favourite too!

Right here and right now.

Later—much later—she knew she would feel totally
differently about that choice, but the two of them were
caught in a moment seemingly out of time, where there
was no past and no future, only now, her body expectantly
aroused, aching with hunger. For Gabriel. For the
touch of his hands. The feel of his lips against her skin.
Everywhere.

She forced herself to make some effort at resisting
that hunger. 'There is the third choice of my just walking
away.'

Gabriel shook his head. 'Not this time.'

'But—'

'No buts, Bryn.' He rested the heat of his forehead
against hers, those brown eyes now mesmerisingly close
to hers. 'It's your choice, Bryn,' he assured huskily. 'But
I advise that you choose quickly!' he added urgently.

Bryn felt surrounded by him, held captive by him—
his physical presence, his heat, the sensual pull of that

muscled body so dangerously close to her own—so much so that she knew that the choice had already been made for her.

CHAPTER SEVEN

GABRIEL FELT AS if time had stopped as he waited for Bryn to answer—an answer that, knowing Bryn, could very well be her deciding to knee him in the groin, rather than choosing either of the two options he had so arrogantly given her!

His only excuse for that arrogance was the need he felt, the burning ache he had, to make love to her—which he doubted the fiery Bryn would see as a reasonable excuse at all.

His jaw was clenched, his forehead slightly damp against Bryn's, his arms rigid as he kept his hands flat on the window on either side of her head. He continued to hold himself back from coming into contact with her body, his arousal a throbbing ache, his shoulders tense as he waited for her to speak. For her to decide, to choose, to determine what happened next.

Bryn's tongue flicked nervously across her lips, only for her to quickly bring a halt to the nervous movement as she saw the way the darkness of Gabriel's gaze was now fixed so intently on those parted and moist lips.

She breathed raggedly, unevenly, her gaze continuing to hold Gabriel's as she spoke in a hushed voice. 'I'm getting a neck ache just looking up at— What are you doing?' She gasped as Gabriel skimmed his hands lightly down her arms, placing them on her waist before moving down onto his knees in front of her. Bryn was forced to reach out and grasp onto the support of his shoulders as she tottered at the suddenness of the movement, Gabriel's eyes now level with her breasts. 'Better?' he murmured throatily.

Better wasn't quite the word Bryn would have used— she would have described their current position as *very* dangerous.

Gabriel was so close now, his face just a breath away, allowing her to see the fire in the depths of those chocolate-brown eyes up close and very personal, the darkness of his hair falling rakishly, enticingly, over his forehead, those sculptured lips parted oh-so-temptingly.

The warmth of his hands on her waist seemed to burn through the cotton of her T-shirt. Big hands. So much so that they almost spanned the slenderness of her waist completely.

Bryn had felt surrounded by Gabriel before, but now she felt totally overwhelmed by his close proximity, the burning heat of his hands on her waist, that same heart burning in his eyes as he looked up at her. 'You do realise this isn't going to change anything, right?'

'I don't want to change anything. I'm more than happy with exactly where we are right now,' he assured huskily, his hands shifting, gaze dropping lower to watch as his fingers slowly pushed up her T-shirt to bare the smooth and silky skin of her abdomen. 'Very happy, in fact....' he murmured throatily, his breath warm against her skin as his lips trailed lightly, caressingly, across her bared flesh.

This wasn't what Bryn had meant, and Gabriel knew it. But she ceased to care at that moment as her every thought, every sensation, came down to the feel of Gabriel's lips and the rasp of his tongue moving caressingly against her skin.

She gasped low in her throat, her back arching, her fingers tightly gripping on to Gabriel's shoulders as his hands now moved up beneath her T-shirt and cupped breasts covered by nothing more than a black lace bra.

'You are so beautiful, Bryn,' he growled softly. 'I've thought of doing this for longer than I care to think about—' he pushed the T-shirt higher so that he could kiss the tops of her breasts '—and this.' He pulled the T-shirt up and over her head before discarding it onto the floor, his eyes dark and hungry. He looked at her appreciatively for several seconds before reaching up to tug the lace cup of her bra down and bare one of her breasts, the rosy nipple already hard and pouting. 'And, oh, God, this!' he groaned, his hands resting on her hips as his mouth closed over the tip of that bared breast and he sucked her roused nipple fully into the heat of his mouth.

Fire surged and swelled inside Bryn, making it difficult for her to breathe at all as she felt that pull on her nipple accompanied by the rasp of Gabriel's tongue, the place between her thighs dampening as her fingers became entwined in the darkness of his hair and she held him closer to her, needing more, wanting more.

Receiving more as Gabriel deftly unclipped and removed her bra completely before suckling and feeding on her other nipple as his hand caressed its twin.

'Could we at least move away from the window? We can be seen from outside the building.' Bryn gasped in half protest, too aroused, too greedy for more, to be able to call a halt to this. Gabriel's breath was hot against the dampness of her breast as he reluctantly released her nipple. 'The windows are reflective. No one can see in. Only we can see out.'

'Oh. Ah!' Bryn gasped breathlessly as Gabriel's hands moved to unfasten the button of her jeans before sliding the zip slowly downwards.

He sat back on his heels, eyes so dark they appeared as black as the lace panties now revealed, the air cool against Bryn's heated flesh as Gabriel slipped off her trainers before slowly pushing her jeans all the way down her legs and removing them completely.

Bryn had never felt so exposed, so desired, as Gabriel glanced up at her briefly, searing her with a single, heated glance, his gaze moving lazily downwards.

Gabriel's hands moved beneath the black lace as he breathed in the scent of her, a perfume that increased his own arousal, demanding that it be set free, to claim what it already knew to be his.

A single glance at Bryn's face had revealed the flush of arousal on her cheeks, the feverish glitter in her eyes. Her fingers tightened almost painfully in his hair as one of his hands cupped her mound, shifting the black lace aside and allowing his fingers to seek out the bare flesh beneath.

Her curls were damp with arousal as his fingers moved lower before moving up and around the roused nubbin. Bryn gasped low in her throat, parting her legs as he slowly stroked her.

Gabriel wanted to taste her, to feel Bryn fall apart as she climaxed. He wanted, needed— 'You do know I just want to rip these panties off you?'

'You're the one who has too many clothes on, Gabriel,' Bryn complained, desperate to touch his naked flesh in the same way he was touching hers. She wanted to run her hands over his bared shoulders, explore the hardness of his chest and stomach, to taste the heat of his skin beneath her lips. 'Please, Gabriel,' she groaned achingly.

'Undress me,' he invited throatily as he sat back on his heels and looked up at her expectantly.

He looked so damned good, wild and seductive as a pagan god, with the darkness of his hair in disarray from her caressing fingers, eyes dark and glittering, his cheeks flushed, lips slightly swollen.

The admiration in Gabriel's eyes as he looked at her dispelled any embarrassment she might have felt at standing almost naked in front of a man for the first time.

Nevertheless, her hands shook slightly as they moved to undo and remove Gabriel's tie, unfastening the buttons of his shirt before pushing it off his shoulders and down his arms to fall onto the carpeted floor with her own clothes.

Bryn's breath caught in her throat as she looked down at his muscled shoulders, a deep V of dark hair covering his chest and leading down over the flatness of his abdomen before disappearing into the waistband of his trousers. 'You're beautiful,' she murmured appreciatively as her hands trailed lightly over all that muscled flesh.

'I believe that should be my line,' Gabriel came back huskily.

She smiled shakily. 'Not from where I'm standing.'

'Then let's not stand any longer.' His grin was entirely roguish as he stood up to sweep Bryn easily into his arms, carrying her over and laying her down on the sofa before straightening to strip off the rest of his clothes.

Bryn watched unashamedly as he slipped off his shoes and socks before unfastening his trousers and allowing them to fall to his feet, carelessly discarding them as if they hadn't cost what Bryn earned in a month.

She had thought him beautiful before, but, wearing only black body-hugging boxers that clearly revealed the lengthy bulge beneath, he had to be the most sinfully gor-

geous man Bryn had ever set eyes on: wide and muscled
shoulders and chest, his waist tapered, thighs lean and
powerful, legs long and lightly sprinkled with dark hair.

Gabriel felt the painful swell of his shaft in response
to Bryn's appreciative gaze on him as he hooked his fingers into his boxers before slipping them down his thighs
and legs, and then straightening.

She drew her breath in sharply as Gabriel stood naked
in front of her, her wide eyes darkening to gunmetal grey
as she gazed up at him with open hunger.

A hunger Gabriel was powerless to resist as he stepped
closer, his breath catching in his throat as Bryn reached
out to trail her fingers lightly down the silken length of
his shaft, her face flushed with passion as she traced
the engorged blood vessels along the length to the bulbous tip.

Gabriel's jaw clenched, hands fisting at his sides, as
Bryn sat up and swung her legs to the floor, her breasts
thrusting temptingly as she leaned forward to curl her
fingers about his erection, her tongue moving distractedly over her lips as the soft pad of her thumb touched the
moistness of that sensitive purple head. She looked up at
him briefly before slowly lowering her head and lapping
up those escaping juices with the soft rasp of her tongue.

'Sweet—' Gabriel muttered as he drew in a hissing
breath, his whole body rigid with tension. 'Are you trying to kill me, Bryn?' he choked as she continued.

'You taste delicious,' she murmured appreciatively.
'Sweet and yet salty too.' The fingers of one hand remained curled about him as she parted her lips before
taking him completely into her mouth.

'You *are* trying to kill me!' Gabriel's back arched, his
hands becoming entangled in Bryn's hair as he began to
thrust slowly, instinctively, into that hot, moist cavern as

Bryn's throaty chuckle of satisfaction vibrated along the length of his pulsing and sensitive shaft.

Bryn hadn't known—had never imagined—anything could taste and feel this good. She felt bold, totally empowered by Gabriel's uninhibited response as her head bobbed in rhythm with his increasingly powerful thrusts, his hips bucking as those thrusts became more urgent still.

'You have to stop, Bryn,' he gasped, his fingers biting into the bareness of her shoulders as he halted her movements. 'Or I'm going to lose this before we've even begun.'

Her lashes rose as she looked up at Gabriel to find him looking down at her, his expression pained; eyes jet-black, cheeks flushed, his mouth twisted into a grimace.

Even so, Bryn was reluctant to release him immediately, moving slowly down his length, lips squeezing just beneath the purple head before she released that pressure. He gave a strangulated groan.

'Now it's my turn to torture you,' he added as Bryn finally sat back to look up at him with wide innocent eyes. 'And I warn you,' he murmured determinedly as he moved down onto his knees between her parted thighs before easing her back against the sofa, 'I'm not going to stop.' His head swooped down as he claimed one pouting nipple into his mouth, suckling deep and hard, as his other hand cupped its twin, finger and thumb plucking, gently squeezing.

Pleasure raged through Bryn like wildfire at this full-on assault to her senses, and she realised that Gabriel had only been teasing her earlier, tantalising her. Her head fell back against the sofa, back arching, as his mouth drew hungrily on her nipple, his thumb and fingers matching that wild rhythm on its twin as heat poured between her thighs like molten lava. The tiny nubbin there pulsing as her hips began to move against him restlessly, pleading, begging for Gabriel's touch.

He growled low in his throat before his lips released her nipple and moved down over her abdomen, his hands moving to grip her hips, holding her unmoving as his lips and tongue sought and easily found the nubbin pouting and swollen amongst her curls.

Her breath caught in her throat, heat engulfing her at the first caress of Gabriel's tongue across that sensitive bundle of nerve endings. He flicked his tongue mercilessly, again and again, across that pulsing nubbin.

Bryn sobbed low in her throat as her hips arched up in rhythm with that torturously flicking tongue, gasping, keening, as Gabriel's hand moved down and he slipped a finger inside her hot and grasping channel, gently thrusting. A second finger joined the first, her pleasure rising to fever pitch as his tongue flattened against her nubbin, pressing to the same rhythm as those thrusting fingers, until Bryn felt the pleasure rising, soaring, completely engulfing her, again and again, until she felt as if she had shattered into a million pieces.

'Are you okay?' Gabriel prompted with concern as he lay down on the sofa beside her and gathered her shaking body close against his.

Bryn in the throes of orgasm had been the most beautiful thing he had ever seen and heard; little throaty sobs had caught at the back of her throat, her face flushed, throat arched, breasts jutting proudly forward, her hips rising to meet each thrust of his fingers as the muscles in her channel gripped tightly with each prolonged spasm of pleasure. A pleasure that Gabriel had drawn out to the fullest until Bryn was sobbing and the tears flowed down her cheeks.

'I'm fine,' she answered him shakily, limp in his arms as she lay draped across his chest. 'Better than fine,' she added. 'That was the most amazing thing— I had no idea— It was truly amazing,' she repeated breathlessly.

'I aim to please, ma'am.' Gabriel chuckled softly.

'Oh, you did! You do,' she amended huskily, hand lightly caressing his shoulder. 'That was truly unbeliev-able. I— Are we going to stop now?'

'Not a chance,' Gabriel assured indulgently. 'I'm just giving you time to recover. You seem a little over-whelmed.'

'A little?' Her laugh was shaky. 'I could become ad-dicted to so much pleasure!'

'You're doing wonderful things for my ego, Bryn,' he murmured wryly.

'I invariably tell the truth too,' she assured quietly.

Gabriel frowned slightly, not wanting either of them to dwell on the reason he had said that to her earlier, not when they were together so intimately. They could deal with the past, and the future, later; right now he just wanted to be with Bryn, with no tension or animosity between them. 'Didn't any of your other lovers pleasure you so well?' he teased.

Her fingers twirled in the curls on his chest. 'What other lovers?'

Gabriel stilled as he looked down at her searchingly, a smile of satisfaction curving her lips as she tweaked one of his nipples and watched as it hardened in response.

She looked up at him. 'Do you like that too?'

'I love it.' He nodded distractedly. 'Bryn—'

'Do we have to talk right now, Gabriel?' She moved to lay between his parted thighs as she flicked her tongue across his hardened nipple, causing Gabriel to draw his breath in sharply as his shaft once again jerked and swelled in response to the caress. 'You do like that,' she murmured with satisfaction, the heat of her breath brushing across his dampened flesh.

'Yes,' he grated between gritted teeth. 'Bryn—'

'Not now, Gabriel.' She glanced up at him pleadingly, her hands looking very pale and slender against his olive skin. 'I don't want to talk—to think—I just want to taste you some more.' She moved sinuously down his body until she knelt between his parted thighs and her hands both curled about the length of his shaft.

Gabriel sat up slightly as he reached down to grasp her wrists and stop those mind-numbing caresses before it was too late. 'Not yet, Bryn. I— Have you had any other lovers at all?' he prompted cautiously.

She frowned as she looked up at him. 'This isn't the part where we confess to past relationships, is it? Because I really would rather skip hearing about all your previous conquests!'

So would Gabriel; there hadn't been so many women for him that he didn't remember their names and their faces, but there had certainly been enough. Not so much during the past five years, but Bryn wasn't ready to hear the reason for that. 'We aren't talking about me, Bryn—'

'Well, we're not going to talk about me either, if this is going to be a one-sided thing!' she assured impatiently. 'Let go of my hands, Gabriel—'

He ignored her request. 'Bryn, are you even on any contraception?' he prompted exasperatedly.

She shrugged. 'I've never had a use for it. Don't tell me a man like you doesn't have a condom or two in his pocket somewhere? Weren't you ever a Boy Scout?'

'Bryn, will you please answer me?' Gabriel sat up, taking her with him, looking down at her intently as he continued to hold both her hands captive in his. 'How many lovers have you had?'

She blinked. 'Why do you need to know?'

'Because this is important, damn it!' he groaned. 'I really need you to answer the question, Bryn.'

She frowned. 'Am I doing something wrong? You seemed happy enough a few minutes ago—'

'I was very happy, Bryn. I *am* happy.'

'You don't look it.'

'That's probably because you keep avoiding answering my question,' he said, sighing his exasperation.

Bryn sat back, completely unconcerned by her own nakedness; Gabriel had seen and touched and licked parts of her that no other person ever had, so it was a little late for her to feel in the least self-conscious now. 'Are you going to make a thing out of this, Gabriel?' she prompted impatiently.

'That would depend on what "this" is,' he answered cautiously.

'Okay, let's just get this out of the way so that we can move on.' She sighed. 'No, I haven't had any previous lovers. Which actually answers your second question, doesn't it, because if I haven't had any lovers then I've obviously never felt the need for contraception either.' She looked up at him uncertainly as he released her to stand up abruptly. A nerve pulsed in his clenched jaw as he stared down at her.

'No lovers?'

'Not until tonight, no.' She slowly shook her head.

'Sweet mother of…' He ran an agitated hand through his already tousled hair as he began to pace restlessly. 'You should have told me, Bryn.'

'Why should I?' she reasoned. 'I should tell you that fierce pacing doesn't have the same impact when you're stark naked.' She fell silent as he quickly pulled on his briefs, trousers and shirt, not bothering to refasten the latter. 'Gabriel?'

He breathed raggedly. 'Just give me a minute, please, Bryn.'

'I believe there were two of us here tonight, not just me,' she continued despite his warning. 'And I don't remember you bothering to ask me any of these questions *before* we both took our clothes off.'

No, he hadn't, had he? Which was more than careless on Gabriel's part. His only excuse—if it could be called one—was that Bryn affected him so deeply he couldn't think of anything else but her when he held her in his arms.

He looked at Bryn now, still unsettled at learning that he was her first lover— Well, her *almost* lover. 'Bryn, I would have— I wouldn't have pushed so hard if I had known of your…inexperience,' he said gently.

She frowned. 'What does that mean?'

He shook his head. 'Well, I wouldn't have made love to you in my office, for one thing.'

'Why not?'

He closed his eyes briefly. 'Your first time should be in a bed, Bryn, preferably a four-poster—'

'I never imagined you as a romantic, Gabriel.'

His jaw tightened. 'Don't mock me, Bryn. Not now.'

'I'm not the one who just spoiled the moment!' She rose lithely to her feet, her face pale as she turned her back on him and began pulling her own clothes back on, her panties and jeans no problem, the bra proving less cooperative, forcing Bryn to thrust it impatiently into her pocket before she pulled her T-shirt on and fluffed out her hair.

'I could have hurt you, Bryn.' He gave a pained frown as he realised what he had just said.

'It's five years too late for you to think of that,' Bryn came back bitterly as she looked up from pulling on her shoes. 'Besides, I don't think either of us was thinking too clearly a few minutes ago. I certainly didn't think I needed to give you a list, or otherwise, of my credentials as a lover before we proceeded.'

He sighed as she stood up to collect her bag in preparation of leaving. 'You can't just leave—'

'Watch me.'

'Why are you so angry, Bryn? Can't the two of us at least talk before you go? Please, Bryn,' he encouraged gruffly.

Her mouth thinned. 'I don't think we have anything to talk about. We had an…encounter, and now it's obviously over.'

It hadn't just been an encounter to Gabriel. No matter what Bryn might think, how many previous lovers he might have had, he had never experienced anything even remotely like the pleasure he had felt with Bryn tonight. She was so beautiful she took his breath away. Responsive beyond belief. And the caress of her hands, the touch of her lips on his body, his shaft, had been so unbelievably arousing he had almost lost control.

He gave a shake of his head. 'I have the feeling that this was your first encounter too?'

Her cheeks warmed with colour. 'I've been a little busy the past five years, okay? Building a new life in Wales for myself and my mother. Getting my degree. Working to pay off the student loans, and the rent, and painting madly in my spare time. Besides which—' she drew in a ragged breath '—I would have felt compelled to explain about the past to anyone I became seriously involved with, and I've never cared enough to want to do that. I'm sorry if that makes me a lousy lover, but I—'

'You're not a lousy lover, Bryn,' Gabriel cut in forcefully. 'Far from it,' he added huskily. 'I just— I'm surprised that you chose me, of all people, to be your first.'

'You of all people,' she echoed bitterly. 'I suppose it is a bit ironic,' she murmured self-derisively. 'But it has a certain rightness about it too, if you think about it. You already know about my past, who I am, who my father was, which means I don't have to confess anything to you.'

In just a few short minutes everything between them had changed once again, and she was back to being her usual defensive and antagonistic self.

Or maybe that responsive woman was the real Bryn?

Gabriel didn't know anymore, and for once in his life he wasn't sure what to do next. Wasn't sure if there was any way they could move forward with Bryn in the mood she was in right now. 'Could we have dinner together tomorrow evening?' he asked tentatively.

Bryn's chin rose stubbornly. 'Not if it's going to result in us having some sort of post-mortem regarding what happened tonight, no.'

'Damn it, Bryn—' He broke off exasperatedly. 'I'm desperately trying to put things right between us, but I could really do with a little cooperation from you.'

'It's a little late in the day for that, isn't it?' she scorned.

'I'm really trying here, Bryn,' he bit out between gritted teeth.

She eyed him suspiciously. 'Put things right between us how?'

He sighed. 'We've skipped over a couple sequences

of a relationship, and I'd like to maybe take those two steps back and start again.'

Bryn looked at him searchingly, not sure where he was going with this. 'We had a sexual encounter, Gabriel, not a relationship.' An encounter that had been life changing for her, although she had a feeling that it was Gabriel himself who had made tonight so special; he was not only an exceptional and experienced lover, but a caring and considerate one too. Even with her own lack of experience Bryn knew that not all men were like that, so maybe she should be thanking Gabriel for the consideration he had shown her, instead of arguing with him.

And maybe she would be—if she didn't feel so confused about how she had allowed tonight to happen in the first place.

Nor did she understand why Gabriel had been thrown so off balance by her lack of experience; didn't men prefer no-ties-no-expectations sex?

And, damn it, she couldn't allow herself to become any more deeply involved with Gabriel than she already was. As it was, she had no idea how she would even begin to explain to her mother about her dinner date with Gabriel, let alone what had happened tonight; accepting another dinner invitation from him would only add to the complication of this situation.

'I appreciate the invitation, Gabriel,' she told him dismissively. 'And I understand what you're trying to say, but I'm really not interested in taking this any further.' She gave him a bright and dismissive smile.

'You're not interested in taking this any further?' he repeated slowly.

'No. You've said you're willing to forget the past, so I suggest we do the same with what happened just now. Let's both just forget it ever happened,' she repeated evenly.

Gabriel had never met another woman even remotely like Bryn Jones. Nor did he ever remember wanting to strangle a woman as much as he did Bryn at this moment.

First, she had aroused him so much that the two of them had almost had unprotected sex on the sofa in his office, of all places, and now she was giving him the brush-off. Unbelievable!

And was that injured pride speaking, or something else?

This woman had him so tied up in knots that Gabriel had no chance of sorting out his emotions. Except to know he wanted to see Bryn again, to be with her.

'Dinner tomorrow evening,' he repeated firmly.

'No,' she refused flatly.

Gabriel's eyes narrowed. 'You already have a date tomorrow night?'

Bryn raised her brows in silent rebuke. 'My shifts at work have worked out that I have three days off together, so I'm travelling home tomorrow morning to see my mother and stepfather. It's also the reason I was working late with Eric this evening,' she added challengingly.

'I see,' Gabriel murmured slowly, not willing to get into that conversation again, or the jealousy he had felt seeing her with Eric.

'How are you getting there?'

'By train.'

'Let me drive you—'

'Don't be ridiculous, Gabriel,' Bryn cut him off sharply, impatiently. 'It's bad enough that the two of us have met again. I don't need to shock my mother by having you turn up on her doorstep with me tomorrow.'

His mouth thinned. 'Are you saying she doesn't even

know about your participation in the exhibition at Arch-angel next month?'

Bryn snorted. 'I wouldn't even know where to start telling her of my reinvolvement with the D'Angelo family!'

'Damn it, Bryn.' Gabriel glared. 'Your mother never hated me in the way that you do—'

'You can't possibly know that,' she cut in dismissively.

As it happened, Gabriel did know that. But it appeared, from what Bryn was saying now, that Mary Harper had never told her daughter of their meetings after William went to prison.

'Bryn, your father—'

'I don't want to talk about him!' Her eyes flashed in warning.

Neither did Gabriel, but at the same time he knew it was a subject they couldn't continue to avoid. 'Bryn, he was a man, not a saint. Just a man,' he repeated heavily. 'His past misdemeanours weren't allowed to come out in court because they would have prejudiced the verdict, but surely you know that your father was a professional conman.'

'How dare you?' she gasped furiously.

Gabriel frowned. 'Not only that, but he brought about his own downfall.'

'You already said that!'

'But I mean this literally.' He sighed. 'Bryn, the reason I came to your home, talked to your father a couple times, was to try to talk him out of going through with trying to sell the painting. Because I knew, deep inside me, here—' he held his hand to his heart '—that the painting was a forgery. I had no proof but that feeling, but that was enough for me to try to stop him from going through with it. The morning after I visited him the second time the headlines of the painting's existence were blazing across half a dozen newspapers.'

'You're saying my father was the one who went to the press?' Bryn gasped.

'Well, I certainly didn't. And if it wasn't me, then it had to be him. If you don't believe me—'

'Of course I don't believe you!' she said scornfully.

He sighed heavily. 'Then ask your mother about him, Bryn,' he encouraged. 'Ask her to tell you about all the years she suffered in silence through William's schemes and machinations. Ask her if he went to the press. You have to ask her, Bryn,' he repeated forcefully.

'I don't have to do anything.' She gave a determined shake of her head. 'I think—' she breathed deeply '—that I may actually hate you for the things you've said tonight.'

Gabriel had no choice but to watch as Bryn left, accepting that if hate was all Bryn had to give him, then he would take even that hate.

CHAPTER EIGHT

'OKAY, YOUNG LADY, time to spill the beans!' Bryn's mother smiled as she placed a jug of fresh lemonade and two glasses down on the picnic table, joining Bryn. They sat outside in the garden at the back of the cottage where she now lived with Rhys Evans, her second husband.

'Spill what beans…?' Bryn straightened in her garden chair as she slowly pushed her sketch pad aside, her expression cautious as she watched her mother pour lemonade into the glasses.

Mary, a slightly older version of Bryn, with shoulder-length brown hair and deep grey eyes, gave her a reproving glance as she dropped down into a seat on the other side of the wooden table. 'This is your mother you're talking to, Bryn. And you've been here for two days already and barely spoken a word since you arrived.'

'I've been busy sketching.' Bryn had found it soothing to lose herself in drawing the beautiful array of coloured flowers that scented her mother's cottage garden, rather than think of the things Gabriel had said about her father before she left London.

'I noticed,' Mary dismissed. 'Now tell me who he is!' she prompted interestedly as she sipped her lemonade.

'He?' Bryn squeaked a reply. She should have known by now how impossible it was to divert her mother's attention once she had made her mind up to something—which she now seemed to have done on the subject of Bryn's distraction these past two days.

'The man who's making my normally chatty daughter so introspective.'

Bryn recognised her mother's tone as being the 'and don't try telling me any nonsense'—in this case, that there was no man—'because I won't believe you' tone.

And Bryn knew she had been unusually quiet since coming home to visit her mother and Rhys, that the last evening with Gabriel had left her in a state of confusion. About the things Gabriel had said about her father as much as about Gabriel himself.

She gave her mother a searching glance now. 'Are you happy with Rhys?'

'Absolutely,' her mother answered instantly, a warm smile curving her lips.

Bryn nodded slowly. 'And were you happy with Daddy?'

Her mother's smile faded and a frown appeared between her eyes. 'Where's this coming from, Bryn?'

'I don't know.' She stood up restlessly. 'I just— I've watched you and Rhys together, the teasing, the easy affection, the total respect you have for each other, and—and I don't remember ever seeing you and Daddy together like that.'

'We were happy in the beginning. When you were little.'

Bryn gave a pained frown. 'But not later on?'

Her mother grimaced. 'It became…complicated. Everything was fine to start with, but then William became restless working in an office day after day, and started coming up with these get-rich-quick ideas—all of which failed miserably. You're old enough to know these things now, Bryn. William used up all our savings on those ideas, and I never knew what he was going to do next. Or whether we would all still have a roof over our heads the following week.' She shrugged. 'That sort of uncertainty in a partner can test even the best of relationships to its limits, and our marriage was already pretty shaky. It very quickly deteriorated into chaos.'

Which was probably why her mother now appreciated Rhys's steadiness, Bryn's stepfather having been the local and much-respected carpenter for all of his working life.

'But you stayed together....'

Her mother smiled. 'We had you.'

'But did you never think of leaving Daddy?' Bryn looked at her mother searchingly.

'Many times,' Mary admitted truthfully. 'And I'm sure, as much as it would have hurt you, it would have come to that in the end.'

Bryn gave a pained frown. 'And yet, even during the trial, you stood by him.'

'He was my husband. And your father,' her mother added pointedly. 'And you adored him.'

Yes, Bryn had adored her father. But she hadn't been able to get Gabriel's outburst that last evening in London out of her mind. To question, to want to know if the things he had said were true.

Her mother's comments confirmed what Bryn had feared—that William had been the petty crook Gabriel had called him, for almost all of her life, involved in one scam or another. A petty crook who had tried to break into the big time by selling the fake Turner—and failed miserably.

And these past few days Bryn had questioned whether she hadn't always known that, and that it was the knowing that had added to her resentment of Gabriel, not because he had kissed her, not because she had fallen in love with him, not even because of his involvement in her father's downfall, but because that involvement had made him part of the disenchantment she hadn't wanted to acknowledge all these years.

'Why the interest in all of that now, Bryn?' her mother prompted softly, her gaze sharp. 'Has something happened? Something that's made you start thinking, questioning the past?'

Gabriel D'Angelo was what had happened! A man who was making it impossible for Bryn not to question the past. But it wasn't Gabriel's fault; Bryn was the one who had chosen to come into contact with him again when she'd entered the exhibition.

No, it wasn't Gabriel's fault, but Bryn's reaction to meeting him again, her response to him, had set in motion those same feelings of guilt inside her that she had felt five years ago when she had looked across that crowded courtroom and known that, despite everything he was saying and all the damage he was causing to her father and her family, she still wanted him.

It had been bad enough then for Bryn to realise she was infatuated with the arrogant and handsome Gabriel D'Angelo, but she found it harder still to realise, all these years later, that she was still attracted to the man who had helped shatter her world.

Admittedly her mother was happily remarried, but still the past had to overshadow, to make impossible, there ever being any sort of relationship between Bryn and Gabriel. A relationship she would have to tell her mother about.

Even if her traitorous body seemed to have other ideas on the subject!

Just thinking about that last evening with Gabriel, of the depth of intimacy the two of them had shared, the way she had totally fallen apart in his arms, climaxing so spectacularly, was enough to make her blush.

'Okay, now I really want to know who this man is if he can make my sensible daughter blush so prettily,' her mother stated firmly.

'I can't tell you,' Bryn groaned.

'Why on earth not?' Mary looked stunned. 'We've always been able to talk about anything in the past— Bryn, if it's a woman making you feel this way, then I hope you know that I'm broad-minded enough not to—'

'It's not a woman!' She gave a rueful smile. 'But I appreciate knowing how broad minded you are!' she added dryly.

'Is this man involved with someone else, then? Maybe married?' her mother added worriedly.

'It's worse than that!' Bryn groaned as she began to pace the lawn Rhys had recently cut. Her mother's brows rose. 'What could possibly be worse than—? Is he older than you?'

'Marginally.' Bryn shrugged. 'Maybe ten years or so.'

'That's nothing.' Her mother sighed her relief. 'But I still don't understand why you won't tell me who he is.'

'Because I can't.' She sighed heavily. 'He's just not— suitable for me to be involved with, okay?'

'No, of course it's not okay, Bryn.' Mary frowned worriedly. 'I've never known you to— He isn't a drug dealer or something like that, is he?'

'Of course not,' Bryn denied ruefully.

Her mother didn't look reassured. 'But he's unsuitable in some other way?'

'Oh, yes,' Bryn sighed.

Mary continued to look at her searchingly for several long minutes, that worried frown between her eyes. 'Does your interest just now, in the past, have anything to do with your reluctance to talk about this man?' she finally prompted.

'I— Maybe.' Bryn's teeth worried her bottom lip. 'Do you know—? Is it possible that Daddy was the one to tell the press about the painting, as a way of ensuring the D'Angelo gallery, or some other gallery, couldn't just dismiss the painting as a forgery?'

'More than possible, I'm afraid,' her mother sighed. 'You know, Bryn,' she said slowly, evenly, 'it took me years to accept this, but your father was responsible for everything that happened to him.' Exactly the words Gabriel had used to Bryn just days ago.

'Not me. Not you,' her mother continued firmly. 'Not anyone else involved in that mess. Just your father. He gambled not just with his own future but with ours too, and he lost. We all lost. But having met Rhys, finding such happiness with him, has shown me that we don't have to continue to let ourselves be the losers, darling.'

'I'm not a loser—'

'Bryn, I've watched the way you've avoided all involvement with men these past five years,' her mother admonished gently. 'And I'm telling you now that the only way of allowing yourself to go forward is to let go of the past.'

Tears blurred Bryn's vision. 'Sometimes that's easier said than done.'

'But it can be done.' Her mother reached out and grasped Bryn's hand tightly in hers. 'I'm living proof of that.'

Yes, her mother's happiness with Rhys now *was* living proof of that. Except... Gabriel had been directly involved in that past her mother spoke of. Not as a spectator, or someone removed from the situation, but as a full participant.

'We'll see.' She squeezed her mother's hand reassuringly. 'But could we just forget about this for now? Talk about something else?'

Her mother looked less than happy with the idea. 'If that's what you really want.'

'It is.'

Mary nodded. 'You know where I am when and if you want to talk.'

Yes, Bryn knew; she just couldn't see a time she would ever be able to tell her mother of the emotional tangle she had got herself into with Gabriel.

'Did you have a good time in Wales last week?' Gabriel's expression was guarded as he looked down at Bryn and saw the way the colour drained from her cheeks. She slowly looked up from the magazine she was reading at the back of the coffee shop, the girl who had prepared his coffee having told him where Bryn was sitting taking her evening break.

Gabriel knew that Bryn had to have been back in London for four days now, but she hadn't come anywhere near the gallery, or him. Mainly him, Gabriel suspected.

The fact that his unexpected appearance at the coffee shop this evening had caused Bryn's face to pale so dramatically, as well as striking her uncharacteristically dumb, would seem to confirm that suspicion.

He pulled out the chair opposite hers and sat down before placing his mug of coffee down on the table between them. 'Everything all right at home?'

Her throat moved as she swallowed before answering him. 'Fine, thank you.'

'That's good.' Gabriel leaned back in the chair to

stretch his long legs out in front of him as he continued to study Bryn.

She appeared somehow fragile to his critical gaze. Her face was pale, and there were hollows in her cheeks that hadn't been there a week ago, implying that she had lost weight since he saw her last. Her eyes were also shadowed and bruised-looking, as if she hadn't been sleeping well.

Because she had been as disturbed by what had happened between the two of them the previous week as Gabriel still was, rather than the things he had said to her?

Had she talked to her mother, as he had advised? Did she now know the truth where her father was concerned? Or did she still hold Gabriel responsible for everything that had happened in the past?

His determination to find answers to these questions had brought him to the coffee shop.

The past week had been a torturous hell for Gabriel, the first three days spent wondering if Bryn would talk to her mother, what she was thinking if she had, what decision she was going to come to in regard to the two of them while she was away. He had then spent the four days since she'd returned from Wales assuming she had decided to cut him out of her life.

A totally unacceptable decision as far as Gabriel was concerned.

Bryn was totally disconcerted at Gabriel's arrival in the coffee shop, not least because his appearance, in a casual cream polo shirt, faded jeans resting low on lean hips and the darkness of his overlong hair falling casually over his forehead, had literally taken her breath away. How she wanted this man.

More so even than a week ago, she acknowledged achingly as she looked at him from beneath lowered lashes, their time together in Gabriel's office, the intimacies they had shared, having for ever changed the way she now thought and felt about him.

A realisation that made a complete nonsense of her avoidance of him this past week.

'You haven't been to the gallery since you got back.' Gabriel's accusing tone echoed some of her thoughts.

She shrugged. 'I've spoken to Eric several times on the phone, explained that I couldn't make it to the gallery because I've been really busy at work.'

'So he told me.'

Bryn found it impossible to meet the dark shrewdness of Gabriel's gaze. 'Then I don't understand why you're here.'

He lost his relaxed pose as he sat forward and grasped both of her hands in his, his nostrils flaring angrily as Bryn instinctively sat back and tried to pull free. A freedom he wouldn't allow her. 'I'm here so that we can have the conversation we didn't finish a week ago.'

Her tone was pleading. 'Gabriel—'

'Bryn, don't try to freeze me out, or put me, and what happened between us, into some convenient little compartment in your brain never to be opened again,' he warned fiercely, 'because, I assure you, that isn't going to happen. I'm not going to allow it to happen.'

She gave another tug on her hands, once again failing to free herself, her throat moving as she swallowed before speaking. 'I don't know what you mean—'

'Like hell you don't,' Gabriel scorned harshly.

A blush warmed her cheeks as she hissed, 'You're causing a scene, Gabriel.' Several people at neighbouring tables had turned to give them curious glances as they had obviously heard the harshness of Gabriel's tone.

He gave a humourless smile. 'We wouldn't be having

this conversation here at all if you hadn't been too much of a coward to come to Archangel when you got back.'

She gasped. 'I told you, I've been really busy at the coffee shop since I returned—'

'Too busy to so much as bother to telephone the man who is your lover?'

'Gabriel!' she warned fiercely, wrenching her hands painfully from his grasp even as she glanced around them before turning back to glare across the table at him. 'You are *not* my lover.'

'More than any other man has ever been,' he stated uncompromisingly.

And how Bryn regretted ever allowing Gabriel to realise that.

Gabriel wasn't enjoying this conversation, not his own part in it, or the fact that it was obviously causing Bryn discomfort. But this past week of not personally hearing so much as a word from her had made him so frustrated that he couldn't seem to help himself.

Just looking at Bryn again as she sat alone in a corner at the back of the coffee shop reading a magazine, taking in the delicate softness of her cheek, the long sweep of her lashes, the silkiness of that defensively spiky hair, had been enough to cause his breath to catch in his throat and his shaft to become hard and aching beneath his jeans—the same painful state of arousal he had been in for most of the past week!

Consequently, he wasn't in the mood to accept the brush-off from Bryn again. 'What time do you finish here tonight?' he prompted.

She blinked. 'Gabriel—'

'We either have this conversation at my apartment later tonight, Bryn, or right here and right now, but we are going to talk sometime this evening,' he assured her.

She gave a shake of her head. 'I'm tired, Gabriel.'

'And you think I'm not?'

Her frown was pained. 'I don't understand.'

'I haven't exactly been sleeping like a baby for the past week as I waited to see what you decided to do about us.'

'There is no "us",' she sighed wearily.

'Oh, yes, Bryn, there most definitely is an "us".'

She gave a shake of her head. 'Doesn't the fact that I haven't bothered to contact you since I returned speak for itself as to how I feel about what happened between us?'

Gabriel gave a humourless smile. 'It tells me you're a coward, nothing more.'

Her chin rose. 'That's the second time you've called me a coward in as many minutes, and I don't like it.'

'Then prove that you aren't one by meeting me once you've finished work tonight.'

She gave him a pitying glance. 'We aren't children playing a game of dare, Gabriel.'

'We aren't children at all, which is why you should stop behaving like one.' His eyes glittered angrily. 'I'm not going anywhere, Bryn, so if you thought I was going to help you get through this situation by going along with pretending last week didn't happen, you were obviously mistaken. It happened, Bryn. I suggest you live with it.'

Bryn had been living with it for the past week. With the knowledge of her complete lack of resistance to this man. With the fact that she'd had no control over what had happened between them in his office a week ago. With the fact that Gabriel had been the one to call a halt to their lovemaking because she hadn't been able to do so.

With the fact that she had only needed to look at Gabriel again tonight to know that she wanted him still.

Her mouth tightened. 'It would have been the gentlemanly thing to do, in the circumstances.'

'Insulting me isn't going to make me get up and walk out of here either, Bryn,' he assured her softly. 'This is way too important for that. To both of us. This past week, waiting, wondering, has been sheer bloody hell.' He ran an agitated hand through his hair.

She looked across at Gabriel searchingly, noting the dark shadows beneath his eyes, the sharp blade of his cheekbones above slightly hollow cheeks, lines etched beside his nose and mouth that she was sure hadn't been there before, and realised that this past week really hadn't been any easier for Gabriel than it had been for her.

'Why won't you just accept that I can't do this, Gabriel?' she groaned achingly.

'Because neither of us knows what this is yet,' he maintained stubbornly. 'And I'm not willing to just give up on it until we do know.'

She gave a shake of her head. 'Isn't it enough that we both know that the events of the past makes this impossible?'

'I refuse to accept that.' His gaze was tormented as he reached across the table to once again take one of her hands in his.

'You have to! We both do.'

Gabriel gave a shake of his head. 'Did you speak to your mother?'

'About you?'

'Obviously not about me,' he drawled knowingly at her shocked expression. 'But did you at least ask her to confirm the things I told you about your father?'

'And what if I did?' Colour warmed her cheeks as she avoided meeting his gaze. 'Knowing who and what my father was, the things he did, changes nothing, Gabriel.'

'It means we can put the past where it belongs—in the past! It can't be undone, or remade, because it is what it is, but if we— If we want each other enough, we should be able to talk about it, to get by it. And I do want you, Bryn, and the trembling of your hand when I touch you is enough to tell me that you still want me too.' His fingers tightened about her shaking ones as she would have pulled away. 'Nothing else matters at this moment but that.'

'And what about later? What happens once the—the wanting has all gone, Gabriel?' Tears glittered in her eyes. 'What happens then?'

'Who says it's ever going to be gone?'

'I do.'

'Then we deal with later when later comes along,' he stated firmly. 'For now I just want us to be together and see where this takes us. Can we do that, do you think?' The soft pad of his thumb caressed the back of her hand as he looked across at her intently.

Could they? This past week had been absolute hell for Bryn too, her desire for this man taking over her every thought as she remembered how it had been between them that night in Gabriel's office. The way they had still responded to each other despite both knowing who the other was, before her feelings of guilt had once again made her deny that desire she still felt for him. A desire that Gabriel so obviously reciprocated and refused to dismiss. Refused to allow her to dismiss.

Could the two of them really have a relationship for however long these feelings lasted and simply ignore the pain of the past?

Could she do that?

CHAPTER NINE

'COME IN AND make yourself at home, Bryn, and I'll pour us both a glass of wine,' Gabriel encouraged huskily as she stood hesitantly in the doorway to the sitting room of his apartment.

He had felt an inner sense of relief earlier, when Bryn had finally capitulated to the idea of the two of them meeting up again when she finished work at ten; he might have deliberately given her the impression he was both confident and unyielding in his demand for them to talk this evening, but inwardly he hadn't been at all sure, until that moment, that Bryn would agree.

Gabriel had been waiting outside in his car for her when she and several of her co-workers left the coffee shop a little after ten o'clock, the two of them not speaking after he climbed out of the car and opened the passenger door for her to get in, or during the short drive to his apartment.

She *had* lost weight, he realised as Bryn finally entered the sitting room, the black denims she wore not quite as figure-hugging as they had been a week ago, her collarbone visible at the open neck of her black shirt, those grey eyes appearing huge in the paleness of her face. Evidence that she was finding fighting the attraction between them as difficult as he was? Gabriel certainly hoped so, because this past week of not seeing her since the two of them had made love together had been sheer torture.

His expression softened as Bryn sank down wearily into the comfort of one of the brown leather armchairs. 'Busy evening?' he prompted as he poured two glasses of pinot grigio.

'Very.' Bryn accepted one of the glasses before taking a welcome sip. 'You have a nice apartment,' she added with an appreciative glance at the obviously masculine decor and original artwork on the walls.

'It isn't mine particularly.' He shrugged. 'We all use it whenever we're in London— Don't worry, Bryn, Michael and Raphael aren't in London at the moment,' he added ruefully as she instantly looked alarmed. 'Michael is in Paris, Raphael in New York.'

Her frown eased slightly. 'They really are wonderful names.'

He nodded. 'The family estate in Berkshire is called Archangel's Rest—and, I assure you, I've heard all the jokes.'

She smiled slightly but it quickly faded. 'Gabriel, I only came back with you tonight because I agree that we need to dispense with this situation once and for all, and then just move on— What are you doing?' she gasped as Gabriel put his glass down on the coffee table before kneeling down at her feet and beginning to unfasten the laces on her shoes.

He looked up to quirk a teasing brow. 'Removing your shoes, obviously.'

'Why?' She tried, and failed, to pull her foot from his grasp as he slipped one shoe off before turning his attention to the other.

Gabriel sat back on his heels after removing the second shoe. 'I'm guessing your feet ache from all that standing?'

'Yes.'

He nodded. 'Then a foot massage should be very welcome about now.'

'A foot— Gabriel, stop that.' She tried to pull away as he took one of her bare feet into both his hands and began to gently knead the aching flesh. 'Gabriel!' Her protest was less convincing this time, and she gave a low sigh of pleasure as his fingers continued to massage the tension from her tired muscles.

'Good?' he prompted.

'Oh, yes.' Her head fell back against the chair, lashes fanning over her cheeks as her lids closed and Gabriel continued to knead and massage her foot.

She had tiny elegant feet, the nails painted a bright— and defiant—red, Gabriel noted indulgently as he turned his attention to her other foot and continued to massage her aching muscles.

Bryn knew she should stop Gabriel doing what he was doing, that his kneeling at her feet was intimate enough, without the sensuous touch of his long fingers massaging her to add to that dangerous intimacy.

She *should* stop him.

But she couldn't.

Because she didn't want to; she was enjoying this far too much to want Gabriel to ever stop.

She had never thought of her feet as being an erogenous zone before now, but they obviously were, the warmth emanating from Gabriel's caressing hands now moving to other parts of her body, her nipples becoming hard and full, a familiar warmth between her thighs. 'You should think about taking this up professionally,' she murmured appreciatively, eyes still closed. 'You could make a fortune!'

Gabriel chuckled throatily. 'I already have a fortune. Besides which,' he added, fingers moving lightly over her ankles and calves now, 'I have no interest in massaging anyone else's feet but yours.'

Bryn raised one lid, her heart beating a loud tattoo in her chest as Gabriel looked back at her, those brown eyes once again as compelling and addictive as chocolate. An addiction Bryn was once again finding hard to resist.

'I think that's enough of that, thank you.' She pulled her feet out of Gabriel's grasp before bending her knees and drawing her legs up into the chair—well away from Gabriel's caressing hands. Her pulse raced as he made no effort to get up from kneeling in front of her. 'It's getting late, Gabriel,' she prompted determinedly. 'I need to leave soon.'

Gabriel sat back on his heels, looking up at her. 'Did you tell your mother that the two of us had met up again?'

'Did I—?' Her eyes had widened. 'Of course not!' Bryn protested impatiently.

His eyes narrowed. 'Why not?'

'Don't be obtuse, Gabriel,' she snapped, glad now that he wasn't still touching her. Because if he had been he would have been able to feel the way just being this close to him caused her to tremble in awareness. 'My mother never knew— She didn't know that we knew each other five years ago. I—I never told anyone about—about that evening you drove me home from the gallery.'

'The evening I kissed you.'

She grimaced. 'I'm surprised you even remember that.'

'It was too memorable to ever forget,' he assured gruffly.

Bryn looked at him sharply. 'I somehow doubt that very much.'

Gabriel looked straight back at her with hot, glittering eyes. 'The timing was all wrong, the circumstances impossible, but even then I wanted to do so much more than kiss you.'

'I— You did?' She was totally flustered by his admission.

He shrugged. 'I was attracted to you then. I'm attracted to you now.'

Bryn gave a scathing snort. 'Five years ago I was a chubby and gauche teenager wearing heavy-framed glasses.' And this man had been lean and sophisticated, with the same dark and wicked good looks that still took her breath away.

He nodded. 'And now you're sleek and elegant, and I'm guessing you wear contact lenses?'

She nodded distractedly. 'Except for when I paint, when I prefer to wear the glasses you returned to me last week.'

'You weren't chubby five years ago, Bryn, you were voluptuous,' he assured her earnestly. 'And your eyes were just as stunningly beautiful behind those glasses as they are tonight.'

She gave a dismissive shake of her head. 'We're veering off the subject, Gabriel.'

'Which is?'

'That just thinking about the distress it would cause my mother if I were to tell her I've met you again now, let alone this—this attraction, between us, is the very reason why it can't continue.'

Gabriel looked up. 'You can't possibly know how your mother would react.'

Bryn frowned her impatience. 'Get real, Gabriel, and

try to imagine how that conversation would go. "Oh, by the way, Mum, guess who I almost had sex with a couple nights ago. Gabriel D'Angelo. How weird is that?"'

Gabriel drew in a sharp breath before pushing up onto his feet to pick up his glass of wine, taking a sip before answering her, knowing Bryn was now spoiling for a fight—probably as her way of putting an end to this situation. But he wasn't about to give it to her, wasn't about to make any of this easy for her after the week of uncertainty he had just suffered through. 'We didn't have sex, Bryn, although we came very close, and, as I said, the location could have been a little more…conventional, but I'm pretty sure there was nothing in the least "weird" about anything we did together.'

Those two wings of colour deepened in her cheeks as she looked up at him with overbright eyes. 'You won't even try to see this from my point of view, will you?'

His jaw tightened. 'I'm not inclined to let you walk away from me just because you *think* your mother might react badly to knowing about the two of us, no.'

'How about if I walk away because *I'm* reacting badly to just the idea of the two of us together?'

His eyes narrowed. 'And are you?'

'Yes!'

'Why?'

She gave an exasperated shake of her head. 'Gabriel, I know you to be an intelligent man—'

'Thank you,' he drawled dryly.

'And as an intelligent man,' she continued firmly, 'you must know how impossible this whole situation is. For goodness' sake, my father went to prison for attempting to defraud you and your family,' she added impatiently when he made no response.

'I'm well aware of what happened five years ago.' He nodded grimly.

'Then you must also be aware— You must have issues of your own about that situation.'

'I deeply regret that I was in the wrong place at the wrong time,' he conceded impatiently. 'But it was sheer coincidence your father chose to bring his painting to Archangel, even more so that I, rather than Michael or Raphael, happened to be in charge of the London gallery when he did.' Something Gabriel had also long had reason to regret.

Except he would never have met Bryn five years ago if not for her father's greed.

She blinked long lashes. 'And you're saying you don't have a problem with that? With the fact that I'm William Harper's daughter?'

'Of course I have a problem with that.' Gabriel swallowed the rest of his wine before placing the empty glass down on the coffee table. 'At the very least it's inconvenient—'

'Inconvenient!' Bryn echoed incredulously.

He nodded. 'Because the past is affecting how you feel about the two of us now.'

Bryn no longer knew how she felt about the past, let alone the here and now.

Five years ago she had been devastated by her father's trial and imprisonment. A month ago she had still been resentful of Gabriel D'Angelo's part in her father's downfall. Even a week ago she had been disgusted with herself for allowing herself to respond to Gabriel in the way that she had.

But Gabriel was asking how she felt about that *now*.

She was still devastated by the events of the past, but the talk she'd had with her mother last week, the things

Mary had told her about the deterioration of her marriage, her daily uncertainty of her own and her daughter's future, how she believed William's get-rich-quick schemes would have eventually caused a complete meltdown in their marriage…

Having spoken with her mother, Bryn now believed that her father, determined to ignore Gabriel's advice to take his painting and just walk away, had instead informed the press of the painting's existence, ballooning the situation beyond anyone's control.

And all of those things put a different slant on that past situation. Bryn had worshipped her father when she was a child, had loved him dearly for the man she had believed him to be. But as an adult she now realised, and was forced to accept, that he had been far from the perfect husband or father.

And, yes, Gabriel had been involved in her father's being sent to prison, but he hadn't done it out of spite, had merely, as he had just pointed out, been caught up in the sequence of events created and executed by Bryn's father, and over which Gabriel himself had no control.

It wasn't the past, or Gabriel's involvement in that past, that made a relationship between the two of them so impossible now; it was how Bryn felt about Gabriel.

Five years ago she had been infatuated, utterly mesmerised, by the dark and devastatingly attractive Gabriel D'Angelo. Since meeting him again, sharing intimacies with him that she had never experienced with any other man, she had realised that it hadn't just been infatuation she had felt for Gabriel five years ago. She had fallen in love with him then, she loved him still, and he—how she felt about him—was why none of the men she had met since had ever held her interest. How could any man compete with Gabriel D'Angelo? Or the fact that Bryn had fallen in love with him all those years ago?

And it was a futile love. Not just because of the past, but because Gabriel, still single at the age of thirty-three, so obviously didn't do falling in love, let alone for ever.

Oh, he was attracted to her, admitted to desiring her, but that was all he felt, and the only way, the only defence Bryn had left against falling even more in love with Gabriel than she already was, was to continue to use the shield of the events of the past to keep him at arm's length.

Gabriel watched through narrowed lids as Bryn swung her feet to the carpeted floor before sitting up.

Her expression was one of cool dismissal. 'I don't feel anything about the two of us now,' she told him coldly.

His jaw tightened. 'That's not—'

'Nor do I think it a good idea for us to be alone together like this again,' she continued firmly. 'You asked that we talk, Gabriel, and we've done that. And I've told you exactly how I feel.' Her chin rose. 'And if anything I've said means you now change your mind about including my paintings in the New Artists Exhibition, then so be it!' she added challengingly as she stood up.

Gabriel eyed her frustratedly, knowing that Bryn was deliberately shutting him out, but he had no idea how to break through the defences she was deliberately putting up against him. The fact that she felt the need to put up those defences at all was surely telling in itself. In what way, Gabriel couldn't be sure. And this stubbornly assertive Bryn obviously wasn't about to enlighten him either.

'I won't change my mind, Bryn,' he assured grimly. 'About anything.' He used the same challenging tone she had to him.

She eyed him guardedly. 'What does that mean?'

Gabriel gave a mocking smile. 'It means that you don't know me very well if you think that anything you've said tonight means I'm going to just walk away from you. It means,' he continued firmly as she would have spoken, 'that, for the two weeks left before the exhibition, I'm going to require that you come to the gallery at least once a day, and that those meetings will be with me, rather than Eric. It means, Bryn, that you can try running away from me, from the attraction between us, but for the next two weeks, at least, I have no intention of allowing you to just ignore me.'

'Why are you doing this?' Tears glistened in those dove-grey eyes.

'Why do you think I'm doing it?' Gabriel rasped, hating being the cause of those tears, but hating even more the idea of giving up on what he knew was between the two of them. Bryn could fight it all she liked, but her responses to him told him that she wanted him as much as he wanted her.

She made a dismissive gesture with her hands. 'Probably because you're the arrogant Gabriel D'Angelo?' she accused huskily. 'Because a D'Angelo doesn't take no for an answer?' She gave a disgusted shake of her head. 'Or possibly because you just enjoy torturing me!'

Gabriel's hands clenched at his sides even as he bared his teeth in a facsimile of a smile. 'Nice try, Bryn, but I've already warned you I'm not backing off because you deliberately insult me.'

'I'm not—'

'Yes, you are, Bryn,' he rasped. 'And yes, I'm arrogant. Enough so that I don't intend taking the answer "no" from the woman I know wants me as much as I want her.'

She drew in a sharp breath.

'You—'

'Your lips might be saying no, Bryn,' he continued remorselessly, 'but the rest of your body, your aroused nipples especially—' he deliberately lowered his gaze to where those hardened nubs were pressed so noticeably against her black cotton shirt '—are definitely saying yes, please!'

Bryn instinctively crossed her arms over her breasts even as she inwardly acknowledged the truth of Gabriel's claim; she *was* aroused from the sensual pleasure of having Gabriel's hands caressing her feet and calves just a few minutes ago, but also because she seemed to be in a constant state of arousal whenever she was in Gabriel's company.

She only had to look at him, into those sultry dark eyes, at those sculptured kissable lips, the long, lean lines of his utterly masculine body, for her own body to become achingly aroused.

And now Gabriel was suggesting—no, ordering—that she spend at least part of every day for the two weeks before the exhibition in his company.

Her eyes glittered with anger now rather than tears. 'I don't even like you very much at this moment, Gabriel.'

He gave another humourless smile as he crossed the distance between them in soft predatory strides. 'If this is not liking me then long may it continue,' he scorned harshly as Bryn took those same steps back, until she could go no farther, her spine pressed flush against the wall as she stared up at him. 'I believe I could become addicted to the way you hate me, Bryn.' Gabriel's expression was grim as he once again held her imprisoned by placing his hands on the wall on either side of her head, his dark gaze deliberately holding hers as his head lowered and his mouth claimed hers.

Bryn groaned low in her throat as, after the briefest hesitation, her arms moved up about Gabriel's shoulders and she met the fierceness of that kiss with a hunger of her own, no room for gentleness as their tongues duelled, Bryn's fingers becoming entangled in the dark thickness of the hair at Gabriel's nape as she moved up on tiptoe to curve her body into his. The softness of her breasts pressed against the hard muscles of Gabriel's chest, her thighs arching as she pressed her mound against the hardness of his arousal, that arousal pulsing in response, growing longer, firmer, as she ground her thighs against his slowly, instinctively seeking that pressure against her hardened nub.

Gabriel wrenched his mouth from hers to hungrily kiss the length of her throat, the tops of her breasts, groaning his frustration as her fastened shirt stopped him from going any lower. A barrier he easily dispensed with by taking hold of both sides of her shirt and simply pulling, several buttons flying off as he pushed the shirt down her arms and let it fall to the floor.

'Oh, yes,' he rasped hotly as he gazed down hungrily at the creamy swell of her breasts visible above a red lace bra. 'I'm going to lick and suck your oh-so-sensitive breasts—' his gaze held hers as one of his hands moved to unfasten the clasp at the back of her bra before dropping it down onto the floor with her shirt '—and I'm going to continue licking, sucking and biting these pretty breasts—' his hands moved up to cup those thrusting globes tipped by swollen strawberry-ripe nipples '—until you come for me again.'

Bryn felt her cheeks pale. 'No, Gabriel—'

'Yes, Bryn,' he ground out harshly, eyes feverish, his skin flushed against the hard blades of his cheekbones. 'You want it as much as I do.'

She did. Oh, yes, she most certainly did. She ached to feel Gabriel's lips and hands on her again, and that amazing, overwhelming feeling when he brought her to climax.

'These are mine, Bryn.' Gabriel's hands squeezed her breasts. 'Do you understand? These are all mine. To lick and suck, to give you pleasure! And I'm not letting you walk out of here tonight until I've proven that to you!' The past few minutes—Bryn's rejection of there ever being a relationship between the two of them, of Gabriel himself—seemed to have stripped him of showing even a veneer of civilised behaviour.

A loss of control that had touched an equally primitive need deep inside Bryn.

Heat gushed between her thighs, the nubbin swelling, pulsing, in the dampness of her curls as Gabriel lowered his head and sucked one nipple deep into the heat of his mouth even as the thumb and finger of his other hand captured and plucked its twin into the same throbbing needing.

Again and again he suckled her nipple, remorselessly caressing and squeezing its twin, both just short of pain, until Bryn was wild, mindless with hunger, with a need that pulsed and ached between her thighs and caused her to groan, to arch her spine, forcing her breast even deeper into the tormenting heat of Gabriel's mouth as he pressed his thigh rhythmically against that swollen nubbin.

'Gabriel?' Bryn gasped in protest as he released her breast to look up at her.

'Come for me, Bryn,' he encouraged throatily. 'Watch me as I take you over the edge. No way, Bryn!' he refused fiercely as she used the last slender thread of her control to defy him by turning her head away. 'Do you want me to stop?' he rasped harshly. 'Look at me now, Bryn, and tell me you want me to stop!'

A sob caught in her throat as she slowly turned back to him, instantly losing herself in the glittering black pools of his feverish gaze.

'Tell me to stop, Bryn, and I will,' he encouraged huskily.

'I—I can't,' she sobbed. 'Don't stop, Gabriel!' she urged achingly as her fingers tightened in his hair, drawing him back towards her breasts. 'Please don't stop!'

'Look at me this time, Bryn,' he encouraged softly, his breath a warm caress across the aching moistness of her swollen nipple. 'I want to look into your eyes as you come for me.' His tongue flicked out, a tormenting lash against her swollen and aching nipple, continuing to rasp that tongue against her, his gaze continuing to hold hers as he released the button of her jeans before sliding the zip slowly down.

Bryn couldn't have looked away if she had tried, her pleasure swelling, rising out of control, at the eroticism of watching Gabriel as he now parted his lips about her nipple before suckling, gently at first, and then more deeply, her breathing hitching, fracturing as she felt his hand against the heat of her abdomen as it slid beneath the red lace of her panties, his fingers lightly circling her swollen nubbin.

Again and again those tormenting fingers stroked, above and then below that swollen nubbin, dipping his fingers into the dampness of her channel before slowly caressing but never quite touching her right where she most craved his touch, never giving her the pressure there that she ached for.

'Please, Gabriel,' Bryn gasped when she couldn't bear the torment a moment longer. 'Please! Oh, yes,' she gasped, her hands clinging to his shoulders, her thighs thrusting up instinctively as his fingers finally brushed lightly over that aching nubbin. 'Harder, Gabriel! Harder!' She cried out as the pleasure built, higher and then higher still as he increased the pressure and speed of his stroking fingers.

'Let go, Bryn,' Gabriel encouraged harshly against the creaminess of her breast. 'Come for me.' He captured the swollen nubbin between his fingers, squeezing as his mouth returned to her breast, drawing greedily on her nipple as he felt that nubbin throb and then pulse between his fingers as Bryn shattered into a shuddering, gasping climax, as he took it all, unwilling, unable to stop, until he had wrung out every last shuddering, trembling ounce of her orgasm.

'Oh, God, oh, God, oh, God!' Her head dropped down weakly onto Gabriel's shoulder as she continued to quiver and shake and cling to him in the aftermath of her pleasure.

Gabriel took her into his arms and held her tightly against his chest, his breathing as ragged and uneven as hers. 'And that, my beautiful Bryn, is why I refuse to walk away from you. From this. From us,' he told her gruffly. 'Not even if you beg me to.'

Bryn wanted to beg, not for Gabriel to walk away, but for him to continue making love to her.

Again and again.

Which was why *she* had to walk away.

CHAPTER TEN

THE NEXT TWO weeks were absolute hell for Bryn, compelled, as Gabriel had promised she would be, to go to Archangel and see him on a daily basis as they dealt with putting the final details of the exhibition into place.

Not that he ever attempted, or even indicated he wished, to repeat the intimacy of that night at his apartment. Oh, no, Gabriel had a much more subtle torment than that, as he took every opportunity to touch her, always seemingly accidentally: brushing lightly against her to emphasise a point, placing his hand on hers, or at the sensitive base of her spine, or the glide of her hips, whenever the opportunity arose.

And he did it all without saying a word or showing outward acknowledgement of the attraction that sparked and burned between the two of them every time they were together.

Bryn quickly realised that Gabriel really was intent on torturing her.

And how well he was succeeding.

As day followed torturous day Bryn's awareness of Gabriel grew to such a degree that she began to tremble and shake even as she approached the Archangel Gallery. Her nerves would be strung tightly, her body tingling with awareness, as she wondered if that would be the day Gabriel would relent and kiss her, caress her, before she went quietly insane with this growing need for him.

By the day of the exhibition Bryn knew she had never been so aware of a man in her life: his smell—that seductive male smell, a spicy musk, that was uniquely Gabriel—the rippling play of muscles across his shoulders and back when he removed his jacket and tie. He'd unfasten the top two buttons of his shirt to reveal a light dusting of dark hair on his chest whenever they weren't in the public galleries, allowing her to fully appreciate that masculinity. Her fingers literally itched to become entangled in the glossy dark hair she could see on his chest, to caress the firm line of his back, the silky hair at his nape.

She only had to get through one more day, just a few more hours of this torture, Bryn told herself on that final morning as she made her way to Archangel and the closed west gallery, where the paintings of the six artists were finally ready to be exhibited at a private invitation-only showing this evening.

Unfortunately, Bryn realised as she came to an abrupt halt in the doorway to the west gallery, today was going to be the most difficult twenty-four hours of the past two weeks of torture. Her breath caught in her throat and her face paled as she saw, and easily recognised, the three men talking quietly together across the room.

Gabriel was instantly recognisable, of course, but the unmistakable likeness between all three men—tall and lean, dark haired, with hewn and handsome olive-skinned faces—told her that the other two men had to be Gabriel's two brothers, Michael and Raphael D'Angelo.

Two men who had absolutely no reason to feel in the least kindly towards Sabryna Harper.

* * *

Gabriel sensed Bryn's presence in the gallery even before he turned and saw her standing pale and still across the room; his senses had become so heightened to her presence during these past two weeks that he now felt a thrum of awareness beneath the surface of his skin whenever she was anywhere near. His shaft would harden, becoming a painful throb just at the smell of her perfume— that exotic spice, and the womanly smell that he knew was all uniquely aroused Bryn—the husky sound of her voice enough to raise the hairs on the back of his neck and send shivers of pleasure down the length of his spine.

Gabriel had lost count of the amount of times he had been tempted to put an end to the torment that made his days a living hell and his nights a sleepless nightmare, to just take Bryn in his arms and make love to her, to keep her there until she admitted she wanted him with the same fierce hunger that he wanted her.

The only thing that held him back from doing that was Bryn herself.

For both their sakes she had to be the one to come to him this time. Through her own choice, and not because of any physical coercion on his part. And if that required that he go quietly out of his mind while he waited— hoped—for that to happen, then so be it!

The fact that Bryn looked small and vulnerable today in a dark grey blouse and black jeans, her eyes apprehensive as she stared across the gallery at the three of them, was enough to tell him that she had found the past two weeks as much of a strain as he had.

'Bryn?' he prompted gently as she made no effort to come farther into the gallery.

Her chin rose. 'I— Excuse me, I just wanted— I didn't realise there was anyone— I'll come back later,' she muttered awkwardly as she turned away with the obvious intention of hurrying from the gallery. And maybe Archangel itself?

'Bryn!' Gabriel called out harshly.

She came to an abrupt halt, her tension visible in the stiffness of her shoulders and spine, her hands clenching and unclenching at her sides as she obviously debated whether or not she was going to turn back and face him or simply continue running.

Gabriel mentally willed her to do the former rather than the latter, to be that strong and confident Bryn that he so admired as well as desired.

Bryn felt slightly light-headed as she forgot to breathe, her heart beating so loud and wildly in her chest that she felt sure the three men standing across the room must be able to hear it.

She hadn't known—hadn't even guessed. No one had thought to warn her—certainly not Gabriel—that his brothers were going to be in London today. For the purpose of attending the exhibition this evening?

Wasn't it bad enough that she had been forced to deal with Gabriel on a daily basis for the past two weeks, that her nerves were shot to hell because of it, without having to now face his two disapproving brothers?

Except there was no escaping the fact that Michael and Raphael D'Angelo were both here, that they were the co-owners of the Archangel Galleries, and as such Bryn knew she had no choice but to face them at some point today. So perhaps it was better if she did so sooner rather than in public later, when the meeting could be even more embarrassing?

Bryn drew in a ragged, steadying breath before turning slowly, her chin tilting defensively as she kept her gaze fixed firmly on Gabriel rather than looking at either of his two brothers. 'I was just—' She moistened the dryness of her lips with the tip of her tongue. 'I thought I would come and take a last look in here before the exhibition this evening.'

'I'm glad you did.' Gabriel nodded, dark eyes hooded, his expression unreadable as he crossed the room in long graceful strides to stand in front of her. 'My brothers would like to meet you,' he encouraged gruffly.

Bryn barely managed to hold back her snort of derision as she looked up at him sceptically; they both knew she was the last person Michael and Raphael D'Angelo would ever wish to be introduced to. 'I thought your brothers didn't approve of my inclusion in the exhibition?' she said loud enough for all three men to hear.

Gabriel's jaw tightened at the directness of her challenge, his gaze dark and disapproving as he frowned down at her.

'We initially questioned your motives for entering the New Artists competition, yes,' one of the two men across the room—Michael or Raphael?—came back just as directly.

'Shut up, Rafe,' Gabriel rasped dismissively.

'Some of us still do.' Raphael ignored him as he strolled across the gallery, dark sable hair long and curling silkily onto his shoulders, more casually dressed than his two brothers in a tight black T-shirt that emphasised the muscled width of his shoulders and chest, faded denims resting low down on the leanness of his hips, heavy black boots on his feet. 'I don't believe Gabriel has bothered to ask you this, but why us and why here, Miss Jones?' He quirked a dark and mocking brow.

'Shut up, Rafe,' the third man instructed harshly—he had to be Michael D'Angelo—as he crossed the room with more forceful strides, his sable hair cropped close to his head, his eyes so dark a brown they appeared black and unfathomable, a three-piece charcoal-grey suit perfectly tailored to his muscular frame, his shirt the palest grey, a darker grey silk tie neatly knotted at his throat. 'I'm Michael D'Angelo, Miss Jones.' His tone was compelling as he held his hand out to her.

Bryn eyed that hand uncertainly even as she felt the compulsion in that voice, enough so that she ran the dampness of her own hand down her denim-clad thighs before raising it to be clasped firmly, briefly, in Michael D'Angelo's much stronger one before he released her again. 'I believe we all know that my name isn't really Jones,' she murmured.

'Confrontational. I like that,' Raphael D'Angelo drawled encouragingly.

'Shut up, Rafe.' Gabriel and Michael spoke together this time, both their tones weary, as if they had suffered years of repeating that same phrase.

Bryn bit her lip uncertainly as she quickly looked at each of the three D'Angelo brothers in turn: Gabriel glowered at Rafe impatiently, Michael also frowned at his sibling while Rafe grinned unrepentantly at both of them before turning to give Bryn a conspiratorial wink.

Her eyes widened as she realised Rafe D'Angelo, rather than seriously challengingly her, was, in fact, deliberately annoying his two brothers.

'I don't understand any of this.' She gave a dazed shake of her head.

'Not even Gabriel?' Raphael came back speculatively.

'Rafe—'

'I know, shut up.' Raphael lightly acknowledged Gabriel's rebuke as he pushed his hands into the front pockets of his denims. 'I don't know why it is, but you and Michael just love to ruin all my fun.' He shrugged.

Bryn really was baffled by Michael and Raphael D'Angelo; she had expected hostility, at least, from the two of them because of who she was and the damage her father could have caused the Archangel Galleries five years ago. A hostility that she realised simply wasn't there.

Admittedly Michael was a little austere, self-contained, restrained, in both appearance and manner, but that seemed to be his normal demeanour, rather than any personal animosity directed towards her.

As for Raphael... Bryn had a feeling, looking into those predatory and shrewd golden eyes, that Rafe D'Angelo was a man who maintained a wickedly irreverent appearance on the outside as a way of keeping his real feelings very close to that beautifully muscled chest.

Gabriel easily saw the bewilderment in Bryn's expression as she looked at his two brothers.

Just as he recognised Rafe's open appreciation for Bryn as he mockingly returned that curious gaze. An appreciation that Gabriel didn't like in the least, following his own two weeks of private hell as he had forced himself not to touch or kiss Bryn.

He put a proprietary hand beneath Bryn's elbow now as he stepped closer to her. 'If the two of you will excuse us, I want to talk to Bryn upstairs in my office for a few minutes.'

'"Talk" to her, Gabriel?' Rafe came back derisively.

He gave his brother a narrow-eyed look of warning. 'I'll see the two of you later this evening.'

'You can count on it,' Rafe came back challengingly. 'I'm very much looking forward to seeing you again this evening, Bryn,' he added huskily.

'For God's sake, Rafe, will you just—?'

'I know, I know. Shut up,' Rafe sighed heavily at Michael's terse admonishment.

Gabriel gave a shake of his head as he and Bryn finally left the gallery together, maintaining his hold on her elbow as the two of them walked towards the private lift at the end of the marble hallway. 'I apologise for Rafe,' he bit out abruptly. 'As you may have gathered, he has a warped sense of humour.' A warped sense of humour that on this occasion had been at Gabriel's expense; Rafe knew and had played upon the fact that Gabriel hadn't liked the interest he had shown in Bryn.

'He seemed…very nice,' Bryn answered him uncertainly as they stepped into the lift together.

'Nice is not a word I would ever use to describe my brother,' Gabriel rasped. 'Annoying, irritating, sometimes infuriating, but never anything as insipid as "nice".' Even as he said it Gabriel knew he was being unfair to Rafe; after all, his brother had been the one to warn him that Bryn Jones was Sabryna Harper after Michael had decided against doing so.

'Both your brothers were far more polite to me than I could ever have expected, in the circumstances,' she murmured softly as they stepped out of the lift and walked down the hallway to Gabriel's office.

Gabriel shot her a sideways glance. 'Than I led you to believe, perhaps?'

'Well… Yes.'

He drew in a sharp breath at the speculation in Bryn's tone. 'I advise you not to complicate an already impossible situation by falling for the charms of one of my brothers!' he bit out harshly.

'I wasn't— I didn't— Why would you even think I might do that?' Bryn reacted with predictable accusation.

'You already know the answer to that question, Bryn,'

Gabriel murmured as they entered his office, closing the door firmly behind them before turning Bryn in his arms, his hands resting lightly on the slenderness of her hips.

'Do I?'

'Yes.' He nodded. 'But just so that there's no misunderstanding—if any of the D'Angelo bothers is going to be allowed to kiss these delectable lips today, then it's going to be me,' Gabriel assured her gruffly as he raised one of his hands to run a fingertip gently over her fuller, sensuous bottom lip.

Her eyes darkened, cheeks suffusing with colour. 'I'm not interested in being kissed by either Raphael or Michael,' she breathed softly.

'I'm glad to hear it.' Gabriel's hand moved beneath her chin and tilted her face up towards his, his other arm moving lightly about her waist as he moulded the softness of her curves against his much harder ones. 'How about me, Bryn? Are you interested in kissing me?'

'Gabriel…' she groaned breathily.

It took every particle of willpower Gabriel possessed not to just take that kiss as he felt the way Bryn's body trembled against his, but he knew that he couldn't, wanting, needing Bryn to make the first move. 'A single kiss, Bryn,' he encouraged throatily. 'For luck. To the success of the exhibition this evening.' His breath caught in his throat as he waited for her answer.

Bryn gazed up at him searchingly, longing, aching to once again feel Gabriel's lips on hers, to lose herself in that pleasure. At the same time as she knew that a single kiss wouldn't be enough, that she wanted so much more from Gabriel than just passion and pleasure. So very much more. And that Gabriel didn't have any more than that to give her.

'I can't,' she breathed softly as she pushed against his chest to be released.

Something dark and primal moved in the depths of his eyes as his arms tightened about her. 'Can't or won't, Bryn?' he rasped harshly.

She closed her eyes briefly before answering him. 'Let me go, Gabriel.'

His mouth thinned, a nerve pulsing in the tightness of his jaw. 'Why are you doing this, Bryn?' he groaned. 'Why are you making us both suffer because of your stubbornness?'

This wasn't about Bryn being stubborn; it was so much more than that—*she* felt so much more than that. 'You know why.'

'Because you're worried about your mother,' Gabriel rasped. 'Because of how you believe she would feel about the two of us being together.'

Tears burned in her eyes. 'And you don't think that's important?' she choked. 'You believe that I should just take what I want and to hell with how it affects anyone else?'

'If I'm what you want, then, yes, damn it, that's exactly what I think you should do!' His eyes glittered darkly.

Bryn gave a shake of her head. 'You said it yourself, Gabriel. This is an impossible situation that doesn't need to be made any more complicated than it already is.'

'And when I said it I was warning you not to take Rafe's flirtation seriously,' he grated harshly.

Bryn blinked back the heat of tears. 'Gabriel, we only have one last day together to get through. Do you think we could try to do that without arguing?'

His expression sharpened. 'You think I'm just going to gracefully bow out of your life after tonight?'

'She tensed. 'I was under the impression— Eric told me weeks ago that you would be returning to the Paris gallery after the opening night of the New Artists Exhibition.'

'Did he?' Gabriel gave a humourless smile.

Bryn looked up at him searchingly, a sick feeling forming in the pit of her stomach as he met her gaze unblinkingly. 'You don't intend going back to Paris tomorrow?' she guessed weakly.

'No, I don't,' he answered with satisfaction. 'In fact, Rafe, Michael and I were discussing that very thing when you arrived. Michael is flying to New York tomorrow to take over the gallery there for a month, Rafe is going to Archangel in Paris and I'm staying right here to oversee the rest of the New Artists Exhibition and auction.'

And Bryn knew that the exhibition was being opened to the public tomorrow, the paintings to be on display until they were included in the next Archangel auction in two weeks' time.

Which meant that Gabriel was going to be in London for at least those same two weeks, possibly longer— and his very presence in London would continue to be such a torment and torture that she wouldn't know a moment's peace.

'Let me go, Gabriel,' she instructed. 'Please,' she added as his arms remained firmly about her waist. 'I have to be at the coffee shop by ten o'clock.'

He frowned darkly as he slowly released her. 'You're working today?'

'Of course I'm working today,' she dismissed impatiently as she stepped away from him, finally able to breathe again now that she wasn't pressed up against the disturbing length of his body. 'I haven't sold any of my paintings yet, and I still have my rent to pay at the end of the month,' she added ruefully.

Gabriel moved to lean back against the front of his desk. 'As of this morning, one of your paintings has a reserved sticker on it.'

Her gaze sharpened. 'It does?'

Gabriel nodded. 'Michael wants it.'

Her eyes widened. 'He does?'

Gabriel smiled ruefully. 'Hmm.'

'Which one?'

'The rose.'

The dying red rose, Bryn's representation of the death of hopes and dreams rather than just the flower itself.

Did the austere Michael D'Angelo, a man who gave the appearance of being so totally self-contained, a man who surely had no hopes and dreams to die, appreciate the full meaning of her painting?

'That's— I'm flattered,' Bryn murmured softly.

Gabriel nodded grimly. 'You should be. Michael's private art collection is very exclusive. I have every reason to believe that Lord Simmons is very interested in purchasing one too.'

'That's…amazing.' Bryn's eyes glowed excitedly as she reached out and grasped his hands impulsively. 'This is really going to happen, isn't it, Gabriel? I'm really going to sell some of my paintings, maybe even be able to paint full-time!'

'It's as real as it gets, yes,' Gabriel confirmed huskily as he pulled her in between his parted thighs before placing her hands against his chest. 'Tonight is your night, Bryn.' His hands cupped either side of her face as he gave in to the hunger and kissed her gently on the lips that had haunted and tormented him for the past five years. 'And I want you to enjoy it. Every single moment of it,' he encouraged.

'Oh, I will,' she assured him happily, her hands warm against his chest. 'I— Thank you, Gabriel, for giving me this chance. I really— I know I've been difficult on occasion—' she grimaced '—but I—I really do appreciate everything you've done for me.'

Gabriel could only hope that Bryn still felt that way after tonight.

The past two weeks of being close to Bryn, but never quite close enough, had been enough of a hell for Gabriel to know that the two of them couldn't go on like this indefinitely, that something had to change, and that it wasn't going to be the way he felt about Bryn.

So he had made his arrangements accordingly. Carefully and quietly. Arrangements that would come to full fruition later this evening.

And he wasn't sure Bryn would ever forgive him.

CHAPTER ELEVEN

'IS IT EVERYTHING you hoped it would be?'

Bryn turned to smile warmly at Eric as he came to stand beside her. 'It's so much more!' Her smile widened as he handed her one of the glasses of champagne he carried.

There were over two hundred people crowded into the west gallery for this invitation-only showing, the men all wearing evening suits, the women chic and glittering in their evening gowns and expensive jewellery. Two dozen waiters circulated amongst them carrying trays of finger food and glasses of champagne and half a dozen huge arrangements of flowers perfumed the brightly lit room, all adding to Bryn's light-headed euphoria.

Bryn had chosen to wear a simple black sheath of an above-the-knee length, her only jewellery a simple silver bracelet about one of her wrists and a silver locket at her throat, both of them presents from her mother.

Her smile faded a little at thoughts of her mother, knowing how much Mary would have loved all of this, how proud she would have been of Bryn's success. Instead, Bryn still hadn't so much as dared to tell her mother about the exhibition; how could she when that exhibition was being held at the Archangel Gallery?

As might be expected, the D'Angelo brothers all

looked amazingly handsome in their evening suits as they stood head, and sometimes shoulders, above the other guests, the darkness of their different lengths of hair becoming a sable sheen below the glittering lights of the chandeliers above them. Michael was as remotely austere as ever when he gave her a brief nod of acknowledgement earlier, Rafe as rakishly devil-may-care as he shot her another wink.

But to Bryn's biased gaze Gabriel was far and away the most distinguished man in the room, and she once again found her gaze shifting to the other side of the gallery where he stood in conversation with David Simmons. His mesmerising and dark good looks drew Bryn's gaze to him again and again as if pulled by a magnet, her heart now skipping a beat as Gabriel laughed easily at something the older man had just said to him.

A heart that ached. To be with Gabriel. To make love with him, just once.

Gabriel stilled as he felt a prickle of awareness, of being watched, at his nape and down his spine. Allowing his gaze to move unhurriedly about the room, he sought the source of that awareness even as he continued his conversation with the enthusiastic David Simmons.

Bryn.

Standing beside Eric on the other side of the crowded gallery, her eyes a deep and misty grey as they looked directly into his, the fullness of her lips curving into an enigmatic smile.

Gabriel raised his champagne glass to her in a silent toast; the exhibition was only an hour old but already Bryn's paintings were noticeably attracting the most attention.

Her smile widened as she accepted his silent toast, her eyes glowing. With happiness? Or something else?

'—keep you any longer when I can see I'm keeping you from where you really want to be,' David drawled dryly.

Gabriel drew his gaze reluctantly from Bryn's as he turned back to the other man. 'Sorry?'

The older man chuckled good-naturedly. 'I advise you go to her, man!'

Gabriel gave a rueful smile. 'Is it that obvious?'

David continued to smile indulgently. 'Lovely-looking girl. Beautiful as well as talented. Deadly combination, hmm?'

'Deadly,' Gabriel accepted heavily.

'Then go to it, man.' David gave him an encouraging slap on the shoulder. 'Before that rascal of a brother of yours beats you to it,' he added with a pointed look at Rafe making his way determinedly in Bryn's direction.

'Damn you, Rafe,' Gabriel muttered impatiently even as he placed his empty champagne glass on the tray of one of the passing waiters before striding forcefully across the room to intercept his brother. 'This isn't what we agreed your role would be this evening, Rafe!' He glowered in warning.

Rafe raised mocking brows. 'I just thought I would keep Bryn company while I'm waiting. She looks absolutely stunning this evening, by the way.'

'Hands off, Rafe,' he growled.

His brother grinned unrepentantly. 'Does Bryn know how damned possessive you are over her?'

'Yes.' He frowned grimly, not sure that Bryn wasn't actually going to hate him by the end of this evening.

Rafe chuckled. 'And have you told her how you feel about her yet?'

'Go to hell, Rafe.'

Rafe looked comfortably unconcerned. 'Of course. Why do things the easy way when you can so easily complicate the hell out of them?' He gave a rueful shake of his head. 'At this rate you're going to end up as cold and remote as Michael!'

Gabriel glanced across to where their older brother managed to remain withdrawn even while mingling with their guests. 'He likes his life that way.' He shrugged.

'But you don't, not anymore. Which is why—' Rafe turned back to Gabriel, brows raised '—complicated or not, you should just grab your woman and to hell with everything else!'

'We both know it isn't that simple where Bryn is concerned.' Gabriel grimaced.

'Then I suggest you make it that simple and put the rest of us out of our misery.'

'Your turn will come, Rafe,' Gabriel warned impatiently. 'And when it does we'll see just how well you deal with it. And her.'

Rafe gave a scornful snort. 'There isn't a snowball's chance in hell that I'm going to let some woman—any woman!—come between me and my bachelor lifestyle.'

'Oh, it will come, Rafe, take my word for it, and when it does I'm going to enjoy seeing you have to eat your words.' Gabriel chuckled with satisfaction. 'In the meantime, keep your lethal charms away from Bryn,' he added firmly.

'Just can't stand the competition, hmm?'

'You're too irritating for me to consider you serious competition,' Gabriel drawled dismissively, his gaze once again returning to, and remaining on, Bryn as she chatted with Eric. 'If you'll excuse me, I think I'll go and talk to "my woman".' But before he could even begin to cross the room to Bryn's side he saw her face pale, her eyes widening in distress as she stared across at the entrance to the gallery.

And Gabriel knew, without needing to turn and look, that the moment of truth had arrived.

'Go now, Rafe!' he rasped harshly as he strode towards Bryn.

Bryn was sure she had to be hallucinating, brought about, no doubt, by the strain of the past two weeks and too much champagne on an empty stomach; she had been too excited about this evening to even think about eating today!

Because she couldn't really be looking at her mother and Rhys standing in the entrance to the gallery; it had to be her guilty thoughts of a few minutes ago that made her imagine she could.

Except… Bryn was sure she would never have imagined Rhys looking so handsome in an evening suit; as far as she was aware her stepfather didn't even own an evening suit. In fact, she didn't think she had ever seen Rhys in anything other than jeans and casual tops, T-shirts or sweaters, depending on the time of year. He had worn a suit at his wedding with Mary, of course, but as far as Bryn knew that had been put at the back of his wardrobe the day after the wedding and forgotten about.

Her mother looked slender and beautiful, of course, in her favourite gown, the same deep grey as her eyes, her ivory skin flawless, pale peach lip gloss on her parted lips.

A smile now curved those peach-coloured lips, grey eyes lighting up with excitement, as Mary looked straight across at Bryn before her attention was distracted by Raphael D'Angelo as he joined them in the doorway, speaking briefly before kissing Mary's hand and shaking Rhys's.

Bryn knew there was no way she could have imagined that.

Which meant her mother and Rhys really were here. How on earth had—?

Gabriel!

Gabriel had to have done this.

But why?

Why would Gabriel do something so potentially destructive to what should have been a glitteringly successful evening for the Archangel Gallery? Was he, despite having consistently denied it, still so absorbed in the past that he was willing to take his revenge against Mary and Bryn at the cost of that success and all the weeks of hard work that had gone into this exhibition?

No.

Bryn couldn't believe that of him. She *wouldn't* believe that of the man she loved and had come to know so well these past few weeks. There had to be another reason, an innocent reason, for Gabriel having deliberately invited her mother and Rhys to the exhibition.

'Bryn? Bryn!'

She turned sharply at the sound of Gabriel's voice, trying to focus through the black spots wavering in front of her eyes. 'Why?' she had time to gasp before those black spots all merged into one huge black hole into which Bryn thankfully fell.

She wasn't aware of being swept up into Gabriel's arms, of the sympathetic gasps of the other guests as he carried her across the room, or her mother's concern as she followed the two of them out of the gallery and up to Gabriel's office, leaving her stepfather and Rafe to deal with providing an explanation for her having fainted.

No, Bryn was aware of none of that as she slowly returned to consciousness and heard her mother and Gabriel talking softly together.

'—should have warned her,' Gabriel muttered disgustedly, holding Bryn's hand tightly in his as he sat beside her limp form on the sofa in his office.

'You wanted it to be a surprise,' Mary soothed.

'And this is the result!' he cursed grimly as he looked down at Bryn, her lashes very dark against the pale delicacy of her face.

'It's just a faint, Gabriel,' Bryn's mother assured ruefully. 'If I know my little girl, she's been too excited about tonight to bother eating today.'

Gabriel stood up abruptly, running an agitated hand through the dark thickness of his hair. 'I just wanted her to have the two of you here tonight to share in her success.'

'I know that, Gabriel,' Mary assured gently. 'And so will Bryn once she's thought things through.'

'You think?' Gabriel knew Bryn well enough by now—knew what she thought of him only too well—to know that she was more than capable of believing he had some Machiavellian reason for inviting her mother and stepfather to the exhibition.

Because he hadn't thought his actions through properly, should have realised the shock it would be for Bryn when Mary and Rhys arrived at the gallery this evening.

'I think,' Mary echoed, having now taken Gabriel's place on the sofa beside Bryn. 'I accept my daughter can be fiery on occasion, Gabriel—part of her Welsh heritage, I'm afraid,' she added ruefully. 'But she isn't so headstrong that she will judge you unfairly. And what you've done for her, in regard to her inclusion in this exhibition at Archangel, and inviting Rhys and I here this evening to share in her success, was incredibly kind of you.'

'Bryn doesn't see me as being in the least kind,' Gabriel drawled ruefully.

'Oh, I think you might be pleasantly surprised at what my daughter sees in you,' Mary murmured dryly.

Bryn knew that last remark was directed towards her rather than Gabriel, that her mother, at least, was aware Bryn had recovered from her faint but was now choosing to appear as if she hadn't.

Mary squeezed her hand to confirm it. 'When she wakes up you need to tell Bryn everything, Gabriel,' she told him—and Bryn—softly. 'She especially needs to know what you did for us five years ago, what you did to help the two of us make a new life together in Wales after William died.'

Bryn frowned at this revelation, at the same time knowing her mother's comment 'when she wakes up' was pointedly directed at her.

And she did need to do that; lying here listening to this conversation was totally unfair to Gabriel. Besides, she very much wanted to hear all about what Gabriel had done for them five years ago.

Mary released Bryn's hand before standing up. 'You're a good man, Gabriel,' she told him. 'And if you give my daughter a chance, I believe you will find she already knows that. Now, I think it's time I returned back downstairs, and left the two of you alone to talk.'

'But—'

'My mother is right, Gabriel,' Bryn spoke at the same time as she opened her eyes and looked up at them both. 'You and I do need to talk.' She swung her legs to the floor and sat up slowly.

'I'm not sure you should do that just yet.' Gabriel stepped swiftly forward and sat down on the sofa beside her before once again taking one of her hands in both of his. 'You're probably a bit shaky still from—'

'Mamma?' Bryn looked up at her mother pointedly.

Mary nodded. 'I'm going downstairs now to bask in some of my daughter's glory,' she murmured indulgently. 'No doubt I will see the two of you sometime later this evening?'

'No doubt,' Bryn nodded distractedly, having eyes only for Gabriel.

'And, Bryn?' Her mother paused in the doorway. 'You're wrong. Gabriel isn't in the least "unsuitable". In any way,' she assured before she left the office and closed the door softly behind her.

CHAPTER TWELVE

'WHAT WAS THAT about?' Gabriel prompted.

Bryn's vision was slightly misty with tears as she turned to look at him, knowing that her mother had been referring to the conversation the two of them had had in Wales three weeks ago, when Bryn had insisted the man she loved wasn't suitable.

She gave a shake of her head. 'It doesn't matter anymore. I— Gabriel, I need to thank you for inviting my mother and Rhys here tonight. It's made my evening so much more special.'

'So much so you fainted, damn it,' Gabriel grated self-disgustedly.

Bryn held on to his hand as he would have pulled away and stood up. 'I want you to stay right here,' she told him firmly as he looked at her questioningly. 'I need to say some things to you, and I want you to be next to me when I say them.'

A frown appeared between his eyes. 'Am I going to need some of my single-malt whisky to get through this?' he drawled.

'I don't believe so, no.' She smiled ruefully, drawing in a deep breath before speaking again. 'I'll admit, when I first realised my mother and Rhys were really here—rather than just a figment of my food-deprived, champagne-induced imagination—that I wondered why you had done it. I only wondered for the briefest of moments, Gabriel,' she assured as his frown darkened. 'The very briefest of moments,' she repeated firmly, 'before my knowledge of you told me that your reason for doing it would be a good one rather than a bad one.'

'Actually, it was purely selfish.' Gabriel grimaced; he wanted this woman so badly he was willing to do anything—anything—to get her.

Bryn gave a firm shake of her head. 'I don't believe that.'

'Oh, but it was. You kept insisting that there could never be anything between the two of us because of how your mother might react if she knew, and so I decided to eliminate that objection, at least.'

Bryn looked at him searchingly for several long seconds before a slow smile curved her lips. 'I accept that might have been one of the reasons, Gabriel—'

'Oh, believe me, it was the prime reason,' he assured her grimly.

Her smile didn't even waver. 'You like people to think you're tough and uncaring, don't you?'

'I am tough and—'

'You are most certainly not uncaring,' she insisted firmly. 'And you may manage to convince other people that you are, but I think you should know I haven't fallen for it for some time now. Not since I realised I was in love with you,' she added softly.

'Bryn?' Gabriel's hand tightened about hers.

'Don't worry, I'm not saying that with any expectation of you returning the sentiment,' she assured ruefully. 'I just think you should know, before we start our affair, that I've realised since meeting you again that I fell in love with you five years ago—'

'You— What affair?' Gabriel demanded sharply as he released her hand before standing up.

'—and that I'm still in love with you,' Bryn continued determinedly. 'And that I have no intention of having any sort of relationship with you now and pretending that I'm not—'

'Bryn, did you really just say you fell in love with me five years ago?' he repeated dazedly.

'I did, yes,' she admitted wryly. 'And the reason I'm telling you this now is because I want you to know how I feel before you tell me in what way you helped my mother and I five years ago. It's time for us to be honest with each other, Gabriel,' she encouraged softly. 'As such, I don't want there to be any misunderstandings about why and when I fell in love with you.'

His eyes widened. 'You heard your mother and I talking just now?'

'Yes.'

Gabriel looked down at her searchingly, Bryn meeting that searching gaze unwaveringly. 'You really fell in love with me five years ago?' he finally murmured.

Bryn nodded. 'On sight, I think. But it was all such a mess after my father was arrested. At the time I wondered how I could possibly still be in love with the man who had helped to put my father in prison,' she added heavily. 'I know the truth about that now, Gabriel,' she assured him firmly. 'I know that you tried to stop him, to save him from himself, and my father's answer to that was to inform the press, and so making it impossible for him to walk away as you wanted him to do. I do believe that, Gabriel.'

'Thank God,' he groaned with feeling. 'You really love me, Bryn?' He looked at her searchingly.

She nodded. 'In fact, I realised a couple weeks ago that you're the reason I'm still a virgin at the grand old age of twenty-three,' she acknowledged self-derisively. 'No other man quite matched up to my first love.' She looked up at Gabriel uncertainly as he still looked stunned. 'Too much honesty for you?'

Too much? It was perfect as far as Gabriel was concerned. Bryn was perfect. For him. She always had been.

'I have no words to tell you how much it…pleased me, to know there's been no one else for you.' Gabriel gave a rueful shake of his head. 'But you should know now that I don't want to have an affair with you.'

She blinked. 'Okay.' She nodded woodenly. 'More fool me for having believed you still did.' She drew in a deep, steadying breath. 'That makes all of this a little embarrassing, but it doesn't change any of what I've said—'

'Bryn, would it surprise you to know that I fell in love with you five years ago too?'

She stilled, staring up at him with wide eyes, a gaze that Gabriel now returned with the same directness as she had a few minutes ago. 'I know you said something like this before but—you couldn't have done,' she finally managed to protest dismissively. 'I was chubby,' she reminded him. 'I wore those unbecoming dark-framed glasses. I was so ungainly I fell over my own feet all the time—' She broke off as Gabriel gave a slow shake of his head.

'To me you were voluptuously sexy,' he corrected firmly. 'And you had—still have—the most beautiful dove-grey eyes I've ever seen, glasses or no glasses. I found your occasional lack of balance endearing rather than ungainly. And I wanted you so damned much I could hardly think straight! You were only eighteen years old, and too damned young for me, but I wanted you anyway. Fell in love with you anyway. Plus,' he continued firmly as she would have spoken, 'after your father was arrested and you refused all my attempts at trying to speak with you again, I also had every reason to believe you hated my guts.'

Bryn stared up at him dazedly, sure that she couldn't have heard him correctly. Gabriel couldn't really have just said— 'I never hated you, Gabriel.'

'Of course you did.'

'I hated the situation, not you,' she corrected. 'Would rather none of it had ever happened. But I know, I accept now, that my father was far from perfect, that he was responsible for what happened to him, no one else.' She looked up at him again. 'Gabriel, what did you do to help us five years ago?'

He grimaced. 'Do we really have to talk about that now?'

'Yes, we really do,' she insisted stubbornly.

He sighed. 'I'd rather not.'

'And I would rather you did.'

'You are so damned stubborn,' he sighed.

'Takes one to know one,' she came back ruefully. 'And if you don't tell me then I'll just ask my mother to tell me instead.'

Gabriel scowled his defeat as he sighed deeply. 'I—' He breathed deeply. 'I paid all your father's legal fees.'

Bryn just stared at him. All this time she had thought— Believed— 'What else…?' she breathed softly.

'Isn't that enough?' he drawled.

'What else, Gabriel?' she persisted.

His mouth thinned. 'I gave your mother enough money for the two of you to be able to move back to Wales. I wanted to give her more, enough to pay for you to go to university, but Mary wouldn't hear of it.'

'I should hope not!' Bryn was absolutely stunned at learning how Gabriel had helped them all those years ago. 'You really live up to your name, don't you?' she said wonderingly.

'Don't give me a false halo, Bryn,' Gabriel rasped harshly. 'I helped the two of you because someone had to.'

'And it had absolutely nothing to do with the fact that you had fallen in love with William Harper's overweight daughter?' she chided, an emotional catch in her throat for the man that Gabriel was, and always had been.

'Voluptuously sexy,' Gabriel insisted. 'Which is exactly how you'll look when you're pregnant with our child. You do want children, I hope?'

'Stop changing the subject.'

'Just thinking of you all round with our child,' he continued gruffly, 'with your breasts so big they spill over the top of your bra, is enough to make me hard.'

'Gabriel!' Bryn stood up abruptly, her breathing uneven as she realised what he had said, what his words implied. A baby? Gabriel was talking about the two of them having a child together?

He quirked a self-derisive brow. 'Too much honesty for you?'

Not enough. Not nearly enough!

She moistened her lips with the tip of her tongue, feeling a thrill run through her as she saw the way Gabriel's eyes instantly darkened at the provocation. 'I— When exactly do you intend us having this baby?'

'I think, for your mother and Rhys's sake, and my own parents', that we should probably wait until after we're married.'

'Married?' she squeaked.

'Married,' Gabriel confirmed decisively.

'But you wanted an affair.'

'You *assumed* I wanted an affair,' he corrected. 'When we met again four weeks ago and I obviously couldn't keep my hands off you, I decided to just take whatever you were willing to give me. But following on from your own honesty just now, you should know from the outset that I am very much in love with you, more so now even than five years ago, and that I won't settle for anything less than the two of us being married to each other.'

Happiness swelled so big and so wide inside her that Bryn felt as if she might actually explode from trying to contain it. Gabriel loved her. Had always loved her. He wanted to *marry* her. Have babies with her!

'I— You haven't asked me yet,' she reminded him breathlessly.

He grimaced. 'I've learned that asking sometimes isn't the right way to go about things where you're concerned.'

'Try me,' she encouraged huskily.

Gabriel looked searchingly into the glowing depths of her deep grey eyes, noting the flush in her cheeks, those slightly parted and oh-so-kissable lips. 'Will you marry me, Bryn?' he prompted huskily.

'Oh, yes, Gabriel. Yes, yes, yes!' She threw herself into his arms. 'Whenever and wherever you want.'

'As soon as it can be arranged.' His arms closed tightly about her.

'We've already wasted five years. I don't want to waste any more, want to spend the rest of my life telling you, showing you, how much I love you, will always love you!'

Bryn glowed with happiness as she imagined the future, a lifetime with Gabriel, years and years together, when they would show and tell each other how much they were loved.

* * * * *

A PRIZE BEYOND
JEWELS
CAROLE MORTIMER

For Peter, as always.

PROLOGUE

St Mary's Church, London.

'IT'S NOT TOO late, Gabe,' Rafe drawled softly. The church was packed with his brother's softly chatting wedding guests as they waited for the bride to arrive.

'I checked earlier. There's a door at the back of the vestry where you can escape…'

'Shut up, Rafe.' His two brothers, one seated either side of Rafe, spoke together; Gabriel with the tension of the anxious bridegroom, and Michael with his customary terseness.

'Hush, Rafe.' Their father spoke with soft warning from the pew behind them.

Rafe grinned unrepentantly. 'The jet is just sitting there on the tarmac at the airport, Gabe, and instead of flying off to the Caribbean for your honeymoon, you could just get the hell out of Dodge.'

'Will you just stop?' Gabriel turned to glare at him, his face white and strained as he waited for the start of the organ music that would announce the arrival of his bride at the church. Bryn was already five minutes late, and each minute had seemed like an hour, deepening the lines of tension in his brow.

Rafe's grin widened as he relaxed back in the pew,

having long considered teasing both of his brothers as being part of his role in life.

'You and Michael would never have had any adventures at all if it weren't for me!'

'Marriage to Bryn is going to be biggest adventure of my life,' Gabriel assured him with certainty.

Rafe was aware of how many years his brother had been in love with Bryn, a love his brother had believed was doomed to remain unrequited until just a short month ago.

'She's gorgeous, I'll admit that.'

'Rafe, will you just stop winding him up?' Michael, the eldest of the three brothers, clipped abruptly as Gabriel's hands clenched and unclenched. 'We don't need a fist fight between the groom and one of the best men to liven up the proceedings!'

'I was only—' Rafe broke off as the ringtone of his mobile jarred loudly in the relative silence of the church.

'I told you to switch that damned thing off before you came into the church!' Gabriel turned on him fiercely, obviously relieved to have something tangible to vent his tension on.

'I thought I had.' Rafe grimaced as he pulled the slim mobile from the breast pocket of his morning jacket and quickly turned it to silent mode before slipping it back in his pocket. 'But seriously, Gabe, you still have time to slip out the back of the church and make your escape before anyone is any the wiser.'

'Raphael Charles D'Angelo!'

Rafe winced, having absolutely no idea how his mother, very petite at all of five feet tall, still managed to silence each and every one of her three six-foot-plus sons, all aged in their thirties, with just their full name spoken in that particularly reproving tone of voice!

Although he was thankfully saved from having to turn and face further admonishment from her as the organ played out the wedding march, announcing Bryn's arrival.

The tension instantly eased from Gabriel's shoulders as the three brothers stood up.

Rafe winced as he felt the vibration of his mobile against his chest to announce another incoming call. He chose to ignore it as he turned to look at Bryn as she walked slowly down the aisle on her stepfather's arm.

'Oh, wow, Gabe, Bryn looks absolutely stunning,' he breathed sincerely. Bryn a vision in white lace and satin, the glow of her smile as she looked down the aisle at Gabriel enough to light up the whole church.

'Of course she does,' Gabriel murmured smugly, an expression of adoration on his face as he gazed at the woman he loved more than life itself.

'Who the hell would be crass enough to phone you during your own brother's wedding?' Michael demanded critically as he joined Rafe to one side of where the wedding guests now stood outside the church in the summer sunshine, watching indulgently as the bride and groom were photographed together. Both Gabriel and Bryn were glowing with happiness.

Rafe grimaced as he looked up from checking his mobile; this was the first occasion he'd had to look for any messages. 'Just a friend calling to warn me that Monique is on the warpath since she found out I won't be returning to Paris after the wedding.'

The three brothers rotated the management of the three privately owned and world-renowned Archangel galleries and auction houses. Michael would be taking over from Rafe at the Paris gallery on Monday, Gabe was to be based in London once he had returned from his honeymoon, and Rafe was flying to New York tomorrow to take over the gallery there.

'You couldn't have just told her that before you left?' Michael barked irritably.

Rafe shrugged. 'I thought I had.'

'Obviously she didn't get the message.' Michael scowled before turning to look over at Gabriel and Bryn between narrowed lids. 'Can you believe our little brother is now a married man?'

Rafe gave an affectionate grin as he also looked over at the happy couple. 'And obviously loving every minute of it!' And Gabriel wasn't such a 'little' brother to them either, only two years younger than Michael's thirty-five, and one year younger than Rafe's thirty-four.

As well as being close in age, the three brothers were alike in their appearance and colouring: all tall and ruggedly handsome, with ebony-dark hair, brown eyes, and olive-toned skin, all courtesy of their Italian grandfather.

Michael was the remote and austere brother, preferring to keep his ebony hair styled short, his eyes so deep brown they appeared piercing black, and just as unfathomable as the man behind those eyes.

Gabriel was quietly but lethally determined, his hair curling about his ears and nape, his eyes a warm chocolate-brown.

Meanwhile Rafe kept his hair styled well below his collar, and much longer than either of his two brothers, and his eyes were so light brown that they glowed with the gold of a predator. He was also considered by most to be the least serious of the three D'Angelo brothers. At least by those who didn't really know him well; those that did were fully aware that Rafe was just as steely as his two brothers beneath that outwardly flirtatious and teasing manner.

Michael raised mocking brows. 'I take it that Monique wasn't the one for you, any more than the rest of the legion of women you've been involved with over the last fifteen years?'

Rafe gave his brother a pitying look. 'I'm not looking for "the one", thank you very much!'

Michael smiled slightly. 'One of these days she might just find you!'

'Hah, in your dreams.' Rafe chuckled. 'I accept that Gabe is ecstatically happy with Bryn, but I don't for one minute believe in that "one love of your life" thing when it comes to myself. Any more than you do,' he added knowingly.

'No,' his brother confirmed emphatically, his eyes an unreadable black. 'I'm not going to be plagued with telephone calls and visits from this Monique woman when I get to Paris, am I, pleading with me to tell her where you are and how she can contact you?'

'I hope not.' Rafe sighed wearily. 'We had fun for a few weeks, but now it's over.'

Michael gave a shake of his head, his expression one of irritation.

'She doesn't seem to realise that.' He gave Rafe a hard stare. 'Perhaps you could turn your charm onto something more useful once you get to New York? Dmitri Palitov's daughter will be coming to the gallery on Tuesday,' he explained at Rafe's questioning look. 'She's personally overseeing the installation of the display cabinets she designed for her father's jewellery exhibition at the gallery next weekend. She will be staying for the duration of the exhibition, along with Palitov's own security.'

Rafe's eyes widened disbelievingly. 'What the hell?'

'Palitov wanting his own security is understandable.' His brother gave a brief shrug. 'Allowing his daughter to design the display cabinets and her continued presence at the gallery before and during the exhibition were also conditions for Palitov agreeing to there being an exhibition at all.'

Rafe was as aware as Michael that it was a coup for the Archangel gallery that the reclusive Russian billionaire had agreed to allow his private collection to be exhibited at all. No one but Dmitri Palitov had seen the majority of that jewellery for decades, some of it reputed to have belonged to the Tsarina herself, after it had disappeared from Russia last century.

'I'm relying on you to keep the daughter sweet for the next few weeks,' Michael added.

'What exactly does that mean?' Rafe frowned incredulously. 'Palitov is pushing eighty, so how old is his daughter?'

'Does it matter how old she is?' Michael dismissed uninterestedly. 'I'm not asking you to sleep with her, just use some of that lethal Raphael D'Angelo charm on her,' his brother drawled mockingly before giving Rafe a patronising pat on the back and strolling away to join their parents.

Rafe gave a disgusted huff, not at all happy at being expected to use his charm on the middle-aged daughter of a reclusive Russian billionaire.

CHAPTER ONE

Three days later. The Archangel gallery, New York.

'WOULD YOU MIND moving? I'm afraid you're in the way.'

Rafe straightened in the doorway of the east gallery of Archangel, where he had been standing for the past few minutes observing the installation of the glass and bronze cabinets being brought in for the displaying of the Palitov jewellery collection. He turned now to look at the young lad who had just spoken to him so abruptly.

He seemed to be in his teens, and a couple of inches under six feet tall, dressed in the same faded denims and bulky black sweatshirt as the other workers, and wearing a baseball cap pulled low over his face.

A face that was a little too pretty for a boy, Rafe realised: arched dark brows above eyes the green of fresh moss, and surrounded by long and thick dark lashes, a pert nose with a light smattering of freckles, high cheekbones above hollow cheeks, with full and lush lips above a pointed and determined chin.

Yes, he was a bit too pretty, Rafe acknowledged ruefully, although he didn't seem to be having any trouble helping to wheel the display cases into place.

Rafe had arrived at the gallery at eight-thirty as usual, only to learn from his assistant manager that the Palitov crew had been here since eight o'clock. 'I was just looking for—'

'If you wouldn't mind moving now?' the boy repeated huskily. 'We really need to bring in the rest of the display cabinets.' Two of the more burly workmen had moved to stand beside and slightly behind the younger man, as if to emphasise the point.

Rafe frowned his irritation with that muscled presence; where the hell was Dmitri Palitov's daughter?

Those green eyes widened as Rafe still made no effort to shift out of the doorway. 'I don't believe your employer would approve of your lack of cooperation.'

'It so happens I'm only here because I'm looking for your employer,' Rafe replied in frustration.

A wary expression now entered those long-lashed dark green eyes. 'You are?'

'I am,' Rafe confirmed with a hard smile. 'It was my understanding that Miss Palitov would be here herself this morning to oversee the installation of the display cabinets.' He raised mocking and pointed brows.

The boy looked even less certain of himself now. 'And you are?'

His mouth thinned with satisfaction. 'Raphael D'Angelo.'

The boy winced. 'I had a feeling you might be.' The youth straightened. 'Good morning, Mr D'Angelo. I'm Nina Palitov,' she added as he made no effort to take her outstretched hand.

Nina had the satisfaction of seeing the man she now knew to be Raphael D'Angelo, one of the three brothers who owned the prestigious Archangel galleries, briefly lose some of his obviously inborn arrogance as those golden eyes widened with disbelief, the sculptured lips parting in surprise.

It gave Nina the chance to study the man standing in

front of her. He was probably in his mid-thirties, or possibly a little younger, with long and silky ebony-dark hair styled rakishly to just below his shoulders, and with the face of a fallen angel. He had predatory golden eyes, sharp blades for cheekbones beneath that olive-toned skin, his nose long and aristocratic, sensuous lips that looked as if they had been lovingly chiselled by a sculptor, his jaw square—and at the moment tilted at an arrogantly challenging angle.

The perfectly tailored charcoal-grey suit and snowy white shirt did nothing to hide the muscled perfection of his taller than average frame—rather, it had no doubt been tailored to emphasise that masculinity! A suit that Nina belatedly realised had probably cost as much as a month's rent on any number of exclusive Manhattan penthouse apartments. The white shirt was of the finest silk, as was the pale silver tie knotted so meticulously at his throat, and his black leather shoes were obviously of the finest Italian leather.

As if all of that weren't enough of an indication of who he was, that softly modulated and educated English accent should have been the giveaway, added to which this man's olive complexion showed he was obviously of Italian descent.

Nina's gaze swept back up to that arrogant—and breathtakingly handsome—face. 'I'm guessing from your expression that I'm not quite what you were expecting, Mr D'Angelo?' she murmured ruefully.

Not what Rafe was expecting?

That had to be the understatement of the decade; it was bad enough that he had thought he was talking to a too-pretty boy, but discovering that boy was in fact a beautiful young woman, and Dmitri Palitov's daughter, was a little hard to accept. Palitov was almost eighty years old, and the woman now claiming to be Nina Palitov could only be in her mid-twenties at the most.

Or maybe Nina was Palitov's granddaughter, and for some reason was here in place of her mother?

Rafe forced the tension to ease from his shoulders.

'Not what, who,' he excused lightly, deciding to keep the 'pretty boy' mistake to himself as he finally briefly shook the hand she held out to him. A warm and artistically slender hand, the fingers long and delicately tapered, the nails kept short.

She looked up at him quizzically with those moss-green eyes. 'And exactly who were you expecting, Mr D'Angelo?'

'Your mother, probably,' Rafe dismissed dryly. 'Or possibly your aunt?'

She gave a rueful smile. 'My mother is dead, and I don't have an aunt. Or an uncle, either,' she added dryly as Rafe would have spoken again. 'Or any other family apart from my father,' she said softly.

Rafe blinked, eyes narrowing as he attempted to process the information this woman had just given him. No mother, no aunts or uncles, just her father. Which meant...

'I'm the Miss Palitov you were told to expect, Mr D'Angelo,' she confirmed huskily. 'I believe I'm what some people might describe as being a child born in the autumn years of my father's life.'

And Rafe would be one of those people!

He'd had no idea that Dmitri Palitov's daughter would be so young. Had Michael known? Probably not, otherwise his brother would never have suggested that Rafe charm her! It was unusual for his big brother not to have all the facts, but this just went to prove that not even the meticulous Michael was infallible.

And this woman's identity probably also explained those two muscle-bound men now standing as silent and watchful sentinels at Nina Palitov's back. No doubt Daddy Palitov kept a very close guard over his young and beautiful daughter.

As if those bodyguards, and the information that this young woman was Dmitri Palitov's daughter, weren't disconcerting enough, she now reached up and swept the baseball cap from her head, releasing a waterfall of fiery red curls that framed the beauty of her face and cascaded over the slenderness of her shoulders before flowing riotously down almost to her waist.

And leaving Rafe in absolutely no doubt that she was a woman.

Rafe's preference in women had always been towards pocket-sized blondes, but as he saw the rueful amusement—at his expense—in those moss-green eyes, the slightly mocking curve to those lushly full lips, evidence, no doubt, that Nina Palitov found his discomfort amusing, he knew that he would enjoy nothing more at this moment than to take this beautiful woman in his arms before kissing that amusement from the sweet curve of those lush and pouting lips.

A move on his part that would no doubt cause those two muscle-bound sentinels to move with lightning speed in her defence.

Nina eyed Raphael D'Angelo beneath lowered lashes, knowing, by the glance he briefly gave at Rich and Andy as they stood behind her, that he had now realised helping to move display cases wasn't their only reason for being at the Archangel gallery.

She had been surrounded by the same bodyguards for most of her life, had grown so accustomed to having at least two of them watch over her day and night that she rarely noticed they were there any more. She now treated the eight men who made up her security detail more like friends than people employed by her father to ensure her safety.

Which was a sad reflection on what her life had become, Nina realised with a frown.

Admittedly her father was a wealthy and powerful man, and Nina knew better than most that with that wealth and power came enemies. But she had often thought wistfully of how nice it would be to be able to do as other people her age did, and just pop out to collect the newspaper or a carton of milk in the mornings, or a takeaway for dinner from a fast-food restaurant, or share a fun evening out with several girlfriends, without her bodyguards having to check out the venue first.

Or maybe go out for a date with an arrogant and decadently handsome man with the face of a fallen angel.

And exactly where had that ridiculous thought come from?

The long years of her father's protection meant that Nina was usually extremely shy when it came to talking to men; she certainly never had erotic fantasies about them the first time she met them!

She frowned up at Raphael D'Angelo, a man who could never be considered as being anything other than an arrogant and decadently handsome man with the face of a fallen angel.

'I have a lot to do here today, Mr D'Angelo,' she told him, hiding her shyness behind the briskness of her tone. 'So if there was nothing else?'

Rafe knew when he was being dismissed. And he also knew when he didn't like it!

He was in charge of the New York gallery at the moment, and it was time that Miss Nina Palitov and those muscle-bound goons standing behind her were made aware of that fact.

'There are a few things I would like to discuss with you first, if you would care to accompany me up to my office on the third floor?'

The blinking of those long dark lashes was the only evidence that she was surprised by his request. No doubt Daddy's money and power ensured that Miss Nina Palitov rarely, if ever, acceded to anyone's request for her to do anything.

Her expression was wistful as she gave a predictable shake of her head, causing that long cascade of fiery red hair to shimmer like a living flame in the sunlight pouring in through the floor-to-ceiling windows behind her.

'I obviously don't have time at the moment. Perhaps later on this morning?'

Rafe's mouth tightened.

'I have several other appointments to deal with today.' But none, he knew, that Michael, at least, wouldn't expect him to cancel in favour of meeting with Dmitri Palitov's daughter, whenever it was convenient for her.

But Michael wasn't here right now, Rafe was, and—

Hell, just admit it, Rafe—the reason you're so damned irritated is because Nina Palitov is utterly gorgeous. And under other circumstances, in a different location—the two of them naked together in a silk-sheeted bed came to mind—he might even enjoy the challenge she represented, both sexually and to his authority.

But they weren't in a bed, that lush mouth wasn't his for the taking, and when it came to Archangel he was the one in charge.

She shrugged dismissively. 'In that case, I'm afraid the discussion will have to wait until tomorrow.'

Rafe took a step closer to her, only to find that the two

men standing behind Nina Palitov took that same step forward, flanking her closely now as they both watched him between narrowed eyes.

'Call off your watchdogs,' he advised harshly.

She eyed him frowningly for several long seconds before slowly turning her head to look at the two men. 'I'm sure Mr D'Angelo poses absolutely no threat to me,' she assured them wryly before turning back to once again look challengingly at Rafe.

As if she believed his wealth and power also rendered him over-indulged and wimpish, a man who wouldn't stand a chance against these two muscle-bound men if they were to take exception to something he said or did.

Admittedly, the two of them together might be pushing it a bit, but Rafe had no doubts that in a one-on-one fight his hours at the gym, and his training in several of the martial arts, would ensure he could best either one of these two men, whether they chose to fight dirty or fair—and their threatening poses indicated it would probably be the former.

He forced the tension from his shoulders as he gave a deliberately wolfish smile as his appreciative gaze swept slowly over Nina Palitov.

'Oh, I wouldn't go so far as to say that I posed absolutely no threat to you, Miss Palitov,' he purred softly, his tone deliberately provocative.

Those beautiful moss-green eyes widened noticeably, a delicate blush creeping into her peaches-and-cream cheeks, and succeeding in making the endearing freckles on the bridge of her nose appear more prominent. At the same time her tongue flicked out nervously to moisten the lushness of those delectably plump lips. Lips that had no need for lip gloss to enhance their fullness or deliciously peach colour.

Those lips thinned now, as if Nina Palitov was well aware that Rafe was playing with her, and she didn't appreciate it.

'Would eleven o'clock be convenient to you, Mr D'Angelo?' she bit out huskily.

'I'll make sure that it is,' he drawled softly.

Nina was very aware that somewhere during the course of this exchange Raphael D'Angelo had taken control of the conversation—and her? His air of lazy confidence and power implied that he preferred always to be in control.

Even when he was in bed with a woman?

Nina felt the colour warm her cheeks for a second time in as many minutes as she realised that Raphael D'Angelo was responsible for bringing those totally inappropriate thoughts into her head.

Why were they so inappropriate?

She was twenty-four years old, with a slender figure, and the way men looked at her told her she wasn't unattractive. And Raphael D'Angelo was dangerously, overwhelmingly handsome in a swarthily Latin way that she realised made her nerve-endings sizzle. They were both over twenty-one, so why shouldn't she indulge in a little light flirtation with him?

Because it wasn't something she was accustomed to doing, came the instant, and sad, reply. Her father was very protective of her, claustrophobically so at times, and it was a little difficult to enjoy a flirtation with an attractive man with two bodyguards always standing at her back. Especially when those same two bodyguards would no doubt report that behaviour back to her father if necessary.

Besides, she might have only just met him for the first time, but it was long enough to know that Raphael

D'Angelo really was too dangerous a man for Nina to practise her relatively inexperienced flirtation skills on.

She knew his reputation, of course; even she had heard the New York gossip about this particular D'Angelo brother, enough to know that Raphael D'Angelo's relationships with women were brief and numerous, and that there was no such thing as a light flirtation where this particular man was concerned.

'Do that.' Nina nodded abruptly, her defensive hackles rising.

Those golden eyes narrowed to steely slits. 'I believe, as it seems we will be required to spend a certain amount of time together over the next few weeks, that you will find me to be much more amenable to your needs if our relationship is one based on mutual respect.'

Nina blinked. 'It's been my experience that respect is earned rather than a given.'

His jaw tightened. 'Meaning?'

Nina kept her expression deliberately blank. 'I don't believe there was any hidden meaning to my comment, Mr D'Angelo, merely a statement of fact.'

Rafe doubted that very much.

Damn, but this woman was irritating. Cool, detached—and damned irritating!

She was also beautiful, in an exotically unusual way; a man could drown in those deep moss-green eyes, become lost in caressing the smooth softness of her skin, and as for those lush and kissable lips? Rafe had no idea what her breasts were like, of course, hidden as they were beneath that bulky black sweatshirt, but her hips and thighs were slender, her legs so long they seemed to go on for ever. As for that abundance of long and curling silkily soft hair, Rafe couldn't ever remember seeing hair of quite that fiery colour before, natural golden and russet highlights visible amongst the red as her sunlit hair surrounded her face like a halo.

Yes, Nina Palitov was all of those things: irritating, beautiful, and desirable—and completely out of any man's reach, if the two heavies standing guard behind her were any indication. And they so obviously were; both men were still eyeing him suspiciously.

She was also, most tellingly of all, the daughter of Dmitri Palitov, the powerful billionaire who took the term reclusive to a whole new level!

She nodded now. 'Obviously I would like the gallery's security to be part of our conversation.'

Rafe looked at her through narrowed lids. 'Archangel's security is my concern, Miss Palitov, not yours.'

She gave a shrug. 'I suggest you read clause seven of the contract your brother Michael signed with my father, Mr D'Angelo. I believe you will find that particular clause states that I have the final say in all security provided for the gallery during the showing of my father's unique jewellery collection.'

What on earth?

Michael had mentioned that Palitov intended to supply his own security for the collection, but at no time had he even suggested that included all of the gallery's security.

Having arrived in New York only the day before, Rafe hadn't yet had time to look in any detail at the contract Archangel had signed with Dmitri Palitov. He had trusted Michael to have dealt with it with his usual ruthless efficiency.

But if what Nina Palitov claimed was true, and Rafe had no reason to believe that it wasn't, then he needed to have a little chat with his big brother.

Admittedly the exhibition of the Palitov jewellery was a coup for Archangel, it would be a coup for any gallery, when the much-coveted collection had never been shown in public before, but that didn't mean they had to allow the Palitov family to just walk in here and take over the whole damned place.

Nina had to hold back a smile as she easily read the frustration in Raphael D'Angelo's expression, inwardly knowing she felt a certain sense of satisfaction in having managed to pierce the confidence of this arrogant man. Raphael D'Angelo was so obviously a man used to issuing orders and having them obeyed without question, and she could see his discomfort now in having been so totally wrong-footed.

And no doubt he would have something to say to his older brother, when next the two men spoke, regarding the concessions Michael D'Angelo had been required to make in order to be able to exhibit her father's jewellery collection.

Nina perfectly understood her father's caution; he had collected the unique and priceless jewellery over many years, and as such it was completely irreplaceable.

'Do you intend trying to change the terms of that contract? If so, perhaps we should call a halt to bringing in any more display cases until after you've spoken with my father?'

'I don't believe I mentioned changing the terms of the contract, Miss Palitov,' Raphael D'Angelo bit out harshly.

'Nina,' she invited softly.

'Rafe,' he countered, golden eyes glittering angrily.

Rafe.

Yes, the shortened version, the rakish version, of this man's name suited him far more than the more formal Raphael.

'Nor do I react well to threats, Nina,' he drawled softly.

'I believe you will find I made a statement rather than

a threat, Rafe,' she replied just as ultra-politely. 'As I also believe you will find that the contract between my father and your brother is completely binding on both sides.'

Nina had been present on the day Michael D'Angelo had met with her father at his Manhattan apartment, both men also having their lawyers present in order to check the details of the contract before it was signed by both of them. Her father never left anything to chance, and the safety of his beloved jewellery collection came second only to his protection of Nina.

'If you have any reservations or doubts, then I suggest it might be preferable if you take them up with your brother before speaking to my father,' she added challengingly.

She had no idea what it was about Raphael, or rather Rafe, D'Angelo that made her bristle so defensively. So uncharacteristically. That arrogant confidence perhaps? Or maybe it was the fact that he was just too dangerously handsome for his own—and any woman's—good? Whatever the reason, Nina found herself wanting to challenge him in a way she never had any other man.

Rafe had more than 'reservations' where Nina Palitov was concerned. Where his attraction to her was concerned.

But he certainly didn't doubt her claim regarding the contract and the security of her father's collection. He knew from the steadiness of that unflinching moss-green gaze that Nina Palitov was telling him nothing but the truth about the contract Michael—ergo, Archangel—had signed with her father. Something else Michael hadn't warned him about, and which Rafe intended taking up with his big brother at his earliest convenience.

He nodded abruptly. 'Very well, I'll make the necessary arrangements for you to view the gallery's full security tomorrow.'

'Today would be more convenient.'

Rafe looked down at her through narrowed lids, easily seeing the challenge in those unblinking green eyes. 'Very well, later today,' he ground out tautly.

'Good.' She gave another terse nod. 'I'll see you in your office on the third floor at eleven o'clock.' She turned away dismissively, gathering up the wild abundance of her hair and pushing it back under her baseball cap as she walked over to rejoin her workmen.

The two bodyguards shot Rafe a warning glance before following hot on Nina Palitov's heels.

A totally unnecessary warning, as far as Rafe was concerned.

He had absolutely no interest in deepening his acquaintance with one Miss Nina Palitov. She was beautiful, yes, and those lips definitely begged to be explored in deeper, more sensuous detail, but the presence of the bodyguards said that wasn't going to happen any time soon, and her dismissive attitude towards Rafe wasn't in the least encouraging either.

No, Miss Nina Palitov was not a woman Rafe had any intention of pursuing on a personal basis.

CHAPTER TWO

A DECISION RAFE had serious reason to question when his assistant, Bridget, showed Nina Palitov into his office two hours later!

Rafe had been extremely busy over those two hours, having no intention of being caught wrong-footed again where this young woman was concerned.

His telephone conversation with Michael hadn't been particularly helpful, his brother showing no interest in the fact that Nina Palitov was aged in her twenties rather than middle-aged, as Rafe had assumed she would be. Michael had simply repeated that it was Rafe's duty to keep Miss Palitov sweet.

The Internet had proved a little more helpful regarding Nina Palitov, revealing that she had been born to Dmitri and Anna Palitov when her mother was thirty and her father in his mid-fifties, which now made Nina twenty-four. It also stated that Anna had died five years after Nina was born, but gave no cause for her premature death.

It also listed the schools Nina had attended, after which she had gone on to Stanford University, attaining a degree in art and design, before taking up a position in her father's extensive business empire.

None of which changed the impact the flesh and blood

Nina Palitov had on Rafe when she walked into his office at eleven o'clock.

Somewhere during the course of her morning's work she had removed the bulky black sweatshirt, revealing a close-fitting white T-shirt beneath. The tightness of the material across her breasts also revealed that she wasn't wearing anything beneath that T-shirt. Her breasts were small and pert, and tipped with darker nipples—the same peach colour as her lips?—as they pressed noticeably against that clinging white material, her abdomen silkily slender as the T-shirt finished just short of her low-rise denims.

She had dispensed with the baseball cap again, that over-abundance of fiery red hair a wild cascade onto the narrowness of her shoulders and down the slender length of her spine. A wild and fiery cascade that now made Rafe's fingers itch to touch it.

And the rising, hardening of Rafe's shaft told him his body had decided, completely in contradiction of his earlier decision to stay away from this young woman, that it also liked what it saw.

'Mr D'Angelo?' Nina prompted as he made no effort to get up and greet her but instead remained seated behind the black marble desk placed in front of the windows across the spacious room.

He had removed his jacket and put it on a hanger some time during the morning, his shoulder-length hair an ebony sheen against the white of his silk shirt. As she had suspected earlier, the broadness of his shoulders, muscled width of his chest, and the tautness of his abdomen owed absolutely nothing to the perfect tailoring of his designer label suit.

Nina deliberately looked away from all that blatant maleness to take in the rest of the spaciously elegant office. Floor-to-ceiling windows made up two of the walls of the corner office, cream silk wallpaper adorned the other two, along with several filled bookcases and a bar, with a comfortable seating area in front of the second wall of windows.

All totally in keeping with the luxurious elegance associated with the world-famous Archangel galleries and auction houses. That reputation and the expensive opulence of this gallery were no doubt the reason her father had chosen Archangel as the venue to exhibit his collection.

Even so, Nina knew that her father would not appreciate the lack of manners Raphael D'Angelo was currently exhibiting towards his only daughter.

'Is this an inconvenient time for you, after all?' she questioned coolly as she turned back to look across the marble desk at him.

'Not at all,' he drawled as he finally stood up to turn away and take his jacket from the hanger and shrug it back on over his wide shoulders before facing her fully, dark brows raised over mocking gold eyes. 'Did you decide to dispense with the bodyguards?'

Nina steadily returned that mocking gaze. 'They're standing just on the other side of that door.' She nodded towards the closed door behind her.

Raphael D'Angelo grinned as he leant back against the front of his black marble desk, arms folded across the width of that muscled chest, every inch of him crying out hot, dangerous male, beware.

'Out of consideration for the fact that I pose absolutely no threat to you?'

Out of consideration for the fact that Nina had told Rich and Andy that that was where they were going to wait for her. They hadn't particularly liked it, but Nina had been adamant. Alone in Raphael D'Angelo's office, very aware of his predatory maleness, and that wicked glint once again visible in those golden eyes, she wasn't so sure of her decision.

Rafe D'Angelo was a dangerously attractive man who even Nina knew had the reputation of being something of a rake when it came to women. An outgoing love-'em-and-leave-'em type of man, in fact, and as such he was completely out of Nina's own limited experience with men.

Which, she knew, was the main reason for her brusqueness towards him earlier this morning; she simply had no previous experience of dealing with men as powerfully attractive as Raphael D'Angelo. With any men at all, other than her father and bodyguards, if the truth be told.

Her father had become something of a recluse after her mother died, at the same time as he had become obsessively protective of Nina. That protection, from men like Rich and Andy, meant Nina had only been out on a few dates these past few years. Always with men her father had first approved of, and who had passed the stringent security checks made on them before Nina could so much as accept an invitation from them to even go out for a pizza.

Rafe D'Angelo, charming on the outside but with a steely and determined inner core, didn't seem like a man who would give a damn about whether he passed security checks or not, if he should decide he was interested in a woman.

Not that Nina thought that he ever would be interested in her; she very much doubted she was beautiful or sophisticated enough to arouse the interest of a man as physically attractive and sought after as she knew Rafe

D'Angelo to be. A man who could have any woman he wanted, and usually did.

But Nina knew instinctively, even from her brief acquaintance with him, that Rafe D'Angelo wouldn't give a damn about whether or not he had her father's or anyone else's approval, or be bothered by the fact that Rich and Andy were standing on the other side of his office door, if he should feel the inclination to kiss her—

What on earth was wrong with her?

Anyone would think that she wanted Rafe D'Angelo to find her attractive. To kiss her, even.

Which was ridiculous. She was only at the Archangel gallery in order to oversee the installation and security of her father's jewellery collection, nothing more. The fact that she was so totally aware of everything about Rafe D'Angelo—the silkiness of his overlong dark hair, that predatory glint in those golden eyes, the hard contours of that sculptured and ruggedly handsome face, the muscled strength of his body—was irrelevant, when she had no intention of allowing her attraction to him to go any further. When her father's protection of her wouldn't allow that attraction to go any further.

'I've made arrangements for you to go down to the basement and view our security at twelve o'clock,' Rafe D'Angelo informed her briskly now, the expression in those golden eyes guarded. 'I trust that time is convenient for you?'

'Perfectly, thank you.' Nina nodded coolly. 'You're also aware, once the collection is in place, that there will be two men from my father's own security detail in the east gallery guarding the collection at all times?'

'So I believe.' He nodded tersely.

Her brows rose at his tone. 'You don't approve?'

'It isn't a question of whether or not I approve,' Rafe

rasped. 'But I find it a tad insulting that your father should feel it necessary, if you really want to know,' he added with obvious impatience.

She shrugged. 'I doubt my father suspects that you, or any of your employees, intend to steal the collection.'

'How reassuring!'

Nina thought they had gone as far as they could on that particular subject; there was no way her father would back off on security for his precious jewellery collection, whether Rafe D'Angelo felt insulted or otherwise. 'So, what was it you wished to discuss with me, Mr D'Angelo?' she prompted lightly.

'I thought we had agreed it would be Rafe and Nina?' he reminded dryly. 'Mr D'Angelo makes me sound like my stern older brother.' He grimaced.

Nina raised auburn brows. 'That would be the Michael D'Angelo who visited my father some weeks ago?'

'You were able to recognise him from my description, hmm?' Rafe drawled ruefully.

Nina shrugged narrow shoulders. 'I found him to be polite, if a little…austere.'

That golden gaze narrowed. 'You've actually met my brother Michael?'

Her eyes widened at the sharpness of his tone. 'I was present when he and my father signed the contracts for the exhibition, yes.' She nodded.

What the hell?

Rafe had spoken to Michael just an hour ago, a conversation in which his brother hadn't acknowledged having actually met Nina Palitov. Admittedly Rafe hadn't actually asked him if he had, but Michael certainly hadn't mentioned having met her, either. Not earlier, or when the two of them had spoken on the subject at Gabe's wedding; a conversation in which Michael also hadn't bothered to contradict Rafe when he had made the assumption that Nina Palitov was middle-aged.

'I saw the beautiful photographs, in the Sunday newspapers, of your younger brother's—Gabriel, is it?—wedding on Saturday. The three of you are very alike.'

Rafe had been studying the tips of his highly polished black shoes, but he now looked up at Nina Palitov, his eyes narrowing as he saw how the sun, shining in through the window behind him once again picked out those gold highlights in that glorious red hair, her eyes a soft moss-green against her creamy soft skin, and as for her lips...

Rafe cursed softly under his breath as he straightened before moving to sit back behind his desk, his already semi-hard erection having given an acknowledging throb in response to his looking appreciatively at Nina Palitov's lushly parted lips.

A totally unacceptable reaction as far as Rafe's intellect was concerned—he had always liked a lack of complication in those tall leggy blondes he was usually attracted to. They spent a few weeks of enjoying each other, mainly in bed, and with no expectations on either side. Nina Palitov, who she was, who her father was, made an attraction to her as complicated as hell.

Unfortunately his once again rapidly hardening manhood still seemed to have an entirely different opinion on the subject.

Rafe chose to ignore that physical reaction as he now looked across the width of his desk at Nina Palitov between narrowed lids. 'Yes, we are,' he bit out dismissively. 'And it was a lovely wedding. As lovely weddings go,' he added with a dismissive lack of interest.

Nina smiled at Rafe D'Angelo's obvious aversion to both weddings and marriage. 'I'm sure it isn't catching, like the measles or chickenpox!'

He gave a hard smile. 'I'm immune if it is!'

'Lucky you,' Nina came back lightly. 'Is that all you wished to discuss with me?'

Rafe D'Angelo blinked thick dark lashes, as if he had briefly forgotten that he was the one who had asked for this meeting, that emotion quickly masked as he gave a shrug. 'Not quite. Why don't you sit down for a few minutes?' he invited lightly, indicating the chair across from him, waiting until Nina was seated before continuing. 'Your father's security aside, I thought we should decide exactly what your role is going to be at Archangel for the period of the exhibition.'

Nina shrugged slender shoulders. 'As I've already stated, you will find that was already decided in the contract signed several weeks ago by my father, and your brother.'

'I've had a chance to read the contract in more detail now.' He nodded. 'And I really can't believe that you want to spend all of your time here for the next two weeks.'

'You can't?' Nina mused.

'No, I can't,' he repeated hardly. 'There's nothing more to do here now that the display cases have been delivered and put in place. I congratulate you on your work, by the way,' he seemed to add grudgingly. 'The display cases are exquisite.'

'Thank you,' she accepted shyly.

Nina had worked on making the display cases for almost four months now, since her father had first proposed the idea of exhibiting his jewellery collection in one of the New York galleries, taking several weeks and consultations with her father to decide on a combination of smooth pewter and bevelled glass, so as not to detract from the beauty of the jewels themselves. Each display case had its own intricate lock and security code, a code known only to Nina and her father. 'They will look even more impressive once the jewellery is inside them.'

'I'm sure.' Rafe D'Angelo nodded abruptly. 'The exhibition doesn't open until Saturday; surely it isn't going to take you more than a day or so to organise the display?'

'It's a very large collection.'

'Even so…'

Nina eyed him teasingly. 'If I didn't know better, Rafe, I would think that you were trying to get rid of me for at least three of those four days?'

And she would be right in thinking that, Rafe acknowledged with rising impatience. Damn it, he had the whole of Archangel to run, not just the Palitov Exhibition, and he didn't have the time—or the inclination—to cater to the whims and demands of the Palitov family. 'Not at all,' he dismissed smoothly.

'I spoke to my father on the telephone earlier, and he wishes me to extend his compliments to you, and invite you to his home for dinner this evening, if that's convenient?' the youngest member of the Palitov family invited formally.

The frown deepened on Rafe's brow at the invitation, knowing that Dmitri Palitov was as socially elusive as he was reclusive, but he now appeared to be inviting Rafe to go to his home for dinner this evening. Understandably so, perhaps, considering Rafe was now the D'Angelo brother in charge of the New York gallery the other man was entrusting his beloved jewellery collection to.

Rafe accepted all of that, he would just prefer not to become any more involved with the Palitov family than he already was, with Nina Palitov in particular. He especially didn't want the watchful Dmitri Palitov to witness Rafe's noticeably physical reaction to the man's daughter.

'Rafe?'

He scowled, his mouth firming. 'I have a previous engagement this evening, I'm afraid.' Thank heavens!

'I see.' Nina Palitov looked more than a little surprised at his refusal.

And no doubt that surprise was due to the fact that not too many people, if they were privileged enough to receive an invitation of any kind from the powerful Dmitri Palitov, would ever think of refusing it. As Rafe knew on a professional level he shouldn't refuse this dinner invitation either, but rather reorganise his date with the actress Jennifer Nichols for another evening instead. No doubt that was what Michael would expect him to do, but, as Rafe was feeling far from pleased with Michael at the moment, he really didn't give a damn what his big brother did or didn't think!

Nina knew that her father, for all that he had made the dinner invitation a request, would still be far from pleased that Rafe D'Angelo had refused that invitation.

At the same time as she, personally, couldn't help but admire Rafe for doing so. She loved her father dearly, but that didn't prevent her from being fully aware of the fact that his power made him far too accustomed to having his own way, to exerting his will on others, and expecting them to ask 'how high' when he said jump. Rafe D'Angelo obviously wasn't one of those people.

She nodded. 'My father suggested, if that should be the case, that you choose another evening convenient to yourself?'

'Let's see.' He made a point of opening and checking the large diary on his desk. 'Tomorrow evening seems to be free at the moment?'

'If that should change you can let me know tomorrow.' Nina nodded, still amused rather than concerned by Rafe's determination not to be dictated to by her father.

He raised dark brows. 'You still plan on coming in to the gallery every day?'

'My father expects it.'

Rafe D'Angelo relaxed back against his high-backed black leather chair as he looked at her through narrowed lids. 'And do you always do what your father expects?'

Nina stiffened at the taunting tone in his voice. 'It causes him less distress if I do, so yes,' she confirmed abruptly.

'Distress?' He quirked one dark and mocking brow.

'Yes.' Nina had no intention of elaborating on that explanation.

Her father's reasons for being so protective of her were none of Rafe D'Angelo's business. Or anyone else's, for that matter. It was what it was, and Nina accepted it as such. If she occasionally chafed against her father's need for that protection, then that was her own affair, and not Rafe D'Angelo's.

His golden, predatory gaze now raked over her with a deliberate, and mercilessly male, assessment, causing Nina's nipples to swell and firm as that gaze finally settled on the pertness of her breasts as they pressed snugly against her T-shirt. Nina drew her breath in softly as the cotton material acted as a mild abrasive against her bared flesh, deepening that arousal, at the same time as she felt a hot gush of dampness between her thighs.

Her body didn't seem to care that Rafe D'Angelo had deliberately set out to cause this response in her, that he was no doubt amusing himself at her expense as the ache in her nipples became an unbearable torture, and between her thighs swelled, became even more moist, as if in readiness for the stroke, the entry, of this man's touch.

But Nina cared. Her father's years of protection might have made her totally inadequate when it came to dealing with men as experienced as Rafe D'Angelo, but she wasn't about to let herself be the cause of any man's amusement, least of all the arrogant and mocking Rafe D'Angelo.

She stood up abruptly. 'I'll inform my father that you've accepted his dinner invitation for tomorrow evening,' she bit out abruptly.

Rafe raised his gaze reluctantly from enjoying the pertness of Nina Palitov's breasts, part of that enjoyment having been knowing, by the sudden tautness and swelling of her nipples, that she was far from immune to his appreciative gaze.

But one look at Nina's face, seeing the pained accusation in those moss-green eyes, the creamy pallor of her cheeks, and the defensive angle of her little pointed chin, and he felt like a complete heel for having behaved so badly. He was angry with his own unexpected physical response to this woman, with Michael for putting him in this position in the first place, even a little with Dmitri Palitov for the same reason, but that didn't give him the right to take that anger out on Nina.

Rafe stood up to move round to the side of his desk, the two of them now standing only inches apart. 'Will you be joining us for dinner tomorrow evening?' he prompted softly.

She looked up at him warily. 'I believe my father will expect me to be there to act as his hostess, yes.'

His brows rose. 'You don't live with your father?'

'Not quite.' Nina smiled slightly as she thought of her apartment. It was located in the same building that housed her father's penthouse apartment, a building that he also owned, and over which he had complete control of all security. Not the complete independence Nina would wish for, but it was better than she had inwardly expected after returning from Stanford.

Rafe D'Angelo eyed her quizzically. 'What does that mean?'

She gave a shake of her head; her father didn't discuss their living arrangements with anyone, and consequently some of that need for secrecy had rubbed off on her. 'It means I will be at my father's apartment for dinner tomorrow evening.'

'But you aren't about to tell me where you live?' Rafe D'Angelo guessed ruefully.

'No.'

'Not even if I were to offer to call for you and drive you to your father's apartment?'

'No,' she refused huskily. 'And I know my father intends to send one of his cars to collect you. He wanted me to confirm that your apartment is still on Fifth Avenue?'

Rafe felt a stirring of unease; Dmitri Palitov seemed to know far too much about him for comfort—far more than Rafe knew about the other man or his beautiful daughter.

'It is,' he confirmed slowly. 'Thank him for me, but I would prefer to drive myself.' Having his own transport meant that Rafe could leave when he'd had enough. He also bridled at the thought of being organised by the arrogant Dmitri Palitov!

Nina Palitov frowned at his refusal. 'I know my father would prefer to have one of his cars collect you.'

'And I would prefer to drive myself,' Rafe repeated unrelentingly.

'I very much doubt you know where he lives.'

'I doubt many people do,' he came back knowingly.

'No.'

He nodded briskly. 'Perhaps you would like to leave

the address with my secretary some time tomorrow? After you've spoken to your father again, of course.'

She chewed on her bottom lip, instantly drawing Rafe's attention to those pouting, slightly reddened lips, and in turn to those captivating moss-green eyes. He realised his mistake as he felt as if he were drowning in those smoky-green depths.

Just as he was aware the rest of him was being pulled, as if by a magnet, towards her, as his head slowly lowered—

'I should go and check security now,' Nina rasped abruptly even as she stepped back and away from him. 'I'll pass your message on to my father.'

'Fine.' Rafe straightened abruptly, inwardly cursing the obviously increasing attraction he felt towards Nina Palitov, and sincerely hoping his date this evening with Jennifer would put that attraction out of his mind—and appease his aching body! 'Do you want me to come down with you to view security in the basement?'

Nina gave a rueful smile at the obvious lack of enthusiasm in his voice. 'I believe that I can find my own way, thank you.'

Rafe eyed her irritably. 'I was being polite.'

'I noticed,' she drawled.

Rafe nodded abruptly before striding across to open the office door for her, a little disconcerted at instantly finding himself the focus of two pairs of wraparound sunglasses, the two bodyguards—Rich and Andy?—standing directly outside the door. 'I assure you, Miss Palitov has come to no harm while in my office,' he drawled mockingly.

There wasn't so much as an answering smile in either of those two grimly set faces, neither man sparing Rafe a second glance as Nina stepped out into the hallway. 'Good day to you, Mr D'Angelo,' she murmured before walking off towards the lift, the two men falling into step behind her.

Which in no way hindered Rafe of the view of Nina Palitov's heart-shaped backside in those tight-fitting denims. A view his once-again throbbing body enjoyed to the full.

He was in trouble—serious trouble!—Rafe acknowledged with a low groan, if just looking at the perfect curve of Nina's bottom in a pair of tight-fitting denims could succeed in making his shaft swell and ache!

CHAPTER THREE

'You like this Raphael D'Angelo who is coming to dine with us this evening?'

Nina tensed, her hand shaking slightly, as she paused in pouring her father's usual pre-dinner drink of single malt whisky from the cut-glass decanter into one of the matching glasses on the silver salver. She waited several seconds for her hand to stop shaking, and to compose her expression, before she finished pouring, and then turned to carry the glass over to her father. 'Have I told you how handsome you look this evening, Papa?' she complimented lightly.

'A man of almost seventy-nine cannot be called handsome,' he drawled dismissively, his English still accented, despite his having lived in the States for more than half his life. 'Distinguished, perhaps. But I am too far beyond the flush of youth to ever be called handsome.'

'You always look handsome to me, Papa,' Nina assured him warmly.

Because he did. Her father might be heading towards his eightieth year, but his habitual air of suppressed vitality made him seem much younger, and his iron-grey hair was still thick and plentiful, his face one of chiselled strength, even if his eyes had faded over the years to a pale green rather than the same moss-green as her own.

Her father gave her a knowing look. 'You are avoiding answering my original question.'

That was probably because Nina had no idea what had prompted her father to ask it.

She had once again spent the day at the gallery, organising the final arrangement of the display cabinets. She'd felt slightly on edge in case she should see Rafe D'Angelo again, and then a certain amount of disappointment when she'd left the gallery at four o'clock without catching so much as a glimpse of its charismatic owner.

A disappointment she had chastised herself for feeling as she lay soaking in a perfumed bath an hour or so later; Rafe D'Angelo was not a man she should become in the least interested in. He was arrogant, mocking, and, even more importantly, not in the least bit interested in her.

Even so, Nina hadn't been able to resist switching on her laptop and looking him up on the Internet once she had finished her bath, sitting on her bed in her dressing gown, her wet hair wrapped in a towel, to scroll through the pages and pages of information and gossip on the highly photographed Raphael D'Angelo. She'd told herself that it was because she needed to know all that she could about the man her father had invited to dinner this evening—other than the fact that he brought out a physical reaction in her that she found distinctly uncomfortable.

It had taken her several minutes of scrolling before she found a photograph of him from the previous evening, as he enjoyed an intimate dinner for two at an exclusive New York restaurant, with the beautiful actress Jennifer Nichols—obviously the 'previous engagement' that had prompted him to refuse her father's initial dinner invitation. Nina had switched off her laptop in disgust.

Nina had decided that Rafe D'Angelo was nothing

more than a rake and a womaniser, and she refused to waste any more of her time—or her emotions—on him.

'You are still avoiding it, Nina,' her father prompted gently.

She gave a rueful shake of her head. 'That's probably because I have no idea what prompted you to ask such a question, Papa.'

'You are looking very beautiful this evening, *maya doch.*'

'Are you saying I don't normally?' she teased.

Her father gave an answering smile. 'You know you are always beautiful to me, Nina. But tonight you seem to have made a special effort to be so.'

Probably because, after seeing that photograph of Rafe D'Angelo with the actress Jennifer Nichols, that was exactly what she had done! Which was pretty silly of her; she could never hope to compete with the beauty or sophistication of the A-list actress.

Nor should she want to.

Rafe D'Angelo meant nothing to her. As she meant nothing to him.

'And I do not believe you have made this special effort on my behalf,' her father added softly. 'So, do you like this Raphael D'Angelo?' he persisted.

Nina gave an exasperated sigh. 'I don't know him well enough to like or dislike him, Papa.'

'You spent some time alone with him yesterday.'

She gave a pained frown. 'I thought we had agreed, after I left Stanford, that I would continue to have my own security detail but that they would only report to you if I was in any danger?'

'We did,' her father confirmed unconcernedly. 'And that has not changed, nor will it. I did not receive this information from your own security detail, Nina. I do not need to do so, when I have my own,' he added softly.

'Let me guess, one of the workmen who accompanied me to the gallery yesterday was one of your men,' she guessed impatiently. 'Papa, you really shouldn't have done that.' She sighed.

He shrugged. 'I am merely interested to know what you and D'Angelo talked about for the twenty-three minutes you were alone with him in his office,' he prompted lightly.

'Twenty-three minutes?' Nina repeated, incredulous. 'You timed how long I was in there?'

'My man did, yes,' her father dismissed unconcernedly. 'Are you aware of D'Angelo's reputation with women?'

'Papa, I'm not going to discuss this with you any further!' She threw her hands up in the air in disgust. 'My meeting yesterday with Rafe D'Angelo was purely business.'

'Rafe?'

She nodded. 'It's what he prefers to be called. And my meeting with him yesterday was on your behalf, I might add.' She felt a blush warm in her cheeks as she remembered those few seconds, just prior to her leaving Rafe's office, when it had almost felt as if he had been about to kiss her. Before, because of her own nervousness, she had put an end to that intimacy.

'I do not want to see you hurt by this man, *maya doch*,' her father said gently.

'And I'm assuring you that isn't going to happen,' Nina insisted firmly. 'I told you, I haven't even decided yet whether or not I even like Raphael D'Angelo!'

'That's a pity, because I've decided I like you, Nina,' drawled an infuriatingly familiar voice.

Nina felt the colour drain from her cheeks as she turned sharply to face Rafe D'Angelo as he stood in the doorway slightly behind her father's butler, obviously having just arrived, and looking breathtakingly handsome in his black evening clothes, with that overlong ebony hair brushed back from his handsome face.

Rafe almost laughed out loud at the look of dismay on Nina Palitov's face as she realised he had overheard her telling remark in regard to him.

But he only almost laughed…

Not only was it not particularly amusing to hear her state her uncertainty of liking him so plainly, but the way she looked this evening had totally robbed him of the breath to laugh even if he had wanted to!

Nina was wearing a gown the same moss-green as her eyes, a knee-length sheath of a gown that clung lovingly to her womanly curves, with two ribbon straps across her otherwise bare shoulders and arms, the swell of her breasts visible above the low neckline, those long legs revealed as being slender and shapely, with three-inch-heeled shoes of the same colour as her gown bringing her height up to six feet. Her fiery red hair, that crowning glory, was held back from her temples with two diamond clips, but otherwise fell in that tumbling cascade of curls down the length of her spine to rest above the shapely bottom he had so enjoyed looking at yesterday as she'd walked away from him.

'Mr D'Angelo, sir.' The English butler maintained a wooden expression as he belatedly announced Rafe's arrival.

'Do come in and join us, Mr D'Angelo,' his host invited smoothly.

Rafe gave the butler a ruefully sympathetic smile as he stepped past him into the sitting room, that smile freezing, becoming fixed, as he looked at his host fully for the first time and realised that Dmitri Palitov was sitting in a wheelchair rather than one of the cream velvet armchairs!

'I trust you will understand why I do not get up to greet you, Mr D'Angelo,' Dmitri Palitov drawled dryly as he obviously saw Rafe's look of surprise.

A surprise Rafe quickly masked beneath a politely bland smile as he strode across the room to shake the hand the older man held out to him. 'No problem. And please call me Rafe,' he invited lightly as he released his hand from the other man's strong grip. 'Despite being unsure as to whether or not she likes me, your daughter already calls me Rafe,' he added softly before glancing challengingly across to where Nina stood silently watching the two men. His glance was slightly censorious, but not because of what Nina had said; Rafe would have appreciated a heads up in regard to knowing her father was in a wheelchair before actually meeting his host this evening.

Although he acknowledged that might have been a little difficult for her to do. Nina had done as he'd asked, and left her father's address with his assistant earlier, but Rafe admitted to going out of his way to ensure the two of them didn't actually meet during the hours she had been at the gallery today.

Because he was annoyed.

With himself, not Nina.

Nina could have no idea that his evening with Jennifer Nichols had gone so disastrously wrong for the simple reason he couldn't stop thinking about Nina. Or, at least, his rebellious body had refused to stop thinking about Nina.

So much so that Rafe hadn't felt an ounce of desire to bed the beautiful actress at the end of the evening, and had instead merely kissed Jennifer on the cheek after driving her home, before then going home alone to his own apartment and his empty bed. Not to go straight to sleep, unfortunately, as a certain part of his anatomy had refused to comply, and even when he had finally slept it had been fitfully, and filled with dreams of bedding flame-haired Nina!

Consequently Rafe hadn't been in the best of moods all day; he'd certainly felt no inclination to actually see or talk to the woman who was causing his present lack of sexual desire to bed another woman. Something that had never happened to him before, and Rafe didn't appreciate that it was happening to him now either.

'Do not blame Nina for her earlier remark,' his host advised ruefully. 'What you overheard her say was merely as a result of my having just teased her.'

Rafe wondered exactly what Dmitri Palitov had been teasing his daughter about to have elicited such a vehement response from her, and that curiosity was added to by the sudden blush that now coloured Nina's cheeks.

'Would you care to join me in a glass of whisky before dinner, Rafe?' his host offered politely.

'Thank you, Dmitri.' Rafe nodded, watching through narrowed lids as Nina silently crossed the room to the array of drinks on the sideboard, that red hair like a living flame as it tumbled down the length of her spine as she kept her back turned towards them while she poured his whisky.

'I trust your previous engagement, yesterday evening, was successful, Rafe?'

Rafe turned back as his host spoke to him once again, knowing by the hardness of the older man's expression that Dmitri Palitov had noticed his interest in his daughter, and wasn't sure as to whether he approved or not.

As the other man was also aware of exactly what—and with whom—Rafe's previous engagement had been last night?

The mockery in those pale green eyes looking so challengingly up into his indicated the answer to that question was a resounding yes. Dmitri Palitov knew exactly where and with whom Rafe had been the previous evening.

'Really, Papa,' Nina drawled mockingly as she crossed the room to hand Rafe his glass of whisky, her hand deliberately not coming into contact with his as she did so. 'We really shouldn't embarrass Rafe by enquiring as to whether or not he enjoyed his evening with Miss Nichols.'

Great; not only did Dmitri Palitov know who Rafe had spent the previous evening with, but it appeared Nina was aware of it too. And the mockery in her expression as she looked at him from beneath thick dark lashes indicated she had drawn her own conclusions about how that evening had ended too.

Nina felt a certain amount of satisfaction in seeing the look of discomfort on Rafe D'Angelo's face as he realised both she and her father were aware he had considered an evening—and night?—spent with the beautiful actress to be more pressing than accepting a dinner invitation from an important client of one of the galleries he owned with his two brothers.

'Not at all,' he finally answered tautly. 'And I had a very pleasant evening, thank you.'

Her father chuckled softly. 'Not much escapes the attention of the press nowadays, Rafe; it is the price one pays when one is in the public eye.'

'Obviously.' He scowled as he took a swallow of the whisky in his glass.

Nina felt a certain admiration for the fact that Rafe made no attempt to try and excuse his behaviour; many men, when confronted by a man as powerful as her father, would have tried to bluster their way out of the situation. Obviously, Rafe D'Angelo had no intention of apologising to any man, or woman, for what he did or didn't choose to do.

'Perhaps you would care to see the jewellery collection before dinner, Rafe?' her father offered lightly.

'I would like that very much, thank you,' the younger man accepted.

Nina accompanied the two men to her father's private sanctuary, impressed as Rafe proceeded to murmur both suitable admiration and knowledge of the beautiful jewellery her father had collected over the years.

It really was a truly amazing and unique collection with dozens and dozens of priceless pieces of jewellery; several necklaces, bracelets and rings had once been owned by the Tsarina Alexandra herself. But every single piece of that magnificent collection had a history of its own, and her father had spent years learning every single one of those histories.

The mood for the evening was much more relaxed once they returned to the sitting room, the conversation over dinner lightly interesting as they all first discussed the exhibition to take place next week, before the conversation moved on to politics, and the inevitable subject of sport, most specifically American Football, as the two men lingered over their brandy and cigars.

Nina had contributed to the first three subjects, but American Football just made her want to yawn.

A reaction that made Rafe D'Angelo smile as he caught her in the obvious act of trying to stifle one of those yawns.

'I believe we're boring Nina, Dmitri,' he drawled teas-

ingly, obviously far more relaxed now than he had been
when he'd first arrived.

'*Doch*?' Her father looked at her enquiringly.

'I'm a little tired, that's all,' Nina assured with a smile.

'It's late.' Rafe nodded. 'Time I was leaving.'

'Please don't go on my account,' Nina protested awkwardly. 'It's been a busy week, that's all.'

'No, I really should go now. I have work in the morning,' he assured dismissively. 'Perhaps I could escort you
home, Nina?' he added huskily.

She felt her heart beat faster, louder, at the thought
of having the rakishly handsome Rafe D'Angelo escort
her to her door, perhaps to even have him kiss her goodnight—

Obviously she had drunk far too much of her father's
excellent wine with her meal, because Rafe hadn't so
much as hinted this evening, by word or deed, that he was
in the least interested in kissing her goodnight!

No, his offer to escort her home had obviously been
made out of politeness, and possibly even as a sop to her
father's obviously old-fashioned manners.

'That is very gentlemanly of you, Rafe.' Surprisingly
her father was the one to answer the other man before
Nina had a chance to do so.

'My daughter has become far too independent, after
her years at university, for my liking.'

Rafe saw the flash of irritation in Nina's eyes before
it was quickly masked. As evidence that she didn't particularly enjoy, or want, to have those bodyguards following her about day, and possibly night, too? He would
well imagine it could feel extremely stifling, as well as
being a complete downer on her personal life.

Which posed the question, did Nina have a man in that
personal life? Rafe would imagine it would take a very

determined man to date the daughter of Dmitri Palitov, let alone put up with the oppressive presence of those bodyguards every time the two of them went out together. And as for moving on to anything more intimate, well, it must be a logistical, and emotional, nightmare!

It also begged the question as to why Nina put up with it. She was a beautiful woman in her mid-twenties, obviously intelligent to have obtained a degree from Stanford, and her comments during the conversation this evening had been both learned and considered. She was also well qualified, and possessed a true talent for design, if those beautiful display cases in the east gallery at Archangel were an indication of her work, so why did she continue to allow her father to limit and watch her movements in the obsessive way that he did?

Another part of the unanswered mystery that Nina Palitov was fast becoming to him...

A mystery, the more time he spent in her company, Rafe found he wanted answers to.

'Nina?' he prompted huskily as he moved to stand behind her chair in preparation for leaving.

'Fine,' she bit out tensely. 'I have no objection to your coming down to the next floor in the lift with me, and walking me to my apartment door, if that's what you want to do.'

Rafe raised his brows. 'You live in this building?'

'Yes.' Her eyes glittered bright with challenge as she looked up at him.

Well, that certainly explained her comment yesterday when Rafe had asked if she lived with her father.

'I see,' he said slowly.

Her mouth tightened. 'Somehow I doubt that very much.'

'Nina,' her father put in reprovingly at the sharpness of her tone.

She closed her eyes briefly, drawing in two calming breaths before opening them again, her smile now one of stiff politeness. 'Thank you, Rafe, I would appreciate your walking me to my door,' she said tightly as he held her chair back for her to stand up, before she moved round the table to kiss her father warmly on the cheek. 'I will see you tomorrow, Papa.' Her voice softened noticeably.

'As always, *maya doch*.' He touched her cheek affectionately before turning to Rafe. 'It has been a pleasure to meet and talk with you this evening, Rafe,' he added formally.

'You too, sir.' Rafe nodded distractedly, his concerned gaze fixed on Nina as she swept from the dining room without so much as a second glance at either man.

'My jewellery collection is very precious to me, Rafe.' Dmitri Palitov spoke quietly beside him.

Rafe turned to look at the older man. 'It's very impressive,' he acknowledged slowly, uncertain as to where this change of subject was going.

'Each piece is priceless.' Dmitri nodded. 'But, beautiful as my collection is, valuable as it is, I value my daughter far above any rubies or diamonds.'

Ah...

'As such,' the older man continued hardly, 'I will always do anything and everything within my power to ensure her health and happiness.'

'Understandably,' Rafe answered non-committally.

'Yes?' Dmitri Palitov spoke with that same hard challenge.

It was the first time that Rafe had ever been warned off a woman by her father, but, yes, he believed he understood this for exactly what it was.

'Nina is a big girl now, Dmitri.' He spoke evenly.

'Yes, she is.' The older man nodded. 'But even so, perhaps you should know that I will not look kindly on any man who chooses to hurt my daughter. Whether it be intentionally or unintentionally.' Those green eyes, so like his daughter's, glittered in warning.

Pretty succinct and to the point—and unmistakably Dmitri Palitov's way of warning him off.

'Thank you for an enjoyable evening, sir.' Rafe held his hand out formally to the other man.

'D'Angelo.' Dmitri Palitov shook that hand briefly, those green eyes pale and hard as some of the jewels in this man's private collection.

Nina wondered if Rafe found the silence between the two of them as uncomfortable as she did as they stepped into the private lift together minutes later. Probably not. His offer to escort her to her apartment had been a politeness, nothing more, and one that she knew would soon be over as the lift halted on the lower floor just seconds later.

'You don't have your bodyguards with you this evening?' he prompted coolly as he walked beside her to her apartment, the heels of her shoes clicking on the marble floor in the otherwise silent hallway.

She gave a tight, humourless smile. 'Even my father accepts that I have no need for them here. He owns the whole building, controls all security, and no one is allowed in or out of the building without his approval,' she explained dismissively as Rafe eyed her questioningly.

He frowned darkly. 'Isn't that taking the protective-father role a bit far?'

'Possibly,' she accepted tightly.

'Why the hell do you put up with it?' he bit out impatiently.

Her mouth tightened. 'I don't believe that's any of your business.'

Rafe scowled his frustration with that reply. 'How long has your father been in a wheelchair?'

Nina flicked him a surprised glance. 'Almost twenty years.'

Rafe nodded. 'And you don't think it might have been a good idea to have told me that before I met him this evening?'

'I don't quite see… It didn't even occur to me. Or your brother, obviously,' she dismissed impatiently. 'I grew up seeing my father in a wheelchair. I don't even notice he's in one now.'

No, of course she didn't, Rafe acknowledged ruefully, and she was right, Michael hadn't thought to pre-warn him either. Yet another thing about the Palitov family that his big brother had forgotten to mention.

'How did it happen?' Rafe prompted softly.

'I— An accident,' she answered stiffly.

Rafe's eyes narrowed. 'What sort of accident?'

'A car accident.' She frowned. 'His spine was severed, and he's been confined to a wheelchair ever since, end of story.' She used her key card to open the door to her apartment. 'Thank you for—'

'Invite me in, Nina!'

Nina looked up quickly, her eyes wide as she saw the intensity of Rafe's expression; those golden eyes glittered down at her, a nerve pulsing in his tightly clenched jaw. 'I— No, I don't think that would be a good idea.'

'Because your father wouldn't approve?' he came back derisively.

She bristled. 'My refusal has nothing to do with my father.' And everything to do with the fact that Nina had been totally physically aware of this man all evening, in a way she could never remember being aware of any other man. Nina had no explanation for it, she just knew that she was drawn to him like a moth to a flame—and probably with the same results; she would get seriously burnt if she gave in to that attraction.

'Oh, I think it has everything to do with him.' Rafe eyed her mockingly.

Nina gave a pained frown. 'You don't understand.'

'You're right, I don't.' Rafe gave an impatient shake of his head. 'I don't understand why a vibrantly beautiful and talented young woman would allow her life to be dictated to by her overbearing father.'

'My father is not—' She broke off, breathing deeply. 'As I said, you can't possibly understand.'

'Then invite me in for coffee and explain it to me.' Rafe raised his hands and placed them either side of her on the doorframe as he leant into her.

She blinked at his sudden proximity, her heart pounding loudly in her chest as she looked up at him searchingly, shaking her head when she found herself unable to read anything from the intensity of his expression. 'You already had coffee in my father's apartment.'

'For the love of—! Will you just invite me into your apartment, Nina?' he ground out harshly.

Her mouth had gone dry, her throat moving as she attempted to swallow past that dryness before answering him. 'I said I don't think that's a good idea.' It was a very bad idea, when Nina was aware of everything about Rafe, from his overlong dark hair, muscled shoulders, flat abdomen, and long, long legs...

'Probably not,' he grated unapologetically. 'But ask me in anyway.'

Nina gave him a puzzled look. 'What's this all about, Rafe?'

He gave a humourless smile. 'One way or another, it's been one hell of an evening. When I arrived I overheard my hostess saying she doesn't like me.'

'That I wasn't sure I liked you,' she corrected, colour warming her cheeks. 'And my father explained the reason why.'

'Partly, yes. An interesting man, your father,' he added harshly. 'The perfect host, so gracious and charming.'

She blinked. 'Why do you sound so mocking when you say that?'

'Probably because I was just very politely but unmistakably warned off by your father,' he rasped exasperatedly.

'I don't understand.' Nina gave a puzzled shake of her head; the two men had seemed to get on well enough during dinner. 'Warned off from what?'

'You.' Rafe glowered down at her.

Her eyes widened. 'Me?'

He nodded grimly. 'Your father took the opportunity, after you had left the dining room just now, to oh-so-subtly warn me that he would prefer it if I stayed well away from his daughter in future.'

'Oh, no.' She felt her face pale, as she knew her father was perfectly capable of doing exactly that.

And for once in her life she resented her father's overprotective attitude. For once in her life she wanted what she wanted. And tonight, watching Rafe surreptitiously all evening, becoming more and more attracted to him by the moment, had revealed to her that she wanted Rafe D'Angelo.

'Yes,' Rafe confirmed hardly. 'Does he do that to every man you come into contact with, or did he just single me out for special attention?'

'I have no idea.' But she intended finding out, intended

having a heart-to-heart conversation with her father first thing tomorrow morning. 'I'll speak to him— He really did that?' She winced.

'He really did, yes,' Rafe confirmed harshly.

'In that case I apologise.' She frowned. 'I have no idea why my father would even think that you— Why he would think there was any possibility of the two of us ever—' She broke off, realising she was just making this situation worse than it already was. If that was possible.

How could her father have done such a thing? How could he have humiliated her in that way, and with a man she might possibly have reason to see on a daily basis for the next two weeks, at least? A man she felt drawn to as if by a magnet.

'Invite me in, please, Nina,' Rafe pressed huskily.

She looked up at him uncertainly, the pulse beating wildly in her throat as she heard the unmistakable husky intensity in his voice and saw the glitter had deepened in those golden eyes.

'I— Why are you so determined I should be the one to invite you into my apartment?' Her acquaintance with this man so far hadn't given her the impression Rafe was a man who waited for an invitation before doing just as he pleased. 'You aren't a vampire, or something, are you?' she added lightly, in an effort to alleviate some of the sexual tension that swirled and swelled around them.

'Hardly.' He gave a humourless smile. 'Although I have been known to bite a neck or two!'

Nina instantly regretted her teasing. 'Why are you so set on my inviting you into my apartment, Rafe?' she repeated determinedly, tempted, oh-so-tempted, by both Rafe and the idea of, for once in her life, thwarting both her father and her bodyguards.

His mouth firmed. 'Because I don't think you need another bossy and dominating man telling you what to do.'

Her cheeks paled. 'My father is— He has his reasons for behaving in the way that he— You don't understand,' she repeated softly.

'You're right, I don't,' Rafe rasped grimly. 'I don't understand why any beautiful and intelligent woman would allow her father to dictate the terms under which she conducts her life!'

How could he? How could anyone understand the fear her father had lived with on a daily basis for the past twenty years, the dread that Nina might one day be taken from him?

As his beloved wife had been so cruelly taken from him.

CHAPTER FOUR

'INVITE ME IN, Nina,' Rafe encouraged gruffly as he saw the indecision in her expression.

She looked up at him wordlessly for several long seconds, before nodding abruptly and turning on her heel to enter the shadowed hallway of her apartment, turning on the soft glow of the overhead light as she did so.

Rafe prowled in after Nina before closing the door gently behind him, his gaze intent on hers as he took her slowly into his arms to mould her curves against his. Her hands moved instinctively to his shoulders as she raised her startled gaze searchingly to his, obviously totally aware of the fullness of his arousal pressing against the softness of her abdomen—that same arousal that had been missing the evening before with Jennifer Nichols.

'There's just no way for a man to hide his reaction to a beautiful woman, is there?' he murmured self-derisively.

Her silky throat moved as she swallowed before speaking. 'I— No, I guess not.'

Rafe's gaze was fixed on her lushly pouting lips. Those same lips that had been driving him insane all evening, when he had been unable to drag his gaze away from watching Nina part them as she sipped her wine, or put food in her mouth, almost groaning out loud when she flicked her tongue across those lips to capture the morsel of lemon mousse that had smeared her bottom lip as she'd eaten her dessert.

Perhaps he had deserved Dmitri Palitov's earlier warning, after all, regarding Nina. No doubt the older man had made a note of every single occasion Rafe had been unable to stop imagining all the ways Nina's lushly provocative lips might give a man pleasure.

She moistened those lips with the tip of her tongue now. 'I— Do you want coffee?'

'No.'

'Oh.'

Rafe could sense Nina's nervousness, just as he could feel the trembling of her body curved so intimately into and against his. He felt the warmth of her hands through the material of his jacket and shirt. Long and elegantly tapered hands that he had ached all evening to press against his bared and throbbing flesh.

Yes, maybe he had fully deserved Dmitri Palitov's warning where Nina was concerned.

There was no way Nina could possibly miss the fierceness of the hunger that now lit Rafe's eyes to a molten, heated gold before his gaze lowered to the swell of her breasts visible above the low neckline of her gown.

'I want to kiss you, Nina,' he groaned harshly.

'Yes,' she groaned, leaning weakly against him as her legs trembled and her hands tightened on his muscled shoulders.

'And then I would like to bare and caress these pretty breasts.' Both his hands moved up to cup beneath their fullness, the soft sweep of the pad of his thumb unerringly finding the swollen tip.

'With my tongue and teeth as well as—'

'Will you stop talking about it, Rafe, and just do it?' Nina groaned softly, almost panting she was so aroused.

Her teeth clenched as she felt that arousal sweep down and through her body, a rush of dampness moistening the already swollen and aching folds between her thighs.

'You aren't afraid to take what you want, after all.' He gave a throaty and appreciative chuckle as he lifted one of his hands and entwined it in the fiery length of her hair, looking deeply into her eyes for several searching seconds before using that pressure to tilt her head back and sideways as he claimed her lips with his own.

Firm and yet softly sensual lips, that sipped and tasted hers for long torturous minutes, his tongue a fiery caress against that melting softness before his kiss hardened, deepened, as his tongue plunged into the heated warmth of her mouth, duelling before entwining sensuously with hers.

Nina's hands moved across Rafe's shoulders to allow her fingers to become entangled in the silky length of his ebony hair as she held him against her. He continued to kiss her deeply, hungrily, his hands moving restlessly down the length of her spine before cupping her bottom and pulling her into the hardness of his arousal, leaving Nina in no doubt as to the length and thickness of that arousal as his shaft throbbed and pulsed against her thighs.

That continued sensual assault, of Rafe's lips and tongue, drove Nina's arousal higher still, until her whole body felt on fire with the need for more. So much more.

She gasped for air, her throat arching as Rafe's mouth released hers to seek out the hollows and dips of her neck. One of Rafe's hand's moved to slip the thin shoulder strap of her gown down onto her arm as the heat of his lips now seared across her exposed skin. The zip of Nina's gown felt cold against her heated flesh as he slid the fastening slowly downwards and allowed both straps of her gown to fall the length of her arms and expose her naked breasts.

The heat of Rafe's lips now followed the slope of her bared breasts, his tongue licking, tasting, tormenting her fevered flesh. Nina's knees buckled, only the strength of Rafe's arm about her waist continuing to hold her up as she felt the heat of his mouth close over the swollen aching tip of her breast before he suckled it deeply into that heat.

Oh, dear heaven!

And it was heaven, dear, sweet torturous heaven, as Rafe's hand cupped, caressed that aching nipple as he turned his attention to her other breast, suckling that swollen nipple deeply and then softly, his fingers and tongue a never-ending torment against her roused and sensitive flesh, pleasuring her, and causing those folds to swell between her thighs as her juices first dampened and then completely wet her panties.

Nina gave a choked sob. She was on fire; she needed— oh, God—she *needed*—

She gasped her disappointment as Rafe's mouth released her and he raised his head slightly, eyes dark as he gazed down at the red and swollen tips of her breasts.

'So pretty,' he murmured gruffly as he touched each of her swollen nipples in turn with the softness of his fingertips.

Nina could barely breathe as she waited to see what Rafe intended to do next. Hoping it was what she wanted him to do.

Rafe gazed his fill of Nina's beautiful breasts, tipped by pretty peach nipples that had become red and engorged from the attention of his hands and mouth. Nipples that still begged for those attentions.

Attention he was more than willing to give her. Just as

he longed to explore the silken folds between her thighs. He could smell Nina's arousal now, creamy and yet with an added enticing spice. And he longed to lap up that creaminess, to drink in her essence even as his lips and tongue explored those swollen folds, and then he wanted to swallow her down, to be able to taste her in his mouth and throat for hours afterwards.

That Nina wanted those things too he was in no doubt as she looked up at him, green eyes dark with her arousal, a flush to her creamy cheeks, and her lips parted invitingly as she breathed raggedly.

And he couldn't do it.

Oh, Rafe knew what the newspapers printed about him—almost on a daily basis when he was in New York, it seemed! That he had a parade of beautiful women passing through his bedroom, women he changed as often as he did his silk bed sheets. And up to a point that was true. There had never been a shortage of women whose bed he might share, for a night or, indeed, several nights or weeks.

Even so, Rafe had his own set of rules when it came to the women who briefly entered his life. He never offered false promises. He never cheated on the woman he was currently sleeping with. And when it stopped being fun, for either of them, he gently brought that relationship to an end.

Nina wasn't like any other woman Rafe had ever known. She was more. So much more. And emotionally complicated, in a way Rafe had always chosen to avoid in the past.

She was much younger than those other women for one thing, had spent all of her twenty-four years sheltered by her overprotective father, and so lacked both the sophistication and cynicism that had allowed those other women to accept the few weeks of a relationship Rafe had to offer them.

There was also the fact, ridiculous as it might seem in the current circumstances, that he was here this evening at the invitation of Nina's father, a man as dangerous as he was powerful, and with whom Rafe's gallery was currently doing business. Rafe had never mixed business with pleasure.

And lastly, even more ridiculously, he and Nina hadn't so much as been out on a date together yet.

'Rafe?' Nina questioned uncertainly as he stood silent and unmoving in front of her, his face set in grim lines as he looked down at her. She felt totally exposed with her gown down about her waist, her breasts still bared, swollen and aching from the touch of his lips and hands.

His jaw was tightly clenched, dark lashes shielding the expression in his eyes as he reached down to pull the straps of her gown back up her arms and into place on her shoulders. Nina was too taken aback by his actions to offer the least resistance when Rafe turned her away from him slightly so that he could refasten the zip up the length of her spine.

Telling her more clearly than any words that this encounter was over.

'Have dinner with me tomorrow evening, Nina?'

She turned sharply back to face him, looking up at him searchingly, but was unable to read anything from the grimness of his expression. 'Why?' she finally breathed.

His brows rose. 'Do you usually ask why when a man invites you out to dinner with him?'

Nina's chin tilted defensively. 'Only when that same man went out to dinner with another woman the previous evening.'

His mouth tightened. 'I have no intention of seeing Jennifer Nichols again.'

'Does she know that?'

'Oh, yes.' His mouth twisted derisively.

She gave a shake of her head. 'I— Our lovemaking just now was—it was…an aberration, Rafe, for both of us, probably.' Although she wasn't sure it could be called 'our' lovemaking, when she had been the one half undressed and Rafe had remained as immaculately clothed as he had been when he first arrived this evening.

Well, perhaps not quite so immaculately. His hair was more than a little tousled from having her fingers running through it, and there was a smear of her peach lip gloss at the corner of Rafe's mouth.

'Don't feel you have to invite me out to dinner because things got a little out of hand just now,' she added firmly.

'An aberration?' Rafe repeated ruefully as he fought back the urge to chuckle.

Which, considering the circumstances, was again more than a little unexpected!

Rafe had been rendered breathless by Nina's appearance when he'd arrived for dinner earlier this evening. He had spent several hours over that dinner politely but nevertheless verbally fencing with her father while unable to take his eyes off Nina, only for Dmitri Palitov to take off the gloves completely at the end of the evening and issue him an outright warning in regard to Rafe staying away from his daughter.

The latter had annoyed Rafe intensely, so much so that he had intended to just walk Nina back to her apartment and then leave, before congratulating himself on being well rid of all of the Palitov family. Apart from their business connection, of course. An intent that had disappeared the moment they had arrived outside Nina's apartment and Rafe had realised he wasn't ready to say goodnight to her quite yet.

'Yes, an aberration,' she insisted firmly. 'I want you to know I'm certainly not in the habit of allowing random men to make love to me.'

'"Random men"?' Rafe couldn't hold back his amused chuckle this time. 'Is that how you think of me, Nina, as just some random man you happened to make love with?'

She frowned her irritation at his humour. 'I obviously drank far too much wine with my dinner.'

'And I believe you're being deliberately insulting now, Nina,' Rafe drawled knowingly.

Yes, she was, Nina acknowledged heavily. Because there was no way she could explain her wanton behaviour just now to Rafe, of all people. To do so would be to admit that he had got under her skin, past her guard, and made her long for things, for the freedom to give in totally to this attraction.

'Maybe,' she allowed tightly. 'But I would like you to leave now.'

'And do you always get what you want?'

Hardly ever, Nina acknowledged ruefully.

Oh, materially she could have anything she wanted; her father's wealth had always ensured that. But she'd had such dreams and plans for her future when she'd returned home from Stanford three years ago, clutching her degree proudly in her hands. Of starting up her own design business. Of making a success of that business. Of meeting a man she could love, and who would love her. Of marrying and one day having a family of her own.

And instead she had been sucked straight back into her father's reclusive and overprotective lifestyle.

No, that was unfair to her father; she was the one who had allowed herself to be sucked straight back into her father's life of bodyguards, who hadn't fought hard enough for the things she wanted for herself.

Because her father had looked so much frailer than when she had left him three years earlier. Because he had obviously needed to have her close to him again and know she was safe. So Nina had put her own dreams and hopes on hold, so much so she had all but forgotten about them until now.

Until Rafe D'Angelo and this attraction she felt towards him had forced her to remember them.

'Nina?' Rafe prompted softly at her continued silence.

She gave a deep sigh. 'Thank you for your dinner invitation, Rafe, but I would rather not.'

'Why not?'

She eyed him irritably. 'Do you usually ask a woman that when she says no to you?'

Those chiselled lips curved up into a smile as she turned his earlier remark back on him. 'That's a little difficult to say, when I can't remember it ever having happened before.'

Nina frowned. 'Well, it's happening now.'

The smile slowly disappeared as he looked down at her searchingly. 'But for all the wrong reasons,' he finally murmured softly.

Her eyes flashed in warning. 'Don't pretend to know the first thing about me, Rafe!'

He shrugged. 'Deny if you can that it's just easier, because of your father, if you refuse to go out with me.'

It was easier. Not only that, Nina knew it was the right thing to do. Except she wanted to accept. This attraction she felt for Rafe made her want to rebel against the limitations her father had imposed on her life.

'And what are your reasons for asking, Rafe?' she asked cautiously. 'Are you asking me out to dinner because you like me, and want to spend time with me? Or are you asking me out to dinner because you're annoyed with my father, because of his warning earlier, and you just want to annoy him back?'

'That isn't very flattering, Nina. To you or to me,' Rafe drawled huskily.

She shrugged. 'Not if the latter is true, no.'

Rafe eyed her thoughtfully, not sure if he felt more irritated by Nina's suspicions regarding his dinner invitation, or by the reality of the life she must have led to make her draw those conclusions in the first place. Either way, he had no intention of backing off. 'It isn't,' he bit out economically. 'So, is your answer to be yes or no, Nina?'

The indecision in those beautiful moss-green eyes made Rafe want to put further pressure on her, to goad or seduce her, whichever worked, into accepting his dinner invitation. But he held back from doing either of those things. It had to be Nina's decision; he had meant it when he told her earlier that he considered one dominating man in her life telling her what to do as being more than enough for any woman.

And so he remained silent, inwardly willing Nina to accept his dinner invitation, at the same time as he questioned himself as to when it had become so important to him that she did.

Maybe when her beauty had rendered him breathless when he'd first arrived this evening? Or as he'd watched and listened to her over dinner? Or perhaps when he had made love with her just now? Or maybe even before any of that? Possibly when he had first seen Nina in the gallery yesterday, and then spoken to her in the privacy of his office later that morning?

Whatever the reason—or when it had happened—his dinner invitation certainly had nothing to do with the irritation he felt at Dmitri Palitov's warning. If anything, being warned off by a woman's father—not that Rafe could ever remember meeting the father of any of the women he had been involved with in the past!—would normally have been enough to cause Rafe to retreat as far as possible in the opposite direction. Not because he would have been in the least concerned by that threat, but because he really didn't do complicated where women were concerned, and having a woman's father warn him off was definitely a complication.

Rafe had a feeling that this unexpected attraction to Nina Palitov was going to complicate the hell out of his life.

Nina drew in a shaking breath, knowing that her answer to Rafe's invitation should be no—and not because of the reason Rafe had just given. Oh, no doubt her father wouldn't exactly be pleased if she were to accept Rafe D'Angelo's dinner invitation, but it was a displeasure her father would have to deal with for once. After the two of them had their talk tomorrow he would know that she wasn't too thrilled to learn that he had warned Rafe off in the first place.

No, the reason Nina knew she should refuse Rafe's invitation had nothing to do with her father, and everything to do with her not being sure it was a good idea to allow herself to become any more attracted to Rafe than she already was. If she spent a whole evening alone with him she had no idea if she would be able to resist him at the end of the evening.

She wasn't a complete innocent, having believed herself in love a couple of times while she was at Stanford, both times with fellow students, one during her second year at university, the other one during her final year.

It hadn't taken her long, however, to realise she wasn't

really in love with either man, possibly because she had found them both less than exciting physically. So much so that she had wondered what all the fuss was about. Nor had she had any particular interest in repeating the experience once she had returned to New York.

Her response to Rafe just minutes ago, to his kisses and caresses, had been nothing like either of those earlier experiences. She had been breathless with arousal, hadn't wanted him to stop touching and kissing her, would have been perfectly happy if Rafe had just carried her off to her bedroom before stripping her completely naked and making love with her. She had ached for him to make love with her.

Just looking at him now, with that overlong dark hair tousled about that perfect, chiselled face, his black evening suit perfectly tailored to the broadness of his shoulders and muscled chest, his waist slender, and hips narrow above long legs, was enough to send a shiver of that same aching longing coursing through her own body.

He quirked one dark, mocking brow. 'Are you usually this indecisive?'

Nina's cheeks warmed with colour as she heard the rebuke beneath that mockery—implying, no doubt, that indecision was responsible for her father having taken over her life so completely.

'Perhaps I just don't think it a good idea to mix business with pleasure?'

Neither did Rafe, but he didn't seem to have any choice in the matter this time, not when it came to Nina Palitov. She was who she was, and he was determined to spend an evening alone with her. Bodyguards or no bodyguards! 'Yes or no, Nina?' he challenged between gritted teeth.

'Oh, okay—yes, I'll have dinner with you tomorrow evening!' She glared up at him impatiently.

Rafe held back his smile of triumph, merely nodding his satisfaction instead. 'I'll make the arrangements and call for you here tomorrow, at seven-thirty?'

She winced, and a frown appeared between those moss-green eyes. 'I'll need to know beforehand exactly where we're going.'

'Small rebellion over— Hey, it's okay, Nina,' he assured her gently as she instantly began to chew worriedly on her bottom lip. Lips that were still temptingly plumped from the kisses they had just shared. 'It really isn't a problem.'

'No?' Her eyes looked huge in the pallor of her face.

'No.' Rafe had already decided not to make life any more difficult for her than her father's stranglehold of security already made it for her. It was enough for Rafe, for now, that she had agreed to go out to dinner with him tomorrow evening. 'I'll let you know at the gallery tomorrow where we're going—I take it that Andy and Rich, or someone very like them, is going to check the place out before we arrive?'

'You make it sound so cloak and dagger.' She frowned.

Rafe shrugged. 'It lacks a certain spontaneity,' he acknowledged ruefully. 'But don't worry about it. We'll make it workable.'

'Thank you,' she breathed.

He looked at her curiously. 'For what?'

'For not—well, for not being difficult. A lot of men would be.'

'I'd hope I'm not like a lot of men, Nina—or even a random one,' Rafe added teasingly, in an effort to lighten the subject for her.

'Stop worrying.' He reached up to smooth the frown from between her brows before bending his head and lightly brushing his lips across hers before straightening. 'I'll see you at the gallery tomorrow?'

'Yes.'

'Smile, Nina, it might never happen,' he cajoled, as she still looked less than happy.

It was already happening as far as Nina was concerned; she was far too attracted to Rafe D'Angelo. Attracted enough that she had allowed him to make love to her.

Attracted enough that she was rebelling against some of the constraints imposed on her life by her father—something that had never happened before.

Attracted enough that she would have to keep reminding herself that no woman had ever succeeded in capturing and holding the long-term interest of the elusive Raphael D'Angelo. That there had only ever been a series of tall, leggy, blonde and sophisticated women, who apparently drifted in and out of his life—and his bed!—with sickening regularity.

And Nina knew herself to be only two of those things—tall and leggy!

Which didn't mean she couldn't enjoy this for exactly what it was: a flirtation on Rafe's part that might or might not eventually lead to them going to bed together.

She smiled as she straightened determinedly. 'I'm really fine, Rafe. And yes, I'll be at the gallery tomorrow.'

'Good.' He nodded his satisfaction with her answer. 'And now I think it's time I was going. There may be no bodyguards following you around tonight but I'm pretty sure the extensive security cameras in this building have already shown your father that I came into your apartment with you earlier but haven't left yet!' he added lightly as the two of them walked the short distance down the hallway to the door to her apartment.

Nina was pretty sure they had too.

Which wasn't to say she liked it, only that this level of security had been in her life for so long she had mainly ceased to even notice it. Maybe it was time she did.

And maybe meeting Rafe, and this attraction she felt towards him, were exactly the wake-up call she had needed to do something about changing it.

Rafe considered telephoning Michael once he got back to his own apartment twenty minutes later, and then dismissed the idea. His brother would be arriving in New York on Friday evening anyway, in time for the invitation-only gala opening of the Palitov jewellery collection on Saturday evening. The brothers attended any new exhibition presented in one of their three galleries. Gabriel wouldn't make it this time, but Michael would certainly be there.

And, amongst other things, Rafe was going to take the opportunity of Michael's presence to discuss a new business venture he had in mind for the Archangel galleries. Not too many people were aware of it, but Rafe was the new ideas man for the Archangel galleries, and always had been. And the reason people weren't aware of it was because Rafe was really quite modest. He didn't mind that the media had him tagged as the playboy.

Only maybe it was now time for that to change.

Rafe brought his thoughts up with a start, having no idea why he'd had them in the first place. Or why now.

It couldn't possibly be because of his attraction to Nina. Could it?

Damn it, he needed to concentrate on learning more about the enigmatic Dmitri Palitov, not his daughter.

Nina had said her father was in a wheelchair because he had been involved in an accident, which probably explained why he had become so reclusive. No doubt it was just as easy for Dmitri Palitov to run his business empire from his apartment on the fiftieth floor of a building he owned as it was to have an actual office in another part of the city.

But an accident didn't explain why Dmitri Palitov was so obsessive about security.

His daughter's security in particular.

CHAPTER FIVE

'I HAVEN'T EATEN here before,' Nina told Rafe as she glanced appreciatively at their surroundings. They had been seated at a secluded table near the window of a fashionable—and wildly exclusive—New York restaurant.

Situated on the top floor of one of New York's most prestigious skyscrapers, with three-hundred-and-sixty-degree views over the city, it was one of the in places for the rich and famous to enjoy themselves in relative privacy. Nina had spotted several easily recognisable TV personalities, as well as actresses and actors, as they were shown to their table. She even recognised a couple of politicians.

As she had said she would, Nina had spent the day at the gallery—most of the time vacillating between going out to dinner with Rafe this evening, as planned, or telling him she couldn't make it after all.

The latter hadn't been because she had received a particularly negative response from her father in regard to the date she had planned with Rafe for this evening; her father's mouth might have tightened with disapproval, but he seemed to know, from the stubbornness of Nina expression, not to comment further.

No, Nina's earlier trepidation, in regard to having dinner with Rafe, had been for a completely different reason. And that reason was Rafe D'Angelo himself.

Rafe was unlike any other man she had ever met. Confident and forceful, but not obnoxiously so, with a wicked sense of humour that was also teasing. He was intelligent without being pompous, and his bad-boy good looks were undiminished by the trappings of civilisation. The elegant black evening suit and snowy silk shirt and bow tie he was wearing this evening did little to temper that impression.

He also showed absolutely none of the awe for her father that so many other men did. Nina had been out to dinner with only three other men since her return to New York three years ago. Without exception all of those men had almost fallen over themselves in an effort to impress her father, with Nina's own preferences or dislikes coming a very poor second.

Rafe, on the other hand, was respectful to her father but at the same time not in the least overwhelmed by the Palitov power or wealth. No, Rafe was most definitely his own man: charming, worldly, wealthy, and confident of himself and his own abilities.

A dangerous combination to a woman who had always known the full force of the effect on other people of the wealth and power of the Palitov name.

'I heard this place was booked up weeks in advance,' she added conversationally, once the waiter had poured them each a glass of the pink champagne that had been delivered to their table the moment they sat down, the bottle now resting in a nest of ice in the bucket beside the table.

Rafe shrugged. 'The owner is a friend of mine.'

Nina gave a teasing smile. 'Was he a friend before you started eating here so often, or did that come later?' It wasn't the same restaurant Rafe had been photographed in with Jennifer Nichols, but Nina was pretty sure she had seen several other photographs on the Internet of him leaving this particular restaurant with other beautiful women.

Rafe shrugged. 'I knew Gerry before he opened this restaurant. Talking of which—he enjoyed having your two men come by earlier,' he added ruefully.

Nina eyed him uncertainly. 'I'm not sure if that's sarcasm or not?'

'Not,' Rafe drawled ruefully. 'Apparently they did a thorough sweep of the place, and then, because they weren't officially on duty for another couple of hours, and the restaurant was still closed, the three of them sat down together and played poker for an hour or so till opening time. Gerry loves playing poker. Especially when he wins,' he added dryly.

Nina chuckled. 'That sounds like Lawrence and Paul; they taught me to play poker when I was ten, and I started beating them when I was twelve.'

Rafe knew his eyes had widened, but otherwise he managed to keep his expression passive. 'You play poker with your bodyguards?'

'Not so much since I started winning.' She laughed.

'Remind me never to play strip poker with you,' he drawled dryly. 'Shouldn't you have still been playing with—oh, I don't know—dolls, or something equally girlish at that age?'

'Sexist!' Nina came back dryly. 'I never played with dolls, and certainly not aged twelve,' she added with a grimace. 'I was more interested in boys then than anything so childishly girlish.'

'And playing poker.' Yet more insight into the strangeness of Nina's upbringing, Rafe acknowledged with a frown. Not only had she grown up alone with her father, but her only other companions during those years appeared to have been her bodyguards.

'Only until I started winning,' she reminded him.

'Hmm.' He frowned. 'Gerry wanted me to thank you for letting your two men stand guard outside the main restaurant rather than inside it.'

'No doubt that's so that they can vet the people coming in.' Nina winced. 'I realise they can be a little intrusive.'

'I told you not to worry about it,' Rafe dismissed easily.

And she was trying, she really was. 'What are we celebrating?' She eyed the champagne curiously.

'Life?'

Nina smiled as she lifted her glass and chinked it against his before taking an appreciative sip; she loved pink champagne, and Rafe had ordered a bottle from her absolutely favourite vineyard. Coincidentally? Or had he known beforehand?

Rafe smiled as Nina gave him a suspicious glance. 'Guilty, as charged,' he drawled in answer to her unspoken question. 'I telephoned your father earlier today and asked him for the name of your favourite wine.'

Nina's eyes widened. 'You did?'

'Hmm.' Rafe rested his elbows on the table, his glass clasped loosely between his fingers as he looked at Nina through narrowed lids.

She looked absolutely stunning tonight. She wore a black sequined knee-length sheath of a dress that clung lovingly to the slenderness of her curves, but left her neck and arms bare. Only a pale green shadow on her lids, her lashes long and dark, a peachy blush to her cheeks, her lips coloured with a deeper peach lip gloss. Her hair was secured in a loose knot at her crown, leaving the long creamy column of her throat vulnerably bare.

Ironically, considering her father's unique and price-less jewellery collection, Nina wore no jewellery this evening. There was nothing to detract from the smooth perfection of her creamy pale peach skin, just a small pair of diamond ear studs.

Rafe had been fully aware that it had been that un-derstated elegance and beauty, in contrast to the other over-jewelled and dramatically made-up women in the restaurant, that had caught the eye of every man in the room when the two of them entered the restaurant to-gether. In response he had placed his arm about Nina's waist, drawing her tightly against his side as they crossed the room to their table.

Not possessively, exactly. Rafe had never felt posses-sive over a woman in his life. But he hadn't wanted any of those men to be under any illusion as to who Nina was with this evening. Or to have any doubts that she would be leaving with that same man at the end of the evening too.

Was that being possessive? Hell if Rafe knew. What he did know was that he hadn't in the least enjoyed hav-ing other men eyeing Nina so appreciatively.

She moistened those full and peach-coloured lips with a nervous sweep of her tongue. 'You spoke to my father today...?' she repeated slowly.

Rafe raised dark brows. 'A courtesy call, to thank him for dinner yesterday evening.'

'That's all?'

He shrugged. 'I told you, I also wanted to know the name and year of your favourite wine.'

Which, Nina accepted, all sounded innocent enough. Except last night her father had warned Rafe to stay away from her, a warning Rafe had taken exception to. And now she was expected to believe that earlier today Rafe had made a thank-you call to her father, and that her father had happily supplied the younger man with the name of her favourite wine for when he took her out to dinner this evening?

She eyed him sceptically. 'And my father just gave it to you?'

'Your happiness is very important to him.' Rafe took another sip of his champagne, those predatory golden eyes quietly watchful over the rim of the glass.

'Rafe—'

'Relax, Nina,' he cut in soothingly. 'Let's look at the menus and order our dinner,' he added as the waiter brought the menus to their table. 'And then, if you still want to, you can ask me more about my conversation with your father earlier today.'

Oh, Nina would still want to. Just as she couldn't help wondering if Rafe's telephone conversation with her father today wasn't the reason her father had made no objections when Nina had told him of her date with Rafe D'Angelo this evening. It certainly explained her father's lack of surprise.

'Spit it out, Nina,' Rafe drawled once they had made their food selections and the waiter had unobtrusively topped up their champagne glasses before leaving them alone together. 'I can tell by your worried expression that you're still questioning my motives for telephoning your father earlier today,' he supplied as she glanced across at him enquiringly.

Nina looked at him beneath lowered lashes. 'Am I such an open book?'

'Hardly!' Rafe chuckled softly. This woman had been

a mystery to him from the first, and the more he came to know her, it seemed the more of a mystery she became.

His forays on the Internet had told him that Nina and her father had lived alone together since she was five years old, and that she had spent her earlier years being educated at home. Her childhood seemed to have been spent exclusively with her wheelchair-bound father, and the muscled men that made up her security detail—making it doubly amazing that she had managed to escape and attend university at all.

Rafe was even more convinced, since meeting Dmitri Palitov, that the other man must have been having heart palpitations over that one. At the same time Rafe couldn't help but admire Nina for having had the strength to break out of that protective cocoon.

And yet, having broken free for three years, Nina had then stepped back into that repressive ring of security when she'd returned to New York. Admittedly she now had her own apartment in the building her father owned, but it was still very much under her father's protection. And the design work she did was always within her father's corporation.

Rafe's efforts last night to find out more about Dmitri Palitov had hit wall after wall after Nina was five and her mother had died. Nor could Rafe find any record of Anna Palitov's death, or the reason for it. As there had been only the briefest mention made of the accident just weeks later that had resulted in Dmitri Palitov being in a wheelchair. A car accident that had apparently killed two of the three men travelling in the other car.

Mystery, after mystery, after mystery.

And Nina, slightly shy, vibrantly beautiful, sexy as hell, as well as intelligent, and incredibly talented in her designs, was front and centre of that mystery.

'I didn't telephone your father, or tell him of our dinner date, with any idea of challenging his warning last night, Nina,' Rafe assured her softly now.

'No?' She winced.

'No,' he replied evenly, having known it would, but hoped it wouldn't, be her conclusion regarding his actions. 'I would hope I'm neither that petty nor that vindictive.'

A delicate blush coloured her cheeks at the reproof in Rafe's tone.

'Then why did you tell him?'

'So that you didn't have to.' Rafe reached over and placed one of his hands on the top of hers as it rested on the tabletop. 'Nina, I'm fully aware of how close you and your father are, and the last thing I want is to be the cause of any tension between the two of you. What I do want is for the two of us to get to know each other better, and I have no intention of doing that by leaving you to be the one who has to do the explaining to your father.'

Nina felt the sting of tears in her eyes. Rafe was already too much for one woman to handle: too wickedly handsome, too charming, too amusing, definitely too sexually attractive for his own good. Or, as she had realised last night, her own good.

And she had been totally physically aware of Rafe this evening from the moment she had opened her apartment door and looked at him standing out in the hallway. His hair had still been damp from the shower he must have taken, he had obviously shaved too, but his beard was so dark there was still a sexy shadow along his jawline. And as for the warmth in those golden eyes as his gaze roved slowly over her...

Adding understanding and compassion to Rafe's al-

ready long list of attractions was just being unfair to
any woman.

And yet Nina had no doubts that whatever Rafe had
said to her father during their telephone call earlier today,
it had helped pave the way for her own conversation with
her father this evening.

'Dmitri and I may not be altogether sure that we like
each other yet,' Rafe continued dryly, 'but I think we respect each other. Which is a start.'

Yes, Nina could appreciate that her father was old-
fashioned enough to have appreciated the fact that Rafe
had been the one to tell him of their dinner date this evening, even if he hadn't particularly liked or approved of
it. Her father admired strength, respected that strength,
and Rafe had it in abundance.

She gave a rueful grimace. 'I'm sorry I was so suspicious of your motives just now.'

'Let's not spend the whole evening apologising to each
other, Nina,' Rafe cut across that apology, giving her hand
one last squeeze before sitting back as the waiter placed
the first course in front of them.

'So tell me what you do at Archangel,' Nina prompted
once the waiter had departed.

'What do I do?'

'Yes.' She nodded. 'I know that you and your two
brothers manage the galleries, but I'm sure that doesn't
take up all of your time,' she prompted interestedly.

Which was how Rafe came to find himself telling
Nina more about the work he did, and about coming up
with new ideas for Archangel. He told her some anecdotes
from his childhood, growing up in a family of three boys.

'Your poor mother!' Nina laughed softly after Rafe
had related one of those stories of his childhood, involving himself and Gabriel placing a frog in their grand-

mother's bed when she came to stay during the summer when he was eleven. 'Michael wasn't involved too?' she prompted curiously as she took a sip of the coffee that had been served to signal the end of their meal.

Rafe gave a shake of his head. 'Even at twelve Michael was the serious one, the responsible one.'

Nina remembered that aloof seriousness from that one occasion she had met Michael D'Angelo. 'Maybe he didn't feel he had a choice, with two mischievous younger brothers?'

Rafe frowned as he seemed to give the suggestion some thought, now wondering if perhaps his older brother chose to live behind a public mask too.

'I've never thought of it quite like that before, but you could be right,' Rafe conceded slowly. 'And talking of Michael, I spoke to him this afternoon, too.'

Her brows rose. 'He's back in New York?'

Rafe shook his head. 'Still in Paris. We spoke on a conference call.'

Nina's brows rose. 'You have been busy today!'

He frowned. 'Didn't the things I've just told you show that I'm busy every day?'

Yes, they had, Nina acknowledged with an inner glow, not sure why Rafe had chosen to answer her questions so candidly, but pleased that he had, now knowing there was so much more to this man, a depth that others wouldn't know was there.

She eyed him teasingly. 'I believe it's the newspapers who prefer to report on your night-time activities rather than the daytime ones!'

'They take delight in reporting what they think are my night-time activities,' Rafe corrected dryly.

'All those photographs of you out with beautiful

women are just a figment of the press's imagination?' she prompted.

Unfortunately, Rafe knew they weren't. And worst of all, of course, was the one of him with Jennifer Nichols two nights ago, when he had refused to cancel his prior arrangements to have dinner with Nina and her father.

'My main reason for talking to Michael...' Rafe abruptly changed the subject '...was because I wanted to see what he thought about my suggestion of asking you to design new display cabinets for all three of the galleries.'

'Me?' She was obviously stunned by the suggestion.

'Why not?' He frowned at Nina's reaction. 'The display cabinets you designed for your father are elegantly beautiful in their simplicity. The same elegance and simplicity that we aim for at Archangel.'

'Well. Yes. I've noticed that these past few days. But...' She was obviously flustered. 'I already have a job.'

'Working for your father.'

Nina could hear the disapproval in Rafe's tone. Perhaps deserved, after all those years she had spent attaining her design degree from Stanford.

But Rafe didn't understand. No one did. Because most people, Rafe included, had no idea what had happened to them nineteen years ago. Nina was well aware that her father had used the Palitov wealth and power to make certain not all the events of that time were ever made public.

'Don't you have any hopes and dreams of your own, Nina?' Rafe pressed determinedly, refusing to back down on the subject. 'An ambition to do something more with your life than stand in your father's shadow?'

She gasped, her face visibly paling at this attack coming so quickly after Rafe had talked to her so candidly. Or perhaps that was the reason for the attack? She very much doubted that Rafe spoke that candidly about himself to many people. 'That was uncalled for,' she murmured softly.

'But true?'

'Thank you for a lovely dinner, Rafe, but I think perhaps it's time I left.' Nina turned away, the bareness of her shoulders defensively stiff as she slowly laid her napkin down on the table beside her empty coffee cup, sure now that Rafe was being deliberately challenging. Because he had so completely let his guard down with her?

Rafe's mouth had thinned. 'I'm driving you home.'

'Lawrence and Paul will take me home.'

Rafe gave a slow, determined shake of his head. 'I drove you here. I'm driving you home.'

'Why?' Her eyes glittered deeply green. 'So that you can insult me some more? Because I asked too many questions? Or because you answered them?' she added astutely as she stood up, black clutch bag in her hand.

Rafe stood up too, grasping her arm as she would have brushed past him on her way to the door. 'And is this what you do, Nina?' he challenged softly. 'Run away every time someone says something that strikes a little too close to home?'

Tears glistened in her eyes as she looked up at him. 'Run home to Daddy, do you mean?'

He winced at the sight of those tears swimming in her pained green eyes. 'I didn't say that.'

'You meant it, though,' Nina said knowingly, attempting to shake off his hold on her arm but not succeeding. 'You're causing a scene, Rafe,' she muttered as she noticed several people at the neighbouring tables were giving discreetly curious glances in their direction.

Not surprising really. The two of them had obviously been getting on so well, talking and laughing together, all the time with that underlying edge of flirtation and awareness, as they ate their delicious meal, and then lingered over coffee, and now this.

And of course Nina had ambitions and hopes and dreams of her own. Lots of them. And one of them had been to go to Stanford. Which she had done.

But she hadn't taken into account how frail her father would be when she returned to New York to live three years later, a frailty she felt partly responsible for, because she knew how much of a strain it had been for him, a worry, while she was away. At the time, the most she had felt comfortable insisting upon was that she be allowed to have her own apartment rather than continue to live with her father in the penthouse apartment.

But that didn't mean that she didn't still long to start her own design business, to be able to take commissions like the one Rafe had just offered her at the Archangel galleries, in London and Paris as well as here. Just thinking of accepting such a commission made her heart soar with excitement.

But it was never going to happen. Not while her father was alive, anyway, and Nina wanted him with her for many more years to come.

'Careful, Rafe—' Nina fell back on mockery as her defence '—or the next thing you'll see in the newspapers is a photograph of you manhandling a woman in your friend's restaurant!'

'Gerry doesn't allow the press inside his restaurant,' he rasped tautly.

So much for mockery! 'Nevertheless, I would appreciate it if you would let go of my arm.' She met his gaze challengingly.

And Rafe would have appreciated it if he could have

just managed to get through a single evening with Nina without the two of them arguing.

Maybe he shouldn't have brought up the subject of having Nina design some display cabinets for the gallery yet. Perhaps he shouldn't challenge her about having hopes and dreams of her own, rather than those imposed on her by her father's security. He certainly shouldn't have accused Nina of running away when the subject became too personal for her!

So why had he?

Because, as she had intimated, she had got too close, Rafe realised. By answering her questions, he had allowed her to see the astute businessman, the 'new ideas' man, behind the façade of the playboy. And it had unsettled him. He'd never allowed any woman to question him so deeply about his work or his family.

But having Nina walk out on him in this way unsettled him more!

'We'll talk about this in the car,' he told her stiffly.

'I told you that I will ride back with Lawrence and Paul.'

'Oh, no, Nina, you don't get to tell me anything when it comes to who's taking you home tonight,' he assured softly, maintaining a hold on her arm as he strode across the restaurant.

He gave Gerry a stiff nod as they paused in the reception area to collect Nina's cashmere wrap, knowing, by his friend's understanding nod as Rafe draped that wrap about the stiffness of Nina's shoulders, that Gerry was more than happy for Rafe to settle the bill at his convenience. Which certainly wasn't now. Anything but Rafe's complete attention and Nina was likely to just walk out of here and not look back.

'We're going to my apartment,' he briskly informed

the two security men waiting near the lifts as he maintained a firm grip on Nina's arm. 'No doubt you're aware of exactly where that is?' he added tersely as he and Nina stepped into one of the lifts together, Rafe pressing the button to close the doors and leaving the two men to follow behind in the second lift.

'Rafe.'

'Not now, Nina,' he bit out through clenched teeth.

'But…'

'Please, Nina.' Rafe's gaze was rapier sharp as he looked down at her. 'I'm trying my damnedest not to—'

He drew in a deep, controlling breath. 'All I want right now is to get you out of here so that we can go to the privacy of my apartment.'

His car was being brought to the front of the building even as they stepped outside. No doubt Gerry had called down to the valets in the underground garage as soon as Rafe and Nina stepped into the lift together. The valet got quickly out of the car to open the passenger door for Nina to get inside, at the same time as the two bodyguards rushed out of the building behind them and hurried off to get their own car from where it was parked further down the block.

The silent drive to Rafe's apartment—doggedly followed by the black limousine occupied by Lawrence and Paul—gave Rafe ample time to think of that last conversation in the restaurant. To accept that he was definitely responsible for the current tension that existed between himself and Nina. And after he had previously decided he would be the one person in Nina's life who didn't cause her hassle or tension.

'I'm sorry,' he murmured on a sigh.

'I thought we weren't going to spend the evening apologising to each other?'

'This one needs to be said. My remark was out of line.'

'It's okay,' Nina said softly.

Rafe gave her a brief glance, his jaw tightening as he saw the tracks of the tears that were still falling down the paleness of her cheeks, before he turned his gaze sharply back to manoeuvring through the late night traffic clogging up the city's streets. 'No, it isn't,' he bit out, disgusted with himself.

No, it wasn't, Nina acknowledged miserably, having now realised that this evening, with Rafe, an evening that had started out with such promise, and which she had been enjoying immensely, was now going to end as disastrously as those dinners she'd had with three other men since returning home to New York.

She had hoped tonight would be different, because Rafe was different from anyone else she had ever known, their conversation this evening showing her he wasn't just the playboy he wanted everyone else to think that he was.

But she could see now that it wasn't going to work. That although he had no intention of sucking up to her father and ignoring what Nina wanted, as those other men had, her attraction to Rafe was pulling her in another direction completely, and one that she knew would ultimately cause her father further heartache. And that was something Nina absolutely refused to do; her father had suffered enough.

And going to Rafe's apartment with him wasn't going to change any of that. No matter how volatile she knew her physical reaction to him was…

CHAPTER SIX

'FEELING BETTER?'

'Yes, thank you,' Nina confirmed huskily as she looked up at Rafe after taking a sip of the brandy he had insisted on pouring for both of them once they reached his apartment.

In the end, Nina hadn't been able to resist accompanying him there; if this was to be their one and only date, as it probably would be, then she intended making the most of it.

The modern décor of Rafe's apartment had come as something of a surprise to her, even a disappointment, with its colour scheme of black, silver and white. The walls in the sitting room were white, as was the carpet, with a black leather sofa and chairs, and a glass coffee table, only the original artwork on the walls and the fantastic view of New York outside the huge windows to prevent it from appearing utilitarian.

It certainly reflected none of the sensuality or larger than life personality of the man who occupied it.

'It's a family-owned apartment,' Rafe dismissed as he saw her curiosity. 'Whichever of the brothers is in New York at the time uses it.'

She blinked. 'Do you change locations a lot, then?'

'Every two months or so, sometimes more often.' Rafe

shrugged. 'Depends what's happening at the time. We have an exhibition coming up in Paris next month, and, with Gabriel away on his honeymoon, Michael decided to take over in Paris for a while. He'll be flying over here on Friday for the gala opening on Saturday, of course.'

Nina knew they were both just talking for the sake of it, that Rafe was trying to put her at her ease. 'My father will appreciate that.' She nodded.

'Michael wouldn't think of not being there.'

And yet Michael had no reservations in leaving Rafe in charge of her father's exhibition. Further proof that Nina really shouldn't believe all that she read about Rafe in the newspapers, that, as she had realised this evening, he really wasn't just the playboy the press had made him out to be.

Rafe placed his glass down on the coffee table before coming down on his haunches beside the chair where Nina sat. He took her free hand in his. 'I really am sorry about earlier. For making you cry,' he told her gruffly. 'I shouldn't have pushed you so hard.'

'It isn't your fault.' Her hand shook slightly inside his as she gave a shake of her head. 'You can't possibly understand, and I can't explain, either,' she added emotionally.

Those golden eyes narrowed. 'Why can't you?'

'It isn't possible.'

His jaw tightened. 'I repeat, why not?'

'Because it isn't my story to tell.'

Rafe had already guessed as much, just as he now believed this story had something to do with whatever had happened to the Palitov family nineteen years ago. When Nina's mother had died, and Dmitri Palitov had been involved in the car accident that had resulted in his being in a wheelchair for the rest of his life.

The timing of those two events, just weeks apart, and Nina's refusal to talk about them, made Rafe wonder if they might actually be linked by more than just Dmitri's distraction at the loss of his wife.

And it mattered to him, Rafe realised. Knowing, what kept the beautiful and talented Nina hidden away from the world mattered to him.

As did the woman herself?

The only thing that mattered at the moment was learning why, whatever might have happened nineteen years ago, Nina continued to allow her life to be so restricted.

Why Dmitri Palitov kept his daughter so protected and sheltered he was in danger of suffocating her.

Rafe had even wondered, as he had allowed his imagination free rein the night before, and having found no actual proof of Anna Palitov's death, if she hadn't just chosen to leave her husband and daughter nineteen years ago. It would certainly go a long way to explaining why Dmitri had become so determined not to lose Nina too.

Nina's smile was sad as she saw the frustrated anger in Rafe's expression; the flash of temper in those amazing golden eyes, chiselled lips thinned as he obviously raged an inner battle with his impatience at her refusal to talk to him, to tell him, the reason she refused to break away from her father's protection.

Nina had no actual memories of what had happened nineteen years ago. She had been five years old at the time, and only knew what had really happened because her father had explained it to her when she was ten, old enough to understand that horrendous sequence of events that had shaped their lives.

And Nina could still remember her father's pain that day, as if it had been just minutes ago rather than five years.

Oh, Nina had been fully aware that her mother had disappeared from her life when she was five. She had cried over it, had pleaded and thrown temper tantrums as she demanded to know where her mother had gone. A demand her father had assuaged by assuring her that her mother hadn't wanted to leave them, that she'd had no choice.

But it had been another five years before her father had explained exactly why Anna had left them.

Kidnapped.

Ransomed.

A ransom Dmitri had gladly paid in his desire to have his beloved wife returned to him, as he had also complied with the kidnappers' demand that he not inform the police or the press of the kidnapping, or his wife would die.

The payment of that ransom hadn't stopped the kidnappers from killing their hostage, anyway. From killing Nina's kind and beautiful mother, and Dmitri's beloved wife.

Or stopped Nina's father from hunting down the three men responsible.

And when he finally found those three men her father had contacted them and arranged to meet with them, only for their two cars to be involved in an accident that had resulted in two of those three men being killed outright, and putting Dmitri in a wheelchair for the rest of his life.

And Nina had always had her doubts as to how that accident had occurred, had always suspected—but never dared ask—that her father had intended those three men to die that day, as retribution for taking his beloved Anna's life.

Which was why Nina knew she could never explain, never tell anyone else about the events of nineteen years ago, without also implicating her father in the death of at least two of the men who had taken Anna from them both. She had always shied away from asking what had become of the third man.

She couldn't explain that to Rafe. She wouldn't. Even if it meant that she now had to allow Rafe, a man she liked and was so attracted to, to walk away from her without a single backward glance.

She drew in a deep, controlling breath before forcing a smile to her lips. 'I think it's time I was leaving.'

Rafe had had an idea that was where all Nina's concentrated thought was going to lead. 'You're running away again, Nina,' he reproved gently.

'Yes,' she confirmed without apology.

He frowned. 'You don't have to leave.'

'Yes,' she sighed. 'I really think that I do.'

Rafe gave a slow shake of his head. 'I don't want you to.' And he didn't.

In fact, Rafe could never remember wanting anything as much as he now wanted Nina to stay, here with him, in this apartment, in his bed.

He reached out and gently took the brandy glass from Nina's unresisting fingers before placing that glass beside his own on the coffee table. Turning back to her and taking both of her hands into his, his gaze seeking and capturing hers as he looked down at her intently. 'Don't go, Nina,' he encouraged gruffly. 'Stay here with me tonight.'

Nina's breath caught in her throat, her heart beating loudly, erratically, in her chest, both at the words Rafe had just spoken, and the intensity of the desire she could see burning in the depths of those glittering golden eyes that looked so intently into hers. 'You'll be disappointed.'

'What?' Rafe stared at her incredulously, obviously startled by her reply.

Heat coloured Nina's cheeks as she avoided meeting

that shocked gaze. 'I—' She moistened suddenly dry lips with a sweep of her tongue. 'I'm not experienced, Rafe. I'm not a virgin either,' she hastened to add, so there should be no misunderstandings. 'But I'm not experienced, not like the other women you've—' She ceased speaking as he pressed his fingertips gently against her lips.

'Nina, all that matters here and now is the two of us,' he assured gruffly. 'No one else, and certainly not the past, but what we both want now. And I want you very much,' he added huskily. 'Do you want me?'

Too much!

Nina had wanted Rafe from the moment she had looked at him that first day, as he stood in the doorway of the gallery in the east wing of Archangel.

It had been so obvious that day that Rafe had assumed she was just another one of her father's workmen, and she had very much enjoyed taking off her baseball cap to release her fiery red hair down her back, in order to shatter that illusion.

Because looking at Rafe had awoken dormant feelings inside her, a physical awareness, a desire that had caused her body to hum with the need for him to see her as a desirable woman.

Exactly the way Rafe was looking at her now. His golden eyes warm with the same desire that coursed through her own veins, an aroused flush to the sharp blade of his cheekbones, those chiselled lips parted, as if he was just waiting for her to say yes so that he could kiss her.

And God knew Nina wanted him to kiss her. Wanted Rafe in a way she had never wanted any other man. To kiss him. To touch him. To make love with him.

And why shouldn't she do just that? Why shouldn't she

take this one night with him? Lose herself in that desire, that arousal, and enjoy Rafe in the way she would never be able to do again?

Because Nina already knew that had to be the ultimate outcome of this evening. That Rafe was far too intelligent, too intensely curious about the past, her past, for her to ever risk incriminating her father by answering any of Rafe's questions.

She moistened her lips with the tip of her tongue before answering, her gaze remaining unwavering on his.

'Yes, I want you, Rafe,' she answered softly, steadily, allowing no room for doubts in her mind. She would take this one night of pleasure, enjoy it, revel in it, with no expectations of anything other than tonight. Men did it all the time, Rafe did it all the time, so why shouldn't she?

'Right now,' she added determinedly.

'Good girl.' It wasn't triumph, but satisfaction, that flared in those golden eyes as he straightened beside her before holding out one of his hands to her invitingly.

Nina placed her own hand unhesitatingly into his as she rose to her feet in front of him. Rafe kept possession of that hand as they turned and walked out of the room together and down the hallway to his bedroom.

Nina felt no reservations, no doubts, as Rafe maintained that hold on her hand as he switched on one of the bedside lamps before turning to cup either side of her face, gazing down searchingly into her eyes before his head lowered towards hers.

'You are so beautiful,' he murmured huskily.

'Kiss me, Rafe,' she encouraged.

'Your mouth has been driving me insane since the first moment I looked at you,' he acknowledged gruffly.

She blinked. 'My mouth?'

'You have the most delicious, lusciously pouting lips,

and I've been imagining kissing them, and having them kiss me, since the moment I first met you. Everywhere,' he groaned.

Her cheeks warmed with colour. 'How can that possibly be true, when you went out with, made love to, another woman that same evening?'

'I didn't,' he drawled. 'Oh, I went out to dinner with her, but bedding her was a different matter, when the woman I wanted was a tall and fiery redhead who enjoys challenging me.'

Nina felt warmed inside just knowing that Rafe hadn't been intimate with Jennifer Nichols two nights ago. Because it was her that he wanted. Her. Nina Palitov. 'In that case, I think I would very much enjoy being kissed and kissing you. Everywhere...'

So would Rafe.

To hell with his rules and the complications of being involved with a woman like Nina; he wanted her. And those complications if that was the only way he could have her!

He continued to cradle the warmth of Nina's cheeks as he kissed her slowly, lingering for long heart-pounding minutes as he sipped and tasted those luscious lips that had taunted and tempted him these past three days. Nina returned the warmth, the heat of those kisses, as her hands glided up his shirt-covered chest beneath his jacket.

Rafe hadn't thought, hadn't dared to hope, that the evening would end like this. End? Damn it, this wasn't the end of him and Nina, but the beginning.

He continued to kiss her, those kisses becoming hungrier, wilder, more heated, as he reached up and took the clip from her hair, allowing those fiery red curls to cascade down the length of her spine. He shrugged out of his dinner jacket and let it fall to the floor. Nina groaned softly in her throat as her body now curved intimately into and against his, her hands now roaming restlessly over his muscled back.

Not close enough. They weren't nearly close enough for Rafe's liking. The barrier of their clothes had to go. He needed to see, to feel the heat of Nina's delicious curves, ached to taste those succulent breasts again, to hear Nina's soft cries of pleasure as he laved those breasts with his tongue and nibbled them with his teeth, before suckling deeply.

His lips raked down her throat in a heated caress as he slid the zip to her gown down the length of her spine, tasting her creamy flesh as he slipped the straps of her gown down her arms before letting it fall to the floor.

'Amazing.' Rafe breathed raggedly as Nina stood before him wearing only a pair of minuscule black lace panties and her high-heeled black shoes, her hair a wild fiery red tumble over her shoulders and breasts.

'You like?' Nina prompted shyly.

That heated gaze roamed over her hungrily. 'Oh, I definitely like!' Rafe assured gruffly. 'Take off the rest, Nina,' he encouraged gruffly.

'I was thinking of you when I wore these,' she revealed huskily as she stepped out of the high-heeled shoes before sliding the black panties down her thighs and dropping them on the carpet beside her gown. She was totally exposed to Rafe now, but not in the least self-conscious as she saw the desire for her burning in those glittering golden eyes. 'Because I wanted this to happen.'

His gaze flicked up to her face, studying her for long timeless moments before he nodded his satisfaction with whatever he saw in her expression. 'In that case, I think it only fair I should be naked too, don't you?' he murmured as he stepped back, arms held slightly away from his body in invitation.

Nina had never undressed a man before. Those two previous encounters had been hurried and unsatisfying, when neither she nor either of those two men had even been completely undressed. Her fingers shook slightly as she removed Rafe's bow tie before unfastening the buttons of his shirt, pushing the white silk down his arms as she gazed her fill of the bareness of Rafe's wide shoulders and muscled chest. His skin there the same olive tone as his face and hands, with a sprinkling of dark hair that covered the flat bronze coins of his nipples, and formed a vee as it tapered down the muscled flatness of his abdomen before disappearing beneath the waistband of his trousers.

'All of it, Nina,' he groaned achingly as he stepped out of his shoes.

Her hands shook even more as she unfastened his trousers before sliding down the zip and allowing them to fall to the floor, gasping as she saw the long bulge of his shaft pressing impatiently against his black boxers. She glanced up at Rafe, before quickly looking away again as she saw the increased heat of the desire burning in those golden eyes.

She could do this. She needed to do this. Needed to be with Rafe, to touch and caress him.

She dropped smoothly to her knees in front of him, Rafe's skin warm to the touch as she hooked her fingers into the waistband of those black boxers, before easing them down and off, baring his arousal.

Rafe was so utterly beautiful, his body as perfect as a huge bronzed statue.

Nina placed one of her hands on Rafe's thigh, the other about the thickness of his shaft as she lowered her head, her tongue flicking out to lap, to taste the salty sweetness of the moisture coating the engorged tip. Encouraged by his low groans of pleasure as his hands moved out to grasp her shoulders, she parted her lips and took him completely into her mouth.

Rafe could barely breathe past the pleasure that engulfed him the moment he felt the lushness of Nina's lips parting before she took him inside the burning heat of her mouth, and then deeper still, taking him to the back of her throat, before moving back again until just the bulbous tip remained imprisoned in that burning heat, her tongue a torturous caress about the rim just below the exposed head, only to repeat that pleasurable lapping of her tongue as she sucked on him greedily, taking Rafe further, deeper down her throat, with each successive motion.

She repeated that caress again and again, humming softly beneath her breast as she lapped and sucked, the pleasure becoming overwhelming, until Rafe knew he couldn't take any more, that he was on the edge of exploding in her mouth.

'No more, Nina!' he groaned achingly as he gently eased her away from him, laughing gruffly as he saw the pout of disappointment on her lips as she looked up at him. 'It's going to be over too quickly for me if I allow you to continue doing that,' he explained huskily as he bent to sweep Nina up in his arms before carrying her over to the bed.

'It's my turn to explore and taste you now,' he assured as he laid her gently down onto the brown pillows and bedcover. Nina appearing a creamily skinned red-haired goddess against that darkness as Rafe moved onto the bed beside her.

Nina's back arched invitingly off the bed as Rafe's

head lowered and his lips parted to capture one hard, engorged nipple before suckling that hardness deep into the heat of his mouth, his hand moving to cup and caress its twin, causing a gush of heated moisture to dampen the swollen lips between her thighs as Rafe's other hand moved caressingly, unerringly, down to her parted thighs to stroke the swollen engorged nubbin hidden there, the dual assault on Nina's senses causing her to cry out as an orgasm immediately ripped through and over her in burning, rippling waves.

Rafe continued those caresses as Nina arched into her climax, suckling deeply on her nipple, deepening the stroke of his fingers as he felt the gushing of her juices against them, lightly squeezing her clitoris between his fingers as he continued to milk and prolong that orgasm until he was sure Nina had taken, enjoyed, every last gasping shudder of her pleasure.

She was so responsive, so open to him as Rafe slid down her body to rest his shoulders between her parted thighs, his hands moving up to capture, caress, pinch her nipples as he lowered his head to lap up the nectar of her juices. The lips there swollen and open, begging for the thrust of his tongue inside her, and causing that channel to ripple and contract as a second, more intensely pro-longed orgasm now caused her to arch her thighs into the deep thrusting rhythm of his tongue. Nina groaned his name over and over again as she came against his mouth.

'I want you inside me, Rafe,' Nina gasped as she reached down to entangle her fingers in his hair, mind-less with that need after experiencing, not just her first ever orgasm but also a second one, her channel still con-tracting greedily as it hungered for more.

'I need you inside me,' she demanded, groaning achingly at the sight of her own juices slicked across Rafe's lips as he raised his head to look up at her.

She whimpered softly in her throat as he rasped his tongue lingeringly over her sensitive nubbin once more before moving up her body, the silky hair on his chest rasping across the swollen nubbin between her splayed thighs, and then her sensitive nipples, as he laid his weight on her, his elbows either side of her head as he looked down at her searchingly.

'So, so beautiful,' he groaned, his hands cradled either side of her face as he kissed her again, deeply, hungrily, the erotic thrust of his tongue filling Nina's mouth with the taste of her own juices even as she felt the nudge of his shaft against her , parting her as his hardness slid inch by slow inch inside those sensitive tissues, the stretching, filling sensation an exquisite pleasure in itself, before he began to stroke slowly inside her, causing Nina to break the kiss as she gasped at each successive slow thrust, the pleasure building, rising, overwhelming in its intensity.

Rafe buried his face in her throat, lips grazing her flesh, his breathing ragged as he continued those slow and measured thrusts. He was threatening to drive Nina insane with the ache building higher and higher inside her.

'Harder, Rafe!' she gasped. 'Oh, please, harder!' she groaned as her nails dug into Rafe's shoulders, her legs curving over the backs of his thighs, pulling him into her as she met his hard thrusts, her body contracting about the long length of him as he filled her completely, her inner muscles squeezing, milking that length as he withdrew, causing Rafe to groan through clenched teeth with each new plunge, until he finally lost control and thrust faster, harder, into that slick heat.

Nina gave a guttural scream, her head thrashing from

side to side on the pillow as she felt another release tearing through her, more intense, more overwhelming even than the last two. She heard Rafe's harsh groan as her muscles tightened about him, clenching, squeezing the long length of his shaft as she convulsed in climax. His back arching, head thrown back, dark hair wild about his shoulders as the intensity of that golden gaze captured and held hers as his own release exploded into her in hot, thick jets, intensifying and prolonging Nina's own release as that heat hit the opening to her womb, filling her, completing her.

Rafe woke the following morning with the feel of the warmth of sun shining on his closed lids, and a smile on his lips. Nina was the reason for that smile as he remembered the night of passion they had just spent together. Hours and hours of making love, their hunger for each other seemingly insatiable.

He had gathered Nina's boneless body up in his arms after the first time, before drawing back the bedclothes and cuddling her beneath them as they fell asleep in each other's arms. But they had woken and made love twice more during the night, slowly, deliciously, wildly, each time becoming more attuned to each other's needs and desires, murmuring encouragements and gasps as they shared their pleasure in each other.

An intensity of pleasure Rafe knew he had never experienced before, with any woman.

A remembered intensity of pleasure that now made Rafe's smile widen as he thought of spending the morning in bed with Nina, or maybe the whole day. He was nowhere near to satisfying the intensity of the desire he felt for her.

Breakfast first, though. He needed to ensure Nina was

fed if they were going to make love all day. Besides, Nina would look sexy as hell walking about the apartment wearing one of his white silk shirts.

As it was, the lack of movement on her side of the king-sized bed told him that she was still sleeping deeply. No doubt she was exhausted after all that nocturnal activity!

Rafe's smile deepened at the thought of waking her, of slowly kissing those luscious lips while caressing that long, lithe body before thrusting deeply, languidly, into the welcoming heat of her sensitive and caressing body until they both gasped out their release.

He rolled over in the bed. 'Nina, I— What the...?'

The other side of the bed was empty, only the indentation in the pillow and the slight warmth of the sheets to show that Nina had been lying there beside him a short time ago.

'Nina?' Rafe called softly as he threw back the bedclothes and got out of bed, padding barefoot and naked out into the hallway as he received no answer from the adjoining bedroom. 'I'm supposed to be the one to make you breakfast,' he teased as he entered the kitchen.

The empty kitchen.

And the rest of the apartment proved to be just as empty as Rafe moved from room to room in search of her.

'Damn it!' he finally muttered angrily as he re-entered the bedroom and realised that Nina's clothes and shoes were no longer on the floor where they had been discarded last night, that there wasn't a single item of her clothing in the bedroom to show that she had ever been there at all.

Because she'd left the bed, the apartment, and Rafe, before he had even woken up.

CHAPTER SEVEN

'WHAT THE HELL did you think you were doing?'

Nina's fingers stilled in arranging her father's jewellery collection in one of the open cabinets as she heard the sound of Rafe's rasping and angry voice behind her. She stood up slowly, her gaze wary as she turned to see that Rafe was indeed angry, if the furious glitter in his eyes and the nerve pulsing in his tensely clenched jaw were any indication.

There wasn't so much as a hint of the passionate and indulgent lover she had spent the night with.

A night of such an intensity of mind-blowing pleasure that it had been an absolute revelation to Nina. It made a complete nonsense of her two previous experiences; she definitely knew what all the fuss was about now!

Rafe had been a tender, fierce and erotic lover, bringing her to climax after climax as he explored and claimed every inch of her body, in the same way that he had allowed, encouraged her, to explore and pleasure every inch of his.

Nina blushed now just remembering the intimacies the two of them had shared during the night. No part of her, not a single inch, left untouched, unsatisfied, by Rafe's caressing hands and mouth, and she was sure she now knew his body more intimately than she knew her own.

'It's okay,' she huskily assured Rich and Andy as she saw they had stepped forward protectively, heads turned towards Rafe as he stood in the doorway of the gallery looking every inch the wealthy and sophisticated Rafe D'Angelo. He was dressed in his custom tailored charcoal suit and pale grey shirt and tie, the darkness of his hair curling silkily onto his shoulders. Much as he had looked the first morning they met. Just three days ago in actual time, but a lifetime away in the changes those same days had made within Nina.

And she wasn't just referring to the physical pleasure she had experienced with him last night.

These last few days with Rafe, and the things he had said to her last night when they argued, had made Nina once again question her own life, and the way in which she lived it.

Heaven knew, she never ever wanted to hurt her father. He had been hurt enough, but some of the things Rafe had said to her last night had settled deep within Nina, breaking open the fragile shell she had placed about her own hopes and dreams for the future, and forcing her to question as to whether or not, after all these years, it really was still necessary for her to live her life under the constant shadow of the past.

Surely there had to be some way of compromising? Some way of reassuring her father as to her safety, while at the same time being able to pursue her own dreams? Of being able to live her life without feeling as if she were in a gilded cage?

'It is not okay,' Rafe snarled as he spared a warning glare for the two burly bodyguards now flanking Nina. 'We're going up to my office to talk,' he rasped as he stood to one side to allow her to precede him out of the gallery.

Nina knew by the glitter in Rafe's eyes, his tight and thinned mouth, tensed jaw, and the angry flare of his nostrils that he was barely holding his temper in check.

A temper Nina hadn't even realised he possessed until this moment, Rafe's usual mood seeming to be one of laid-back charm and private amusement at the world.

Neither did Nina understand the reason for his current mood. The two of them had been out to dinner together yesterday evening, after which they had spent the night together, enjoyed each other to the full—as the pleasurable aches in Nina's body testified!—so what was Rafe's problem this morning?

Surely this was the way the game was played? No strings, no attachments, no expectations, on either side? Rafe's past history with relationships certainly said that was the way he liked to live his own life. And it was the way Nina had decided she would treat their relationship.

'I'm busy, Rafe.'

'Now, Nina!' he bit out harshly, a nerve pulsing in his tightly clenched jaw.

'I don't think you should be talking to Miss Palitov in that tone of voice, Mr D'Angelo.'

'Stay out of this!' Rafe turned fiercely on the bodyguard. Rich or Andy—they were interchangeable as far as he was concerned!

He was just relieved to have something else—someone else—to vent his frustrations on.

Rafe's imagination had run riot once he accepted that Nina had left his apartment without so much as saying goodbye. He wondered if in the clear light of day she was angry or upset about last night, or maybe a combination of the two.

He had become even more frustrated when he realised he didn't even have a personal telephone number on which he could contact her, and he had been in no mood to speak with her father to get to her, either. No doubt the older man would have been informed, and have an opinion, on where his daughter had spent the previous night.

Not that Rafe gave a damn how Dmitri Palitov felt about that. He just wanted to talk to Nina, and he was pretty sure, after the previous warning Dmitri had given him in respect of his daughter, that the older man wouldn't be in the least helpful in that regard.

Showering quickly before dressing and driving over to Nina's apartment hadn't been in the least productive either. The two men manning the reception desk—obviously yet more of the Palitov security—refused to tell Rafe anything other than Miss Palitov was 'currently not at home'.

An ambiguous answer that caused Rafe to question whether or not Nina really wasn't in her apartment, or just not at home to him, in particular?

Annoyed, frustrated, and more than a little concerned as to the reasons Nina had decided to leave so abruptly, and with no way of knowing and no one to answer those concerns, Rafe had driven to Archangel, deciding he would contact Nina again later today. Only to be told when he entered the gallery that Nina was here, as she had been for the past three days, working in the east gallery organising the display of the Palitov jewellery collection.

Rafe had gone straight to the east gallery, where he found Nina down on her hands and knees calmly arranging her father's jewellery collection in one of the display cases—as if last night hadn't happened. As if she hadn't left Rafe's apartment this morning before he had even woken up, as if he hadn't been worried as to why she might have done that! It had turned his churning emotions, his worry and concern, into a burning fury.

A fury that he realised was all the more deeply felt because he had opened up to this woman last night. Let his guard down, confided things in her, in a way he had never done with any other woman.

He was certainly in no mood to deal with her two overprotective, over-muscled security guards. 'We can have this conversation here, Nina, or we can have it upstairs in my office,' he bit out coldly. 'It's your choice.'

Nina wasn't at all reassured by the anger she could see blazing in Rafe's eyes. Although she was still puzzled as to the reason for it; she had thought he would be relieved when he woke up alone in his bed, that it was the way these things were done.

But she did accept that continuing this conversation in front of Rich and Andy wasn't a good idea. The two men looked ready to physically attack the other man, if they deemed it necessary. And that challenging glint in Rafe's eyes said he would welcome a show of the aggression.

'Fine.' Nina removed the thin cotton gloves she had worn for her work. 'You had better stay with the collection,' she instructed Rich and Andy. 'I'll only be a few minutes,' she assured them lightly.

'I wouldn't count on it,' Rafe muttered as she passed him in the doorway.

Nina gave him a frowning glance, her own anger stirring as Rafe continued to look grim as he fell into step beside her. Her anger deepened as he made no effort to explain himself, either outside in the hallway, or as they walked up the stairs to his office.

All of that changed the moment they had crossed through his assistant's office and closed Rafe's office door behind them. Nina suddenly found herself with her back pressed flush against that door, with Rafe towering over her, his hands either side of her head as he glowered down at her.

She frowned her displeasure as she felt imprisoned, both by Rafe's hands placed either side of her and pinning her in place, and his close proximity. A proximity that her traitorous body instantly reacted to by becoming achingly aroused, her nipples tightening into swollen, aching buds beneath her T-shirt, that familiar dampness gushing between her thighs.

'What's this all about, Rafe?' Her voice was sharp with irritation, at her physical response to him rather than Rafe's incomprehensible behaviour.

His eyes narrowed. 'You left.'

'What?'

'Why did you leave this morning, Nina?'

She gave a puzzled shake of her head. 'I don't understand the question.'

'Do I take it from your answer that you're in the habit of sneaking out of a man's apartment, without so much as a goodbye, after spending the night with him?' he grated harshly.

Nina's eyes flashed. 'I didn't sneak.'

'What the hell else would you call it?' Rafe snarled.

'I would call it your still being asleep when I woke up and my needing to get back to my own apartment to shower and change before coming in to work!' she snapped back dismissively.

'Without saying good morning or goodbye?'

She shrugged. 'As I said, you were asleep.'

'And we had just spent an incredible night together. You didn't consider waking me before you left?'

'No.' Her chin rose challengingly as she reminded him, 'You told me Michael would be arriving today.'

'This evening, not this morning,' he rasped impatiently. 'Besides which, I doubt my brother would go into shock at finding a woman in the apartment.'

'Probably not, no,' she drawled, sure that it was an occupational hazard for the three charismatic D'Angelo brothers, if they shared the same apartments around the world.

Not so much for Gabriel, of course, now that he was married, but Nina had no doubts that the brothers were used to stumbling across each other's lovers in the morning. Even the aloofly austere Michael, although no doubt more discreet about his relationships than his two younger brothers, was too charismatically handsome not to have a succession of women in his bed. That very austereness with which he surrounded himself was a challenge to any red-blooded woman.

'I would prefer it if he didn't find me there,' Nina added decisively.

Rafe looked down at Nina searchingly for several long seconds before pushing away from the door to move sharply away from her and stand in front of the window with his back towards the room. He thrust his clenched hands into the pockets of his trousers as he resisted the urge to grasp hold of her shoulders and shake her.

He was more than a little annoyed with himself because he wanted to kiss Nina again, make love to her again, rather than continuing with this less than satisfying conversation.

And it was playing havoc with his self-control that Nina still managed to look so damned fresh and alluring, despite the lack of sleep during the night of pleasure they had just spent together. Low-rise skinny black denims rested low on her hips, below a T-shirt the same green as her eyes. Her fiery red hair was caught up in a ponytail at her nape, her face appearing bare of make-up, and revealing those endearing freckles across the bridge of her nose.

Rafe, on the other hand, now had irritation to add to the blackness of his mood, the worry he had suffered after waking and finding Nina gone obviously completely unnecessary. 'Why did you leave, Nina?' he repeated harshly.

Nina frowned as she looked across the room at the stiffness of Rafe's back, her own anger at his behaviour now still burning low in her stomach. 'Is that what all this is about?' she questioned incredulously. 'Because I dared to leave Rafe D'Angelo's apartment this morning without his say-so?'

He turned abruptly, a dark scowl on his brow. 'You didn't need my permission to leave.'

'No?' Nina challenged, hands on her hips. 'That isn't the impression I'm getting right now!'

Those golden eyes narrowed. 'And what impression are you getting right now?'

She gave a scornful smile. 'That Rafe D'Angelo is usually the one who does the leaving. That it's all right for him to sneak out of a woman's apartment the morning after, but damned infuriating for a woman to dare to do the same thing to him!'

That there was some truth in her accusation didn't help Rafe's current mood of frustrated anger. Going to bed with a woman, spending part of the night with her in her apartment, had never been a problem for him, but he rarely—in fact, never!—stayed the whole night. He always left before he had to go through the awkward-ness of sitting across a breakfast table, trying to make conversation with the woman he had just had sex with.

Nina had been different. Not only was she the first

woman he had ever confided in, but she was also the first woman he had taken back to the family-owned apartment. He had actually been looking forward to making her breakfast, to talking and laughing with her as they shared that breakfast, in bed or out of it. Just as he had been anticipating how sexy she would look dressed only in one of his own shirts, before he carried her back to bed and made love with her again.

That he had never wanted that intimacy with another woman only made Nina's leaving all the more frustrating. Finding her calmly working at Archangel, as if nothing had happened between them last night, certainly hadn't improved his mood. Nevertheless…

'I never take women back to my apartment.'

She blinked. 'You don't?'

'No.'

'And yet you took me there?'

A nerve pulsed in his jaw. 'Yes.'

'Why?'

'At this moment I have absolutely no idea!' he rasped coldly.

'Oh.' Nina eyed him uncertainly.

'Yes,' he bit out succinctly.

She rallied determinedly. 'That's still no reason for you to have behaved like a Neanderthal downstairs!'

'A what?' Rafe prompted incredulously, eyes wide beneath his raised brows.

'A Neanderthal,' she repeated. 'Primitive man. As in "you woman, me man".'

'I know what it is, thank you,' Rafe drawled, some of his anger evaporating, to be replaced by amusement at hearing Nina accuse him of behaving like a caveman.

Which, with hindsight, he could see that he had done, and still was.

Just because Nina had walked out on him this morning? Or something else? Something more?

Nina had certainly got to him in a way no other woman had, but surely that didn't mean—

'Then why bother asking?' Nina snapped impatiently, hands thrust into the back pockets of those tight-fitting denims as she glared across the office at him, thrusting her breasts forward.

And instantly causing Rafe's body to throb and ache with the desire to make love to her all over again.

What was it about this woman, this woman in particular, that he had told her those things about himself last night? That he became aroused just looking at her flashing green eyes, those lushly full lips, the challenging tilt of that stubborn little chin, and those breasts tipped by hard little points visible against her T-shirt? Damned if Rafe knew, he only knew that he did.

He sighed heavily. 'Okay, so I might have come on a little strong downstairs.'

'A little strong?' Nina echoed scathingly as she began to pace the office like a caged tigress. 'You not only embarrassed yourself but you embarrassed me too.' She glared at him. 'Rich and Andy know exactly where I spent the night, an awkwardness I already have to deal with. I certainly didn't need you bursting into the gallery just now behaving like some prehistoric—'

'I think I got that part of the conversation,' Rafe drawled dryly.

'Then I suggest you make a note of it for any future relationships you might have,' she snapped. 'Because women have moved on a long way since we all lived in caves.'

His brows rose. 'I'm perfectly happy with the relationship I have at the moment, thanks very much.' And he wasn't sure he felt altogether comfortable discussing any future relationships with the woman he was currently involved with, either. The woman he had spent such an amazing night with. The woman he wanted to spend many more nights with.

'We don't have a relationship, Rafe,' Nina told him evenly.

'Last night—'

'Was last night,' she insisted firmly. 'And one night does not a relationship make,' she added decisively.

Rafe stilled as he eyed her guardedly. 'Then what does it make?'

Nina shrugged slender shoulders. 'It made for a few very enjoyable hours in bed together.' She deliberately used the past tense, knowing she would never forget those precious hours, at the same time as she accepted she had been just another conquest for Rafe, just another woman to fall for his charm.

But she had known that when she went to bed with him, so no recriminations there. It wasn't Rafe's fault that her emotions had become involved to a degree where Nina wasn't sure if she wasn't already half in love with him.

Rafe didn't care for the past tense in Nina's statement. 'And is that your usual modus operandi? Spend the night with a man and then just walk away?' he persisted, now wondering exactly what Nina had meant the previous evening when she had told him she 'lacked experience'? That inexperience certainly hadn't been apparent last night when the two of them had enjoyed each other so completely.

He'd assumed at the time that Nina had meant that she'd had a couple of previous lovers, but nothing serious; her offhand attitude towards him this morning, to the night the two of them had spent together, seemed to imply otherwise. And he didn't like it; he didn't like it at all.

Nina didn't like the sneer she could hear in Rafe's tone. At the same time she wasn't willing to back down on the stance she had decided to take where he was concerned.

Rafe might give the outward impression of a relaxed and charming playboy, but after their conversation last night Nina now knew there was another man behind that façade. A man of astute business acumen and deep intelligence. And curiosity.

And intelligence and curiosity were things she simply couldn't afford where her father and the past were concerned.

But that didn't stop her from wishing it could have been otherwise.

She had woken a little after six this morning, her body a pleasurable ache as she'd turned to find Rafe sleeping soundly beside her. She hadn't been able to resist lingering, for just a few minutes, in order to study him in the early morning sunlight streaming in through the windows.

His face had appeared almost boyish in his relaxed state, the overlong darkness of his hair a silky curtain about those relaxed patrician features. Long lashes a dark sweep above the sharpness of his cheekbones, chiselled lips curving in a smile even in his sleep.

The sheet had fallen down to his waist, leaving his bronzed and muscled chest bare. His chest was covered in that light dusting of ebony hair that formed a vee down to the flatness of his navel, and lower, to where his shaft already lay aroused against his stomach.

Rafe was, without a doubt, the most beautiful man Nina had ever seen.

And last night he had been all hers, to kiss and touch.

Their lovemaking was beyond anything Nina had ever imagined it could be, their bodies seeming to be totally attuned to pleasuring each other, each kiss, each caress a symphony of that pleasure.

It had been a beautiful night. One that Nina never intended to forget. But, as she had lain beside Rafe, drinking in her fill of him, she had known that it was over. That, for her father's sake, it had to be.

She certainly wasn't about to put her father at risk and become Rafe's 'sometimes' girl. She knew Rafe well enough, his history with women well enough, to know that, despite their closeness last night, he had no intentions of settling down with one woman.

She gave a dismissive smile. 'There's nothing worse than waking up the morning after and turning over and being sorry that the person beside you is there.'

Rafe drew in a hissing breath, his eyes as hard as the gold they resembled. 'And is that what happened to you? Did you wake up this morning and look at me and regret last night had ever happened?'

'Don't be silly, Rafe.' She forced a tinkling, dismissive laugh, knowing she would never, could never, regret waking up beside Rafe this morning. But if he wanted to think that was what she had done, then perhaps she should just leave him under that misapprehension.

'The two of us have a business relationship, and I think it's more important we continue to maintain that than pursuing any fleeting pleasure we might find in going to bed together for a few days or weeks.'

'A business relationship,' he echoed softly.

She nodded. 'There's my father's exhibition, and you asked me to consider designing some display cabinets for the Archangel galleries,' she reminded him.

'An offer I seem to remember you refused.'

Nina avoided meeting his piercing gaze. 'And which I'm now reconsidering. Unless you've changed your mind?'

'I haven't, no. But I'm curious as to why you've changed yours,' he prompted shrewdly.

It was a good question. And the simple answer to that lay in the decision she had made during the night regarding her future. No matter how much her father might fight against it, it really was time, past time, for her to start to break free of the confines that had been put on her life. Rafe's barbs had shown her she needed to start to make a life of her own.

And the best way Nina could think of to start doing that was to make that career for herself. Without the help of her father. And certainly without continuing to sleep with the man responsible for offering her the commission that would be the stepping stone to her starting that career.

The Archangel galleries, in New York, Paris and London, were the most prestigious privately owned galleries in the world, and having her work on show there, by designing display cases for each of the three galleries, would bring her work to the attention of collectors and other galleries.

'Why not, when it seems I already have my first commission?' she came back dismissively.

Rafe couldn't say he didn't feel a certain satisfaction in hearing Nina say she had finally decided to break away from her father, to do something she wanted to do. He just questioned the reasons as to why she was choosing to do it now.

He was also far from pleased at the way Nina so easily dismissed the idea of there being any future relationship between the two of them.

'If you feel it could be a problem for us after last night,' she continued lightly, 'then I can always discuss my ideas with Michael when I see him tomorrow evening.'

Rafe tensed as he felt a sharp pang of— Of what? Jealousy? He had never been jealous over a woman in his life!

His emotions had never been engaged enough in the past with any of the women he had been involved with to ever feel anything so basic as jealousy because of them.

Another way in which his feelings towards Nina were different from anything he had felt before?

His mouth thinned at the suggestion. He liked Nina, had very much enjoyed making love with her last night, but that was all he felt for her. He certainly wasn't jealous of her suggestion she spend time with Michael tomorrow night. 'It was my idea, my project, which means that Michael will also insist you deal directly with me, and not him.'

Nina's eyes widened at the harshness of Rafe's tone. She was unsure as to the reason for it. Any woman, unaware of Rafe's aversion to emotional entanglement, might have thought that he was expressing jealousy at her suggestion of talking with his haughty but equally handsome older brother. Because Rafe D'Angelo didn't do emotions like jealousy; why should he, when he could have any woman he wanted just by crooking his little finger at them?

No, Rafe was obviously still annoyed with her for having left his apartment this morning without saying goodbye. As annoyed, it seemed, as Nina was relieved that she'd found the strength to do so.

It would have been so much easier not to leave, to wake Rafe instead, to spend the morning in bed with him, making love with him. But she felt far too much for him already to allow herself to become any more deeply involved with him; she also knew she was just asking for her heart to be broken if she continued to be intimate with him.

If it wasn't already too late.

She had never met anyone like Rafe before. A man who had everything, it seemed. A successful business-man. Confident and wealthy and so handsome he made her heart beat faster just to look at him. So charming it took every effort of will on her part to resist giving him whatever he asked of her. So indulgent and experienced a lover that Nina had lost count of the amount of times she had climaxed in his arms last night.

Just so everything that Nina was afraid she might al-ready, stupidly, have fallen in love with him.

'Fine,' she accepted abruptly. 'Was that all? It's the gala opening tomorrow night, and I really need to get back to the gallery now and finish placing the jewellery in the cabinets.'

Rafe barely managed to bite back his irritation, his frustration, with this conversation. With Nina. With the fact that she had somehow managed to answer, and yet at the same time not answer, a single one of the ques-tions he had asked her.

Why had she left so abruptly this morning? Was that how she usually reacted after spending the night with a man? If she had been the one to wake up beside him this morning and regretted spending the night with him? And lastly, why had she chosen today, of all days, to decide to begin to break away from her father, to pursue her own career, by accepting Rafe's commission to design the display cabinets for the three Archangel galleries?

All of her answers to those questions had been either outright avoidance or glibness. Two behaviours Rafe had never before associated with Nina.

Two behaviours he found damned irritating, if he was honest with himself. Because they stopped him from reaching Nina. They erected a barrier between the two of them, and one that she seemed determined to keep firmly in place.

He sighed his frustration with the situation. 'Is there going to be any fall-out for you, with your father, because you stayed at my apartment last night?' he prompted impatiently.

Nina hadn't seen her father yet today, but she had no doubt he would know by now that she had spent the previous night at Rafe D'Angelo's apartment. Just as she had no doubts he would mention it to her when she saw him later this evening.

And Nina had absolutely no idea what he was going to say to her on the subject.

She was close enough to her father that she usually knew how he would react in any given situation, but her having stayed the night at Rafe's apartment was so unusual that Nina really had no idea what her father's opinion on that was going to be. No doubt she would find out later this evening.

'It's a little late to think about that, isn't it, Rafe?' she said dryly.

He shrugged. 'I'll talk to him if that would make it easier for you.'

Nina eyed him scathingly. 'And say what, exactly?'

'That it's none of his damned business where you spent the night.'

'No, thanks, I think I can handle it.' She chuckled wryly, recalling the phone conversation she'd had with her father the first time he realised she had been with a man. It had been embarrassing for them both, but that was all it had been; much as he wanted to protect her, to keep her safe, her father also wanted her to enjoy what other twenty-something women enjoyed. As long as it was in the circle of his protection.

'This isn't the first time it's happened, hmm?' Rafe rasped knowingly.

'Now you're being deliberately insulting again.' A frown creased Nina's brow as she looked across at him reprovingly.

'Am I?' He crossed the room in restless strides before sitting down in the chair behind his desk. 'Maybe that's because I'm finding the whole of our present conversation insulting. We spent an enjoyable evening together—apart from when I made you cry,' he acknowledged tightly. 'But we got over that, and spent an even better night together. And yet this morning you're telling me that you don't want to go out with me again, because you want to concentrate on your career.'

'I don't recall your having asked me to go out with you again,' Nina replied. 'But you're quite right in assuming my answer would have been no if you had,' she continued firmly as he would have spoken. 'We did have a lovely evening, and a fantastic night, and now it's time to get back to the real world.'

'And your real world doesn't have a place in it for me.' It was a statement rather than a question.

The only place Nina wanted Rafe in her life was one she could never have, nor was it one he was interested in her occupying. Despite the other side of Rafe she had discovered last night as they talked together, he had never pretended to be anything other than what he was: a thirty-four-year-old very eligible and handsome bachelor, who enjoyed women—lots of them.

Unfortunately Nina knew she wasn't made that way, which was why it was better, for both of them, if this

ended now. And not just because of her father. She had
to end this now, before she lost her pride, as well as her
heart, to the point she was completely broken when Rafe
ended their affair in a few weeks' time. As he surely
would.

She raised her chin determinedly. 'Not at this point
in time, no.'

He raised dark brows. 'And do you ever see a time
when that might change?'

'No.'

'Fine,' Rafe rasped harshly. He wasn't about to beg,
like a starving man asking for the scraps from Nina's
table. If one night was all Nina wanted from him, then
one night was all they would have.

All they'd had.

Because Nina had left him in no doubts that she considered the two of them to already be in the past tense.

CHAPTER EIGHT

'NOT GOING OUT this evening?'

Rafe turned to scowl at his older brother as Michael looked up at him from reading through the paperwork he had brought with him from Paris. He'd been working on it since he'd arrived at the apartment an hour or so ago.

'The clothes gave it away, huh?' Rafe scoffed. The faded denims and black T-shirt Rafe had changed into when he got back to the apartment that evening weren't something he would ever have worn to go out in on a Friday night.

'Somewhat,' Michael drawled. 'Rafe, will you stop pacing, damn it, and tell me what's wrong?' he added impatiently as Rafe continued to prowl restlessly around the sitting room.

Because Rafe felt too unsettled to join his brother by sitting down in one of the armchairs. As he had been too unsettled all day to be able to tackle any of the work piling up on his desk. How could he possibly concentrate on work when he knew that Nina was down in the east gallery, calmly arranging her father's jewellery collection in the display cabinets she had designed? And probably without so much as giving Rafe a second thought.

He had to admit, it was a little unusual for the woman to be the one to walk away from him. Unique, in fact.

And frustrating as hell, when Rafe was nowhere near to being ready to let Nina go.

She had been so damned cool this morning. So distant and in control as she'd told him their relationship—such as it was—was over.

Was that how he had appeared to all those women he had said goodbye to over the years? So cool and uninvolved emotionally as he told them he didn't want to see them again?

And had those women hated his guts in the same churning, furious, frustrated way that Rafe now—?

Now what?

Hated Nina?

Of course he didn't hate Nina. How could he possibly hate her when he still wanted her so damned much?

He was angry and frustrated, that was all, at having Nina end their relationship so abruptly. But it was his ego that had taken the knock, nothing else. And for no other reason than this had never happened to Rafe before, and he hadn't been ready to let Nina go, he assured himself.

'Rafe?'

He glanced across at Michael, knowing by his brother's perplexed frown that he really was concerned by his uncharacteristic distraction. 'It's nothing,' he dismissed impatiently. 'Do you want to order something in for dinner?' He moved to the desk to take out the menus for the restaurants he usually ordered food from the rare evenings he spent at home. The brothers' comings and goings were far too erratic for them to have ever considered taking on a full-time housekeeper.

Rafe wondered what Nina was doing for dinner this evening. No doubt she'd had some explaining to do to her father this evening. An explanation Rafe had half been expecting all day to have to make to Dmitri Palitov himself.

And Rafe readily admitted he had felt disappointed when the expected phone call from Dmitri, demanding an explanation from him, hadn't come. He had been spoiling for a fight with someone all day, and he would very much have enjoyed telling the older man to stay out of his own and Nina's business—endangering the exhibition of the unique Palitov jewellery collection, be damned!—as well as exactly what he thought of the older man for screwing up Nina's life.

Only to be left with a feeling of disappointment when he hadn't seen or heard from either member of the Palitov family all day.

'Rafe, what in the hell is wrong with you this evening?' Michael demanded impatiently.

'What?' Once again Rafe scowled his irritation as he turned back to his brother.

Michael put the paperwork aside. 'You've been holding those menus in your hands for the past five minutes, not looking at them, and not saying a damned word, just staring off into space.'

Yes, he had, Rafe realised self-disgustedly. 'So?' he challenged as he handed the menus to his brother.

'So it's the sort of taciturn behaviour I'd grown to expect from Gabriel pre-Bryn, but not from you.'

Rafe's mouth thinned. 'What does that even mean?'

'It means you've been mooning about all evening.'

'I do not "moon about",' Rafe rasped scathingly. 'I'm just a little distracted, that's all.'

Michael's gaze sharpened. 'Are you having problems with the Palitov family?'

Rafe stiffened defensively, wondering how Michael

could possibly have known? Michael didn't know; he had to be referring to Dmitri Palitov rather than Nina Palitov.

'Not that I'm aware of, no,' he answered carefully; no doubt Dmitri Palitov would have something to say to him when the two men next met, but at this moment Dmitri hadn't told him how he felt in regard to the night Rafe had spent with his daughter.

Pure semantics, Rafe knew, because he could easily guess how the older man felt about it; he just didn't know for certain.

Michael nodded acceptance of his answer. 'Did you talk to the daughter?'

Rafe's tension increased. 'About what?'

'About your idea of commissioning the display cabinets for all the Archangel galleries from her, of course,' Michael answered impatiently. 'For God's sake, get a grip, Rafe. It was your recommendation that we ask her!'

Yes, it was, and it was a recommendation Rafe now had reason to regret. It very much looked as if Nina was going to accept the commission, and how the hell was he supposed to work on the design of those display cabinets with Nina when he only had to look at her to want her?

'She's on board with the idea.' He nodded. 'She said she would talk to you about it at the gala exhibition tomorrow night.' He bleakly recalled his own less than happy response to that suggestion.

A response that continued to fester and grow after Nina told him she didn't want to continue seeing him.

'Me?' Michael echoed blankly.

'Yes—you,' Rafe confirmed with hard derision. 'Obviously Miss Palitov considers, as you're the senior D'Angelo brother, that you're the one she should be talking to about this rather than your disreputable younger brother!'

'She doesn't realise that I'm the businessman in the family, Gabe's the artistic one, and you're the new ideas man for all the D'Angelo galleries?'

Rafe's mouth twisted. 'Does anybody?'

'And whose fault is that?' Michael frowned.

'Mine,' Rafe sighed. 'And it's never really bothered me before.'

'But it does now?'

It did, yes. Because for the first time in his life Rafe wanted someone, Nina, to see him not for who he was perceived to be but who he really was—the 'ideas man' of the D'Angelo family, as Michael had just called him.

Just earlier this evening the two brothers had discussed another new project of Rafe's that he had been thinking about the past few days, one in which they took Gabriel's original idea of a competition for new artists and broadened the spectrum to include all new artistic talent, from sculpture to the design of jewellery, giving over a room each month in the three galleries for displaying that talent.

The two previous competitions in the Paris and London galleries had been a great success, and a third was due to take place here in New York later in the year. Based on these successes, Rafe couldn't see any reason not to expand the idea.

It would mean a lot of hard work for each of the brothers, but Rafe believed the rewards, of discovering and exhibiting new artistic talent, would ultimately be well worth it. Instead of just selling or exhibiting great art, they would be discovering it.

Michael was already enthusiastic about the idea, and the two of them would discuss it with Gabriel once he was back from his honeymoon.

'Maybe,' Rafe conceded hardly.

'Becoming a little tired of the playboy label?'

'I believe I am, yes.' Especially so if it meant that was all Nina saw him as being!

'It's about time!'

'It is?' Rafe came back dryly.

His brother nodded. 'It was okay in your mid and late twenties, but it's good to see that it isn't enough for you now. You're a brilliant ideas man, Rafe, have always read the market perfectly, known in exactly which new direction we should take Archangel. I'd like other people to appreciate that as much as Gabe and I do. And I'll talk to Miss Palitov tomorrow evening, by all means.' Michael shrugged. 'But only to tell her that you're in charge of the project. As you're in charge of all new projects at Archangel.'

Oh, yes, Nina was going to learn that Rafe was very much 'in charge' when it came to anything to do with her, and anyone else, working within the realms of the Archangel galleries.

It might be sheer torture for Rafe to work with Nina, desiring her as he still did, but there was absolutely no way he was going to let her bypass him in favour of working with Michael.

Nina might not like it, but, as far as Rafe was concerned, if she was serious about wanting to design the new display cabinets for the three galleries, then she was stuck with him for the duration.

He looked across at his brother now. 'Ni— Someone made a comment to me a couple of days ago, implying that maybe the reason you've always had to be the serious one is because you had two mischievous younger brothers.'

Michael arched a dark brow. '"Someone"?'

'Someone,' Rafe insisted. 'Is it true?'

Michael gave the idea some thought. 'Maybe,' he finally conceded. 'As the eldest I always felt I had to be more responsible than you and Gabe.'

'Not much fun for you, though?'

'Has being the middle brother, feeling as if you have something to prove all the time, or constantly being the joker in order to grab your share of the attention, been any more fun?'

Rafe grimaced. 'Not really.'

Michael looked at him searchingly. 'You really are tired of that role, aren't you?'

Yes, he really was, and if he wasn't careful Michael was very soon going to ask why it was he suddenly felt that way. 'Let's order dinner, hmm?' he encouraged lightly, determined to change the subject and not to think about Nina, or anything she had said, again tonight.

Tomorrow night at the gala opening of her father's jewellery collection would be soon enough for that.

'If you have something to say, Papa, then I really wish you would just say it!' Nina frowned across at her father as the two of them travelled in the back of the limousine together on their way to the gala opening at the Archangel gallery on Saturday evening. The New York traffic was as dense and noisy as usual, the early evening sun shining into the smoked glass windows of the car through the gaps in the surrounding skyscrapers.

'About what, *maya doch*?' Her father returned her gaze steadily, his expression unreadable.

Nina gave a shake of her head. 'Don't be coy, Papa.'

He raised grey brows. 'In what way am I being coy?'

She sighed. 'You haven't said anything, but let's neither of us pretend you don't know about my having spent Thursday night at Rafe D'Angelo's apartment.'

It was a statement rather than a question. After all, she had been waiting thirty-six excruciating hours for her father to so much as mention the subject of her having spent the night with Rafe.

Her father shrugged. 'That is your affair, no?'

Her eyes widened. 'The other evening you warned him to stay away from me,' she reminded.

'Ah, he told you about that.' Her father nodded ruefully.

'Oh, yes,' she recalled with feeling.

'He was not pleased by my warning.' Her father nodded. 'As I fully expected he would not be.'

'And you knew I wouldn't like it either, so why do it?' Nina frowned.

'To see how Rafe would respond, of course,' he answered with satisfaction.

She stared at her father incredulously. 'You were testing him?'

'I was attempting to see what manner of man he is, yes,' her father acknowledged unapologetically.

'And?'

Dmitri gave a half-smile. 'And by inviting you out to dinner, spending the night with you, despite that warning, he has obviously shown himself to be a man who is not cowed, by me, or the Palitov name.'

Knowing Rafe, as she now did, Nina knew he was a man who wouldn't be cowed by much at all, least of all her father or the Palitov name.

And, much as she loved her father and didn't want to hurt him, she knew it was time for her to do the same.

She drew in a determined breath. 'Rafe approves of the display cabinets I designed for your collection, so much so he's asked me if I would design more for all the Archangel galleries,' she revealed huskily.

Unreadable emotion flickered in her father's eyes before it was quickly masked. 'And you wish to do this?'

Nina sat back as she met those guarded eyes a paler green than her own. 'I do, yes.'

'You now like him.' It was a statement rather than a question.

'Enough to spend the night with him, at least!'

'Perhaps we should discuss this further once we have returned home later this evening?' her father suggested as the limousine pulled up at the back of the Archangel gallery.

Her father had expressed a wish to be lifted from the car and into his wheelchair there, rather than in the full glare of the photographers crowded about the front steps of the gallery, eagerly snapping photographs for tomorrow's newspapers of the glittering array of personalities invited to attend this private showing of the Palitov jewellery collection.

'There is much I still need to tell you. About the past, *maya doch*,' he continued huskily. 'But this is not the place or time in which to do it.'

Nina gave her father a searching glance, noting the pained expression in his pale green eyes, the lines of tension beside his nose and mouth, the pallor of his hollowed cheeks. 'Are you quite well, Papa?' She placed a hand on his arm, feeling the way it trembled slightly beneath her fingertips. 'If you're unwell we don't have to attend the gala.'

'I am as well as I can ever expect to be in regard to my health, daughter,' he assured gruffly. 'My heart and mind are another matter, however. Not now, Nina.' He placed his hand over hers and squeezed lightly as he saw her anxious expression. 'We will attend and enjoy the gala together, as planned, and talk of these things

again later tonight. I only hope you will be able to forgive me—' He broke off, his expression anguished as he
looked across at her.

'Forgive you for what, Papa?' she prompted, fearing
his anxiety had something to do with the fate of the three
kidnappers.

'We will talk later,' he repeated determinedly.

She would have to be satisfied with that answer, for
the moment.

Except she wasn't.

There had been something in her father's eyes just
now, a darkness that spoke of pain, a deep-rooted pain
he had never revealed to her before. But not of a physical kind, as he had assured her it wasn't, but one that bit
deep into his heart and mind.

Not that Nina had any more time to think about that
right now, when she had the ordeal of the gala exhibition
at Archangel, and seeing Rafe again, to get through…

'I don't recall her being quite so beautiful.'

Rafe was only half listening to Michael, far too busy
studying Nina as she arrived with her father. He was
too busy looking for any signs in her expression that she
found this evening as much of a strain as he did to give
his brother his full attention.

Her eyes were that clear unshadowed green, her skin
glowing with health and vitality, and she smiled brightly
as her father introduced her to the two men who had just
joined them, all of the guests having been waiting in anticipation for the arrival of the reclusive Dmitri Palitov.

Rather than strained Nina looked sensational. Absolutely, breathtakingly, sensational.

She had left her hair loose again tonight, a moving
river of flame as it fell silkily over her shoulders be-

fore cascading down the length of her spine to her waist. Her emerald-green eyes dominated the creaminess of her face, and there was a deep rose gloss on those temptingly pouting lips. Her gown was a gold shimmer that clung lovingly to her curves, leaving her arms bare, and finishing several inches above her knees to reveal those long and shapely legs, her four-inch-heeled shoes the same rich gold colour as her gown.

And Rafe hadn't been able to take his eyes off her since the moment she had appeared in the doorway of the gallery beside her father's wheelchair, his eyes narrowing now as she laughed huskily at something said to her by one of the two men her father had introduced her to.

'Rafe, are you listening to me? Rafe!'

'What is your problem now, Michael?' He turned on his brother fiercely, his hands clenched into fists at his sides.

Michael raised calm dark brows at that show of aggression. 'I merely remarked on the fact that I don't remember Nina Palitov being quite so young or so beautiful. A remark which you obviously didn't hear. Or just didn't want to comment on,' he added shrewdly.

Rafe's scowl deepened. 'If you recall, I did mention the little fact of her beauty in my telephone call to you after I'd met Nina for the first time, after I had discovered she wasn't the middle-aged spinster you'd allowed me to expect!'

Michael grimaced. 'I didn't "allow" anything. I just wasn't taking a lot of notice of how the daughter looked when I last met Dmitri Palitov. But I'd have to be dead not to have noticed now.'

Rafe's eyes narrowed. 'What's that supposed to mean?'

His brother's gaze was still on the beautiful Nina as she stood beside Dmitri Palitov, so he didn't see the displeasure on Rafe's face. 'We should go over and greet our guest of honour,' he added distractedly.

Rafe placed a warning hand on his brother's arm. 'Keep your restrained but lethal charm to yourself around Nina!' he warned harshly.

Michael turned back to look at him, narrowed gaze raking slowly over Rafe's face. 'What the hell?' he finally muttered softly. 'Rafe, please tell me you didn't— Oh, hell, you did.' He grimaced as Rafe quirked one dark, pointed brow. 'I asked you to keep Dmitri Palitov sweet and you slept with his daughter!'

'Keep your damned voice down.' Rafe glared at him.

Michael continued to scowl at him. 'Is Nina Palitov the reason for your distraction yesterday evening? The reason you've been walking around growling at everyone at the gallery today? More to the point...' his brow slowly cleared '...is she the reason you've suddenly tired of the playboy image and decided it has to go?' he probed shrewdly.

'Mind your own damned—'

'It is my business, Rafe,' his brother cut in coldly. 'Anything that affects Archangel is my business. And Gabriel's too.'

'This has nothing to do with Archangel.'

'And what is "this", precisely?' Michael bit out softly. 'What does Nina Palitov mean to you?'

'None of your damned business.'

Michael gave an impatient sigh. 'Does Palitov know about the two of you?'

'There's nothing to know.'

'Does he know?' Michael grated harshly.

Rafe's jaw clenched. 'Yes. But it's already over between the two of us.'

'Why?' Michael's brows rose.

'Shouldn't you just be pleased that it is rather than asking why it is?'

'Not if it's not what you want, no.'

Rafe's brow cleared. 'You know, Michael, you really do live behind a mask as much as I do.'

'Meaning?'

'Meaning that you hide your emotions behind that mask. Meaning that maybe our little brother getting married has got to you.'

'As it's got to you?'

Nina was what had 'got to' Rafe. Just Nina. And he still had no idea what he was going to do about it. About her.

'Do you think he's just lulling you into a false sense of security by showing up here this evening?' Michael was staring across at Dmitri Palitov. 'And that maybe he intends to set some of his bodyguards on you in a dark alley one night?'

'I don't know how I've survived all these years without a daily dose of your sunny disposition.' Some of Rafe's own normal good humour returned. 'Let's go and say hello to them—and perhaps later you could let me know if you still think he intends having me discreetly eliminated.' He didn't wait to see what else his brother had to say on the subject as he made his way through the crowded gallery to where Nina stood beside Dmitri's wheelchair as Dmitri now chatted with several business acquaintances.

Nina found it slightly intimidating to have not one, but two, of the formidably handsome D'Angelo brothers bearing down on her. Or, to be strictly accurate, one of them was bearing down on her in that intimidating way; Michael D'Angelo's attention was obviously more focused on her father.

But the D'Angelo brothers were without doubt the two most arrestingly handsome men here this evening, their perfectly tailored black evenings suits and snowy white shirts emphasising the width of their muscled shoulders and the lean strength of perfectly toned bodies. Rafe's hair was a silky ebony curtain onto his shoulders, Michael's hair as dark but styled much shorter, and revealing stark and arresting features dominated by obsidian-black eyes.

And she was deliberately delaying looking at Rafe by keeping her gaze fixed firmly on his austerely handsome older brother.

She knew she had good cause for that delay when she finally turned the coolness of her gaze on Rafe and saw the angry glitter in those predatory gold eyes, and a nerve pulsing in his tensely clenched jaw.

Predatory golden eyes that held Nina's gaze captive as she distractedly acknowledged Michael D'Angelo's formally polite greeting before he turned to shake her father's hand with warmer familiarity. Rafe remained noticeably silent as he continued to look down at her with that piercing coldness.

What on earth was wrong with him? Admittedly the two of them had parted badly yesterday morning in his office, and they hadn't spoken a single word to each other since, but did Rafe have to make the tension that now existed between the two of them so obvious to other people? To her father? To his brother?

His next actions would seem to confirm that he did.

'If you will excuse us, gentleman, I just need to steal Nina from you for a few minutes,' Rafe rasped determinedly, not waiting for either man to respond as he reached out and circled one of Nina's wrists with steely fingers before he turned and walked in the direction of the gallery doorway.

Nina stumbled along beside him as she found it difficult to keep her balance in her four-inch-heeled shoes.

'You're making a scene again, Rafe!' she hissed as she saw the curious glances being sent their way.

His eyes glittered dangerously as he spared her the briefest of glances. 'Maybe you would rather I caused even more of a scene by pushing you up against the wall right here and taking you in front of everyone?'

'Rafe!' Nina wasn't sure whether her breathless gasping of his name was in shocked outrage or aching longing for him to do just that.

She had a sinking feeling it was the latter.

CHAPTER NINE

THE NEED TO kiss Nina again, to touch her and to make love to her again had been like a burning ache inside Rafe for the past thirty-six hours. He'd been kept in a state of arousal for almost all of that time too, until something had snapped inside him just now, just from looking at the way that clinging, glittering gold gown clung so lovingly to every curve of her delicious body, with her hair tumbling like a living flame over her shoulders and down the length of her spine. As for those lushly pouting lips…

'Don't even think about it,' he tensely instructed the two Palitov bodyguards on duty just outside the gallery as they stepped forward at first sight of Nina.

'It's okay, Andy,' Nina added ruefully as the larger of the two burly men turned to her enquiringly. 'Stay with my father. Mr D'Angelo and I are going for a little walk,' she added lightly as Rafe continued to pull her down the hallway.

Walk, be damned. Rafe needed to taste Nina again, to touch her again so badly, that he opened the first door he came to once they had turned the corner into another hallway, uncaring that it appeared to be some sort of small service cupboard containing brooms and buckets. He pushed her unceremoniously inside before following her in and shutting the door behind them, immediately throwing them into complete darkness.

'Rafe!'

'I need to kiss you, Nina!' he groaned as he lowered his head and fiercely captured her mouth unerringly with his, moaning his satisfaction at the first delicious taste of her.

All of Nina's annoyance at Rafe's high-handed behaviour in having dragged her from the gallery—very much in the manner of that Neanderthal she had accused him of being yesterday morning!—evaporated as if it had never been at the first touch of Rafe's mouth against hers. Her own desire for him was instantaneous, combustible.

Her lips parted beneath his, and she let her clutch bag slide to the floor before moving her arms up and over his shoulders to allow her fingers to become entangled in the darkness of Rafe's hair. She pressed the length of her body against his and returned the hunger of that kiss, her breasts swelling, nipples pebbling, between her thighs heating, as Rafe's hands roamed restlessly along the length of her spine before cupping her bottom and pulling her heat in tight against the hardness of his arousal.

He wrenched his mouth from hers, his hand fisting in her hair as he pulled back slightly, arching her neck to allow his lips and tongue to seek out the silky hollows and dips of her throat. 'Your father isn't going to be happy about this.' he acknowledged unconcernedly, his breath hot as his tongue rasped moistly against her skin, tasting her, drinking her in.

Nina gave a soft, breathless laugh. 'I'm not sure my father has any place here.'

'Hell, I hope not,' he muttered distractedly, his body throbbing with heat as he pressed into her more intimately still, moving his hips in a slow arousing rhythm, pressed up between the dampness of her thighs, even as one of his hands slipped beneath the hem of her gown to caress the length of her thigh. 'I need to feel your heat against my fingers, Nina.' He groaned as his fingers lingered at the lacy edge of her panties.

'Rafe!' Heat suffused the whole of her body in anticipation of her own need for the pleasure promised by those questing fingers.

'Are you wearing panties beneath this gown?'

'Yes,' Nina answered uncertainly.

'Minuscule ones, I'm guessing?'

'Very,' she confirmed dryly.

Rafe breathed deeply. 'And I just want to rip them off you, stroke and caress you and feel you as you climax! Then I want to lick my fingers and taste—'

'Rafe, please...' Nina groaned helplessly, unsure if she was pleading for him to stop or continue as just his words caused a gush of that hot moisture between her thighs.

'Oh, I want to please you, Nina,' he assured gruffly. 'I want that more than I want my next breath.'

Nina wanted it too. It didn't matter that they were squashed into what had looked like a cleaning storeroom before the door had closed and plunged them both into darkness. Nor was it important that just metres away from this small room there were two hundred people attending the jewellery exhibition, including her own father, all of whom had seen Rafe drag her out of the gallery just minutes ago.

All that mattered at this moment was being with Rafe, making love with Rafe, having Rafe kiss and caress her.

'Do it, Rafe,' she encouraged achingly, needily. 'Just do it!'

The words had barely left her lips when she heard the

delicate sound of lace and silk ripping as Rafe caught the side of her panties and pulled, a rustle of movement telling her that he had disposed of the ripped panties.

'You're so beautiful here,' Rafe murmured gruffly as he parted and then stroked the silky bareness of the flesh between her thighs, his face buried against her perfumed throat. 'So, so beautiful,' he groaned.

He began a gentle, teasing stroking, able to feel the way those swollen folds parted greedily with each measured caress. Nina's clitoris pulsing, swelling, as he pressed harder, caressed faster, before thrusting one, and then two fingers inside the heat of her, his fingers curling as he found that sensitive spot inside her. His thumb continued that sweet caress as she began to buck into those thrusts. Rafe's other arm tightened about Nina's waist as he felt those inner contractions deepen, lengthen, as her legs began to tremble and threatened to buckle beneath her.

'Yes, Nina,' Rafe encouraged hoarsely as he felt her climax hit with the force of a tsunami. 'I want it all, damn it. Give me every last measure of your pleasure,' he pressured fiercely.

Nina cried out as that pleasure ripped through her body in ever-increasing waves, her nipples hard and aching pebbles, her core tightening, grasping greedily at those thrusting fingers as they filled her time and time again. She felt completely boneless, incapable of standing, by the time the last wave of her climax had rippled through her. She would have collapsed down onto the floor if Rafe hadn't continued to hold her up with his arm about her waist.

Nina groaned, another wave of pleasure rippling through her as Rafe slowly eased his fingers out from the heat of her.

'Mmm, delicious,' he murmured appreciatively seconds later.

'What?'

'You taste like honey, Nina.'

'God...!' She rested the dampness of her forehead against the shoulder of his jacket, her cheeks burning at the thought of the intimacy of having Rafe licking his fingers, of his tasting her.

'The name's Rafe,' he came back with teasing softness as both his arms moved about her now.

'Egotist!' She gave his other shoulder a half-hearted punch. She simply didn't have the strength left to do any more than that. Her body was one big pleasurable ache. 'No doubt you're feeling almighty and powerful now.'

He chuckled huskily. 'No doubt.'

'You could try a little harder for modesty, Rafe,' she admonished ruefully.

'Not while I'm holding my very satisfied woman in my arms, I couldn't,' he drawled lightly.

His satisfied woman?

What did that even mean? Rafe had made it obvious that relationships weren't for him, that fun was his only aim, and that when the fun was over it was time to say goodbye.

Nina's life was too complicated to ever be thought of as fun.

She knew she should be feeling indignant at this further display of Rafe's arrogance, knew that she should pull out of his arms and tell him that this changed nothing between them. That she was determined to keep to her decision not to become any more involved with him. That she would never be any man's woman.

Except she couldn't do it. She didn't have the strength

right now to stand up unaided, let alone walk away from Rafe for a second time in as many days.

Later, she told herself. She would make him understand later.

'Come to my apartment tonight,' Rafe instructed gruffly—seeming to have picked up on some of her thoughts, at least. 'This should all be over by eleven o'clock. Spend the night with me, Nina, please,' he urged.

'What about Michael?' she questioned huskily.

'Michael can get his own woman.'

'I meant—'

'I know what you meant, darling Nina,' Rafe drawled indulgently. 'And the apartment is big enough that he doesn't even have to know you're there.'

Could she do that? Was it possible? Could she take, steal, another night in Rafe's arms, in his bed?

How could she refuse when he had given her such pleasure just now and taken nothing for himself? Her past experiences might not have been good ones, but she had never been a selfish lover.

'Because you want to, Nina, not because you feel obligated to give something back to me because of what happened just now.' This time Rafe seemed to pick up on all of her thoughts.

At the same time as he had managed to strip away all of the arguments Nina had been giving in order to justify to herself going to his apartment later tonight.

She moistened her lips before speaking. 'I think the more immediate problem is how are we going to walk out of this closet and go back into the gallery, having left together so abruptly a few minutes ago, without everyone knowing exactly what we've been doing?'

Rafe gave another chuckle. 'There's little chance of that happening. I happen to know exactly what you look like after pleasure, Nina, and believe me the hot, sultry glitter in your eyes, the blush in your cheeks, and those roused and puffy lips are a dead giveaway as to exactly what we've been doing.'

'Oh, very attractive,' she muttered. 'You make me sound like a wild woman.'

'No, just my woman.' His arms tightened about her. 'And I like you wild. I like it a lot.'

Nina liked the way Rafe made her feel wild too. A lot. Too much so to have the strength to deny herself just one more night in his arms.

'Even so, I think you should return to the gallery on your own now, and then I'll come back in a few minutes, when I've had a chance to tidy my appearance.'

'That's not going to change the fact that I will be aware for the rest of the evening that your ripped panties are sitting in my jacket pocket.'

Her cheeks felt warm at the knowledge that she was now completely naked beneath her gown, a gown that moved silkily, sensuously against the heat of her skin, and that it would also ensure she was aware of that fact for the rest of the evening.

'Okay, I'll come to your apartment later— Damn, I forgot! I have to go home with my father first,' she realised with a wince. 'We started a conversation on the way over here which we have to finish tonight,' she explained ruefully.

'Anything serious?' Rafe murmured softly, not completely happy with Nina's answer, but willing to settle for what he could get for the moment. He had seduced her once, he would do it again, and again, if necessary.

'I'm not sure,' Nina acknowledged slowly.

He frowned. 'Does it have anything to do with your

staying with me on Thursday night? Because if it does maybe I should—'

'No,' she assured him firmly. 'This is just something my father needs to discuss with me. But hopefully it won't take too long,' she assured lightly, 'and I can be with you before midnight.'

Rafe nuzzled his lips against the warmth of her throat. 'I'll see what I can do about persuading Michael into going straight to bed when we get home. Maybe remind him of his jet lag along with his advancing years.'

'He's only a year older than you are!'

'Only in calendar months. Still he wasn't particularly happy with me before I dragged you off into my cave,' Rafe mused ruefully.

'Why?' Nina prompted slowly.

'Because I told him about us.' He shrugged. 'Because he has the idea that your father might arrange to have me disposed of in a dark alley one night.'

Nina moved back slightly in his arms. 'My father isn't some sort of gangster, Rafe.'

He chuckled as his arms tightened about her. 'I never said he was.'

'But you and Michael think of him as being one?'

'Hey.' Rafe sobered as he heard the strain in Nina's voice. 'It was just Michael's idea of a joke, Nina.'

'If you thought that about him, I'm surprised either of you wanted to risk sullying the name of Archangel by displaying my father's jewellery collection,' she came back sharply. 'After all, he might have stolen some, if not all, of it.'

'Nina, don't—' He broke off as she pulled completely out of his arms. 'Nina?'

'We should get back.'

'Not like this,' Rafe groaned in protest at the distance

he could feel yawning between them again, Nina refusing to allow him to take her back into his arms. 'I didn't mean to upset you just now, Nina. My remark really was meant as a joke. Obviously it was in poor taste,' he added regretfully.

Unfortunately, Nina's suspicions in regard to her father's accident nineteen years ago prevented her from seeing anything in the least humorous in Rafe and Michael's comments about her father.

'I really have to go, Rafe.' She opened the door before bending down to pick up her clutch bag from where she had allowed it to fall to the floor earlier, only to straighten and find herself prevented from leaving because Rafe had moved to stand in the doorway in front of her.

Allowing her to see now that the darkness of his hair was slightly tousled from where her fingers had been enmeshed in it just minutes ago, but otherwise Rafe looked as handsome and impeccable in his appearance as he had before their little sojourn to the supply cupboard.

Whereas Nina was pretty sure her own appearance was one of total dishevelment, and that she definitely looked like a woman who had just been made love to fully and well.

And there was no denying that feeling of satisfied heaviness between her thighs, or the fact that she was fully aware of the fact that she now wore no panties beneath her short and clinging gown!

'You'll still come to me later?' Rafe looked down at her searchingly.

She really should say no. Should keep to the decision she had made yesterday morning, not to see or be with Rafe again, and so give him the opportunity to probe and push into the past.

That was what she should do.

Unfortunately, that ache in her body said otherwise. 'I'll still come to your apartment later,' she confirmed huskily.

'Good.' He nodded his satisfaction with her reply. 'I suppose you're right, and we have to go back to the exhibition now.' He grimaced.

Nina had to smile at his obvious lack of enthusiasm for the idea. A lack of enthusiasm she echoed.

'Nina?' The hand Rafe placed lightly on her arm halted her as they stepped out into the hallway together.

She glanced up at him warily. 'Yes?'

His hands moved up to cup either side of her face, his gaze holding hers captive as he slowly lowered his head to brush his lips lightly against hers. 'Thank you,' he murmured huskily.

Nina's heart beat a wild tattoo in her chest at the touch of his lips and his close proximity. 'For what?' she breathed softly.

'Just thank you.' Rafe wasn't a hundred per cent sure himself what he was thanking Nina for.

Maybe for not slapping him in the face earlier, when he had dragged her out of the gallery like the caveman she had accused him of being yesterday?

Or perhaps because, once they were alone together, she hadn't even attempted to deny the attraction that still burned so fiercely between the two of them?

Or maybe because of the pleasure her uninhibited response gave him. Rafe was certainly no longer suffering with that same frustrated anger he had been plagued with for the past thirty-six hours.

Or maybe he was thanking her for simply being Nina?

Rafe had the rest of the evening to get through before he could even begin to give that revelation any deeper thought.

* * *

'Are you sure you're quite well, Papa?' Nina prompted concernedly as she saw how pale her father was looking when she rejoined him in the gallery. She hoped that his pallor was due to the effort of socialising, after so many years of avoiding it, rather than her own disappearance with Rafe just a short time ago.

She had done what she could to tidy her appearance once she reached the ladies' room, but brushing her hair and reapplying lip gloss had done nothing to hide that sultry glow Rafe said she had after lovemaking. A glow that had noticeably darkened her eyes to deep emerald, rendered her cheeks a delicate peach, and left her lips plump and rosy from Rafe's kisses.

'I am quite well, *maya doch*,' her father assured as he looked up at her searchingly. 'You and Rafe D'Angelo are…friends again?'

'I wasn't aware we were ever anything else.' Nina avoided meeting her father's probing gaze as she blushed.

'I believe we have passed the stage of coyness in regard to your relationship with D'Angelo, Nina,' he reproved softly.

There was every reason for Nina to blush, when she could so clearly remember the wildness, the heat, of the lovemaking between her and Rafe such a short time ago.

It was as if they had been starved for each other, wild with need.

Rafe compelled to touch her and Nina desperate to feel his touch. She had been completely aware of the heat still throbbing between her bare thighs as she crossed the gallery to rejoin her father.

She glanced across to where Rafe stood in conversation with his brother, just in time to see him put his hand in the pocket of his jacket where he had placed those ripped panties.

As if he sensed her glance Rafe's gaze rose to meet hers, those predatory golden eyes glittering with memories, chiselled lips slowly curving into a smile that was a promise of yet more pleasure to come when she joined him at his apartment later.

'You're pacing again.'

Rafe shot a malevolent glare across the kitchen to where Michael sat at the breakfast bar enjoying his morning tea and toast as he read the business section in the Sunday newspaper.

And of course Rafe was pacing, damn it, because Nina hadn't turned up at the apartment last night as she had said she would.

He and Michael had arrived back at a little before midnight the previous evening, Michael needing no persuading in taking himself off to bed—perhaps because he had guessed that Rafe was expecting Nina to join him?

Rafe had waited for Nina to arrive until one o'clock before phoning down to the security desk on the ground floor, to see if he had somehow missed her, only to be told that there had been no visitors for him at all that evening.

Rafe had waited another hour before telephoning security again. Only to be given the same answer.

At which time he had realised Nina wasn't going to come to him tonight, after all.

But even then, remembering the seriousness of her tone when she had mentioned the conversation she needed to have with her father before she could join him at his apartment, Rafe had been more worried than annoyed. He didn't at all like the possibility of Nina being upset and alone in her own apartment.

Although a call from her, telling him of her change of plans, might have been nice.

Even so, worry niggled at Rafe, until in desperation he had called her apartment building, asking the security guard on duty to put him through to Nina's apartment, only to discover that she wasn't in her apartment to answer his call. Nor would the security guard on the other end of the line reveal whether or not she had returned to the building with her father earlier, or whether or not she had gone out again.

And there was no way Rafe was going to call Dmitri's apartment and ask him where his daughter was.

Instead Rafe had finally gone to bed. Alone. But not to sleep.

Because, no matter how much he punched and pummelled his pillows to get comfortable, sleep had eluded him. Rafe simply lay in the bed, wide-eyed, his brain working overtime as he went over and over the events of the rest of yesterday evening, trying to find some reason, something he might have done or said, to make Nina change her mind about spending the night with him.

The only thing he knew she had taken exception to was that remark he had made about her father, but even that didn't make sense, because Nina had confirmed that she would come to his apartment after Rafe had made that foolish joke.

Which was the reason it was now ten o'clock on a Sunday morning, and he was pacing up and down the kitchen on bare feet, still wearing the black T-shirt and grey sweats he had slept in, his hair standing on end from where he had run his fingers through it so often in the past ten hours, while at the same time suffering Michael's penetrating and knowing gaze.

'I fully expected to see Nina here with you this morning,' Michael prompted softly.

'Well, obviously you expected wrong!' Rafe scowled at him darkly.

Michael nodded. 'Obviously. Rafe—' He broke off as the telephone rang.

Rafe crossed the kitchen quickly to snatch up the receiver, hoping—praying—it was Nina. 'Yes?' he snapped impatiently.

'There's a visitor waiting down in Reception to see you, Mr D'Angelo,' Jeffrey, the doorman informed, sounding slightly nervous.

'Send her right up,' Rafe barked sharply.

'But—'

'Now, Jeffrey.' Rafe slammed down the receiver, his pacing restless now rather than angry, as he waited impatiently for Nina to ring the doorbell.

'I think I'll go shower and dress ready for leaving for the airport shortly—' Michael rose to his feet '—and leave you two alone to talk and sort out whatever it is you need to.'

'Thanks,' Rafe answered distractedly, barely aware of his brother leaving as he strode out into the hallway to wait for Nina.

Whatever the reason for Nina's no show last night, she was here now, and that was all that mattered.

The doorbell had hardly finished ringing when Rafe threw open the door, the welcoming smile freezing on his lips as he saw the two burly bodyguards standing shoulder to shoulder outside in the hallway, their eyes once again hidden behind those wrap-around sunglasses. That probably explained Jeffrey's nervousness on the telephone just now.

Rafe couldn't say he was particularly happy at seeing the two bodyguards either. 'What—?'

'I'm sorry for the intrusion, Rafe.' The two bodyguards had parted to reveal Dmitri Palitov sitting in his wheelchair in the hallway behind them. 'I wondered, if my daughter is here with you, if I might speak with her?' His expression was hopeful rather than condemning.

That told Rafe that Dmitri Palitov had no more idea where Nina was than he did.

CHAPTER TEN

NINA HELD HER head confidently high as she walked into the Archangel gallery late on Monday morning, her smile conveying that same confidence to the receptionist, in her right to be here, as the other woman nodded in recognition as Nina walked towards the staircase that would take her up to Rafe's office on the third floor of the building.

Rafe...

Nina had no doubt that he was going to be far from happy with her, for not having turned up at his apartment on Saturday night, and for not getting in touch with him since then to explain why she hadn't.

Rafe might have claimed to have been joking on Saturday evening, as to the possibility of her father being some sort of gangster, but Nina had always had her own suspicions that weren't so far from the truth. Her conversation with her father late on Saturday evening hadn't gone far enough to confirm that, but it had certainly proved to her how powerful a man her father really was.

As a result, Nina knew there was no way she could ever tell Rafe of those new and shocking truths about her mother that her father had revealed to her late Saturday evening. Nina was having trouble accepting that truth herself, so how could anyone else possibly be expected to understand?

Which was why Nina had decided—again!—that from now she and Rafe could only have a business relationship. She would design the new display cabinets for the Archangel galleries, and as one of the owners of those galleries Rafe could approve those designs. Straightforward. Simple.

At least, it had seemed straightforward and simple when Nina had made that decision in her hotel room yesterday. She'd spent most of the night sitting dry-eyed in a chair beside the window looking sightlessly out at the New York skyline, wondering how, after the things her father had told her about her mother, she was going to get through the next few hours, let alone all the days that were to follow.

Here and now, with Rafe just a staircase away, her decision seemed far from simple. Rafe had already shown that he wasn't the type of man to just accept what she said at face value, that he would want to prod and probe in order to learn the reasons for her having made that decision. Reasons Nina couldn't possibly share with him. That she couldn't share with anyone.

Her footsteps slowed, grew heavier, the closer she got to Rafe's office. To the confrontation she had decided she had no choice but to face if she really was serious in her intention to make a life for herself. She planned to start by setting up her own business, well away from her father's influence. This work for the Archangel galleries was her door into doing that, at least.

All she had to do, before any of that became possible, was to fend off or dismiss any of Rafe's demands for the answers she couldn't give him.

All she had to do!

Just standing here outside the door to Rafe's office

made her heart pound louder and her palms grow damp, so how much worse was it going to be once she was face to face with him?

'Bridget, I thought I told you no interruptions—Nina!' Rafe rasped in recognition as he looked up from the catalogue he had been studying and saw it was Nina standing in the doorway rather than his assistant.

He stood up to move swiftly around his desk and cross the room in long strides before taking one of her hands in both of his, his gaze roaming over her face searchingly—hungrily!—easily noting the pallor of her cheeks and the distance in those cool green eyes that looked into his so steadily.

'Have I come at a bad time?' Her voice had that same distance and coolness.

He continued to look at her searchingly, wanting, needing to see some of 'his Nina' in the pained depths of her eyes. 'Are you okay?' Stupid question, Rafe instantly rebuked himself impatiently; of course Nina wasn't okay!

If Nina was 'okay' she wouldn't have walked out of her father's apartment on Saturday night. If she was 'okay' she would have come to Rafe that same night, as they had agreed she would. If she was 'okay' she wouldn't be looking at Rafe now as if he were a stranger to her rather than her lover.

She shrugged dismissively. 'Why wouldn't I be okay?'

Rafe didn't know the full answer to that; Dmitri Palitov hadn't been exactly forthcoming on the details yesterday, and would only reveal that Nina was upset about something he had told her, and had been missing since the previous night.

'Come inside.' Rafe kept a firm hold of her hand as he pulled her further into the room before shutting the door behind her. 'I can't tell you how pleased I am that you came here, Nina,' he added huskily.

'Why?'

Because now at least Rafe knew she was alive. Because now he knew she was safe.

Just because he needed her here with him, damn it.

'Nina, your father came to see me yesterday.'

Emotion flickered in the cool depths of those green eyes before it was quickly quashed. 'Did he?' she dismissed uninterestedly as she firmly but determinedly removed her hand from within Rafe's before walking away from him to stand in front of his desk. 'That must have been pleasant, for you both,' she added tersely.

Rafe continued to look at Nina searchingly, seeing the brittle fragility beneath her cool exterior. A fragility that was all the more apparent to him because she wore her hair up today, clearly revealing the hollows of her cheeks, the dark shadows beneath her eyes, and the delicate arch of her throat.

It was a fragility that Rafe believed might snap and break, shattering Nina along with it, if he said or did the wrong thing to her.

Which was the only reason Rafe hadn't taken Nina into his arms and kissed her senseless the moment he had closed the office door behind her.

Nina looked so brittle at the moment she was only capable of showing two responses to any attempt Rafe might make to hold her in his arms. One, she would fight him, biting and scratching with every bit of strength she possessed. Two, that fragile outer shell she held so tightly about her would crack wide open and she would disintegrate in front of his eyes. The first Rafe would withstand gladly, the second would utterly destroy him.

As it would destroy Nina.

And he didn't want that to happen. Nina's shy but rebellious spirit was one of the many things he had admired about her from the moment he first met her—was it really only a week ago?

That initial admiration had widened, and now included her unassuming beauty, her gentle sense of humour, her passion, the warmth of her heart, so evident when she spoke of her father.

A warmth so noticeably missing today whenever she spoke of Dmitri.

Rafe drew in a slow, measured breath, determined not to do or say anything that would shake the fragility of the tight control Nina had over her emotions. 'Nina...'

'I realise it would have been more businesslike to have made an appointment first, but I've brought in some sketches of my designs to show you,' she told him briskly, indicating the folder she carried in her left hand.

His brows rose at her use of the word 'businesslike'.

'Your designs?'

Her smile lacked any warmth or humour. 'I found myself with a lot of time on my hands over the weekend.'

Rafe winced.

Not only had Nina not spent the day with him yesterday, as he had hoped she would following the two of them spending the night together, but he also knew that after walking out of her father's apartment on Saturday evening Nina had gone down to her own apartment, packed a suitcase, and left the building altogether.

Because of something Dmitri had told her after they had returned home from the gala opening on Saturday evening. A conversation Nina had found so painful that she apparently walked out of her father's apartment, swearing she would never forgive Dmitri for what he had done.

Quite what that was Rafe had no idea. Dmitri had remained close-mouthed about the details of that conversation when Rafe had repeatedly pressed him for answers. All Dmitri was interested in was finding Nina, and, as Rafe had shared that concern, the two men had reached an uneasy truce on the reasons for her disappearance.

Nor, it seemed, had Nina come to Rafe today for any other reason than to show him her designs.

When Rafe had been hoping she had come to be with him because she needed him.

As he needed her.

Rafe had been shocked yesterday to learn that Dmitri hadn't seen Nina since Saturday night either. Having discovered Nina was missing on Sunday morning, after eluding her security guards, Dmitri had gone straight to Rafe's apartment to look for her.

Only to learn that Rafe hadn't seen her since Saturday evening either.

Michael had walked in on the heated argument that followed as Rafe and Dmitri threw accusations at each other, out of their concern for Nina rather than any real anger towards each other. Having calmed the situation down enough to find out what the problem was, Michael had even offered to cancel his flight back to Paris in order to help them look for Nina. An offer Rafe had thanked him for but refused, knowing that he and Dmitri were the ones who had to look for her. Who had to find her. They had to ensure that she was safe.

The two men had spent most of yesterday calling any and all of Nina's friends or acquaintances to see if they had seen or heard from her. None of them had. Following that they had called hotel after hotel to see if a Nina Palitov had booked in late on Saturday night. When those calls had turned up nothing, they had widened the search to the suburbs, to any and all places Nina might have stayed since she had walked out on him.

All to no avail; Nina was out there somewhere, but she obviously didn't want to be found.

Rafe had hoped that didn't include by him, but her comment just now would seem to imply that she hadn't even been aware he would bother looking for her when she hadn't arrived at his apartment on Saturday night, as she had said she would. And maybe he deserved that dismissal; Nina had no way of knowing that Rafe had thought of little else but her since the moment he first met her.

And now, when she was hurting so badly, because of the things her father had told her, wasn't the right time for Rafe to tell her how he felt, either.

'You know, Nina…' he spoke softly '…whatever your father has done, whatever he's said to you, nothing and no one is ever as completely black or completely white as they appear, and those shady areas of grey can be—'

'Oh, please!' Nina cut him off disparagingly. 'He got to you, didn't he?' she continued with knowing derision. 'And no doubt he told you just enough to excuse his behaviour.'

'He told me nothing, Nina, made no excuses for whatever it was he's done to upset you,' Rafe assured gruffly.

'Because there aren't any!' Her eyes glittered deeply green as the first crack began to appear in her defensive shell, a lapse she quickly brought under control as she straightened her shoulders determinedly. 'There just aren't any excuses for what he did, Rafe,' she repeated evenly.

'He loves you very much. He was only trying to protect you.'

'He's protected me from life all of my life!' Angry colour appeared in the pallor of her cheeks.

'Yes, he has,' Rafe acknowledged gently. 'And maybe that was wrong of him.'

'Maybe?' She moved restlessly. 'There's no maybe about it!' Her eyes continued to glitter angrily. 'He must have told you something, Rafe,' she continued scornfully. 'Enough that he's the one you feel sorry for, obviously.'

'It isn't a question of feeling sorry for anyone.'

'Isn't it?' she dismissed harshly. 'Well, believe me, I don't feel in the least sorry for him after hearing the things he's kept from me all these years.'

Rafe looked at her searchingly, the glitter of tears in her eyes enough to tell him that she wasn't as immune to her father's pain as she claimed to be. 'This isn't really you, Nina,' he cajoled huskily. 'You love your father, and you don't have it in you to be deliberately cruel, to him or anyone else.'

She gave another humourless laugh. 'What do you really know about me, Rafe? That I like having your hands on me? That I liked it so much on Saturday evening I let you drag me into a damned cupboard full of brooms just so that you could pleasure me?' She gave a disgusted shake of her head. 'That isn't knowing me, Rafe, that's just enjoying having sex.'

'Don't,' he warned harshly, knowing exactly what she was going to say next, and totally unwilling to allow her to reduce what they had to that basic level. 'You came to me today, Nina,' he reminded her gruffly, hands clenched at his sides to prevent himself from reaching out and taking her in his arms. 'Whatever excuse you may have given yourself for coming here, you came to me, damn it!'

Yes, she had, Nina acknowledged heavily. This morning, as she'd showered and dressed in her hotel room, she had convinced herself she was going to see Rafe today because she wanted the commission for the display cabinets from Archangel galleries. That securing those designs was more important than her pride if she was really serious about launching her own design company.

Now that she was here, with Rafe, Nina wasn't so sure she had been altogether truthful, even to herself.

There was comfort for her in being in Rafe's company, in that quiet strength he had, and it was already acting as a balm to her shattered emotions. It fed the need she felt to be with someone who desired her, at least, and who could warm her even a little; at the moment her heart felt like a heavy block of ice in her chest.

So, yes, she had come to Rafe this morning, had needed, wanted to be with him. To be with the man she had realised that she had fallen in love with.

Not all of the last thirty-six hours had been spent thinking about that last conversation with her father. She had thought of Rafe too. A lot. Of what their relationship meant to her. Of the fact that she not only desired and wanted him, but that she liked him too. That she had fallen in love with him.

Her desire for Rafe's dark good looks was undeniable, and she liked that fun person he could so often be, but she also knew, after this past week, that there was so much more to Rafe than that charming rogue persona he chose to show to the world at large.

Rafe cared.

About the Archangel galleries.

About her...

And he loved his family deeply. And it was a love, after her conversation with Michael on Saturday evening, which she had no doubts his family returned.

The serious Michael had made a point of talking to her

alone about his brother Rafe, casually at first, and then of how hard and diligently Rafe worked for the success of the galleries, of how they all owed much of the galleries' continued success to Rafe's ideas and innovations.

It was a caring part of Rafe that had already shone through bright and clear to Nina no matter how hard he tried to hide it.

Enough that she had already fallen in love with him.

A love that Rafe would never return.

She straightened her shoulders determinedly. 'The only reason I'm here today is to show you my designs,' she assured him coolly. 'If you're still interested in seeing them, that is?'

'Nina, we can't just sit down together and discuss your designs as if your conversation with your father on Saturday night had never happened.'

'I don't see why not,' she cut in icily.

'Nina—'

'Exactly what did he tell you about that conversation, Rafe?' she prompted again, harshly. 'How much of the truth, having known you for a week and me my whole lifetime, did he decide to confide in you?'

Rafe straightened, his tone soothing. 'You have to calm down, Nina.'

'No, Rafe, I really don't. I don't have to do anything, not any more.' Her eyes had a reckless glow. 'From now on I intend to do exactly as I damn well please. Now, do you want to see my designs or not?'

He winced at the aggression in her tone. 'Of course I want to see your designs.'

'Then could we do it now, please?' She handed him the file. 'I have business premises and an apartment to find this afternoon.'

'You aren't returning to your own apartment?' He frowned.

Her jaw tightened. 'No.'

Rafe was at a complete loss to know how to deal with this hard, unreachable Nina. He barely recognised her as the woman who had occupied most of his waking thoughts this past week—and quite a few of his sleeping ones too.

The woman he only had to look at to feel aroused. The woman who teased him and made him laugh. A woman of warmth and gentleness. A woman he had confided in. A woman so unlike any other that Rafe felt beguiled by her. The woman he knew he wanted to be with.

The same woman who was hurting so badly right now she was falling apart inside.

Because whatever Dmitri had told her on Saturday night it hurt her. Deeply.

Rafe didn't know all the facts—no matter what Nina might think, Dmitri really hadn't been willing to go quite so far as to confide in him—but Rafe knew enough to know that whatever secrets the other man had been keeping from Nina all these years it was breaking her apart.

If it hadn't already broken her heart.

'Nina—'

'Please, Rafe.' Her voice cracked emotionally. 'If you care anything for me at all, then help me do this.'

If Rafe cared?

He had realised, during these past two days that he cared more for Nina, about Nina, than he ever had for any woman. Than he ever would again for any woman. 'Nina…'

Both of them turned as the door to his office was suddenly thrown open without warning. Rafe groaned inwardly as the two burly bodyguards entered the room before parting to allow Dmitri Palitov to enter in his wheelchair.

One look at Nina's white and accusing face, and Rafe knew that she believed he'd had something to do with her father's unexpected arrival.

CHAPTER ELEVEN

'DID YOU INSTRUCT your assistant to inform my father if I came here?' Nina looked at him with hurt accusation.

'No.'

'Rafe has absolutely nothing to do with my being here this morning, Nina.' Dmitri spoke quietly, the two body-guards once again instructed to wait out in the hallway, the door firmly closed behind them. 'I've had both Rafe's apartment and this gallery under observation since yesterday, on the off-chance that you might come to him.'

Rafe scowled darkly. 'You have one hell of a nerve!'

Which wasn't to say, despite the outrage Rafe felt now on Nina's behalf, that he didn't still feel a certain inner warmth in the knowledge that, whatever reason she claimed for being here today, Nina had come to him.

'My apologies, Rafe. But it was necessary,' the older man added.

'In your opinion,' Nina snapped, though she was relieved that Rafe hadn't had anything to do with her father being here. She wasn't sure she was strong enough to face another betrayal by one of the two men who meant so much to her.

Her father looked at her calmly. 'Where have you been for the past two days, Nina?'

'Right here at a hotel in New York.'

'We checked all the hotels.'

'I booked in under the name Nina Fraser,' she said, feeling no sense of satisfaction as she saw the way her father flinched at hearing she had booked into the hotel using her mother's maiden name.

She was hurt and angry with her father, yes, for the things he had kept from her, but Rafe was right, she wasn't, and never could be, deliberately cruel to anyone, least of all her father. 'You should have told me the truth about Mama from the beginning, Papa,' she said softly.

A spasm of pain passed over his already strained features. 'You were only five years old, and far too young to understand, let alone accept that truth.'

'But later, you should have tried to explain it to me when I was older,' she came back emotionally.

'I thought of it, of course I did. But it was not pleasant, *maya doch*.' Her father looked haggard. 'Better, I decided, that you had the good memories of your mama and not the bad.'

Rafe had no idea what the two of them were talking about, but that didn't prevent him from feeling as if he was intruding on something very personal to the two of them. 'Perhaps you would like me to leave so the two of you can talk privately?'

'No.'

'No!'

Rafe nodded as both Palitovs spoke at the same time, Dmitri with resignation, Nina with an edge of desperation. And if Nina needed him to be here, then that was exactly where Rafe was going to be.

'Let's sit down, shall we, Nina?' Rafe encouraged gently, sitting down beside her as she perched on the edge of the sofa.

Nina gave Rafe a quick glance as he lifted one of her

trembling hands to lace his fingers with hers, a wave of gratitude sweeping over her at this tacit show of his support. Overwhelming love for him bubbled up, swelled to overflowing inside her, for the gentleness Rafe showed towards her.

Because Nina now knew, beyond a shadow of a doubt, that she did love Rafe, that she was in love with him.

Which was why, much as she might have protested at the thought of Rafe leaving a few minutes ago, she now had to be fair to him and give him a chance to do exactly that.

'I'm aware this is your office, Rafe, and I'm sorry for the way we've intruded.' She spoke quietly. 'But you really don't have to be here to listen to this if you would rather not.' She looked up, appealing to her father.

He understood her silent plea as he gave a slight nod before turning to the younger man. 'You may prefer not to be here, Rafe.'

'I want whatever Nina wants.' Rafe's expression gentled as he turned to look at her, once again noting the tension she was under, how the shadows seemed to have deepened in those deep green eyes. 'I want to be here for you,' he told her huskily. 'If it's what you want too?'

'Yes, please,' she breathed.

He nodded before turning back to Dmitri. 'Then I'm staying right here,' he told the older man firmly.

Nina's fingers tightened about his in gratitude before she turned to look at her father with tear-wet eyes. 'It was cruel of you to keep the truth about Mama from me all these years, Papa. Surely I had a right to know? A right to choose for myself?'

'I did what I thought was best at the time.' He sighed heavily. 'And this conversation must be very confusing for Rafe,' he added. 'Which, as we are in his office, seems a little unfair.'

The tears were falling silently down Nina's cheeks as she turned to Rafe. 'It's not too late, you can still leave.'

'I'm staying,' he stated grimly, wanting, needing, to know exactly what had reduced his Nina to this emotional state.

She drew in a deep breath. 'Then you should know that nineteen years ago my mother was kidnapped.' She nodded abruptly at Rafe's harshly indrawn breath. 'The kidnappers contacted my father immediately, demanding that he keep the police out of it, but that if he paid their ransom within one week my mother would be safely returned to us.'

Now Rafe understood the reason Dmitri Palitov had been, and still was, so protective of his daughter; his wife had been taken from him nineteen years ago, and he had no intention of the same thing ever happening with his young daughter.

Rafe felt a hard jolt in his chest just imagining how Dmitri must have suffered all those years ago. The pain and agony of having his wife taken from him followed by days of wondering if he would ever see her again.

Imagining how he himself would feel if it had been Nina!

The knuckles on Nina's hands showed white as she held on tightly, painfully, to Rafe's hand. 'My father obeyed their instructions, paid the men their ransom, but—but—'

'This is where our stories start to diverge,' Dmitri put in softly, heavily, as Nina faltered. 'At the time I told Nina nothing about the kidnapping, only that Anna had died. And then when Nina was ten years old I told her of the kidnapping, as a way of helping her to understand why I was so protective of her, but not— Until Saturday evening I was still not completely truthful about her mother's fate.'

Rafe looked at the older man searchingly, eyes widening in shock as he read the truth in Dmitri's agonised expression. 'Anna didn't die when Nina was five,' he breathed, remembering how he hadn't been able to find any record of Anna's death when he did an Internet search on Dmitri Palitov.

Dmitri's jaw tightened. 'Anna died five years later, in the private nursing home I had been forced to place her in just days after she was returned to me. She is buried in the churchyard nearby. Her mind had gone, you see, so that she no longer knew me. She had retreated to a place neither I nor anyone else could reach her, for ever broken from what those animals did to her in the week they held her captive.'

'Don't, Papa!' Nina choked emotionally, reaching out to him with her other hand, aware of the cracking of the ice that had encased her heart since she had learnt the truth two days ago.

That ice now broke wide open, shattered completely, before melting away as she saw the agony of that shocking past in her father's pained green eyes.

It had been too much for Nina to take in on Saturday night, for her to be able to fully comprehend what his having kept that secret all these years had done to her father, emotionally. All she had heard then, all that had mattered, was that her mother had been alive for five years more after Nina had believed her to be dead.

But she realised, as she looked at her father now, how alone he must have been in his grieving for the wife who had never completely come back to him. Of the five years he had suffered, visiting Anna once a week at the nursing home where she had lived out the rest of her short life, so lost in the safety of the world she had created for herself that she hadn't even known who Dmitri was, let alone that she had a young daughter who loved her too.

And Nina realised now that he had done that for her. So that she might grow up with only the happy memories of her mother.

'It was wrong of me.'

'Don't put yourself through having to say it all again, Papa!' Nina pleaded emotionally. 'It isn't. I was the one who was wrong on Saturday evening, for not understanding.' She released Rafe's hand so that she could stand up to go to her father, her arms moving about him protectively as the tears now trailed down his weathered cheeks.

'I'm so sorry, Papa. So very sorry that I walked out on you on Saturday night. For putting you through yet more pain by disappearing for two days.'

'I would forgive you anything, *maya doch*, you know that.' He spoke gruffly. 'Anything, as long as you are safe.'

Nina began to cry in earnest now, no longer able to shut out the thought of all the years her father had suffered, unable to share or express his grief for the wife who still lived but no longer had any knowledge of him or their young daughter.

'There's more, isn't there?'

Nina kept her arms protectively about her father as she turned to look across at Rafe.

'Not that this isn't already enough.' Rafe stood up abruptly, too restless to continue sitting any longer.

His hands were clenched at his sides as he resisted the impulse he had to take Nina in his own arms, knowing that this was a time of understanding, of healing, for Nina and Dmitri. A time when Rafe's own emotions had to be kept firmly in check. Which wasn't to say he didn't feel them.

He gave a shake of his head. 'I can't even begin to tell you how sorry I am that this happened to all of you. It's incomprehensible. Too huge to take in completely.' He ran a hand through the shaggy thickness of his hair as he gave a shake of his head, wondering how Dmitri had ever managed to live with the pain.

Rafe had grown up in the security of the deep love his own parents had for each other, and he knew, without a doubt, without needing to ask, that his own father would have acted in exactly the same way Dmitri had in these same circumstances. That having lost his wife, Giorgio would have done everything in his considerable power to care for his wife, and ensure his three sons were protected from the truth.

Rafe also knew that Gabriel, so in love with Bryn, would tear the world apart looking for anyone who dared to hurt her.

Just as Rafe knew, if that had ever happened to him, that once the initial shock had receded he would be filled with that same rage. That he would want to find the men responsible, to destroy them, to tear them apart with his bare hands, for what they had done to the woman he loved, and to make sure they were never able to hurt another woman, to destroy another family in the way that they had.

He drew in a hissing breath. 'Your car accident wasn't an accident, was it?'

'No,' the older man confirmed as he drew himself up stiffly while retaining a tight hold of Nina's hand. 'It took time, but I hunted the three kidnappers down until I found them, and then I arranged to meet with them.' He drew in a controlling breath. 'It was my intention to kill them that night, at a secluded spot far from the city, to make them suffer, as my Anna had suffered—' He broke off as Nina gave a pained cry. 'I did not succeed, *maya doch*,' he assured her huskily.

'You didn't?' Nina gasped. 'But all these years I've thought—believed— We never spoke of it openly, but I always assumed…?'

Dmitri gave a rueful shake of his head. 'It would seem they had the same intention in regard to me. They did not wish to have anyone left alive who could identify them.' His jaw tightened. 'They rammed my car on the way to that meeting, attempted to drive my car off the road. Instead it was their own car which bore the brunt of the impact.' His mouth tightened. 'Two of the men were killed instantly, the third died a year later, as a result of the injuries he had received.' Dmitri made the statement evenly, unemotionally, and with no apology for what he had intended.

As far as Rafe was concerned no apology was necessary. Dmitri had done what he felt he had to do. What most men would have done in the same situation.

What Rafe would have wanted to do given those same circumstances.

'I think,' Rafe spoke slowly, 'that if I had known you then, Dmitri, young as I was, that I would have wanted to help you in your search for the kidnappers.'

Nina felt so grateful to Rafe at that moment, for not judging, for not condemning her father for what he had intended, that she could have kissed him!

She wanted to kiss him anyway. Had been longing, aching, to do exactly that since the moment she had entered his office half an hour earlier.

Just as she had longed to go to Rafe on Saturday night, despite the things her father had told her. She had needed

Rafe then, had been desperate to feel his arms about her, to lose herself in their lovemaking rather than dwell on those lost years with her mother.

But she had known instinctively that it was the wrong thing to do.

Knew that if Rafe ever learned the details of the conversation she'd had with her father he would feel she had been using him that night, rather than what was true—that she had just ached to be with him, to be held by him that night. Because she loved him.

'You are an impressive young man, Raphael D'Angelo.' Dmitri spoke appreciatively.

Rafe raised dark brows. 'I happen to think your daughter is the impressive one.' He looked at Nina with open admiration. 'All these years she's secretly wondered if you killed those men that night, and yet she's held her own counsel, never speaking of it to anyone.'

'Yes.' Dmitri's pride glowed in his eyes for his daughter.

Nina winced. 'Maybe if I'd spoken to my father about it before now I wouldn't have been left secretly wondering. I feel so ashamed now, for thinking what I did, Papa. I'm sorry. I really believed—thought that...'

'It was only fate that decreed it otherwise, *maya doch*,' her father soothed gently. 'I left our apartment that night with every intention of ridding the world of those three men.'

'But you didn't do it.' She clasped her father's hands tightly in hers as that truth finally sank in completely, Nina feeling as if a weight had been lifted from her shoulders. 'You didn't do it, Papa!' And that weight lifted even higher as she realised what that knowledge meant to her own life, and the freedom, the choices it now gave her.

'No, I did not,' he conceded gruffly. 'Because as I

drove to the meeting point that night I realised that I could not do it. Because of you, Nina.' He squeezed her hand. 'Much as I wished to rid the world of such vermin as those men, I would then have had to pay for my crime, and so left you completely alone. And that I could not do, *maya doch*. I could not leave you without both your mother and your father.'

Tears blurred Nina's vision as she wept silently.

Tears for the deep love her father felt for her, and which she returned.

Tears of joy because she now knew her suspicions all these years, regarding who had been responsible for her father's accident, and the deaths of those three men, had been wrong.

Tears for the freedom that knowledge now gave her in her own life, allowing her to give her heart, her love, to the man she was already so deeply in love with.

It didn't matter that Rafe would never return that love; it was enough that Nina could now allow herself, was finally free, to be with him for as long as he wanted her.

If he still wanted her?

Rafe felt a jolt in his chest as Nina turned to smile at him. A smile of such sweet, unadulterated joy that he had to blink as it made his own eyes sting with emotion.

But there was still one question Dmitri had left unanswered.

'Why now, Dmitri?' he prompted huskily as he turned to look at the other man. 'Why did you decide now was the right time to tell Nina the truth about her mother?'

The older man smiled up at him sadly. 'Why do you think, Rafe?'

Rafe looked at Dmitri searchingly, not sure, uncertain still—

But he could hope, couldn't he?

Yes, he could certainly hope that this was Dmitri's way of letting Nina go. Of allowing her to have her own life at last. Of allowing her to live. To love.

Because Dmitri had realised, already knew, that Rafe was in love with her.

'I realise that you and Nina still have a lot to discuss, Dmitri.' He spoke huskily to the older man while all the time turning to look at Nina. 'But would you mind very much if I were to steal her away for a few hours? I very much doubt she's bothered to eat very much the last two days, so I could feed her lunch at least,' he added ruefully as he saw Nina's puzzled glance.

'I think that would be an excellent idea, Rafe.' Dmitri nodded. 'And Nina and I have the rest of our lives in which to talk more of all these things.'

'Nina?' Rafe prompted as he held his hand out to her, holding his breath as he waited for her response.

CHAPTER TWELVE

'DID YOU NOTICE that my father stopped Andy and Rich as they moved to follow us?'

Rafe glanced at Nina as she sat beside him in the passenger seat of his car, looking so vulnerable and young at that moment, her eyes slightly red from where she had cried earlier, her face completely bare of make-up.

'I did, yes.'

'It's really going to be okay, isn't it?' she murmured shakily.

Rafe reached out to briefly squeeze her hand before returning his own hand to the steering wheel. 'Yes, it's really going to be okay.'

She relaxed back against the leather seat. 'I'm sorry you had to listen to all of that.'

'I didn't have to do anything, Nina, I chose to do it,' he corrected firmly. 'And I think it's time you stopped apologising. To me. To your father. Or to anyone else. Because you have absolutely nothing to apologise for.' He glanced at her again, and saw the frown between those beautiful emerald-coloured eyes. 'Do you have any idea how much I admire you right now?'

Rafe admired her?

It wasn't exactly the return of her love that Nina longed

for, she acknowledged ruefully, but it was high praise indeed coming from the enigmatic Rafe D'Angelo.

'That's nice,' she accepted huskily.

'Nice?' he echoed dryly.

'Very nice?' She quirked a teasing brow, happier than she had ever been at this moment, just knowing there were no more misunderstandings, nothing left unsaid, between her and her father.

More importantly, she was with Rafe. The man she loved. A love that had grown deeper, even stronger, during this past hour as he gave her his strength to lean on.

Those chiselled lips twisted laughingly. 'The first time I tell a woman I admire her, and all she can say is, "That's nice,"' he muttered disgustedly.

'I did expand it to very nice,' Nina reminded lightly, desperately trying not to read any more into his statement than Rafe actually meant. Because it would be all too easy for her to do exactly that, and the last thing Nina wanted to do was embarrass Rafe, or herself, by overreacting to his comment. 'Isn't admiration something you feel for talcum-powder-smelling maiden aunts?'

He frowned. 'I don't have any maiden aunts!'

'That explains why you've never said it before, then.' She nodded.

'Exactly where are we going for lunch?' She changed the subject to something less open to misunderstandings. Or hope, on her part, not Rafe's.

Rafe bit back his feelings of impatience with Nina's determination to keep their conversation lightly teasing.

He might have received Dmitri's tacit approval just minutes ago, but it was too soon for Rafe to expect, to ask, for anything from Nina other than the physical attraction between them that she had never tried to deny.

He sensed that was all Nina needed from him right now: to be able to lose herself in desire, passion and pleasure.

'To the best restaurant in New York,' he answered her lightly.

'Am I dressed appropriately?' She looked down uncertainly at the business suit she had worn to his office this morning. Like a suit of armour.

'I thought we might go to my apartment. Do you think you're dressed appropriately for there?' Rafe prompted huskily.

Nina's cheeks flushed a fiery red as she recalled that the last time she'd been in Rafe's apartment she'd been completely naked! 'I didn't know you could cook?'

'I can't,' he admitted unapologetically. 'It will just be fruit and cheese, I'm afraid. It's where we're going to eat the food from that's going to make it the best restaurant in town.'

The warmth deepened in her cheeks. 'Would you care to enlighten me?'

'Oh, I'd care to do a lot of things to and with you, Nina,' Rafe assured huskily as he parked the car in the private underground parking beneath his apartment building, before turning in his seat to look at her. 'First I want to strip you naked. Second I want to lay you down on my bed before arranging my lunch on selected parts of your delectable body. Thirdly I want to then taste, lick, nibble each tiny morsel of pleasure.'

'Rafe!' Nina gasped breathlessly, her heart leaping in her chest just thinking of the intimacies he'd described.

He reached up to release the clasp from her hair, allowing it to cascade loosely onto her shoulders and down her spine. 'Too much?' he prompted huskily.

Not enough! It would never be enough for her where Rafe was concerned.

But this, here and now, with Rafe, anticipating the lovemaking yet to come, was exactly what she needed after the last two emotionally traumatic days.

'Do I get to eat my lunch in the same way?'

He quirked one dark brow. 'Do you want to?'

'Oh, yes,' she breathed longingly.

Rafe nodded. 'I'm starving for you,' he murmured huskily, his golden gaze easily holding hers captive. 'How about you?'

Nina moistened the softness of her lips before answering. 'Ravenous.'

'Thank God!' he groaned his satisfaction with her answer before getting out of the car and moving quickly round to her side of the vehicle to open her door for her, taking a firm hold of her elbow as they crossed the car park to the lift.

The lift doors had barely closed behind them before Rafe took her in his arms and kissed her. Deeply, hungrily, as if he couldn't get enough of her. As if it was her he wanted to eat and to hell with lunch!

They were still kissing greedily as they stepped out of the lift into Rafe's apartment. Their lips locked together as they hurriedly threw off their clothes, moving erratically towards Rafe's bedroom, clothes left scattered down the hallway, both of them completely naked by the time they fell on the bed together and they lost themselves in the pleasure of each other.

'So much for lunch,' Nina murmured a long time later, fingers toying with the damp vee of dark hair on Rafe's muscled chest and abdomen as they lay entwined together between the silk sheets.

'Oh, we're still going to eat lunch, Nina,' Rafe assured her huskily, his hair rakishly tousled as he moved up onto his elbow to look down at her, thoroughly enjoying see-ing the satisfied glow in her eyes, the flush to her cheeks, her lips lush and full, and her hair a wild and silky red tangle. 'I just—I needed you too much this first time to be able to take things slowly,' he acknowledged gruffly.

Her eyes widened. 'You did?'

'I did,' he admitted. 'I wasn't too rough with you, was I?' He lightly caressed the dampness of her hair back from her temple.

'Not at all.' She smiled shyly. 'Was I too rough with you?'

'Not at all,' Rafe echoed softly. 'Nina—' He broke off to chew uncertainly on his bottom lip.

'Yes?' she prompted curiously. The Rafe she knew and loved was never uncertain, always seemed to know exactly what he was doing, and why.

He drew in a deep and ragged breath. 'I promised myself I wasn't going to do this today, that you've had enough trauma for one day...'

Nina's stomach tied up in tense knots as she looked up at him searchingly, as she wondered if the intensity of Rafe's lovemaking just now hadn't been because, for him, this was the end of their relationship.

If it was, then she would accept his decision, had no intention of making Rafe feel in the least guilty about ending their affair. He had been there for her this morn-ing when she had needed him, so strong and so kind. He'd listened without judgement as her father talked of the past, and at the same time been totally supportive of her. So much so that the least Nina owed him was to make a dignified exit from his life, if that was what he wanted.

'You don't want to see me any more,' she accepted lightly.

'What?' Rafe's face tensed. His eyes had darkened to molten gold, his skin taut across the sharp blades of his cheekbones, nostrils flaring, his lips having compressed to a thin, uncompromising line.

'It's okay, Rafe.' She touched his chest lightly, reassuringly, determined to remain strong. There would be plenty of time later for her to break down. As her heart was already breaking at the thought of not being with Rafe like this again. 'I knew going into this that you don't do long-term relationships. Or complications,' she added ruefully. 'And it seems that my life is just one shocking complication after another!'

Rafe scowled darkly. 'You don't want to be with me any more?'

'You don't want to be with me!' she corrected emotionally.

'I didn't say that,' he rasped harshly.

'But...' Nina frowned up at him. 'It sounded as if you did.'

'Absolutely not!' Rafe threw back the bed sheet to climb restlessly out of bed, unconcerned by his nakedness as he began to pace the bedroom, at the same time as he ran an agitated hand through the unruly darkness of his hair. 'The timing of this is all wrong,' he muttered crossly.

'The timing of what is all wrong?' Nina looked completely baffled by his behaviour.

Rafe gave an impatient shake of his head. 'You're naturally upset, traumatised after learning your mother lived.'

'Rafe, I'm fine,' she cut in gently. 'I really am,' she assured huskily as Rafe stopped pacing long enough to look across the bedroom at her. 'In fact, I'm better than I've ever been,' she added ruefully as she also threw back the bed sheet and climbed out of bed. 'I know the truth now, all of it. Don't you see, Rafe, for the first time in years I feel free of the emotional baggage I've been carrying about with me for most of my life?'

'Free to do what?' Rafe prompted searchingly, trying his damnedest not to be distracted by the beauty of Nina's nakedness. A battle he knew he was destined to lose as he became instantly aroused. For Nina. Only for Nina.

'To live. To love,' she added huskily as her gaze seemed drawn, as if by a magnet, to the physical evidence of Rafe's rapidly lengthening arousal.

Rafe's breath caught in his throat as he couldn't look away from the provocation of seeing Nina's little pink tongue sweep moistly across the plumpness of her bottom lip. As if in anticipation of licking him!

He wasn't even aware of having stepped towards her until he realised he was now standing only inches away from her, not quite touching her, but wanting to. Dear God, how much he wanted to just take Nina in his arms and make love to her again, to keep her in his arms, in his bed, until she promised never to leave.

He swallowed before speaking. 'I'm in love with you, Nina.' He gruffly spoke the words he had never imagined he would ever say to any woman, but desperately needing to say them now, to Nina, more than he needed his next breath.

'I love you.' It was much easier saying it the second time, something seeming to lighten, to ease deep inside Rafe, a heaviness, a restraint, he hadn't even known was there until it lifted.

'I love you, Nina Palitov,' he murmured again with satisfaction as he took her into his arms at last and curved the heat of his body against hers. 'I love you, Nina. I love you. I love you!' His voice rose joyfully as he announced his love for her over and over again, knowing he would never grow tired of saying it.

Nina stared up at Rafe wonderingly, almost afraid still to believe, to hope that he was saying these wonderful words to her when just seconds ago she had thought he was saying goodbye.

'I love you too,' she breathed softly. 'I love you too, Rafe.' She spoke more strongly now too as her hands moved up to rest on the warmth of his chest, allowing her to feel the wild beating of his heart beneath her fingertips.

Rafe's arms tightened about her.

'Marry me, Nina,' he urged forcefully. 'Marry me!' His eyes blazed fiercely down into hers.

She stared up at him unblinkingly. 'Raphael D'Angelo doesn't do love and marriage.'

'He didn't do love and marriage,' he corrected gruffly. 'Until you. But you should know right now that I'm not going to settle for anything less when it comes to you.' His arms tightened about her. 'I want you for always, Nina. As my wife. As the mother of my babies. God, just thinking of you pregnant with our child makes me hard!' he acknowledged huskily as his arousal surged against her. 'I want a lifetime with you, Nina. Want to wake up beside you every morning, to have the freedom to be able to tell you how much I love you a dozen times a day!'

Nina gazed up at him wonderingly. 'Yes, Rafe. Oh, yes, of course I'll marry you!' Her arms moved about his waist. 'I love you so much. So very much, Rafe!' She raised her face to meet the fierce possessiveness of his kiss.

The rest of the world drifted away, ceased to exist, as they revelled in the depth of the love they had found with and for each other.

* * * * *

A D'ANGELO LIKE
NO OTHER
CAROLE MORTIMER

Our Son, Matthew, A Man to be Proud of.

PROLOGUE

St Gregory's Church, New York.

'WEREN'T THE THREE of us sitting together in a church very like this one just a few weeks ago?' Michael spoke mockingly to his youngest brother Gabriel as they sat in the front pew of the church crowded with wedding guests, their restless brother Rafe seated on his other side.

'I believe we were, yes,' Gabriel confirmed dryly. 'Except on that occasion you and Rafe were my best men, and now we're Rafe's.'

'How many weeks ago was that, exactly?' Michael arched derisive brows.

'Five wonderful, glorious weeks.' Gabriel smiled at the thought of his own recent marriage to his beloved Bryn.

'Hmm.' Michael nodded. 'Did I ever tell you of the conversation I had with Rafe that day, in which he assured me, most emphatically I believe, that he didn't believe in this "one love of a lifetime" thing, and certainly had no intention of getting married in the immediate, or even distant, future?'

Gabriel glanced at their brother Rafe, holding back a smile as he saw the tension in Rafe's white face as he waited for his bride to arrive at the church. 'No, I don't believe you did...'

'Oh, yes.' Michael settled more comfortably on the pew. 'It was as we were standing outside the church together, when you and Bryn were posing for photographs. I seem to remember that Rafe had just received a call from one of his women, and—'

'And this is hardly the time, or the place, for you to so much as mention any of that!' A tense Rafe turned on them both fiercely, his brief relationship with the Parisian, Monique, having ended several months before he had even met his future bride.

The three D'Angelo brothers owned and ran the three prestigious Archangel galleries and auction houses, in New York, London and Paris. Until recently they had run those galleries on a casual two-to-three-month-rotation basis, depending on what exhibitions or auctions were taking place in each gallery, but Gabriel's marriage to Bryn now meant that he was based mainly in London, Rafe would be spending most of his time in New York once he and Nina were married, leaving Michael in charge at the Paris gallery.

'Nina is now five minutes late,' Rafe muttered after another glance at his wristwatch, the tenth such glance in almost as few seconds.

'It's the bride's prerogative to keep the man waiting,' Gabriel dismissed unconcernedly. 'A case of "how the mighty have fallen", don't you think?' he calmly continued his conversation with Michael.

'Oh, most definitely.' Michael nodded. 'From what I've observed, he's been totally off his head since the day he met Nina.' He grinned unabashedly in the face of Rafe's scowl.

'Love does that to you.' Gabriel nodded wisely. 'It will be your turn next, Michael.'

His humour instantly faded. 'I don't believe so,' he assured with grim certainty.

'Famous last words...?'

'Fact,' Michael corrected tersely. 'I can't imagine ever willingly allowing any woman to get me into that state.' He gave a pointed glance in Rafe's visibly agitated direction.

'When you two have quite finished!' Rafe's hands had clenched into fists, his expression one of pained tension as he turned to glare at his two brothers. 'Nina is late, damn it!'

'We heard you the first time...' Michael arched one dark brow. 'Do you think she might have changed her mind about marrying you?'

Rafe's already pale face seemed to take on a greyish tinge as he groaned. 'Oh, God...!'

'Stop teasing him, Michael,' Gabriel chided affectionately, his five-week marriage to Bryn having completely mellowed him. 'Personally, I'm longing to see the beautiful matron of honour!' He smiled at the thought of his wife.

Michael shrugged broad shoulders. 'Calm down, Rafe. Nina will be here,' he assured his brother dryly. 'For some strange reason the woman is in love with you!'

'Ha ha, very funny.' Rafe scowled.

'The limo is probably having trouble getting through the New York traffic, that's all.' Michael grimaced.

'Lord, I hope so.' Rafe's face had taken on a slightly green tinge now. 'I knew I should have gone ahead with my original plan and just persuaded Nina to elope!'

'Not if you had wanted to continue living, Raphael Charles D'Angelo!' his mother warned from the pew directly behind them, the whole of the D'Angelo family having once again gathered together to see another one of the three brothers married.

Which left Michael, the eldest brother at thirty-five, as the only remaining bachelor…

A state he intended to continue!

Oh, Michael was pleased for both of his younger brothers, had absolutely no doubt that Rafe and Gabriel loved the two women they had chosen as their wives, and that those two women loved them in return, that the two couples would have long and happy lives together. It just wasn't a state, the love or the marriage, that Michael wanted for himself.

Ever.

He had been in love precisely once in his life, fourteen years ago, disastrously as it turned out, and it wasn't an experience he had ever felt the slightest inclination to repeat. All that angsting and heartache had just made him miserable, the betrayal even more so, and he certainly hadn't enjoyed the unpleasant feeling of having lost control of his emotions.

A feeling that he would find even more unacceptable after all these years of doing exactly as he pleased, when he pleased, with whomever and whatever woman he pleased.

No, as far as Michael was concerned, Rafe and Gabriel could provide the next generation of D'Angelos, because he had no intention of having his well-ordered life complicated by either a wife or children.

'Oh, thank God…' Rafe breathed his relief as the organist began to play the Wedding March announcing Nina's arrival at the church, the three men standing up to turn and look at the bride as she walked down the aisle at her father's side. Nina was a vision in white satin and lace, her smile radiantly beautiful, love shining in her eyes as she walked towards her bridegroom.

Michael felt a slight pang in his chest as he realised that

his decision not to marry meant that no woman would ever gaze at him with such open adoration.

A pang he quickly quashed and buried, in the knowledge that *he* had no intention of ever falling victim to loving any woman in the way his brothers now loved their wives...

CHAPTER ONE

Archangel gallery, Paris. Two days later

'WHAT THE—?' MICHAEL looked up to scowl his displeasure as he heard what sounded like a baby crying in the office opposite his own. He stood up quickly behind his desk as several voices now clamoured to be heard above the noise.

The sound of raised voices, so close to the inner sanctum of Michael's private third-floor office, was unusual enough, but a baby crying…? In one of the private areas of the prestigious Paris Archangel gallery and auction house? It was unheard of! And Michael had little patience for it having occurred now.

He continued to scowl as he strode forcefully across his office to wrench open the door into the hallway, only to come to an abrupt halt, his verbal protest dying in his throat at the pandemonium that met his narrowed gaze.

His secretary, Marie, was fiercely gabbling away in French, as was his assistant manager, Pierre Dupont. Both of them, as was usual with the French, communicating as much with their hands as with their mouths.

And standing between them, holding a young baby in her arms, was a young girl—woman?—with ebony shoulder-length hair, dressed in the *de rigueur* tight denims and fitted T-shirt of her generation. Her top was a bright purple, the expression on her flustered face flushed as she ignored both Marie and Pierre and instead attempted to soothe and cajole the crying baby into silence.

An attempt that failed miserably as the baby's cries seemed to grow even louder.

'Will you two please lower your voices?' The young woman turned impatiently on Marie and Pierre, her voice throatily husky. 'You're scaring her. Now look what you've done…!' she fumed as a second baby began to cry.

Michael looked around dazedly for the source of that second cry, his eyes widening as he noticed the pushchair parked just inside Marie's office. A double pushchair, in which a second baby was now screaming at the top of its considerable lungs.

What the—?

Pandemonium? This situation, whatever that might be, was like some sort of hellish nightmare, the sort every man wished—prayed!—to wake up from. And sooner rather than later!

'Thank you,' the disgruntled young woman muttered accusingly as Marie and Pierre both fell silent as she hurried over to the pushchair before going down on her haunches to coo and attempt to gently soothe the second baby.

Michael had seen and heard enough. 'Will someone, for the love of God, tell me what the hell is going on here?' His voice cut harshly through the cacophony of noise.

Silence.

Absolute blissful silence, Eva realised with a sigh of appreciation for her aching head, as not only the two employees of the Paris Archangel remained silent, but even the babies' cries both quietened down to a soft whimper.

Eva remained down on her haunches as she turned to look through sooty black lashes at the source of that harshly controlling voice, her eyes widening as she took in the appearance of the man standing across the hallway.

He was possibly aged in his mid to late thirties, his short black hair was neatly trimmed about his ears and nape, and framed an olive-skinned and handsomely etched face that any of the male models Eva had photographed at the beginning of her career would surely die for. Dark brows arched above eyes of obsidian black, his nose a long straight slash between high cheekbones, with sculptured, slightly sensual lips above a firm and determined chin.

His wide shoulders, muscled chest, tapered waist, and lean hips above long legs also ensured that *he* wore the expensively tailored dark suit, white silk shirt and grey tie, rather than the clothes wearing him.

And leaving Eva in no doubt, along with the deference on the faces of the two silent gallery employees, and the fact that he had come from the office across the hallway, that this man had to be D'Angelo. The very man she had come here to see!

It was a realisation that ensured there was absolutely no deference in Eva's own expression as she straightened before crossing the room to thrust Sophie at him. 'Take her so I can get Sam,' she instructed impatiently as he made no effort to lift the baby from her arms but instead looked at her incredulously, down the long length of his aristocratic nose, with those black-on-black eyes.

Michael found himself having to look a long way down. Goodness, this woman was small, only an inch or two over five feet tall compared to his own six feet three inches. She had a coltish slenderness that was saved from appearing boyish by full and thrusting breasts tipped by delicate nipples, breasts that were completely bare beneath the purple T-shirt, if Michael wasn't mistaken. And he was pretty sure that he wasn't.

Those full breasts, along with the confident glint in those violet-coloured eyes surrounded by thick sooty lashes, were enough to tell Michael that she was indeed a woman rather than a girl, and possibly aged in her early to mid-twenties.

She was also, he acknowledged grudgingly, extremely beautiful, her face dominated by those incredible violet-coloured eyes, a short pert nose, and full and sensuous lips, while her skin was as pale and delicate as the finest porcelain. Dark shadows beneath the violet eyes gave her an appearance of fragility.

A fragility that was somewhat nullified by the stubborn set of the woman's full lips above an equally determined and thrusting chin.

Michael dragged his gaze away from that arrestingly beautiful face to instead stare down in horror at the pink-dress-clad baby this young woman held out in front of him; horror, because he had absolutely no experience with holding young babies. How could he have, when he had never been this close to a small baby since being one himself?

He recoiled back from the now-drooling infant. 'I don't think—'

'I've found that it's best not to think too much around Sophie and Sam, especially now they're teething,' he was assured dryly. 'You might want to put this on your shoulder to protect your jacket.'

The woman handed him a square of white linen as she dumped the baby unceremoniously into his arms before turning to stride back across the office, giving Michael a perfect view of her curvaceous denim-covered bottom as she bent down to unclip the strap that secured the second, still-whimpering baby into the pushchair.

Michael held the first baby—Sophie?—at arm's length, totally at a loss as to what to do with her, and more than a little disconcerted to find himself the focus of eyes the same beautiful deep violet colour as her mother's. A steady and intense focus that seemed far too knowing, almost mocking it seemed to him, for a baby of surely only a few months old.

Eva lifted Sam up out of the pushchair as she straightened, more than a little annoyed that the two gabbling Archangel employees had woken the babies up at all; it had taken the whole of the walk from the hotel to the gallery to lull them into falling asleep in the first place, after a disjointed night of one or other of the twins—and consequently Eva—being woken up with teething pains.

As a result both Eva and the babies were feeling a little disgruntled this morning. Which didn't prevent her from almost laughing out loud as she turned to find D'Angelo was still holding Sophie with both arms straight out in front of him, a look of absolute horror on his face, as if the baby were a time bomb about to go off!

But Eva only almost laughed…

Because there had been very little for her to laugh about these past few nightmarish months.

Those memories sobered Eva instantly. 'Sophie doesn't bite,' she snapped impatiently as she cuddled a denim-and-T-shirt-clad Sam in her arms. 'Well…not much,' she amended ruefully. 'Luckily they both only have four teeth at the moment…'

Michael wasn't known for his patience at the best of times—and right now, in the midst of this chaos, was far from the best of times. 'I'm more interested in knowing what they, and you, are doing in the private area of Archangel, than in hearing how many teeth your children have!'

The woman's pointed chin rose as she looked at him with hard and challenging violet eyes. 'Do you really want me to discuss that in front of your employees, Mr

D'Angelo? I take it that you are Mr D'Angelo?' She quirked a derisive brow.

'I am, yes.' Michael scowled darkly. 'Discuss what in front of my employees?' he prompted cautiously.

Her mouth thinned. 'The reason I'm in the private area of Archangel.'

He gave an impatient shake of his head. 'As I have absolutely no idea what your reasons might be I can't answer that question.'

'No?' she scorned.

'No,' Michael bit out harshly. 'Perhaps you would care to come through to my office…?'

Pierre, a man several years his junior, voiced his concern by launching into all the reasons—in French, of course!—as to why he felt it inadvisable for Michael to be alone with this woman, with several less than polite references made as to whether or not she was quite sane, along with the suggestion that they call security and have her ejected from the building.

'I understood all that,' their visitor answered in fluent French as she turned her glittering violet and challenging gaze on the now less than comfortable Pierre. 'And you can call security if you want, but, I assure you, I'm quite sane,' she mocked Michael.

'I never doubted it for a moment!' Michael drawled, equally mockingly. 'It's fine, Pierre,' he assured in English. 'If you would care to come through to my office…?' he prompted the woman again, before stepping out of the doorway to reveal the room behind him, still having no idea what to do with the baby in his arms. Especially as the baby—Sophie—was now smiling up at him beguilingly as she proudly displayed those four tiny white teeth.

'She likes you,' the baby's mother announced disgustedly as she continued to carry Sam at the same time as she manoeuvred the pushchair past Michael and into his office.

He hastily placed the piece of white linen on his shoulder and hefted the baby into one arm before he was able to close the office door behind him on the wide-eyed and slightly worried stares of Marie and Pierre.

'Wow, this is some view…'

Michael turned to see the violet-eyed woman gazing out of the floor-to-ceiling-windows at the view up the length of the Champs Élysées to the Arc de Triomphe; that view, and the prestigious address, were the main reasons for choosing this stunning location for the Paris gallery. 'We like it,' he drawled with hard dismissal. 'Now, if you wouldn't mind explaining yourself…?' he added pointedly. 'Beginning with who you are?' Michael had wondered briefly if she wasn't the persistent Monique from Rafe's past, but the English accent seemed to say not.

Eva turned, still holding a now-quiet Sam in her arms. 'My name is Eva Foster.'

'And?' D'Angelo prompted when she added nothing else to that statement, those obsidian-black eyes blank of emotion.

Eva eyed him impatiently. 'And you obviously have absolutely no idea who I am,' she realised with horror.

He arched dark brows. 'Should I have?'

Should he have? Of course he should, the arrogant, irresponsible jerk— 'Perhaps the name Rachel Foster would be more helpful in jogging your memory?' she prompted sweetly.

He frowned darkly even as he gave a slow shake of his head. 'I'm sorry, but I have absolutely no idea what—or who—you're talking about…'

A red tide seemed to pass in front of Eva's eyes. All these months of heartache, chaos, heartache, loss, and, yes, just plain heartache, and this man didn't even remember Rachel's name, let alone Rachel herself—!

'What sort of man are you? Don't bother to answer that,' Eva added furiously as she began to pace the office. 'Obviously so many women pass in and out of your privileged life, and your no doubt silk-sheeted bed, that you forget about them as soon as the next one takes up occupancy—'

'Stop right there,' D'Angelo advised harshly. 'No, I didn't mean you, little one,' he added softly as Sophie gave a protesting whimper at the tone of his voice. His eyes were as black and piercing as jet as he turned back to Eva. 'Are you implying that you believe I've been... involved with this Rachel Foster?'

Eva's eyes widened angrily, her cheeks warming with temper. 'This Rachel Foster happens to be my sister, and, yes, you've been "involved" with her. In fact, you're holding part of the evidence of that involvement in your arms right now!'

Michael instantly stared down at the baby he held. Not a newborn, certainly, probably a few months old, possibly five or six, and very cute, as babies went, with her mop of black hair, those violet-coloured eyes, and her little face screwed up in concentration as she played with one of the buttons on the jacket of his several-thousand-pound suit.

If this woman, this Eva Foster, was trying to say that he was somehow responsible?

Shades of yesterday...

'I've never met your sister,' Michael stated firmly. 'Let alone—I've never met her,' he repeated coldly. 'So whatever scam the two of you are trying to pull here I would advise that you forget it—' He broke off abruptly as one of Eva Foster's hands made loud and painful contact with one of his cheeks, causing the baby in his arms to let out another deafening wail. 'That was uncalled for,' he bit out between gritted teeth, his jaw clenched as he jiggled the baby up and down in his arms in an effort to silence her screams.

'It was very called for,' Eva Foster insisted heatedly, her face having become even paler as she moved forward to soothingly stroke the back of the baby in Michael's arms. 'How dare you stand there and deny even knowing my sister, accuse the two of us of trying to pull a scam on you, at the same time as you're holding your own daughter in your arms?' Her eyes flashed deeply violet in contrast to the emotional shaking of her voice.

'I am not—' Michael broke off to draw in a deep, controlling breath, his cheek still stinging from that slap. 'Sophie is not my daughter.'

'I assure you she is,' she snapped.

'Do you think we could both just take a couple of deep breaths, maybe step back a little, and try to calm this situation down? It's distressing the babies,' Michael added firmly as Eva Foster opened her mouth with the obvious intention of continuing to argue with him.

It was unusual for anyone to argue with him, period, Michael being accustomed to issuing orders and having them obeyed rather than have people dispute them. Nor did he appreciate the added complication of this woman— a feisty young woman he acknowledged as being irritatingly beautiful—continuing to accuse him of fathering her sister's babies.

It was an accusation Michael didn't appreciate. He'd learnt his lesson many years ago when it came to the machinations of women. And he had Emma Lowther to thank that, for teaching him to never, ever trust a woman, when it came to contraception or anything else.

How many years ago was it since Emma had tried to blackmail him into marriage by claiming she was pregnant?

Fourteen. And Michael still remembered every moment of it as if it were yesterday.

Not that he had ever thought of shirking his responsibility. Oh, no, Michael had been stupid enough to think he was actually in love with Emma, had even been pleased about the baby, and the two of them had been making wedding plans for weeks when he introduced Emma to an acquaintance at a party, and she had decided within days of that introduction that Daniel, his family richer even than Michael's, would be a far better choice as a husband. Which was when she had told Michael there was no baby, that she had been mistaken. Three months later she had tried to use the same trick on Daniel.

The scene that had followed, once Emma had learnt that Michael had warned Daniel of her machinations, that there was no baby this time either, had not been pleasant!

Emma's pregnancy had been a sham, a trick to make Michael marry her, and it had been enough of a warning for him never again to trust any woman to take care of contraception...

Which was why he could now confidently deny Eva Foster's claim in regard to her sister's babies.

'Twins,' she now corrected softly. 'The babies are twins.'

They certainly looked of a similar age and colouring: both had silky heads of ebony dark hair and the same amazing violet-coloured eyes as their aunt. Their features weren't completely formed as yet, but there were certainly enough similarities for Michael to accept Eva Foster's claim that they were twins.

But whether they were twins or otherwise, they were not—most definitely not!—Michael's children.

'How old are they?' he bit out tightly.

'Trying to jog your memory?' she scorned.

'How old?' Michael repeated through those gritted teeth.

She shrugged. 'Six months.'

And if Rachel Foster had gone full term with her babies that would mean nine months to be added onto the six months, making it fifteen months ago he was supposed to have—

Damn it, why was Michael even bothering to do the maths? No matter what this woman might claim to the contrary, he had not impregnated any woman fifteen months ago or at any other time!

'And you believe they're mine because…?' He kept his voice soft and even as Sophie's lids began to flicker and her head dropped down sleepily onto his shoulder, the infant obviously tired out by her previous screeching.

That pointed chin rose another challenging notch. 'Because Rachel told me they were.'

Michael nodded. 'In that case, would you care to explain why your sister hasn't come here and confronted me with this information herself?'

'Because— Careful!' Eva warned as she realised Sophie had fallen into the completely boneless sleep only babies seemed able to do, and was almost slipping off one of those broad shoulders as a result.

'How did you do that?' she breathed ruefully as she looked at the sleeping Sophie.

Usually the twins only fell asleep after she had walked them in their pushchair or bounced them up and down for hours; Eva couldn't remember the last time she'd had even one uninterrupted night's sleep. And those lazy Sunday mornings of dozing in bed until lunchtime, which she had once taken so much for granted, now seemed like a self-indulgent dream, a mirage, and one Eva was sure she was destined never to know again.

'Do what?' D'Angelo rasped softly.

'Never mind,' Eva muttered irritably. 'Just put Sophie in the left side of the pushchair. She doesn't like sitting on the right side,' she supplied wearily as he paused to raise dark, questioning brows.

'She's asleep, so what does it matter?'

'She knows when she wakes up,' Eva dismissed impatiently.

'Right,' Michael drawled dryly, willing to take this woman's word for it that a six-month-old baby was aware of which side of a pushchair she was sitting in.

He looked down at the baby after he had somehow managed to ease her down into the pushchair without waking her. Sophie was like a dark-haired angel, ebony lashes fanning across her flushed cheeks, her mouth a little pouting rosebud.

He straightened abruptly as he realised what he was doing. 'What about that one?' He indicated the baby in Eva Foster's arms.

'*His* name's Sam,' she supplied somewhat tartly. 'And he's just fine where he is.' She looked down indulgently at the baby now snuggled into her throat. 'Sam is more placid than Sophie,' she explained waspishly as she obviously saw Michael's mocking expression. 'What did you say?' she prompted softly as he muttered under his breath.

'I said that's probably because he's a man,' Michael repeated unabashedly.

Eva Foster gave a scathing snort. 'It's been my experience that men tend to be lazy, not placid!'

'I beg your pardon?' Michael's brow lowered.

'I'm sure you heard me the first time,' she came back with feigned sweetness.

He had, and he hadn't liked it either; he and his two brothers had worked damned hard the past ten years to develop the one gallery they had then owned into three, spread across London, New York and Paris, and to build them up to become some of the most prestigious private galleries and auction houses in the world. And the three brothers were now reaping some of the benefits of that hard work, all of them extremely wealthy and able to live a lifestyle befitting that wealth, then it certainly wasn't because it had just been handed to them on a silver platter.

The scornful expression on Eva Foster's delicately lovely face showed she obviously thought otherwise!

As she was also under some strange delusion that Michael was the father of her niece and nephew...

It was time—past time!—that he took control of this situation. 'In your opinion.' He nodded tersely as he moved to sit behind his black marble desk. 'You were about to tell me why you're here instead of your sister...?'

Eva was well aware of the fact that D'Angelo had deliberately chosen to resume his seat behind his desk, as a way of putting some distance between the two of them at the same time as it put their conversation onto a businesslike footing. Although how anyone could think, or talk, of babies in a 'businesslike' way was beyond her!

D'Angelo wasn't at all what she had been expecting of the man who had first charmed and then impregnated her younger sister. Rachel had been fun-loving, and, yes, slightly irresponsible, having decided to travel around the world for a year once she had finished university, only to come back to London ten months later, alone and pregnant. With this man's baby—which had turned out to be babies, plural.

The man seated behind the desk wasn't what Eva had imagined when her sister had talked so enthusiastically of her lover's charm and good looks, and the fun they'd had together in Paris. Oh, this man was certainly handsome enough, dark and brooding—dangerously so, she would hazard a guess, and causing Eva to give an inner wince as she looked at the mark her hand had left on one of those perfectly chiselled cheeks. No doubt that dangerous aura this man exuded was counteracted by the tight control he also showed, otherwise she might have found herself with a similar imprint on her own cheek!

His was such an austere handsomeness: icy black eyes, harshly etched features, his manner rigidly controlled, and there was a cool aloofness to him that it was difficult for Eva to imagine ever melting, even—especially!—when he made love with a woman.

She certainly couldn't imagine him and the slightly irresponsible Rachel as ever having gone out together, let alone—

Maybe it would be better, for all concerned, if Eva's thoughts didn't dwell on the physical side of Rachel's relationship with this man. A physical relationship he continued to deny!

Her mouth thinned as she answered him. 'I'm here instead of Rachel because my sister is dead.'

He gave a visible start. 'What…?'

If Eva had thought to make him feel guilty, to get some reaction other than shock with the starkness of her statement, then she was disappointed; he looked suitably shocked, but in a distant way, rather than as a man hearing of the death of an ex-lover.

Eva drew in a sharp, shaky breath as she attempted to keep her own emotions under control. It was some weeks since she had needed to explain to anyone that her sister had died, and to do so now, to the man who had once been Rachel's lover—even if he denied all knowledge of it—was particularly hard.

Just as Eva still found it impossible to believe, to ac-

cept, that her sister Rachel, only twenty-two, and supposedly with all of her life still ahead of her, had died, quite
peaceably in the end, just three short months ago.

And Eva had been trying to cope ever since with her
own grief as well as the care of the twins. It was a battle
she had finally had to accept she was losing, physically as
well as financially. First Rachel had been so ill, and then
she had died, and it had been—and still was—almost impossible for Eva to work when she had cared for Rachel
and then had the full-time day-to-day care—and the sleepless nights—of the twins to cope with. Her savings had
now dwindled almost to nothing, certainly quicker than
she was able to replenish them with the few photographic
assignments she had been free to accept these past six
months. Assignments when she had been able to take the
twins with her, which was becoming increasingly difficult
the bigger and more vocal they got.

Which was why Eva had decided, rather than giving
D'Angelo the opportunity to fob her off in a telephone call,
to instead use the last of her savings to fly herself and the
twins over to Paris yesterday, so that she might confront
the babies' father face to face with his responsibilities.

Much as Eva might hate having to do it, after much
soul-searching, she knew she no longer had any choice
but to try and seek D'Angelo's help from a financial point
of view, at least, for the good of the twins.

Michael stood up abruptly as he saw how pale Eva
Foster's face had become, adding to that air of fragility.
Her sister's death, caring for the twins, went some way to
explaining those dark shadows beneath those beautiful
violet-coloured eyes.

He crossed economically to the drinks cabinet in the
seating area of his office to look at the array of bottles,
deciding against offering her alcohol and instead choos-

ing to bring her a bottle of water from the small fridge. He very much doubted Eva Foster would have accepted drinking a more reviving whisky, when she had two young babies in her care.

'Here, let me take Sam, while you sit down over here,' he rasped abruptly as he saw Eva Foster was swaying slightly on her canvas-shod feet. Not waiting for her reply, he took the baby from her unresisting arms before placing his free hand lightly beneath her elbow to guide her over to the seating area and eased her down onto the black leather sofa.

'Sorry about that,' Eva murmured shakily after taking a much-needed sip of the ice-cold water. It was very warm outside, and it had been a long walk to the Archangel gallery from the cheap hotel she had booked into with the twins yesterday. 'I think I'm doing okay and then suddenly the grief just hits me again when I'm least expecting it.'

Although she should have realised that this meeting with Rachel's lover was going to be far from easy. Just as coming to Paris at all, seeking out D'Angelo, hadn't been an easy decision for her to make in the first place. In Eva's eyes, it almost smacked of defeat.

But she'd had no other choice, she assured herself determinedly; this was for the twins' benefit, not hers. As it was, she would far rather spit in this man's eye than so much as have to speak to him, let alone ask him for help!

'I'm sorry for your loss,' D'Angelo murmured gruffly.

Was he? Considering he had denied all knowledge of Rachel just minutes ago, Eva found that a little hard to believe!

She still couldn't quite come to terms with Rachel ever having been involved with this austerely cold man at all; Rachel had been outgoing and warm in nature, and this man was anything but. But maybe it had been a case of opposites attracting? D'Angelo was certainly attractive enough, and he possessed an inborn confidence, an arrogance, that Rachel might have found attractive, even challenging. This man's controlled aloofness would represent a challenge to any red-blooded female.

Even Eva?

The last thing she wanted was to find the man who had fathered the twins in the least attractive!

Eva sat forward to place the bottle of water on the coffee table in front of her. 'I think you can put him down too now...' she drawled ruefully as she realised that Sam—the traitor!—had also fallen asleep on one of D'Angelo's broad and muscled shoulders. All those hours of pacing and walking, a twin on each of her shoulders, and D'Angelo just had to hold them to have the twins instantly fall asleep!

Because they instinctively recognised who he was? Maybe. As Eva had learnt these past few months, babies were far more intuitive than she had ever realised; the twins had both certainly quickly picked up on Eva's own nervousness in caring for them twenty-four seven, making a battle of their first few weeks together.

Michael turned to look at Eva Foster after he had secured the sleeping Sam in the pushchair beside his sister, relieved to see that, although the shadows beneath her eyes remained, those porcelain cheeks had at least regained a little of their colour, that pallor having been emphasised by straight and glossy ebony hair to just below her shoulders.

He was more than a little troubled himself to learn of the death of this woman's sister, the mother of the sleeping babies. 'How old was she...?'

Eva Foster looked at him blankly. 'Who?'

'Your sister Rachel.'

Derisive brows rose over those violet-coloured eyes. 'The two of you were too busy to discuss ages?'

Michael drew in a sharp breath at the obvious derision in her tone. 'I repeat that, to my knowledge, I didn't so much as even meet your sister in order to be able to discuss our respective ages, let alone father her twins!'

'And I repeat, I don't believe you,' Eva Foster stated coldly.

'I can see that.' Michael nodded grimly.

She drew in a shaky breath. 'Rachel was just twenty-two when she died, three years younger than me,' she stated huskily.

'In childbirth?'

'No.' She grimaced. 'They discovered, during a routine scan partway through the pregnancy, that Rachel had a tumour.'

'God!'

Eva Foster nodded abruptly. 'Rachel refused to have the pregnancy terminated, or to have treatment for the tumour, because of the danger of harming the babies. She...died when they were three months old.' And the pain of that loss, of the consequences of her sister's decision, was now etched into that creamy brow and in the lines of strain beside those violet eyes and sensuously sculptured mouth...

'What about your parents...?' he prompted huskily.

'They both died in a car crash eighteen months ago.'

Michael folded his lean length down into the armchair opposite the sofa, uncomfortable towering over Eva Foster in the circumstances, at the same time as he recognised she wouldn't appreciate him sitting down beside her on the sofa. There was currently a defensive aura about Eva Foster, an invisible barrier that was preventing her from breaking down completely.

Not surprising, when first her parents had died and she had now lost her younger sister so tragically. Michael was the eldest of the three D'Angelo brothers, and he couldn't imagine—didn't want to imagine—the devastation he would feel if he should ever lose his parents so suddenly, or Gabriel or Rafe before they had all grown old and grey together.

Which still didn't change the fact that he had absolutely no knowledge of Rachel Foster, or her babies. 'Where did Rachel and the babies' father meet?' he prompted gruffly.

Eva Foster shot him an impatient glance. 'Right here in the gallery.'

Michael did some mental arithmetic. 'I wasn't in Paris, or the gallery here, fifteen months ago.'

'What...?' Eva looked at him blankly.

He grimaced. 'I wasn't in Paris fifteen months ago, Eva,' he repeated gently. 'Until recently, my brothers and I have moved around the three galleries on a rotation basis,' he added as she still stared at him dazedly. 'I was at the New York gallery fifteen months ago, organising a gala exhibition of Mayan art.'

She gave a slow shake of her head. 'I don't— My sister said—'

'Yes?'

Eva could barely breathe, a sinking, nauseous sensation in the pit of her stomach as she prompted warily, 'Exactly who are you...?'

He gave a tight smile. 'Isn't it a little late to be asking me that when you've already accused me of having been "involved" with your sister and fathering your niece and nephew?'

Eva's mouth had gone so dry she didn't even have enough saliva left to moisten the stiffness of her equally dry lips. 'I assumed— Who are you?' she demanded to know shakily, her hands tightly clenched together as they rested on her thighs.

'Michael D'Angelo.'

*Michae*l D'Angelo? *Michael* not—

Eva thought she might actually be physically sick at the realisation that all this time she had been accusing the *wrong* D'Angelo brother of fathering the twins!

CHAPTER TWO

OH, GOOD GRIEF, why hadn't Eva thought to ask this man for his full name? To find out which of the D'Angelo brothers she was actually talking to before—before—well, at least before she had launched into her accusations?

Unfortunately, Eva knew exactly why she hadn't done any of those things...

Because this man—Michael D'Angelo—brought out a response in her, a physical awareness, she had considered as being entirely inappropriate in regard to the man she had believed to have been involved with Rachel.

Not that it was any less inappropriate now; he was still the *brother* of the man who had fathered the twins!

He was just so much larger than life, exuded a confidence, an aura of power, that caused Eva to be aware of everything about him: the way his hair was inclined to curl slightly at his ears and nape, the intensity of those black-on-black eyes, the harsh and yet somehow mesmerising sensual lines of his finely sculptured face, and as for the way his shoulders and chest filled out his perfectly tailored jacket, and the slim cut of his trousers emphasised the lean length of his long legs—

'Drink some more water.' Michael was suddenly down on his haunches beside Eva holding out the water bottle towards her.

Eva took the bottle with shaking fingers, drinking thirstily as she realised she was starting to hyperventilate just thinking about the way this man looked. At the same time she inwardly cringed as she recalled all of their conversation, the things she had said, the accusations she had made—and all *to the wrong man*!

His identity as *Michael* D'Angelo certainly explained why Eva hadn't been able to imagine her fun-loving sister Rachel ever being attracted to such a coldly aloof man who was also so much older than her, let alone involved in the passionate affair with him that had resulted in the birth of the twins!

None of which helped the awkwardness of the situation Eva now found herself in. 'It seems I owe you an apology,' she murmured stiffly. 'I— Obviously I made a mistake. I— It— I don't know what else to say...' She groaned self-consciously, unable to look Michael D'Angelo in the eye now.

Unable to look into that coolly arrogant face at all. A face, a man, she shouldn't find in the least attractive.

Except Eva knew that she did...

She couldn't stop herself from giving him a brief sideways glance, once again struck by the chiselled perfection of Michael D'Angelo's features: those black obsidian eyes that revealed so little of the man's thoughts or feelings, those sculptured cheekbones, his mouth—dear Lord, this man's mouth was pure perfection, the top lip fuller than the bottom.

Possibly as an indication he had a deeply sensual nature?

If it was, then Eva was sure it was a sensuality this coldly aloof man always kept firmly under his own iron control!

This man...

Michael D'Angelo.

A man Eva knew she had to guard herself against being any more attracted to.

He straightened abruptly. 'As I said earlier, maybe we should both take a few deep breaths, a step back, and calm this situation down?'

Eva still felt as if she was on the edge of hyperventilating again rather than calming down!

Having made the hard decision to come to Paris in the first place, she had planned out in her mind exactly how her meeting with D'Angelo was going to proceed once she arrived here.

She would find a way to confront D'Angelo.

Which she had done.

He would deny any and all involvement with Rachel.

Which he had done.

Eva would then scorn that denial, with the twins as proof of that 'involvement'.

Which she had done.

D'Angelo's accusation that she and Rachel were trying to pull some sort of scam on him, by claiming the babies were his, had been unexpected...

As much as Eva's response, slapping his face, had been; she had never thought of herself as being a person capable of violence until today!

And the conversation had seemed to go downhill from there...

She drew in several deep and steadying breaths before speaking again, determined not to lose complete control of this situation.

'That's all well and good, Mr D'Angelo, but I think you're still missing the point here.'

Michael D'Angelo quirked one dark and arrogant brow. 'Which is?'

Eva straightened her shoulders determinedly as she met

his gaze unblinkingly. 'That you may be correct in claiming not to be the twins' father—'

'I assure you, I am not their father,' he bit out hardly.

'—but that doesn't change the fact that one of your brothers most certainly is,' Eva continued firmly, her gaze meeting his challengingly now.

At the same time, she inwardly questioned just how Michael D'Angelo could speak so certainly of never having fathered a baby by Rachel. Eva certainly didn't believe it was from physically abstaining. Beneath this man's aloofness she sensed that sensuality, deep and dark, an indication that, once aroused, he would be the type of lover who would demand and possess a woman completely.

He was also, Eva acknowledged with a frown, a man who would need to be in control at all times, and as such he would no doubt ensure that he would never forget to take the necessary precautions to ensure that no unwanted pregnancy ensued from any of his relationships with women.

Something Eva should probably have realised *before* she accused him of being the twins' father!

Michael's breath left him in a hiss as he took in the full ramifications of Eva Foster's revelations. Almost wishing now—almost!—that he *had* been the one responsible for fathering Rachel Foster's twin babies. Because for either of his younger brothers to be the father—his now both very much married younger brothers—would be a disaster of unthinkable proportions.

Not that Gabriel or Rafe had been married fifteen months ago, when the twins were conceived, but they were now, Gabriel for just five weeks, Rafe for only a matter of days. And it would surely be asking a lot—too much, perhaps—for either Bryn or Nina to accept that either of their respective husbands had fathered the now six-month-old twins with another woman!

His mouth thinned. 'I think, having already made one mistake, that you need to be a little more certain of your facts before you go around making any more accusations.'

Colour warmed Eva Foster's porcelain cheeks. 'My mistake—for which I've apologised—' she added uncomfortably, 'doesn't alter the fact that one of your brothers fathered Sophie and Sam.'

Michael turned away to give himself the privacy for the emotions he was sure must be apparent on his face: dismay, concern, and not a little anger, all of them directed towards whichever of his brothers had caused this current situation.

He thrust his hands in the pockets of his trousers as he walked over to stand in front of the windows, for once totally blind to the magnificent view outside. Because he could never remember feeling quite so helpless, so out of his depth with a situation. Until now.

As the eldest brother, even if only by a year and two years respectively, he had always been protective of Rafe and Gabriel—sometimes too much so for their liking. But in this present situation—surely a disaster just waiting to happen, no matter which of his brothers Eva Foster was accusing?—he couldn't think of any way in which to avert the coming disaster.

But for which one of his brothers…?

The outwardly light-hearted but inwardly determined and assertive Rafe, who had finally found, fallen in love with and married the beautiful Nina, the perfect woman to counterbalance those apparent contradictions in his mercurial nature?

Or Gabriel, in love with Bryn for the past five years but thinking it an impossible love, a lost love, that he had no right to, only for the two of them to meet again and learn that it wasn't, now happily married to each other?

Whichever of his brothers was responsible it was sure to cause—

'Rafe.'

Michael's eyes were narrowed as he turned sharply back to face Eva Foster. 'What?' he rasped harshly, coldly, already knowing what her answer was going to be but wishing—so much wishing—that he didn't.

'It was Rafe that Rachel was involved with fifteen months ago,' Eva Foster supplied abruptly.

Michael had already worked out in his mind which of his two brothers had been in charge of the Paris gallery fifteen months ago, and it now took tremendous effort of will on his part to keep his expression remote and unemotional as Eva Foster confirmed his worst fear.

Oh, Michael had no doubt that Nina loved Rafe unconditionally, and that his brother loved Nina in the same way, and that somehow, between the two of them, they would find a way to deal with this situation, for their marriage to survive the blow.

But Nina's father, the rich and powerful Dmitri Palitov, was another matter entirely. His protection of his daughter was absolute, and he would not look kindly on anyone who dared to threaten Nina's happiness.

Michael knew that Rafe was more than capable of taking care of himself; it was Eva Foster for whom he now felt concern…

'I hope you'll forgive me if I'm still a little sceptical as to the accuracy of your accusation!' Michael now rasped scathingly.

While inwardly his heart was beating erratically, and his thoughts racing, as he tried to think of some way to come up with some proof that Eva Foster was wrong for the second time in regard to the identity of the twins' father.

Except…

Until Rafe met and fell in love with Nina, he had played fast and loose with dozens of beautiful women—something Michael had warned him about on more than one occasion.

And there was no changing the fact that Rafe had been here at the Paris Archangel fifteen months ago.

Most importantly of all—despite her initial mistake in having thought Michael was Rafe—Eva Foster seemed very certain of the name of the man responsible for having fathered her niece and nephew...

'Be as sceptical as you like,' she came back evenly. 'We'll both know the truth once I've had a chance to speak to your brother.'

That was what Michael was afraid of! 'Obviously he isn't in Paris at the moment.'

'I suppose you're now going to tell me that I need not have put myself through the trauma of flying to Paris with the twins,' she drawled self-derisively, 'because Rafe is currently at the London Archangel gallery?'

Michael was having trouble speaking at all, his thoughts were so chaotic. Unusual for him, but then this situation was beyond anything he'd ever had to deal with before.

One thing he was sure of, and that was that he didn't want Eva Foster roaming about, here or in London, repeating her accusations to anyone else. Not till he'd had the chance to talk to Rafe. Something Michael had no intention of doing for the next two weeks, at least!

'No.' He spoke softly. 'I'm not going to tell you that.'

'Please don't tell me he's at the New York gallery!' Eva groaned. She couldn't bear even the thought of flying all the way to New York with six-month-old twins who were cranky most of the time because they were both teething. Although to look at the two of them now, both sleeping like little angels, no one would ever believe it!

'No, I'm not going to tell you that, either...' Michael D'Angelo answered slowly.

Eva looked at him between narrowed lids, finding it impossible to read anything from his closed expression; those black-on-black eyes were completely without emotion, the harshness of his features set into hard, uncompromising lines. 'And we've already established he isn't here, either, so where is he?' she prompted suspiciously.

'Unavailable.'

Her brows rose at the terseness of Michael D'Angelo's answer. 'That isn't an acceptable answer, I'm afraid.'

His mouth tightened grimly. 'It's the only one you're going to get for the moment.'

Eva eyed him shrewdly. 'Why "for the moment"...?' she finally prompted guardedly.

This woman was too astute for her own good, Michael recognised impatiently. For his good too. And most certainly for Rafe's!

'It just isn't,' Michael bit out between clenched teeth.

Obviously this woman hadn't seen the photographs in the Sunday newspapers of Rafe and Nina's marriage on Saturday, no doubt because caring for six-month-old twins didn't leave her a lot of time for doing anything else. But Michael knew that he couldn't keep that truth from her indefinitely.

Eva Foster bristled. 'I need to speak to him urgently.'

He nodded. 'Anything you have to say to Rafe you can say to me.'

'Having already made that mistake once, I don't think so!' she bit out.

Michael's nostrils flared his impatience. 'I will naturally pass on your...concerns, to my brother, when I next speak to him, but other than that—'

'No,' Eva Foster stated firmly as she stood up abruptly.

'That simply isn't good enough, Mr D'Angelo,' she answered his questioningly raised brows. 'I need to talk to him now,' she insisted, 'not after you next happen to speak to him.'

Michael had to give this woman credit for tenacity—all five feet and a dot of her!

That determined glitter in those violet-coloured eyes said she wasn't about to back down any time soon either, not from him, or her demand that she speak to Rafe. 'I've already said that isn't possible.'

Her eyes flashed. 'Then I suggest you *make* it possible, Mr D'Angelo!'

'I don't care for your tone,' he bit out harshly.

Eva shrugged. 'Then maybe you should stop trying to prevent me from speaking with your brother.'

Michael bit back his own anger. 'The twins are now six months old, so why this sudden urgency to speak to the man your sister told you was their father?'

'He is their father,' Eva insisted stubbornly.

And why the sudden urgency...? Because Eva, much as she had tried, much as she hated having to admit defeat, knew that she just couldn't cope any more without help. Financially. Or emotionally.

Although she had no intention of admitting the latter to the aloofly controlled and ultra-self-confident Michael D'Angelo, a man who looked capable of dealing with any situation...

How could a man like him possibly understand the crippling heartache that washed over Eva like a dark and oppressive tide whenever she allowed herself to dwell on the death of her sister Rachel, let alone how inadequate Eva felt, no matter how much she might love the twins, for the task of caring for two rapidly growing babies?

And all of that was apart from the fact that she simply

didn't have enough money coming in to be able to afford the care the twins needed now, or in the future.

There was no way Eva could go away on photographic assignments any more, because she simply couldn't leave the twins for any length of time. Even taking local assignments, going back to the well-paid but monotonous photography of weddings and christenings was becoming problematic as the twins grew older, making it increasingly difficult for Eva to take them with her; brides tended to frown at having the photographer's twin babies scream at their wedding!

And even if Eva could manage to find a child-minder that she trusted it was going to cost yet more money, and so eat into any of the fees she might earn from her work.

No, Eva had thought long and hard before seeking out Rafe D'Angelo, considered her options carefully, and, unpalatable as this alternative might be, she couldn't see any other way out of this problem other than asking the twins' father for financial help.

It wasn't as if she wanted anything else from him, just a way of being able to care for the twins without having to worry where the next penny was coming from. But that was all she wanted.

After meeting and speaking with Michael D'Angelo, Eva was convinced the less physical interaction any of the D'Angelo family had with the twins—and her!—the better she would like it!

She gave a shake of her head. 'It's your brother Rafe I need to speak to, Mr D'Angelo, not you.'

Michael had no idea as to the thoughts that had been going through Eva Foster's head these past few moments, but he did know they hadn't been pleasant ones. Her face was once again as pale as bone china, those deep shadows under her violet-coloured eyes more prominent, and the fullness of her mouth appeared to be trembling slightly, as further evidence of her vulnerability.

An air of vulnerability Michael had a feeling this woman would hate intensely if she was made aware of it!

He narrowed his eyes. 'Have you eaten anything today?'

She gave him a startled look at this sudden change of subject. 'Sorry?'

He shrugged. 'It's almost lunchtime, and you're looking a little pale, so I wondered if you had eaten anything today.'

She blinked long sooty lashes. 'I— Yes, I believe I did manage to grab a piece of toast while I was feeding the twins their breakfast.'

No doubt she only managed to grab something to eat a lot of the time with two small babies to care for! 'At your hotel?'

She gave a slightly derisive smile. 'I believe you would call it more of a *pension* than a hotel. It was the best I could afford, okay?' she added defensively as Michael's frown deepened. 'We can't all live in penthouse apartments in major cities around the world and fly about in private jets, you know!'

There was no denying that Michael did exactly that, as did his two brothers. Which was no doubt one of the reasons Eva Foster had decided to seek out the twins' father and ask for his help... 'And where is this pension?'

'It's in a back street just a short walk away from the Gare du Nord,' she revealed reluctantly. 'Look, if I could just speak to your brother—'

'I take it you intend to ask him for financial help when you do speak with him?'

Her cheeks flushed. 'It's my intention to remind him of his financial responsibility towards his two children, yes— Don't look at me like that!' she snapped sharply, her slender hands clenched so tightly together her knuckles showed white.

'How am I looking at you?' Michael prompted evenly.

'As if you still think I'm some sort of gold-digger out to fleece your brother out of some of his millions!' She gave a disgusted shake of her head. 'It wasn't easy for me to come here, you know.' She began to pace the office restlessly. 'The last thing I want is any contact with the twins' obviously reluctant father—'

'Are you saying that Rafe knows of the twins' existence…?' Michael looked at her through narrowed lids. If his brother had known of Rachel Foster's pregnancy and not told him, or, more importantly, not told Nina…!

Eva Foster came to an abrupt halt. 'I— No. I don't think so.'

'But you aren't sure?'

'Not absolutely, no.' Eva grimaced. 'But I'm assuming not. Rachel wasn't exactly forthcoming on the subject, except to tell me the name of her lover, and that the relationship was over by the time she found out she was pregnant,' she added heavily. 'I was out of the country when Rachel first realised she was pregnant, and she never so much as mentioned it during our weekly telephone conversations. By the time I returned to England she was already five months pregnant and had been diagnosed with the cancer.' She sighed. 'Pressing Rachel for more details of the babies' father, other than to tell me his name before she died, didn't seem very important at the time.'

'I imagine not.' Michael nodded. 'Returned from where?' For some reason he found himself more than a little interested as to why Eva Foster should have been out of her native England for several months.

She frowned. 'Does that matter?'

He shrugged. 'Just filling in the details.'

Eva shot him an irritated glare, sure that this man wasn't usually a man who cared for 'details', that he usually left such trivia for other people to deal with; he commanded, others obeyed! 'My work often takes me out of England. At least, it did,' she added with a grimace.

'Rachel was so ill the last six months of her life, and since then I've been caring for the twins on my own.'

'You haven't been able to work since your sister died?'

'Not properly, no.' It was the truth, so what else could she say?

'What—?'

'Look, my career, my life, none of this is up for discussion,' she snapped irritably.

She loved the twins, adored them actually, not just for themselves, but because they were all she had left of Rachel.

But Eva had trained and worked hard to become successful in a career that was dominated by men, and these past nine months of being unable to do that career had taken their toll, on both Eva personally, and the respect she had worked so hard to achieve for her photography.

'I disagree,' Michael D'Angelo bit out coolly. 'If—and it's still a big if, as far as I'm concerned—' he warned hardly, 'it should transpire that Rafe is the twins' father, then your career, and your life, would certainly both be very much up for discussion.'

Eva stilled as she looked across at him searchingly, a panicked fluttering beginning in her chest as she saw the hard, uncompromising jet of his eyes and the grim set of those sculptured lips.

She gave a slow, guarded shake of her head. 'Rachel made me the twins' legal guardian before she died...'

Dark brows rose. 'And their biological father would naturally take precedence over their maternal aunt.'

That panicked flutter turned into a full surge as Eva's heart seemed to be squeezed tightly inside her chest. 'Are you threatening to take the twins away from me, Mr D'Angelo...?'

Whatever it was Michael was doing, he certainly wasn't deriving any pleasure out of it. Inwardly he felt as if he were kicking an already starved and abused kitten.

Although this particular starved and abused kitten would probably spit in his eye as soon as look at him...

CHAPTER THREE

MICHAEL KNEW THE reputation he had, that most people believed him to be both cold and ruthless, an automaton without a heart, and in business perhaps that accusation was true. And no doubt many of his past lovers would also agree with that sentiment; several of the women he had been involved with over the years had accused him of lacking that particular organ when he had ended their relationship!

But Michael loved his family dearly—his parents and his two brothers, and now their two wives—and he would do anything he had to do in order to protect each and every one of them.

Even to the extent of browbeating a young, defence-less woman who only wanted to do what she believed was right for the only family she had left, namely her orphaned niece and nephew?

Unfortunately, yes.

But only because Michael didn't feel he had any choice. Because he dared not allow Eva Foster to repeat this wild accusation to anyone else until he'd had a chance to speak with Rafe, and he wasn't going to do that until Rafe and Nina returned from their honeymoon. And if the only way to achieve Eva Foster's silence was to put the fear of God into her, by giving her the impression that Rafe, if he should be the twins' father, might want custody of them, then that was what he'd do.

His brother was headstrong, yes, had deliberately earned himself the reputation of being something of a playboy these past fifteen years, but falling in love with Nina had changed his need for that armour. They were two very small, adorable babies, Michael acknowledged as he looked down at the angelically sleeping twins. The truth was Michael had absolutely no idea how Rafe would react to knowing, if it were true, that he had fathered twins with a woman other than Nina.

Michael only knew how he would feel in the same situation!

No matter what the cost to himself, to any other relationship he might have in his life at the time, Michael knew he would want his children with him. And Rafe, despite the outward differences in their personalities, was enough like him to feel the same way. Which was the reason Michael, at least, was convinced Rachel Foster hadn't told Rafe anything about her pregnancy or the twins' birth.

'I'm merely stating a fact, Miss Foster,' Michael answered her abruptly. 'Not that I'm saying that would definitely be the case, only that you should consider it as a possibility.'

Eva didn't want to even consider the idea of the twins ever being taken away from her!

Yes, she found it difficult, all-consuming, to care for two small babies night and day, but she would dare any woman in the same situation, even the natural mother, to deny that it was hard work.

And yes, caring for the twins had also put her career on semi-permanent hold.

But that didn't mean she would ever willingly give them up.

The opposite, in fact; she knew she would fight tooth and nail to prevent that from ever happening.

She strode over to take control of the babies' pushchair. 'Perhaps I made a mistake coming here.'

'I'm afraid it's too late for that, Eva.'

She stilled, as much at hearing Michael D'Angelo speak her name in that husky, nerve-tingling tone as at the words he had spoken.

And how stupid of her was that?

Michael D'Angelo was too arrogantly handsome for his own good, wealthy beyond belief, extremely powerful—worse, he was using those last two things to threaten her—and her only response was to once again feel that quiver of awareness down the length of her spine, to feel her breasts swelling beneath her T-shirt, and the nipples tightening, engorging, in physical arousal.

More humiliating still, they were no doubt engorged nipples that Michael D'Angelo would be able to see pressing against the tightness of her T-shirt!

Eva couldn't quite meet the darkness of his gaze as she gave him an over-bright smile at the same time as she turned the pushchair towards the office door. 'I'm sure I've taken up enough of your valuable time for one day, Mr D'Angelo—'

'You aren't leaving, Eva.'

She gave him a startled glance as she came to an abrupt halt. 'What do you mean? Of course I'm leaving.'

'This office, maybe—'

'There's no "maybe" about it—'

'—but I'm afraid I can't allow you to leave Paris until I've spoken to Rafe,' Michael D'Angelo continued as if she hadn't spoken, the authority in his voice unmistakable, despite the even softness of his tone.

'You can't *allow* me!' Eva stared at him incredulously.

'Forgive me, Mr D'Angelo, but at what point in this conversation did you think I gave you the right to tell me what I can or can't do?'

He gave a tight smile. 'I believe, Miss Foster, that it was at the point you told me it's your belief that my brother Rafe is the father of your niece and nephew.'

Eva's eyes narrowed. 'I think that's for Rafe and me to discuss further, don't you?'

'And that's where the problem lies.'

'I still fail to see why...?'

Michael drew in a deep controlling breath, hating what he was doing, but knowing he had no real choice. The fact that Eva Foster was so far unaware of Rafe's recent marriage didn't mean that she would remain so, and for Rafe and Nina's sake Michael had no choice but to keep an eye—a very close eye—on the young woman who could put a serious strain on his brother's recent marriage. And for Michael to be able to do that Eva Foster had to remain in Paris...

His mouth thinned. 'I've already told you my brother isn't available for either of us to talk to right now—'

'And very mysterious you were about it, if you want my opinion!' Those violet-coloured eyes snapped with temper. 'Which you probably don't,' she added scathingly as he continued to look at her coolly. 'I have the distinct impression you don't care for anyone else's opinion but your own!'

'I don't believe resorting to insults to be in the least constructive to this situation, Miss Foster,' he bit out icily.

'It's making *me* feel better,' Eva came back tartly.

Michael D'Angelo raised dark brows. 'And why is that?'

Why was that? Because the power this man exuded unnerved her. Just as his dark and charismatic good looks unsettled her. Worst of all, she found her physical reaction to him deeply disturbing.

And Eva didn't want to be unnerved, unsettled, or disturbed. She had realised, after this single meeting with Michael D'Angelo, that she would need to keep all of her wits about her when dealing with any of the D'Angelo family.

'You threatened me a few minutes ago,' she reminded tautly.

'I asked that you remain in Paris until Rafe returns.'

'As I remember it you didn't ask, you ordered,' Eva corrected dryly. 'And exactly where in the world is your brother Rafe that you can't just pick up a mobile phone and speak to him right here and right now?'

Michael D'Angelo sighed, his expression grim. 'It isn't the where he is, it's the why.'

'Why what?' Eva was completely puzzled by Michael D'Angelo's evasive behaviour; he didn't seem like the sort of man who would feel the need to avoid any situation.

'Why I consider Rafe to be currently unreachable as well as unavailable,' he revealed tightly.

'And are you going to tell me what that "why" is…?'

'It would seem I have little choice in the matter, when you could pick up any newspaper or simply go online and find out for yourself!' he bit out with exasperated impatience.

'You're starting to alarm me…' Eva frowned uncertainly.

'That wasn't my intention.' Michael sighed his frustration with this situation.

His day had started out like any other, the alarm going off at seven o'clock, allowing him time to shower and dress before leaving his apartment to walk to his favourite coffee shop, to sit down at his usual table and enjoy two cups of their strong coffee with delicious buttery croissants, before then strolling further along the street at eight-thirty to enter Archangel, and begin his day's work.

At no time in the past four hours had Michael had so much as a single indication that his day, his week—his year!—was going to be shot down in flames by a tiny violet-eyed firebrand and her baby niece and nephew!

But it had been, it still was, and would continue to be so until so he had a chance to speak with Rafe, so for the moment he had no choice but to deal with this situation as best he could...

Eva felt a sinking sensation in the pit of her stomach as Michael D'Angelo lifted his arrogantly chiselled chin to look at her with those glittering onyx-black eyes, telling Eva that whatever he was about to say to her she wasn't going to like it!

His jaw tightened. 'Rafe was married two days ago and is currently away on his honeymoon.'

Eva felt herself pale even as she reached out to grasp the back of one of the leather armchairs in an effort to stop herself from collapsing completely, her knees having gone weak, a loud buzzing sound inside her head.

'Here, sit down in this chair!'

Eva barely heard Michael D'Angelo's rasped instruction over the increased buzzing inside her head, offering no resistance as he took a light grasp of her arm to ease her down into one of the leather armchairs before straightening to step back and away from her, seeming to realise that she needed time and space in which to deal with her turmoil of thoughts.

Not that any amount of time or space was going to make this situation seem less disastrous!

Rafe D'Angelo was now married.

Worse than that, he had only been married for two days.

Just forty-eight hours!

If Eva had sought him out just a week ago, even three days ago, then it might have been different, but as things stood this now seemed like an impossible situation. It was one thing to approach Rafe D'Angelo and ask for his financial help with the twins, something else completely for Eve to possibly wreck his marriage before it had even begun.

Despite Eva's urgings for her to do so, Rachel hadn't really wanted to talk about Rafe D'Angelo after revealing the name of her babies' father. As far as her sister was concerned it had been a holiday romance, the two of them not in love with each other, just enjoying a couple of weeks' fun together in Paris.

Rachel had been totally realistic about the whole affair. It had happened, and it was over when she left Paris, and that was the end of the relationship as far as she was concerned. Learning of her pregnancy hadn't changed Rachel's mind about that in the slightest.

The decision to now seek out Rafe D'Angelo, to ask for his financial help with the twins, at least, had been completely Eva's own idea.

And she couldn't have chosen a worse time to do it!

Much as Eva needed Rafe D'Angelo's help with the twins, she wasn't a vindictive person, was well aware of the chaos it would cause if she was to force her way into his life now, with the twins in tow. As for his poor wife—!

Eva tried to imagine how she would feel if confronted with twin babies belonging to her new husband. Oh, God…!

No wonder Michael D'Angelo had been so adamant that neither he nor Eva could talk to Rafe 'right here and now'. He could hardly contact his brother on his *honeymoon* and tell him of Eva's presence in Paris, along with his son and daughter!

She drew in a deep breath, her head clearing slightly as she did so, willing her pulse to slow as she looked up at the broodingly silent Michael D'Angelo. 'I couldn't have come here at a worse time.' It was a statement rather than a question.

'Oh, I don't know,' he drawled dryly. 'I have a feeling that four o'clock in New York on Saturday would have been an even less welcome time for you to break the news. Rafe and Nina were married there at three o'clock,' he explained in response to Eva's puzzled frown.

And she didn't appreciate it if that was supposed to be Michael D'Angelo's attempt at humour—from a man who looked as if he very rarely found anything to smile about! 'What do I do now?' She gave a slightly dazed shake of her head.

'What do *we* do now?' Michael corrected hardly.

As far as he was concerned his decision not to let Eva Foster roam around Paris or London like a loose cannon, and in the process possibly arouse people's curiosity as to her reason for doing so, still stood. Marie and Pierre's obvious curiosity about her earlier was an example of exactly how that could, and no doubt would, occur!

No, until it became possible for Michael to talk to Rafe he intended keeping Eva Foster, and these two babies, well away from the public and curious eye. At great inconvenience to himself, he might add. Rafe had better appreciate what he was doing for him, because Michael had no doubt the next couple of weeks were going to be excruciatingly painful ones for him. His brother was certainly going to owe him—big time!

'I don't understand...' Eva Foster looked up at him blankly, obviously still suffering under some degree of shock at learning of Rafe's recent marriage.

Michael grimaced. 'How long did you intend staying in Paris...?'

She blinked. 'My return flight is booked for three days' time—I didn't think it would take more than a day or two to speak with your brother,' she added defensively as Michael frowned.

'Cutting it a little fine, weren't you?' he rasped impatiently. 'Never mind, we can cancel that flight and—'

'I have no intention of cancelling my flight.' Eva stood up abruptly. 'Coming here at all was a risk, and I have even less reason to stay on in Paris now that I know your brother isn't even here.' Or likely to be available anywhere any time soon for her to be able to talk to him, when he was currently on his *honeymoon*!

She should have telephoned before coming to Paris, of course, at least established that Rafe D'Angelo was actually in the city before flying over here and coming to the Archangel gallery and insisting on seeing him.

That was what Eva should have done. Except she hadn't wanted to alert the man to her imminent arrival, had hoped to catch him off guard, preventing him from leaving Paris before she had even arrived.

And instead Rafe was away on his honeymoon and she was faced with Michael D'Angelo in his stead. A man who Eva already knew she had to guard herself against becoming any more disturbed than she cared to think about!

Michael D'Angelo now narrowed those piercing black-on-black eyes. 'You have some reason for hurrying back to London, perhaps? A boyfriend? Live-in lover? Or maybe even a husband?' He raised dark brows.

'I believe I introduced myself as Eva Foster, the same surname as Rachel's, and we've already established that she wasn't married when she died.'

'Not every woman changes her surname to that of her husband when she marries.'

He had a point, Eva conceded grudgingly. 'Not that it's any of your business, but no, I don't have a boyfriend, a live-in lover, or a husband I need to hurry back to,' she dismissed impatiently. 'I hadn't had the time for the latter before the twins were born, was too busy working, and then latterly caring for Rachel and the twins, and now I can't see any man being interested in taking on both me and my ready-made family!'

He nodded his satisfaction with her reply. 'Then there's no reason why you can't stay on in Paris for a week or two.'

'Stay on in Paris for a week or—!' Eva eyed him incredulously. 'There's one very good reason why I can't do that, Mr D'Angelo, and that reason is financial.' Honestly, did this man not live in the real world at all?

It had taken the last of Eva's savings to pay for the flight to Paris and the four nights' stay at the pension, and she simply couldn't afford to stay on any longer than that. It had all been a waste of her time and money anyway, which made the whole situation even worse!

'I wasn't for a moment suggesting—' Michael broke off what he had been about to say as a knock sounded on his office door. 'Come in,' he invited tersely, his scowl not lessening in the slightest as his dark-haired assistant manager opened the door to stand in the doorway. 'What is it, Pierre?' he demanded irritably as the other man looked at them both hesitantly.

Pierre grimaced his obvious discomfort at the interruption. *'Excusez-moi—'*

'You may as well stick with English, Pierre.' Michael tersely reminded the younger man that Eva Foster understood his French perfectly.

The younger man nodded. 'In that case, I thought I should remind you that you have a luncheon appointment with the Comte de Lyon at one o'clock, and it's twelve-thirty now,' he said in his perfect, unaccented English.

Michael gave an impatient glance at his wristwatch. 'So it is,' he realised impatiently. 'I'll need you to go to lunch with the Comte in my stead, Pierre,' he instructed briskly. 'Give him my apologies, and explain that—that an urgent family matter came up, which I had to deal with.'

Eva's cheeks burned with colour as she literally felt Pierre's curious brown gaze turning towards where she now stood near the floor-to-ceiling windows. When her own colouring and the twins' was so similar he would naturally jump to the conclusion, as most people did, that Eva was their mother.

Not that she thought for a moment that this elegant, handsome assistant of Archangel would press Michael D'Angelo on the subject; she doubted too many people ever dared to question this arrogantly decisive man on anything!

Besides which, Eva really wasn't interested in Michael D'Angelo's relationship with his staff, or his luncheon appointment with some French count. She was more concerned with finishing the conversation the two of them had been having before they were interrupted.

Was Michael D'Angelo seriously suggesting that she stay on in Paris for a week or two? What for? Whatever his reasoning he had better explain himself soon, because the twins would shortly be waking up and demanding their own lunch—probably at the top of their healthy lungs!

'And if the Comte is…unhappy with this arrangement?' Pierre prompted his employer.

'Then he'll just have to be unhappy,' Michael D'Angelo snapped. 'Just reschedule if that should be the case, Pierre,' he added dismissively as the younger man still looked uncertain.

A man, Eva realised, who had in all probability been working at Paris Archangel at the time Rachel was involved with Rafe D'Angelo…

'How long have you worked at Archangel, Pierre?' she

prompted curiously, and instantly earned herself a frowning glance from Michael D'Angelo.

The younger man shot his employer a slightly startled
glance before answering Eva's question. 'I—I have had
the pleasure of being Assistant Manager here for almost
four years now,' he answered her guardedly.

Eva gave a rueful smile at the man's tactful reply; she
somehow doubted that was altogether true during the times
when the forceful Michael was the D'Angelo brother in
charge!

Her smile faded as she frowned. 'In which case, you
will have been here—'

'We should let Pierre go to lunch now, Eva,' Michael interrupted her firmly, easily guessing where she was going
with this conversation. And having Eva question the Archangel staff, or anyone else for that matter, as to whether or
not they had known of her sister's relationship with Rafe
fifteen months ago was exactly what Michael was trying
to avoid happening.

'I'm sure Pierre doesn't mind my interest, Michael,'
Eva returned the familiarity with saccharin sweetness.
'Especially when he finds it such a pleasure to work here.'

Michael eyed her sceptically, not fooled for a moment
by that sweetness; Eva Foster had a tart little tongue in
her beautiful head, one that he, and no doubt most of the
men who met her, could easily imagine being put to better use. Eva Foster was seriously underestimating her own
beauty and attraction if she believed having custody of the
twins would deter most men from being attracted to her!

It was obvious, from the admiration gleaming in Pierre's
gaze, that even a married man with two small children
wasn't totally immune to the attraction of that glossy dark
hair and those violet-coloured eyes!

'I'm afraid I have to insist,' Michael rasped harshly

before turning to look at the younger man with narrowed eyes. 'I'm leaving now, Pierre, and won't be coming back to the gallery again today,' he informed the other man dismissively. 'So if you could see to the cancelling of my appointments for the rest of the day, and make sure that everywhere is locked up and ready for security before you leave this evening...?'

'Of course,' the younger man confirmed slightly dazedly. 'Mademoiselle,' he added politely to Eva Foster before leaving and closing the office door behind him, both men fully aware that hadn't been Michael's intention before Eva Foster had arrived at the gallery.

'You shouldn't have stopped me,' Eva Foster protested impatiently. 'He might have met Rachel, been able to confirm her relationship last year with your brother Rafe—'

'The only person I'm interested in confirming that relationship—or otherwise—is my brother Rafe,' Michael assured grimly.

'And he's unavailable!'

Michael scowled across at her. 'What do you want from me, Eva? Do you want me to interrupt Rafe's honeymoon and tell him about the twins—is that it?'

'Yes! No! I don't know...' she groaned unhappily.

'I can do that, if you demand it.' Michael nodded grimly; it was what most women would demand, so why should he expect this one to be any different? He didn't... 'No doubt it will irrevocably damage his marriage, but, yes, I can certainly contact Rafe right now if you insist upon it!'

'Stop trying to make me out to be the bad guy here!' Her eyes glittered with her own anger.

'Yes or no, Eva?' he pressed scathingly.

'I— No, of course I don't want to—to damage your brother's marriage before it's even begun, or hurt his wife, I just—'

'You've waited three months to come here looking for Rafe. Why can't it wait another couple of weeks?'

'Because it can't!'

'Why can't it?'

'Because—because—if you must know, because I'm almost broke! Okay?' she snapped defensively. 'The babies are very draining financially, and I haven't been able to work properly, and—and I'm broke!' she repeated emotionally.

Some of the tension left Michael's shoulders. 'And I'm suggesting you let me worry about that for the moment. If you wouldn't mind waiting here for a few minutes? I just have a few instructions I need to give to my secretary before we leave.' He strode over to the door.

'I— What do you mean, before "we" leave?' It had taken Eva several seconds to regroup, but now that she had...! It was one thing to agree that she wouldn't speak to Rafe D'Angelo until he came back from his honeymoon, quite another to accept any help from his arrogant brother. 'The only place I'm going is back to the *pension*, so that I can feed the twins and then call the airline to see if I can get our tickets changed to an earlier flight!'

'You're correct in assuming we're going back to your *pension*.' Michael D'Angelo nodded abruptly, his expression still grim.

Eva stilled as she eyed him warily across the office. '*We* aren't going anywhere. At least, not together.'

'Oh, but we are, Eva,' he assured in a tone that brooked no argument.

Well...it might have brooked no argument from either Pierre or this man's secretary, but, as Eva wasn't one of Michael D'Angelo's employees, she had absolutely no intention of being browbeaten by this overpoweringly dominant man.

'No, we're not,' she answered him just as firmly before once again crossing the room to take charge of the handles of the double pushchair. 'If you wouldn't mind opening the door for me…?' She looked at him pointedly.

Michael frowned back at her with pure frustration. Did Eva really think that having come here and dropped this bombshell on him—on Rafe, and possibly the whole of his family—she was going to be allowed to just walk out again?

Perhaps she hoped that he would allow her to do just that, after Michael's threat earlier as to Rafe possibly wanting custody of the twins?

It certainly seemed that way…

And it was impossible for Michael not to admire her audacity as well as her stubbornness, as much as he had admired her beauty just minutes ago. Not too many people would dare to even attempt to thwart him, but Eva Foster obviously felt no hesitation in attempting to do just that!

As she had seemingly taken on the responsibility of her sister's two children without a thought for the impact it would have on her own life…?

It would seem so, he acknowledged begrudgingly.

Not only had it affected her ability to work at the career the warmth in her voice implied she loved—and which Michael had every intention of learning more about at the earliest opportunity, just as he intended learning much more about Eva Foster altogether—but she also believed it played a part in her inability to have a man in her own life.

Michael still thought she was seriously underestimating herself in that assumption, but nevertheless he also felt grateful that a man in her life was one less immediate complication he had to deal with.

And was that the only reason for him feeling an inner

sense of satisfaction at knowing there was no man, either currently or in the recent past, in Eva Foster's life…?

Michael liked to keep his emotions guarded from the outside world, but that didn't mean he wasn't also completely honest with himself, and that honesty now demanded that he admit, inwardly at least, that he was deeply attracted to the fiery Eva Foster. And it was an attraction that annoyed him intensely.

And yet the attraction to her was there, nonetheless…

Possibly because at this moment he was clenching his hands into fists at his sides in order to stop himself from reaching out and touching the silkiness of her dark hair. And wanting to smooth those glossy black strands back from the pale perfection of her face as he gazed into those unusual violet-coloured eyes before he lowered his head to taste her soft and full lips with his own!

Also knowing that just a single taste wouldn't be enough, that he wanted to taste, to explore all of Eva Foster, from her glossy black head to her no doubt elegant toes.

Not only was this attraction particularly stupid on his part, in the current circumstances, because Eva Foster had openly admitted she wanted Rafe's financial help with the twins, but it also complicated the hell out of what Michael was planning to do next…

CHAPTER FOUR

'YOU CAN'T DO this!'

Michael sat in an armchair, elbows on the arms of that chair, fingers steepled together in front of him. He appeared totally relaxed and calm as he watched Eva pace restlessly up and down in the sitting room of his apartment, her eyes blazing like violet jewels, her cheeks flushed with temper. 'Forgive me for pointing this out…but, as the twins are already taking their afternoon nap in their cots in one of the bedrooms, it looks as if I already have done it.'

Eva faltered slightly before coming to a complete stop to glare across the room at him. 'And looking mighty pleased with yourself about it too!' she acknowledged disgustedly.

Michael shrugged his shoulders. 'I like it when my plans come together, yes.'

Eva looked as if she were about to explode at his latest 'plans'. 'You can't force me to stay here!'

Michael bit back his disappointment that the halt in her pacing had also put an end to his admiration of her curvaceous denim-clad bottom, something he had been enjoying immensely. 'I don't remember using any force?' He looked up at her between narrowed lids.

No, he hadn't, Eva acknowledged with frustration. Mainly because she hadn't realised what he was doing until it was too late, and she and the twins were already safely ensconced in the luxurious D'Angelo apartment, just a few minutes' walk down the Champs Élysées from the Archangel gallery!

Not that they had walked here immediately after leaving the gallery. Oh, no, first Michael had arranged for his car to drive them both to the *pension* where she and the twins were staying, and while she had been occupied feeding the twins their lunch he had been busy packing up the things she had taken out of the two suitcases when she arrived in Paris yesterday; she had packed as lightly as she could, but had still needed to bring two suitcases to carry all the paraphernalia necessary for travelling with two small babies.

By the time she had finished feeding the twins, and changed them both into clean clothes, Michael had been waiting at the door of her shabby room with those two suitcases already packed and sitting on the floor beside him.

Even then Eva hadn't realised exactly what his intentions were, had innocently imagined—as the sneer on his lips as he looked around the room had shown that neither it nor the pension came anywhere near this man's high expectations of accommodation—that he had decided to move them into a hotel until it was time for their flight back to England.

Never in her wildest dreams had Eva imagined that Michael intended moving her and the twins into the D'Angelo apartment. With him.

Or that one of those 'few instructions' he had needed to give his secretary before they had left the gallery was actually the buying of two cots, and the bedcovers to go with them, to be delivered immediately to his apartment for the twins to sleep in.

As for the D'Angelo apartment…!

Eva had been too nervous earlier, and then too agitated,

to completely take in the elegance of Michael's office at the Archangel gallery, only registering that it was luxuriously chic.

But this apartment—the D'Angelo family apartment, and used by all of them whenever they were in Paris, Michael had explained when they arrived here a short time ago—was the ultimate in elegant opulence.

It was also huge, taking up the whole of the top floor of this historic building, brown carpets on the floors, the walls papered with silk and pale cream throughout. There were original paintings and elegant mirrors adorning those walls, with gold filigree work to separate the panels down the hallway and in the sitting room, and crystal chandeliers hanging from every ceiling. Eva had no doubt that each and every piece of ornamentation or statuary was also a genuine antique.

The furniture in the sitting room was Georgian in design, an elegant chaise-longue in one of the bay windows looking down the Champs Élysées, with several other sofas and chairs covered in pale pink and cream striped silk, placed conveniently beside several delicate spindle-legged tables, each adorned with a unique and delicate ornament.

Eva's first thought, as she stood looking around that beautiful elegance, was that the twins, both able to crawl now, would demolish a beautiful room like this in just a few minutes. The brown carpet would be safe from their dribble and often food-besmeared fingers, but she didn't hold out the same hope regarding the silk-covered furniture and walls...!

Michael D'Angelo obviously had no appreciation of the destructive force of two six-month-old babies. And why should he? Eva very much doubted that he came into contact with babies at all in his day-to-day life. She hadn't appreciated the mess involved herself until she had sole custody of the twins. It hadn't taken her long to make her apartment in London babyproof: covers on the chairs, and everything moveable—knick-knacks, photographs, books et cetera—now put at a height Sophie and Sam couldn't reach.

All of those objections to the three of them staying here were without taking into account Eva's own, the primary one being she didn't want to stay here in this apartment with Michael D'Angelo!

He was too forceful, too unsettling, too disturbingly male, just too *everything* for Eva to even be able to think of sharing an apartment with him, even for the short time he demanded!

The bedroom Michael had informed her would be hers for the duration of her stay was beyond anything Eva could ever have imagined; the décor was all in gold and cream, delicate white furniture, gold covers and drapes on the white ornate four-poster bed, the carpets and curtains also gold, the painted ceiling an ornate display of cherubs and angels. It was the ultimate in luxury.

She gave a shake of her head. 'As soon as the twins wake up we're leaving.' She should never have allowed Michael to persuade her into putting them down for their afternoon nap in the first place. And she wouldn't have done if the twins, having eaten their lunch and ready for their nap, hadn't both been decidedly bad-tempered by the time they arrived at the D'Angelo apartment.

Michael arched dark brows. 'To go where, exactly?'

Eva's eyes narrowed. 'A hotel, or another *pension*, anywhere but here.'

'I thought you said you were low on funds?'

Her mouth thinned. 'You know, if I didn't already dislike you intensely, then your smug attitude right now would certainly ensure that I did!'

Michael eyed her mockingly. 'Isn't it a little early in our acquaintance for you to have decided you dislike me as strongly as that?"

'Oh, I assure you, a little of your company goes a long, long way!' she snapped. The less she had to do with Michael D'Angelo in future, the better she would like it.

And not because she disliked him, intensely or otherwise...

Eva hadn't shared an apartment with anyone since her university days, and the thought of staying in this apartment now, night as well as day, with a man as physically charismatic as Michael D'Angelo, even with the twins as chaperones, made her feel decidedly uncomfortable.

Not that Eva thought for one moment that Michael would ever return that physical attraction; she just didn't think it was a good idea for her to be alone with him here. If nothing else, she stood a good chance of making a fool of herself if he should ever realise her attraction to him!

Nor did she completely understand the reason for him insisting that she and the twins stay here with him...

'I have absolutely no idea why you're smiling,' she bit out irritably, annoyed with herself as much as with Michael. For having noticed that he looked even more dangerously male when he smiled. Those black eyes became the colour of warm chocolate when he smiled instead of that cold black, and they were edged with laughter lines. Those same laughter lines beside curved and parted lips, showing very white and even teeth, and all revealing Michael D'Angelo for exactly what he was: a predatory male in his prime!

Michael didn't understand why he was smiling either. Laughter wasn't a predominant part of his nature at the best of times, and even more rarely when in the company of a beautiful woman. But Eva, with her apparent lack of a verbal filter, seemed to have found the ability to amuse him.

Even, it would seem, when she was telling him she disliked him intensely...

His humour faded as quickly as it had appeared. 'Neither do I,' he bit out coolly. 'But as you've agreed not to talk to Rafe until he returns from his honeymoon, I feel it best if you, and obviously the twins, stay here.'

'With you.'

'With me,' he confirmed evenly.

Warmth coloured her cheeks. 'That's hardly appropriate.'

Michael eyed her curiously, noting that telling colour in her cheeks, and the way her gaze refused to quite meet his. 'I wasn't suggesting that the two of us should share a bedroom, Eva, just the apartment,' he finally murmured slowly.

She looked even more flustered. 'I didn't think for a moment— It hadn't even occurred to me— You're being ridiculous!' she accused agitatedly.

The deepening blush in Eva's cheeks as he looked up at her was in complete contradiction to her claim of not having thought that for a moment...

'Am I?' Michael mused as he rose slowly to his feet, a hard smile of satisfaction curving his lips as he saw the way Eva instantly took a step back. Confirmation of her nervousness of being too close to him?

'Of course you are,' she snapped irritably.

'Why is that?' Michael knew that most women wouldn't hesitate to take every advantage of their present situation.

Eva frowned her impatience. 'For one thing we don't even know each other—'

'And what we do know we dislike?' he suggested helpfully.

'I think the fact that you suspect me of being some sort of gold-digger, looking to fleece your brother out of his millions, and have treated me accordingly, speaks for itself!'

'You've openly admitted you want Rafe to give you money.'

'For the twins, not me!' she came back defensively.

If Michael was completely honest he was no longer so certain of Eva's motives, knowing it was his own past experience with Emma that had caused him to jump to that conclusion originally.

Admittedly he could see no similarity to Rafe in either of the twins, except perhaps the dark hair, but as Eva also had ebony-coloured hair it was logical to assume that her sister might have had similar colouring. But just because he didn't see any similarity to Rafe in the two babies didn't rule out the possibility of the twins being his brother's children. Eva seemed so certain that he was their father and there was no disputing the fact that Rafe *had* been in Paris fifteen months ago…

Michael grimaced. 'I'm willing to give you the benefit of the doubt on the subject. For the moment,' he added hardly.

'That's big of you!' she snapped sarcastically.

'I thought so,' he answered mildly.

'That's still no reason for you to deliberately embarrass me by making ridiculous remarks about the two of us sharing a bed!' She glared at him with those incredible violet-coloured eyes.

'And yet your blush would seem to imply you weren't entirely averse to the idea…?' he prompted hardly.

Eva looked nonplussed for a moment, and then that

rebellious light came back into her eyes. 'Of course I blushed,' she bit out impatiently. 'The last thing I expected when I came to Paris was to…to be propositioned by Rafe D'Angelo's older brother!'

Michael shrugged. 'You would have found the idea less disturbing if I weren't Rafe's older brother?'

'I— You— But you are,' she finally managed to accuse impatiently. 'And, for the record, I find your warped sense of humour offensive.'

His mouth twisted derisively. 'You may not have known me very long, Eva, but I think you know me well enough to realise that I rarely, if ever, joke about anything…'

Yes, Eva did know that, had realised from the first that Michael D'Angelo was altogether too serious, which was the reason she'd had such difficulty imagining him and the fun-loving Rachel together. Correctly, as it happened.

But if Michael rarely, if ever, joked about anything did that mean that he was being serious now?

Of course he wasn't, she instantly chastised herself for her naiveté; Michael D'Angelo was just enjoying seeing her feel uncomfortable! And more fool her for allowing him to do so.

She snorted. 'If—and it's still a big if—I should decide to accept your offer and stay here with you until your brother gets back from his honeymoon, then you can be sure the two of us will be occupying separate bedrooms!'

'Let me know if you change your mind,' he drawled softly.

Eva looked at him searchingly, her stomach giving that lurching roll, palpitations in her chest, as though her heart was beating far too rapidly. She was unable to look away from the intensity of that jet-black and unblinking gaze. 'Why are you doing this?'

He raised dark brows. 'Maybe because I'm not averse to the idea of sharing a bed with you.'

Maybe, but he didn't look at all happy about it if that was the case, Eva realised slightly dazedly.

He grimaced on catching sight of her frown. 'Eva, I'm too old and cynical to play guessing games with a woman—'

'How old?' she put in quickly.

His mouth quirked into another smile, no doubt because of the incongruousness of her question; what did it matter how old Michael was, when Eva had no intention of becoming involved with him?

'Thirty-five,' he supplied softly. 'Too old for you?'

'I was just curious—' She broke off as she heard the sound of one of the twins crying out, quickly followed by another cry as the second baby was woken by the first.

'Babies *interruptus*...' Michael murmured mockingly. 'Let's put a "to be continued" sign on this conversation, hmm?'

'Let's not,' Eva dismissed firmly even as she turned and hurried from the sitting room to go to the twins.

Ran from the room better described it, Eva acknowledged ruefully as she gathered up both babies in her arms and quickly halted their crying.

Michael might have started out mocking her, but that conversation, the very air they both breathed, had seemed to become altogether too fraught with physical tension a few minutes ago.

With physical awareness...?

A physical awareness that would seem to imply Michael really might be attracted to her under all that cynicism...?

Despite the sudden intimate turn of their conversation, Eva had great difficulty believing that!

It wasn't just that Michael D'Angelo was such an aloofly

arrogant and forceful man, there was also the fact that he so obviously didn't trust her, as well as the fact that he was way out of Eva's league, and she didn't just mean because of his immense wealth.

Ten years her senior, he was also a man of experience and sophistication, and, while Eva knew herself capable of being comfortable in any social setting, she certainly didn't play the sort of bed-hopping games so many other people enjoyed. People like Michael D'Angelo...

She wasn't a prude and nor was she a virgin, having been involved in one year-long relationship a couple of years ago, before the two of them had decided, quite amicably, that their two careers, hers in photography, his in accounting, made the relationship impossible to sustain; Eva had been away far too much on assignments, and they had eventually just drifted apart.

Eva hadn't been seriously involved with anyone since—hadn't so much as been out on a date since taking custody of the twins! She didn't think Michael D'Angelo, a man who so obviously had issues where trusting women was concerned, would be a good choice for her to think of taking the plunge with now either.

He might be as handsome as sin, but he was also far too dominating, too intense in nature, too cold to be the sort of man Eva was attracted to. Most importantly of all, Michael was Rafe D'Angelo's brother!

And yet she was attracted to him, Eva acknowledged with a sinking heart. Maybe in part, because Michael was such a dominating, intense, and cold man...? There was a certain satisfaction in thinking that such a coolly self-contained man might find *her* attractive.

In wondering what sort of lover he would be...

Despite what she had thought earlier, would Michael lose that outer coldness when making love to a woman?

And how would it feel to have the freedom to touch and caress the hard planes of that lean and muscled body, to have Michael's long and elegant hands caressing her breasts, her thighs, and to have his lips and tongue explore and taste—?

'Everything okay?'

Eva spun round guiltily, her cheeks flushing a fiery red as she looked across at Michael standing in the bedroom doorway, at the fully clothed man who had just been at the centre of her erotic and very naked fantasy.

'Eva...?' He quirked a questioning brow as he obviously saw that guilty blush colouring her cheeks.

'Everything's fine,' she snapped irritably.

He continued to look at her searchingly between narrowed lids for several long seconds before nodding abruptly. 'I'm just going to change out of these formal clothes, and then we can decide what to do about our own lunch.'

Eva looked at him blankly. 'What to do about it...?'

'Whether to eat in or eat out,' he dismissed tersely. 'How much of Paris have you seen since you arrived?'

She grimaced. 'The inside of the *pension* and the scenery on the walk to your gallery this morning.'

Exactly what Michael had thought Eva would say. 'Then we'll eat out. If you would like to get together anything that the twins might need while I'm changing...?'

She gave a slow and wary shake of her head. 'I'm not expecting you to—to entertain me.'

'I thought we had agreed to put that particular conversation on hold...?' Michael gave a hard smile of satisfaction as he saw the becoming blush that instantly coloured those ivory cheeks.

'You know I didn't mean it in that way!' She shot him an irritated glare.

Of course Michael had known that. He just enjoyed seeing Eva blush. Just as he liked the idea that it was his teasing that had caused that blush.

Which was strange, because teasing, bantering word play wasn't something he usually bothered with where a woman was concerned. He had always preferred a more straightforward approach. Knowing that beneath a woman's desire there were always those pound signs.

And Eva Foster was no different in that regard, he reminded himself impatiently, the only difference being that it was Rafe she wanted money from.

His humour faded. 'I have no intention of entertaining you,' he bit out abruptly. 'We both need feeding, I don't cook, there's no housekeeper here, so the two of us going out to lunch is the logical answer.'

And Eva had a feeling that 'logic' was an important part of Michael's personality. That he preferred cool, calm practicality to any form of spontaneity. Quite where their previous conversation fitted into that cool logic she had no idea.

Although his mention of there being 'no housekeeper here' confirmed that, apart from the twins, the two of them really would be completely alone in his apartment...

'The four of us,' she corrected pointedly. 'And I think you might find that eating out with two small babies isn't as easy as it sounds,' she added ruefully.

That dark gaze flickered to the two currently quiet and contented babies Eva held in her arms. 'They seem happy enough at the moment.'

Eva smirked inwardly. He had no idea.

'I did try to warn you.' Eva gave the stony-faced Michael an amused glance between sooty lashes as they left the elegant restaurant situated along the embankment of the Seine, where he had decided they would stop and eat lunch.

It was a far less pristine Michael than the one who had left the apartment two hours ago, orange juice now visible down the front of his plain blue shirt, his casual black trousers damp from a glass of water Sam had knocked over, and slightly creased from where he'd had Sophie sitting on his knee for almost all of the meal.

If Michael had thought that Sophie and Sam would sit happily in their pushchair playing with their toes and gurgling happily while the two of them ate their meal, then he had been in for a rude awakening. The twins had fretted to be picked up within minutes of the two of them sitting down at the table, Eva knowing from experience that it was better for all concerned—namely the other people trying to eat their meals in peace—if she just picked them up rather than trying to reason with them. As Michael had tried to do initially. And very quickly learnt that six-month-old babies hadn't yet developed the capacity to be reasoned with.

It had been a very trying couple of hours.

Not least for Michael, who had obviously been totally at a loss as to how to amuse Sophie, let alone eat his food with one hand, which was all he'd had free when he was holding the baby in his other arm. It was a skill Eva had perfected in the past three months, always seeming to have one or other of the twins on her knee, sometimes both of them, whenever she tried to eat her meals.

'If you insist on us continuing to stay at your apartment, then perhaps we should shop for food and eat there in future...?' Eva suggested lightly as she wheeled the pushchair along the sun-dappled riverbank beside him, the majesty of the Eiffel Tower visible on the other side.

It was a view Eva would have loved to stop and photograph, if not for the fact that she had the broodingly silent Michael D'Angelo walking along beside her!

He shot her an irritated glance from beneath lowered dark brows. 'I am not about to let a six-month-old baby—or even two of them!—dictate where and when I eat my meals.'

'No?'

'No!'

Eva laughed softly at his determination. 'Even if it's easier?'

His mouth thinned. 'Easier doesn't make it acceptable.'

No, it didn't, and Eva could imagine that this man, so controlled, so serious, rarely took the easy way out in anything he did. Which was probably the main reason—surely the only reason—he had insisted that she and the twins stay at the apartment with him in the first place.

It was something Eva had been mulling over in her mind a lot during lunch.

Michael obviously wasn't convinced by her claim that his brother Rafe was the father of the twins. But he clearly had enough doubts that he was willing to accept this upheaval in his own life in order to keep them all exactly where he could see and hear them, until he was able to straighten things out once Rafe had returned from his honeymoon.

Because, she had realised, Michael had no intention of allowing her to repeat her claim about the twins' paternity to anyone else but him.

Oh, she had accepted that this couldn't have happened at a worse time for Rafe D'Angelo. She really wasn't a marriage wrecker, even if the marriage happened to be that of a man responsible for fathering the twins. She even understood Michael's reasons for deciding to keep her firmly under his watchful eye. But that didn't mean she had to like it.

Which was why Eva had felt a certain amount of amusement at Michael's obvious discomfort during lunch. He was inconveniencing her by insisting on detaining her in Paris; it seemed only fair that he should suffer a little of that same inconvenience himself.

And Eva knew from caring for the twins full time for the past three months that this was only the beginning of that inconvenience.

With any luck, Michael would be begging the three of them to leave Paris in just a few days' time...

CHAPTER FIVE

'IS IT LIKE this every night?'

'Like what...?' Eva turned from tidying up to look at Michael as he appeared in the doorway of the sitting room several hours later, pressing her lips together in an effort not to smile as she saw the disgusted look on his face as he eased the soaking wet front of his *third* clean shirt of the day away from his chest. 'Maybe you should go and change that,' she suggested, barely disguising a smirk.

'I intend to, but I'm seriously in need of a whisky first. Leave the tidying for now, and I'll help you do it later,' he advised as he walked over to the drinks cabinet. 'Like one?' He held up the decanter.

Why not? 'With lots of water, thanks,' she accepted lightly as she took his advice, and made herself comfortable on the sofa. 'Sophie appears to have taken a liking to you.' To the extent that her niece had squealed with pleasure when Michael had appeared in the bathroom doorway at bath time, Sophie smiling at him endearingly as she had held her arms up to him to be lifted out of the bath. A charm even the coolly self-contained Michael hadn't been immune to as he had then helped to put Sophie into her nightclothes before putting both babies down in their cots for the night.

'And you've been doing this on your own for three

months?' He handed her the drink before sinking down gratefully into one of the armchairs.

Michael was surprised at how tired he felt; there was a lot more to this baby minding than he had ever realised.

For one thing, he had learnt that it was damned danger- ous to take your eyes off crawling babies for even a few seconds, as Sam had proved when he had gone over to in- vestigate the Venetian standard lamp and almost pulled it over on top of himself. And Sophie was into everything, constantly having to be distracted away from one disaster or another as she explored the room in detail.

Michael looked around that room now, too weary to even care that it was no longer the neat and tidy haven he had left this morning but now looked as if two mini tor- nadoes had swept through it.

'I really will finish tidying up in here in a minute,' Eva promised as she obviously saw his grimace.

'As I said, it will keep,' Michael dismissed. 'Is caring for babies always this…frenetic?'

She smiled ruefully. 'Today was a good day.'

Michael frowned as he recalled the chaos in the restau- rant earlier today, the need to constantly pry little fingers away from danger since they had returned to the apart- ment, the coaxing necessary to get the twins to calm down enough to eat their tea, the splashing and squealing at bath time before the babies were placed clean and angelic-look- ing into their cots, both children having drifted off to sleep as Eva sang to them.

He gave a shake of his head. 'How have you managed on your own all these months?' This evening had been so chaotic he was seriously questioning his suspicions that Eva Foster was a gold-digger; surely no woman would will- ingly put herself through three months like the day he'd just spent with the twins if she didn't love them intensely!

She slipped off her shoes before tucking her legs up beneath her on the sofa. 'If you remember, I didn't have any choice in the matter.'

No, she hadn't, Michael acknowledged. With no parents, her sister also dead, and no help forthcoming from the father of the twins, there had only been Eva left to care for her niece and nephew. Michael was exhausted after spending only a few hours with them, and he hadn't been their main carer, just helping out occasionally when Eva obviously hadn't had enough hands to deal with them both at once.

How would Michael have coped in the same circumstances?

It was different for him, of course. He could afford to hire a nanny for the twins, two, if necessary. Eva, on the other hand, had not only lost her beloved sister three months ago, but she had also been left with the sole care of the twins, and obviously didn't have the money to pay for a single nanny to care for the babies, let alone two. Any more than she had enough money to pay for childminders while she continued with her career. Whatever that career was…

And the strain of that had taken its toll, he realised as he looked across to where Eva now sat with her head leaning back against the sofa. Her eyes were closed, that ebony hair falling silkily onto the cream sofa cushions.

There were deep shadows beneath her closed lids, hollows in the paleness of her cheeks. Her face was all sharp angles, the skin stretched taut across high cheekbones, as if she had recently lost weight. Just as the clothes she had changed into after putting the babies to bed, a pale lemon T-shirt and black denims, seemed slightly loose on her slender frame.

If Eva really was a fortune-hunter then surely she would

have sought out the twins' father—be it Rafe or some other man—much sooner than this? She certainly wouldn't have put herself through the hellish months of trying to cope with her sister's children on her own.

That was unfair. Eva hadn't just *tried* to cope; she had succeeded!

Until it had all become too much for her. Which was when she had decided to seek out the help of the father of the twins...

A man she claimed was his brother Rafe.

Michael still had a problem believing that.

Because he didn't want to believe it, because of the complications it would cause in Rafe's life, in all their lives? Or because that was what Michael really believed?

Hell if he knew any more.

He did know that Eva believed it.

Just as he knew, by the way her whole body had now gone lax, the glass almost slipping from between her fingers, that Eva had fallen asleep!

Michael rose quickly to his feet to gently pluck the glass from her fingers before it fell to the carpeted floor and woke her up. He placed it gently down on the coffee table beside her before moving quietly about the room turning off most of the lamps, leaving only the Venetian lamp in the corner to cast a warm green glow over the room.

It was the perfect time for him to go to his bedroom and change out of his wet shirt—again—but he paused beside Eva for several seconds before doing so, frowning darkly as he looked down at her. She looked very young and vulnerable without that fierce pride glittering in those violet-coloured eyes and the defensive and angry flush to her cheeks, the stubborn set to her mouth, and the determined thrust to her pointed chin.

Eva had said this morning that she was in her mid-twenties. And already burdened down with two small babies that weren't even her own—although Michael now thought Eva might take exception to him using that phrase in reference to her custody of the twins she so obviously adored!

As she seemed to take exception to a lot of the things he had said to her today.

His previously well-ordered life was now in chaos, his workday totally destroyed, his apartment now invaded by three interlopers.

Because, until he had spoken to Rafe, Michael dared not do anything else but make sure this young woman stayed exactly where he could see her. No matter what the inconvenience or discomfort to himself.

And that was all without adding in the fact that Michael found himself unaccountably drawn to her, physically aroused by her, and in such a way that he knew having Eva's presence in his apartment for the next week or so, even with the twins as chaperones, was also going to play hell with his self-control...

She was light to his dark. Softness to his hardness. Warmth to his coldness. Laughter to his grimness.

In a word, Eva Foster was *dangerous*...

Eva woke slowly, momentarily disorientated as she stretched before opening her eyes to look about the unfamiliar and elegantly appointed room, taking several seconds to remember exactly where she was and why. And with whom.

Michael D'Angelo...

All six feet plus dark and broodingly disturbing inches of him!

Which posed the question, where was he?

Quickly followed by the realisation that she had fallen

asleep without plugging in and turning on the vitally important baby monitor that would allow her to hear the twins cry out if they needed her.

Eva swung her legs quickly to the floor before sitting up abruptly, her head swimming slightly with the suddenness of the movement.

'Relax, Eva, the babies are both fine.'

She turned so suddenly towards the source of that voice she strained her already stiff neck, putting up a hand to soothe that stiffness as she frowned across to where Michael D'Angelo stood in the doorway. His hair looked dark, presumably from a recent shower, and a black T-shirt now stretched tautly over his muscled chest and flat abdomen, a pair of faded denims resting low down on his lean hips.

He looked…different, in informal clothes. More… Darker. Leaner. Sexier. So much more of the latter that Eva instantly felt the increased rate of her pulse as she continued to look at him, at the same time as she resisted the impulse to fold her arms to conceal the plumping arousal of her breasts.

'You shouldn't have let me sleep,' she accused defensively as a glance at her wristwatch showed it was almost nine o'clock.

'You were obviously tired…' Michael's eyes had narrowed, not at the aggressiveness of her tone, but because he was wondering what had caused the becoming flush that now coloured Eva's previously pale cheeks, her eyes a dark and unfathomable violet between sooty lashes. 'Dinner should be delivered in a few minutes,' he added distractedly.

She pushed back the dark swathe of her hair, revealing the delicate network of veins at her brow. 'Pizza?'

He smiled slightly. 'A four-course meal and the appropriate wines from André's.'

She raised dark brows as she obviously recognised the name of one of the most exclusive restaurants in Paris. 'Normal people just order pizza...'

'I would hope I'm a normal person, Eva. I just also happen to like good food.' Michael gave an unapologetic shrug. 'I also thought we both deserved more than a snack for dinner as our lunch was such a disaster.'

'Oh, I'm not complaining,' she assured ruefully. 'And I hate to tell you this, but lunch was a typical example of mealtimes with the twins!'

Michael had already guessed that, which was another reason he had decided to order the meal from André's; Eva's slenderness was a clear indication that she was in need of an uninterrupted meal, cooked by someone else.

Although Michael wasn't quite so sure, with his increasing physical awareness of her, about the two of them eating dinner alone together in the intimacy of the adjoining dining room... 'I thought we could eat in the kitchen?' he prompted briskly.

'Fine with me.' Eva nodded as she stood up to stretch her cramped limbs. 'I can't remember the last time I slept so deeply...' she added with a frown.

He shrugged broad and unconcerned shoulders. 'You obviously needed it.'

Yes, she had. She had been with her sister constantly during the last seven months of Rachel's life, and the past three months had been spent sleeping with half an ear open in case one or both of the twins needed her.

Eva had no doubt that she owed the deepness of the nap she had just taken to the fact that she had known instinctively that she could trust Michael D'Angelo to deal with any emergency that might occur while she was sleeping.

He exuded an assured self-confidence that seemed innate, Eva acknowledged as she now looked at him beneath lowered dark lashes. An air of competence as well as confidence.

Just as he also exuded an inherent sexual aura that Eva knew would prevent her from ever feeling completely relaxed in his company...

It was the fact that Michael seemed so unaware, or more likely just uninterested, in the impact of his own sexual attraction on women that made that attraction all the more lethal.

In fact, Eva could never remember being so totally physically aware of a man as she was of the enigmatic Michael D'Angelo at this moment.

Maybe it was because his hair was still damply tousled from the shower, and the informality of the fitted T-shirt and denims made him appear far removed from the cold and incisive businessman she had met at the gallery earlier this morning.

Either way, this awareness, this pulse-pounding body-heating attraction she now felt towards Michael, was totally inappropriate in the circumstances!

'I think—'

'I'll just—'

Eva's cheeks flushed slightly as she looked across at Michael questioningly.

'I'll just go and put out the cutlery and glasses in the kitchen,' he finished dryly.

Eva nodded. 'And I'll go and check on the twins and then finish tidying up in here.' It wouldn't take her more than a few minutes; the wreckage the twins left in their wake always looked worse than it was.

Michael grimaced. 'I would have done it, but I didn't want to wake you.'

She smiled. 'Thanks.'

Michael continued to look at Eva for several long seconds

as he found himself slightly transfixed by the brightness of her smile; her eyes now glowed a warm violet, her cheeks were rosily flushed, the lushness of her lips relaxed and slightly parted to reveal straight and even teeth.

Eva Foster, when she wasn't looking angry or harassed, was indeed a very beautiful woman.

Damn it, she was still beautiful even when she was looking angry or harassed!

And this was only day one of his self-imposed nightmare...

Day one became day two, and then day three, and with each successive day Michael's awareness of Eva Foster deepened to the point he had felt himself more than once balanced on the edge of taking her in his arms and kissing her. He had nothing but admiration for the selfless way in which she had devoted herself to caring for her sister's twin babies.

Michael spent his days at the gallery, but Eva and the twins were there waiting for him in his apartment when he returned each evening, and the two of them had fallen into the routine of feeding and bathing the twins together before Michael ordered dinner to be delivered from one of the exclusive restaurants he usually frequented but was currently unable to do so.

They talked as they ate those meals together, exchanging views on everything and nothing. But, as if by tacit consent, neither of them talked of Rafe, or what would happen when his brother returned from his honeymoon.

It was...domesticated. Pleasantly so, in fact, when Michael had always believed that domesticity wasn't for him.

As for Eva...

Each minute, each hour, Michael spent in her company

only served to deepen his attraction to her, to increase his physical awareness of her, to a degree that he had begun to take cold showers before going to bed in an effort to resist the ever-increasing desire he felt to walk the short distance down the hallway that separated their two bedrooms!

By the third evening of Eva's stay Michael knew his normally rigid control was seriously shaken, so much so he was no longer sure a cold shower was going to be anywhere near enough of a deterrent for the increasing ache he felt to make love with her...

'That was another delicious meal.' Eva gave Michael a smile of satiation as he sat across the kitchen table from her watching her intently as she finished the last of the lemon mousse he had ordered for their dessert; Michael certainly knew some amazing Parisian restaurants to order food from!

To her surprise the past two days had been more relaxed than she could ever have hoped for in the circumstances, her days spent sightseeing with the twins, her evenings enjoying eating a leisurely and always delicious meal with Michael.

And, Eva realised, she had enjoyed Michael's company as much as, if not more than, the delicious food!

He had proved to be both an intelligent and provocative dining companion as they discussed but respected their often differing views on everything from education to global warming. And art. They discussed art, in all its forms, a lot. Which Eva especially loved; it had been too long since she had been able to sit down with another adult and enjoy any intelligent conversation, let alone about her favourite subjects.

And if all of that conversation and those amazing and companionable meals had succeeded in heightening Eva's awareness of this relaxed and informal Michael D'Angelo, then that was her problem to deal with, because, her own reservations aside, she knew she was the last person Michael would ever *allow* himself to be attracted to.

He looked across at her quizzically now. 'You still haven't explained how it is you've travelled so extensively...?'

Her smile became wistful. 'It was part of my job. I used to be a photographer,' she explained at Michael's questioning look.

'Well...I suppose I'm still a photographer. Of sorts,' she added with a grimace. 'Only I've taken a step backwards, and now just do the occasional wedding and christening!'

Michael gave a slow shake of his head. 'And what did you used to photograph?'

'Oh, this and that.' Eva shrugged dismissively, reluctant to talk about what she used to do.

Because it was too painful.

Much as she loved the twins, and was more than happy to stop travelling on assignments while they were so young and needed her with them, she still couldn't help but feel a pang of longing for the career she had necessarily put on hold. It wasn't for ever, Eva consoled herself—the twins would grow up, go to school, and then maybe she could think about resuming at least part of her career.

In the meantime having the twins meant she still had part of her sister with her. That she could enjoy watching the twins grow up, and telling them, when they were old enough, of the mother who had loved them. Loved them so much she had been willing to die to give them life...

Michael eyed her searchingly as he noticed the sudden sheen of tears in those violet-coloured eyes. 'Why the reluctance to talk about your work, Eva?'

She shrugged. 'I just don't see the point in talking about the past, that's all.'

No, that wasn't all, Michael recognised shrewdly. Whatever Eva's photographic career had been, her reluctance to talk about it now would seem to indicate it was something she had loved doing.

Something she'd had to give up in order to care first for her sister, and then the twins.

Which forced Michael to acknowledge that he hadn't carried out his initial decision: to find out everything he could about Eva Foster...

Not surprising when his days had been spent so busily at the gallery and his evenings just as busy with Eva and the twins!

Or maybe, inwardly, he had been harbouring the hope that Eva would be the one to tell him about herself...?

'And if I'm interested...?' he prompted softly.

'That's just too bad,' she dismissed impatiently as she stood to begin collecting up the last of the dishes from their meal before carrying them over to the counter.

Michael turned in his chair so that he could continue looking at her, watching the suppleness of her body as she loaded the dishwasher, even as he tried to puzzle out this woman who had somehow managed to fascinate him, in spite of himself.

These past few days had been unlike any others he had ever known, and not just because the twins had burst into his life. No, the main reason was Eva, and his interest in her, his attraction to her in spite of himself, and his enjoyment in her company.

He loved his family, enjoyed his work at the galleries, but the women who came briefly into and then out of his life never even came close to knowing the real Michael. Probably because he chose those women for their physical and social attributes, and they chose to be with him, however briefly, because he was one of the wealthy and influential D'Angelo brothers.

At a little over five feet tall, with a lean, slender figure —apart from those firm and thrusting breasts!—Eva Foster was nothing at all like the sophisticated spa-and-beauty-parlour-enhanced women he briefly dated.

Just as Eva had made it clear from the beginning that she didn't consider his being one of the wealthy and influential D'Angelo brothers as being an asset as far as she was concerned!

As a result, these past few days had been the first time, ever, that Michael had felt as if he and a beautiful and desirable woman had talked openly, honestly, to each other.

And he didn't want that to change by having Eva clam up on him now.

'Perhaps if you— Wait a minute!' Michael sat forward alertly as an idea suddenly occurred to him. An idea that maybe should have occurred to him much sooner than this! 'Eva Foster...' he murmured slowly, sharply. 'Is it possible that you're the photographer E J Foster?' He looked across at her searchingly.

Eva blinked as she straightened from loading the dishwasher, her shoulders tensed defensively. 'How do you know about E J Foster?' she prompted as she looked across at him warily.

'I co-own and run three art galleries, Eva,' Michael reminded dryly. 'And I consider E J Foster's photographs to be art in its purest form!'

'You do...?' A delicate—and pleased?—flush now coloured her cheeks. As evidence that she was indeed E J Foster?

'I do.'

Eva couldn't help but feel a certain amount of pleasure in Michael's praise of her work. After all, no matter what her personal gripe was against the D'Angelo family, he *was* Michael D'Angelo, one of the three brothers who owned the prestigious Archangel galleries, and a man, an expert, whom she knew the art world held in deep respect.

Michael stood up abruptly. 'Come with me.' He held out his hand to her.

Eva's wariness increased, her expression guarded as she still held back. 'Come where?'

'With me,' Michael pressed decisively as he continued to hold out his hand invitingly.

Eva wasn't at all sure about this. Admittedly the two of them seemed to have reached an uneasy truce, considering that Michael suspected her of trying to coerce money out of his brother, and the fact that she wasn't at all happy about his suggestion that his brother Rafe might perhaps want a hands-on role in his children's lives.

But Michael was certainly acting very strangely now…

Nor did she feel in the least reassured when she reluctantly took his hand—a strong and firm hand that swallowed up her much smaller one as he curled his fingers about hers—and he led her out of the kitchen and down the hallway in the direction of the bedrooms.

His own bedroom, Eva realised as he opened a door at the end of the corridor and flicked on a light switch, illuminating two paintings on the opposite wall, but otherwise leaving the room in darkness.

Even so Eva could see that the décor was in browns and creams, the carpet a dark chocolate-brown, the drapes at the windows of cream brocade, the four-poster bed a dark and masculine mahogany and draped with the same cream brocade.

But the added giveaway to this being Michael D'Angelo's own bedroom was the suit he had been wearing earlier draped over the mahogany chair in front of the masculine dressing table, a pair of highly polished black leather shoes tucked neatly beneath that chair, and a set of gold cufflinks glittering on the dressing-table top.

Eva instinctively pulled back from entering his obviously personal domain, although she didn't succeed in freeing her fingers from his. 'I don't know what you have in mind, but I think I should warn you that I'm really not— What are you doing?' she protested as Michael released her hand, only to take a firm hold of her arms and push her further into the bedroom. 'Michael...?'

'There!' Michael stood behind her, keeping that light grasp on both her arms as he faced her towards one of the paintings illuminated on the bedroom wall.

Except it wasn't a painting.

There, on Michael D'Angelo's bedroom wall, was a large, framed, limited edition photograph. A photograph Eva easily recognised. Because she had taken it...

CHAPTER SIX

IN THE FOREGROUND of the photograph was a young African woman, her baby strapped to her back with a wide strip of coloured material, and above and behind her, silhouetted in the setting sun, was a lioness lying on the flat rock of an escarpment, her cub at her feet. A small gold plaque on the base titled it 'Harmony'.

Eva blinked back the tears as the photograph brought back memories of that last evening of her stay in Africa. She had spent over a week at the tribe's encampment, listening to their stories, and had taken dozens of photographs. But this particular photograph, of the woman and her baby, the lioness and her cub atop that escarpment, she had taken on her last evening there, and it held special meaning for her.

It represented the harmony of man and nature, living together, each respecting the other's right to be there. Even if that occasionally led to one or other of them being killed...

'There's something more to the photograph, isn't there?' Michael prompted gruffly, intensely, the photograph affecting him emotionally, as it usually did.

Eva looked at him sharply. 'How did you know that?'

He shrugged broad shoulders. 'I just did.'

Moisture dampened her eyes as she nodded before turning back to the photograph. 'The mother had lost her older child when this same lioness attacked the village a few weeks earlier.' She spoke in a hushed voice, as Michael had, as if they might disturb the mother or the lioness if they spoke too loudly. 'The men of the village tracked the lioness down, left her unharmed, but killed one of her two cubs.

'They saw it as balance, that with only one cub to feed the lioness would not be hungry enough to attack their village a second time.' She gave a shake of her head. 'I talked to the mother for hours, and, while she deeply mourned her lost child, she harboured no ill will towards the lioness for wanting to nurture her own children, and, as you can see, she felt no fear either. She just accepted the balance, the—the—'

'Harmony,' Michael murmured softly, appreciatively.

Eva swallowed. 'Yes. I don't think I could be as…understanding of that balance or harmony, if it had been one of the twins who had been taken.'

'No,' he accepted huskily, understanding that Eva's perspective would certainly have changed with the advent of the twins into her own life. 'But even so, at the time you understood, totally encapsulated this mother's acceptance of that balance and harmony, in your photograph.'

Eva breathed softly. 'I— How did you get this?'

'The same way every other lucky person at the E J Foster exhibition in London eighteen months ago acquired their own exclusive photograph—I bought it,' Michael stated with satisfaction, remembering how he had been drawn to this image that evening. He had been determined, compelled, to own it.

He'd had no idea he would one day meet the photographer under such unusual circumstances.

'You weren't at the gallery that evening…?' If she had

been Michael would have made a point of being introduced to her. And, in view of his attraction to her now, it was anyone's guess where that introduction might have led…

She drew in a sharp breath. 'No. I— It was the night of my parents' car accident.' She gave a shake of her head. 'They were on their way to the exhibition when another car went through a red light and hit them head-on. They were both killed instantly. The exhibition didn't seem important after that.'

'God, I'm sorry…' Fate, it seemed, had found a cruel way to intercede in the two of them not meeting before now.

'That was the first, and last, exhibition of my work,' Eva acknowledged wistfully.

'Why?'

She smiled ruefully as she shrugged. 'Life—and obviously death—got in the way.'

Michael nodded. 'Your parents, then the twins and your sister.'

'Yes.'

'You said you were out of the country when Rachel discovered she was pregnant…?'

'Tibet,' Eva confirmed.

'Photographing for another exhibition?'

'Yes,' she sighed.

'An exhibition that never happened.'

'No.' Eva still had the photographs on her camera, but hadn't had the time, or the inclination, to do anything with them since returning to England.

And she now found it weird, too uncomfortably strange, that Michael D'Angelo, of all people, should have one of her earlier photographs displayed on his bedroom wall. She couldn't even attempt to dismiss or make light of it.

Stranger still that Michael had sensed, known, there

was more to the photograph than could be seen with the naked eye...

It was an intuition, a sensitivity, she would never have expected from the coldly brisk businessman she had met at Archangel that first morning, in his expensive tailored suit, silk shirt and soft Italian leather shoes.

The same man who had initially treated her with such suspicion, and who still didn't trust her not to bring shock waves of scandal to his family, simply because she could. To the point that Michael had preferred to invite her and the twins to invade his own personal space, namely this Parisian apartment, rather than allow her to return to England before he'd had the opportunity to confirm or deny her claim by speaking to his brother Rafe.

That man, that coldly aloof and arrogantly forceful man, had exhibited none of the inner sensitivity Michael had revealed to her these past two days, and had just reinforced, by his complete understanding of one of her African photographs...

Because, as Eva had come to realise, Michael D'Angelo was a man of many layers. Layers she now suspected he had deliberately put in place in order to guard himself and his emotions. She had no idea what—or possibly who— had caused this reaction in him, only knew that they were layers he allowed very few, if any, to peel away to reveal the sensitive man hidden beneath.

No doubt his family knew the real Michael.

And the twins, in their innocence, had recognised, had known instinctively from the beginning, the emotionally sensitive man that lay beneath that outer veneer of cold urbanity, and they had been drawn to him, had trusted him.

Eva would have preferred, it would have been safer, if she had never so much as glimpsed that man beneath those layers...

Because she was far too aware of Michael already. Against her will—her loyalty to her sister—she had found him overpoweringly attractive as the co-owner of the Archangel galleries, dressed in his dark and exquisitely tailored business suits. But she found him even more so in the casual T-shirts and faded denims he changed into in the evenings, both emphasising the lean strength of his body, while at the same time doing nothing to diminish the leashed sensuality of the man wearing those clothes.

'I had always assumed E J Foster was a man.'

Eva turned to him in surprise. 'Why?'

'I have no idea,' he acknowledged gruffly, eyes glittering darkly as he continued to look up at the photograph rather than at Eva. 'I really should have known... It's so obvious to me now that a woman took this photograph,' he added ruefully. 'It's there, in the gentle way the fading light picks up the darkness of the baby's eyes as its head rests tiredly against its mother's shoulder, in the smooth turn of the mother's cheek as she gazes up at the lioness with its own cub. I believe a man would have concentrated on the majesty of the lioness and cub, rather than the more gentle beauty and calm of the mother and her baby.'

Eva felt slightly...unnerved—*very* unnerved!—by this further example of Michael's insight into what her feelings had been that evening in Africa, because those had been exactly her emotions as she photographed the woman and lioness. And Michael had known that just from looking at the photograph. So much so that he had wanted to own it...

Her discomfort, her awareness of him, in this dimly lit bedroom, increased exponentially.

It was so quiet in this part of the apartment, no sound of traffic or people, just the soft sound of their joint breathing, and the dim lighting to add to the air of intimacy.

An intimacy Eva knew she desperately needed to break—before she did something incredibly stupid!

In fact, now would definitely be a good time for one of the twins to cry out for attention!

No such luck, she realised, as the rest of the apartment outside this bedroom remained completely, eerily, silent…

Eva moved abruptly to look at the second illuminated frame, frowning as she found herself looking up at a painting of a single red rose. A dying rose, the blood-red petals falling softly down onto the base of the canvas. 'This painting is…' She broke off, lost for words as to both the poignant beauty and starkness of the subject of the painting.

'Allegorical,' Michael provided huskily.

'Yes.' Eva nodded, having known immediately that the painting represented so much more than the dying of that beautiful, perfect rose.

Just as she knew that the death of the rose would represent different things to different people. In some, the death of hopes. In others, dreams. And to many, love…

The question was, which of those things did it represent to Michael, a man Eva hadn't initially believed to be capable of any of those softer feelings, but had come to see differently?

He was a wealthy and successful businessman, so she very much doubted that he had any unfulfilled hopes and dreams in the professional side of his life.

Which left his personal life, and the possible death of love. Or perhaps trust…? Which would go a long way to explain his distrust of her initially, a distrust she had realised was slowly fading…

Michael was still single. And completely unattached romantically? Eva had never thought to ask! Had he once hoped for more? Had he loved and lost, a loss this painting represented to him?

Eva couldn't imagine any woman wanting to walk away from the intensity of emotions she was now so sure Michael was capable of feeling.

So perhaps it wasn't the painting itself, but the artist, that meant something to him?

'Bryn Jones.' She read the name of that artist in the bottom right corner of the painting. 'I saw pictures of some of the pieces from her exhibition online. She's an amazing new artist, isn't she?' And perhaps meant more than that to Michael?

'And my sister-in-law,' he provided huskily. 'Bryn is now married to my youngest brother Gabriel,' he added as Eva looked at him curiously.

'Oh.' Eva frowned as that theory crashed and burned. 'It's…a beautiful painting.'

Michael chuckled. 'But sad,' he acknowledged wryly. 'So very sad…'

'Yes.' What else could she say? It *was* a sad painting. Very much so. And a reflection of Michael's own inner emotions? Of his disillusionment, with life or love? Or possibly both?

Eva would much rather not think of Michael in that way. Much preferred to keep him at arm's length, emotionally as well as physically, rather than finding herself, as she now believed she did, understanding the emotional man that lay beneath that outer veneer of cold severity.

A veneer that Eva found she saw less and less the more time she spent in Michael's company…

'Bryn tells me she's painting its opposite—a red rose in full bloom—for her next exhibition,' he revealed.

Eva arched dark brows. 'In the hopes you'll buy it?'

'Apparently not.' He gave a rueful shake of his head. 'The painting will make an appearance at the exhibition, but it won't be for sale; Bryn insists on giving it to me as a gift. In the hope, she says, that it will help me to eventually see and feel love the way she and Gabriel do.' He grimaced. 'It's a little sickening to hear someone as lovely as Bryn talking about my little brother in those terms!'

And Michael, Eva realised shrewdly, with that last remark, was deliberately deflecting the conversation away from what his first comment had revealed…

Michael *had* once loved and lost, Eva acknowledged uncomfortably. It might have been many years ago, rather than recently, but Eva had no doubt that an artist of Bryn Jones' calibre would also have been able to see, as she now did, the man beneath that outer shell of cold aloofness. A veneer he had chosen to adopt because of that lost love?

It was significant, Eva thought, that Michael kept the painting in the privacy of his bedroom rather than on public view in any of the main rooms of the apartment.

As he did her African photograph…

Eva felt another quiver of awareness down the length of her spine, an increase in the tension in the air, at the intimacy of knowing Michael kept one of her photographs on the wall of his bedroom. She had always felt that all of her photographs were a part, an extension, of herself. And it was a little unnerving to know that all this time Michael would have looked at this particular photograph on a daily—and nightly—basis!

Of course he wouldn't, she instantly chastised herself. Not only was Michael a businessman, which meant he no doubt considered both the painting and the photograph as investments, but he had told her himself that he and his two brothers rotated the management of the three Archangel galleries, here, New York and in London. Which meant that Michael would only be in Paris for a maximum of four months a year—

'The painting and the photograph travel on the D'Angelo plane with me wherever I live,' he said huskily.

Eva frowned her impatience as she turned. 'Why did you tell me that?' she snapped irritably.

Because Michael had been able to see, to know, the thoughts that had been running around in Eva's beautiful head just now. Because all of Eva's thoughts, and her emotions, were becoming easier for him to read.

And a few minutes ago she had definitely been in the process of putting both Bryn's painting, and her own photograph, in a neat little box, no doubt marked 'Michael D'Angelo's investments'!

Oh, there was no doubting that the painting and photograph could both be classed as investments; they just meant so much more to him than that, to a degree that Michael knew he would never sell either one of them.

To have now realised, to know, that Eva was E J Foster, the photographer of 'Harmony', was...unsettling, to say the least.

Michael had attended the exhibition of E J Foster's photographs that night eighteen months ago without too much hope of finding anything to interest him. His acceptance of the invitation had been more of a courtesy to a fellow gallery-owner than anything else. Photography wasn't a medium that had ever particularly meant anything to Michael. It had certainly never touched him emotionally, the way a painting or sculpture could.

He had been impressed by the E J Foster photographs at first glance, and totally hooked the moment his eye had caught 'Harmony'. Had felt himself being drawn into the photograph, along with an instant affinity with the raw emotion and majesty of the subject.

And the photographer?

Perhaps.

But until this evening Michael had assumed that E J Foster was a man, allowing his own emotions to be centred on the photograph rather than the photographer. To now know that Eva was that 'man', and the history behind the photograph, a history he had only been able to guess at before this evening, somehow now seemed to give Michael that same affinity with her...

'Michael...?'

He looked at Eva through narrowed lids, his breath catching in his throat, his pulse pounding loudly, as he saw how beautiful she looked in the dimmed lighting of his bedroom, her eyes a deep and drowning purple.

It had been a serious mistake to bring her to his bedroom at all, Michael now realised as another part of his anatomy began to pulse and harden to the heated rhythm of the blood that now pounded through his veins as he found himself captured, ensnared, by those deep purple wells of emotion.

Deep purple wells of desire?

The same desire that now held Michael in its thrall?

Eva could almost feel, touch, the intensifying, the thickening of the air as it now seemed to still about them, as she and Michael continued to stare at each other in the semi-darkness of his bedroom, only the light spilling in from the hallway and over the two picture frames to illuminate the room.

Eva barely felt able to breathe, certainly couldn't look away, or move so much as a finger in protest, as Michael's gaze continued to hold hers and his head slowly began to lower towards hers.

Her heart leapt in her chest, electricity now charging the air about them as she felt the first, exploratory, questioning touch of those chiselled lips against her own, before they hardened, taking control, as Michael obviously felt her response.

Eva's hands moved up to grasp onto the broadness of Michael's shoulders as her knees went suddenly weak, instantly feeling the heat of the hard flesh beneath her fingers, and the muscled strength of Michael's chest as his arms moved about her waist and he pulled her in closer against him.

She groaned low in her throat even as her lips parted to the moist and rasping brush of Michael's tongue, that marauding tongue instantly seeking, exploring, the heat of her mouth as he held her even closer, making Eva fully aware of the throbbing heat and fullness of his arousal as it pulsed long and thick against her abdomen.

It was a desire Eva knew she felt too as her breasts swelled with arousal, the nipples becoming hard and aching berries as that heat now swelled, dampened, between her thighs, her whole body on fire with need as she returned the intensity of Michael's kisses.

Heated kisses that deepened, grew hungrier still, as Eva felt the warmth of Michael's hand against the bare flesh of her abdomen beneath her T-shirt, moving slowly and caressingly upwards, until that hand cupped the fullness of her breast, the soft pad of Michael's thumb a soft caress against the aching tip.

Eva wrenched her mouth from Michael's in a gasp, her throat arching as the heat of his mouth trailed across her cheek to the sensitive column of her throat, and then lower still as he pushed up the barrier of her T-shirt before taking the fullness of her nipple into the heat of his mouth, suckling deeply even as his tongue moved in a rough and sensuous rasp across the plump nipple.

Eva's knees threatened to buckle as desire coursed through her body in hot, pulsing waves, her fingers becoming entangled in the dark thickness of his hair as between her thighs swelled, ached, moistened in invitation, Eva needing, wanting more.

And Michael gave her more as he transferred the attention of his mouth and tongue to her other breast, the v between her thighs becoming an urgent needing throb as his hand moved down to cup her there.

'I need—oh, God, I need—Michael…?'

'Do you trust me to know, to give you what you need, Eva?' Michael groaned urgently.

'Yes…! Just— Please!' She was going out of her mind with desire, with aching need, had to have relief from the pleasure that now surged and swelled inside her in hot and consuming waves.

Michael's lips and tongue returned to caressing and suckling her sensitive breast as he curled one arm about her shoulders, the other beneath her knees, before he lifted her up into his arms and carried her over to the bed, placing her gently down on top of it before joining her there.

He moved up on his knees between her parted thighs as he pulled her T-shirt up and over her head before throwing it to one side as he then feasted his eyes on the bareness of her breasts. Full and swollen mounds that fitted perfectly into the palms of his hands as he cupped them, and tipped by deep rose-coloured and engorged nipples.

Michael's gaze held Eva's as he slowly lowered his head to suckle first one nipple and then the other, knowing he had never tasted anything so exquisite; her skin was so soft, and tasted of warmed honey.

It was a taste he could all too easily become addicted to!

He continued to hold Eva's gaze as he kissed down the leanness of her abdomen, her eyes dark and glittering between sooty lashes, her cheeks flushed, her lips red and moistly swollen from their earlier kisses.

Would those lips between her thighs be as swollen, as red, as glistening with that same arousal? Would they have the same honey taste?

Michael ached to know!

Had to know.

To *taste*…

Michael looked down at her between narrowed lids as he sat up on his knees once again before releasing the button on Eva's denims and slowly sliding the zip downwards, allowing her the opportunity to stop him if she wanted to; he had never forced himself on a woman in his life, and he wasn't about to start now. No matter how much he might want, *ache*, to taste Eva.

Thankfully, she made no move to stop him, not when he shifted to one side to take off her shoes before peeling her jeans down her thighs and removing them completely, nor when he hooked his fingers into her tiny black silk panties and they met the same fate. Instead she closed her eyes completely, her hands falling to the bedcovers beside her as Michael once again knelt between her legs, allowing him to look his fill between her parted thighs.

Her curls here were as ebony as the hair on her head. Silky soft and slightly damp curls that revealed her mound and the glistening and swollen lips beneath.

'Beautiful…' he groaned huskily as he parted her legs even wider before slowly moving to lie between her thighs and lowering his head.

Eva groaned just at the feel of the warm heat of Michael's breath against her sensitivity, that groan turning to a soft keening, her hands moving up instinctively to become entangled in the dark thickness of his hair at the first hot sweep of his moist tongue.

She lost all sense of where she was, who she was, as that plundering tongue continued to lathe hot and rhythmically, endlessly, hard and then soft, circling and then pressing, and almost, but not quite, taking her over the edge into the maelstrom of release.

'No…!' she groaned in protest as Michael raised his head, only to groan anew as he moved lower and she felt his fingers moving to caress, to stroke her most sensitive spot, as the moist length of his tongue probed, and then pierced through the throbbing lips at the entrance to her sheath, before plunging hotly, deeply inside. Taking her, possessing her as his other hand moved up to her breast, capturing, caressing, gently squeezing the fullness of her nipple between finger and thumb in the same rhythm as his thrusting tongue and stroking fingers.

Eva's hips arched up off the bed as she once again felt the hot sweep of Michael's tongue against her pulsing core, even as his fingers parted her swollen folds before thrusting inside, first one, and then two, stretching those quivering muscles, fingers curling slightly as he sought, and found that place deep inside her to stroke with each thrust of his fingers.

Eva's hips continued to arch up, again and again, as she met each and every one of those thrusts, until she cried out, sobbed, her fingers tightly clasping the coverlet as the fierceness of her orgasm surged through her whole body in hot and burning release, threatening to tear her apart with its ferocity. Tears burned down Eva's cheeks as wave after never-ending wave of pleasure took her beyond anything she had ever known before.

As *Michael* took her beyond any other pleasure she had ever known before…

CHAPTER SEVEN

'DID I HURT you?' Michael frowned his concern as he moved up the bed to lie beside Eva, fingers gentle as he touched the tear-wet cheeks beneath the dark sweep of her lashes.

Her eyelids remained closed. 'No.'

'Then what—Eva...?' he prompted sharply as she turned her head away from him. Damn it, he hadn't meant things to go this far—had never intended— 'Eva, speak to me, damn it!' he pressed worriedly as he smoothed the tangle of dark hair back from the dampness of her brow.

'And say what?' she prompted bitterly. 'I came to Paris because I believe your brother seduced my sister, and now—'

'Now I've seduced you,' Michael realised heavily.

'Hardly!' Eva scorned. 'I was there too, Michael. Oh, God, I was there too...!' More tears escaped her lids and fell down her pale cheeks.

'Eva, look at me, damn it!'

She raised her lids slowly, those violet-coloured eyes appearing bruised and slightly haunted as she looked up at him. 'What did we just do?' She groaned. 'What did I just do?' She gave an agonised moan before turning away from him again and curling up into a huddled and defensive ball.

She looked so small and fragile, lying naked on her side

with her back turned towards him. Michael could see the vulnerability of her hunched shoulders, the ridges along her slender spine, the gentle curve of her bottom.

'I've only known you a matter of days!' she continued to berate herself disgustedly. 'I don't really know you at all!'

'You know me, Eva,' Michael contradicted gruffly, knowing that it was true. Eva did know him, better than most people did or ever would.

It might have been only days since they first met, but they had been days when Michael knew he had revealed more of himself to Eva than he had to anyone for a very long time. If ever.

Just as he now knew Eva in that same deep and penetrating way...

And not just on a physical level.

He had come to like, not just to desire Eva these past few days, and discovering she was E J Foster, the photographer of 'Harmony', had ensured he had even further insight into exactly who and what Eva Foster was.

She was a woman who felt things deeply. A woman who was honest with herself to the point that she exposed the rawness of her emotions in a way Michael had never been able to do. Or, at least, not for many years.

And, it was that realisation, the honesty and rawness of Eva's emotions, that confirmed the complete nonsense of Michael's initial accusations to her. Much as he did not wish it to be true, he knew that Eva did truly believe that Rafe was the father of her sister's babies.

Just as the honesty of her emotions just now had allowed her to give herself over to him so completely...

Michael could still taste her nectar on his lips as he slowly ran his tongue across them. Just as he could still feel the velvet softness of her skin beneath his hands, and the way she had come alive beneath his caresses, as she made no attempt to hide her responses to him.

Just looking at her now, her skin a pale unblemished ivory in the dim lighting, her hair ebony silk, Michael knew he wanted to touch and taste her like that again!

'Eva—'

'Don't touch me again,' she warned tautly as he placed a gentle hand on her shoulder. He had no need to remove that hand as she scooted across the bed away from him. 'I can't believe I'm lying here stark naked and you're still fully dressed!' she added with self-loathing.

'What does that matter...?' Michael's hand dropped to his side as he fell onto his back against the pillows, watching regretfully between narrowed lids as Eva quickly pulled on her T-shirt, panties and jeans to cover that nakedness before standing up.

'It matters because—' Her hair was a silky tangle about her shoulders, her eyes dark and haunted as she looked across the bed at him. 'You didn't— It was selfish of me to take and not give—'

'Have I said that concerns me?' Michael rasped harshly. No doubt he would pay for that lack of physical release after Eva had left him, but for the moment he was content in having given her pleasure, in having enjoyed her pleasure.

'No...' She gave a dismissive shake of her head as she avoided meeting his gaze before straightening her shoulders determinedly.

'But that doesn't mean I don't feel— It's far too late to move the twins tonight but tomorrow I'll find somewhere else for us all to stay.'

His jaw tightened. 'No.'

Eva's gaze flickered in his direction before quickly moving away again, her cheeks very pale and luminescent in the dimmed lighting. 'What do you mean no...?' she prompted warily.

'Exactly what I said,' Michael bit out grimly as he swung his own legs to the floor before standing up. 'What happened between us tonight—'

'Was a mistake,' she finished tautly, her chin held defensively high as she still refused to look him in the eye. 'You and I both know that,' she added miserably.

Michael wasn't yet sure what tonight was, needed time—and solitude—in which to decide that for himself.

And the repercussions it might have, if any, on what was already a delicate situation...

He did know he didn't like hearing Eva describe it as having been a mistake! 'Let's just both sleep on it, hmm, and then talk again in the morning?' he prompted gruffly.

Eva didn't want to sleep on anything; she wanted to leave this apartment—and Michael—right now. Except she couldn't. Because, for once, the twins were both sleeping peacefully in their cots, and there was no way she was going to disturb them by moving them out of the apartment tonight. After all, where would she go?

How could she have allowed this to happen? *Why* had it happened?

Oh, she had known from the beginning that she found Michael broodingly attractive, that physically he affected her more deeply than any other man she had ever known, but she hadn't realised it was to the extent—to a degree that—

Eva would have laughed scornfully if someone had told her that she and Michael D'Angelo would ever have ended up making love together!

Or, to be more accurate, that Michael would make love to her...

How awkward was that? How *embarrassing* was that?

Eva wanted to curl up in a mortified ball—again!—just thinking of Michael's lips and hands on her, of the *intimacy* of having his lips and hands on her, *in* her...!

And, much as she tried to avoid admitting it, Eva knew exactly why it had happened.

Eating dinner together these past few evenings, talking together about everything and nothing, had been more relaxing than she could ever have imagined, but it had been looking at the painting and her photograph, both hanging on Michael's bedroom wall, that had pushed their third evening together over into intimacy.

Because in that moment Eva had *seen* Michael for exactly who and what he was. And that who and what he was really wasn't, as she had already suspected it might not be, the coolly remote man he chose to present to the public.

Oh, she might not know the reasons for the veneer Michael had erected on top of his emotions, or when he had done so, but his obvious attachment, to both the painting of the dying rose and her African photograph, had confirmed that it really was the veneer she had suspected it might be.

And behind that veneer were deep and complicated emotions. Emotions that this evening had touched some echoing depth inside Eva, and it was a connection she ultimately hadn't been able to deny. So much so that she'd had no thought of denial when the two of them began to make love.

And the bitter aftermath of that connection was these feelings of disgust at herself and humiliation...

She knew what Rachel, with her complete joy of life, would have said—and that would have been, *Go for it, sis.* And Eva had certainly gone for it. Had she ever! Her body still quivered and quaked in the aftermath of the first orgasm she'd ever experienced. An orgasm that had left her with a lingering hunger for more.

An impossible hunger, when Eva considered her reason for being in Paris in the first place.

Her chin rose. 'I really think it would be for the best if the twins and I were to move out—'

'No,' Michael repeated grimly.

She shot him an irritated frown. 'I don't think that's for you to decide—'

'On the contrary.' Michael straightened determinedly. 'If those two babies are, as you claim, my niece and nephew, then they, and you, will remain here under my protection until I am able to speak to Rafe.'

She arched challenging brows. 'And who's going to protect me from you?'

Michael's jaw tightened. He didn't appreciate the comment, but knew it was deserved, nonetheless. Who was going to protect Eva from him?

Or him from Eva…?

Because Michael had no doubt that if they continued to stay in this apartment together what had happened tonight would almost certainly happen again…

The answering throb in his still engorged shaft, when he was just thinking about making love with Eva again, was confirmation of that!

'Aren't you overestimating your own attraction?' Michael's tone was deliberately scathing as he looked her coldly up and down. But he wished he could take that coldness back as soon as he saw her flinch, and caught the way the shadows darkened beneath those beautiful violet-coloured eyes. However, putting some distance between the two of them, verbally at least, was what he needed to do for now. For both their sakes.

Her mouth tightened. 'Am I?'

'I believe so, yes,' he drawled dismissively. 'Tonight was an…interesting diversion, no doubt brought about by close proximity, but I doubt it will ever be repeated. Now, if you wouldn't mind leaving my bedroom...?' He turned away abruptly. 'Some of us have to go to work in the morning.'

Eva hadn't thought she could feel any more humiliated than she already did, but Michael's cold dismissal of her now proved that she could. And did.

Michael was behaving as if the past half an hour had never happened, was nothing at all like the passionate lover who had so generously gifted her with that incredible, earth-shattering orgasm. And it *had* been a gift, a totally unselfish one.

Just as Michael was now using his fall-back indifference as a defence in his cold dismissal of her...

'Fine,' Eva snapped just as coldly. 'As you say, we'll talk again in the morning. And tomorrow the twins and I will be moving elsewhere until our flight back to England—'

'I've already cancelled your original flight,' Michael informed her arrogantly.

'You've done *what*?' Eva's hands curled into fists at her sides.

He gave an unconcerned shrug. 'I told you that I would.'

'Yes, but— I can't believe— You overbearing, arrogant ass—'

'Language, Eva,' he drawled mockingly.

'—hat,' she finished scathingly. 'How dare you just—? Well, you can just rebook it,' she instructed furiously.

'I don't think so,' he came back mildly.

'Then I will,' she assured forcefully.

'You can try, I suppose,' he nodded unconcernedly. 'But when I spoke to the woman on the booking desk she thanked me for letting her know so promptly, as they have a long waiting list on that flight. So I'm pretty sure you won't be able to get back on that flight, at least.' He looked across at Eva challengingly.

The shortness of Eva's fingernails now dug into the palms of her hands as she clenched them even more tightly. 'You really are an arrogant bast—'

'For the twins' sake I really would suggest you try to curb the tenure of your language,' Michael bit out distantly. 'Also, I believe that children, babies in particular, are very sensitive to the moods of the adults around them, and behave accordingly...?'

Eva had learnt that to her cost over the past three months; if she was in a cranky mood, through lack of sleep or whatever, then the twins tended to pick up on that mood and started to misbehave themselves. And trust the arrogant Michael, who admitted to having no more experience with babies than she had until three months ago, to know that!

Eva wasn't sure that she didn't actually hate him at that moment. She certainly disliked him. Intensely. 'Then I advise you to stay away from me for the rest of our stay here,' she warned fiercely before turning sharply on her heel and leaving the bedroom, not bothering to close the door behind her as she headed for her bedroom that adjoined that of the twins.

Any clearing up still left to do in the kitchen Michael could deal with himself, because Eva had had more than enough of him for one evening!

'Have a croissant, Eva.' Michael held the basket of pastries out to her enticingly as they sat in the dining room eating breakfast. The twins were strapped in the two high chairs he'd had delivered to the apartment the first morning of Eva's stay here, when it had become obvious they were needed, along with a playpen. 'I went out, as usual, this morning to buy them,' he encouraged dryly, having accepted a couple of days ago that his morning routine of strolling out to enjoy a leisurely breakfast at his favourite cafe would have to be put on hold for the duration of Eva and the twins' stay with him. Which didn't mean he couldn't still enjoy the café's delicious croissants, even if he had to go out each morning and buy them!

Breakfast with two six-month-old babies was certainly an experience, as usual half their fruit purée and oats having landed down them rather than in their mouths, as had the milk they were drinking from lidded and spouted cups. They were now gumming their toast more than chewing it with the four teeth they displayed so proudly every time they smiled. Which was often. Enchantingly so.

Michael had quickly learnt not to dress in his suit for work until after breakfast, but instead wore the faded denims from last night and a white T-shirt—currently decorated with some of the twins' breakfast!

But they certainly were a cute pair of babies, Michael allowed ruefully as he politely refused the piece of soggy toast Sophie now offered him.

Their enthusiastically noisy presence also had the added benefit of masking some of the tension that so obviously existed between Eva and Michael this morning.

As expected Michael hadn't slept well, as he first attempted to drive away his still raging erection, an exercise in will power that certainly wasn't helped by the fact that he knew Eva was in another bedroom just that short distance down the hallway.

Another cold shower had helped a little, even if it hadn't succeeded in dispelling that desire for her completely. That had only been achieved when Michael mulled over how best to continue this living arrangement with Eva.

His surprise in realising she was E J Foster, to the extent he had taken her to see her photograph hanging on his bedroom wall, along with Bryn's painting, had meant he had now revealed far too much of his inner self to Eva.

A realisation that now made Michael feel almost as emotionally exposed as Eva no doubt had after the intimacies they had shared the previous night.

The proof of that was in the bristling hostility Eva had shown him this morning when he first entered the kitchen with the bag of pastries, her chilling politeness causing Michael to become equally guarded.

'Thank you.' Eva's gaze avoided meeting his as she now took one of the croissants from the basket.

At least they were still showing a semblance of politeness to each other in front of the twins!

A stilted politeness, maybe, but it was better than the two of them not talking at all, which was what Michael had feared might be the case. Because he had enjoyed Eva's company last night, as he had the previous two nights.

And he had more than enjoyed making love with her!

Despite Eva's chilling demeanour clearly communicating that she would endeavour to ensure it was never repeated.

When Michael was certain that it would…

Mainly because he was having difficulty keeping his hands off her right now!

Eva looked more fragile than ever to him this morning, her eyes darkly shadowed, her face pale, and the tight-fitting denims and purple T-shirt she was wearing today clearly outlining her too-slender figure.

What Eva needed—

Michael was pretty sure that Eva had absolutely no interest in knowing what *he* thought she needed—even if it was something as innocent as several long and uninterrupted nights' sleep, and having someone looking after her for a change.

Michael had certainly been aware of the twins both waking up twice in the night, had even thought of going to their room and taking over while Eva went back to bed, but thought better of it. He knew he had exacerbated the distance between them when his own defences had fallen into place and he had allowed his coldness to hide both his thoughts and feelings.

And so he had remained in his own bedroom last night, aware of Eva talking softly to the twins as she tried to get them both to settle, frustrated at not being able to do anything to help her. Knowing she would reject that offer of help even if he were to make it.

He had something important he needed to discuss with her today, though. But not here, and not when her attention would be divided. 'I would like you to come to the gallery later this morning.'

Eva glanced up from putting honey on her croissant, her gaze wary as she looked across the table at Michael. 'Why?'

'I need to talk to you.'

She frowned. 'We're talking now.'

'And we have a demanding audience,' he pointed out ruefully as Sam gleefully threw his toast across the table.

Eva absently picked up the toast and placed it on the side of her own plate before answering Michael. 'Why at the gallery?'

'Why not?' He shrugged. 'I might even be able to persuade Marie or Pierre to watch the twins while we talk. Pierre has a couple of children of his own.'

She looked at him searchingly, but as usual wasn't able to read anything from Michael's closed expression; he really could be as inscrutable as a sphinx when he chose to be. And he was choosing to be so now.

Eva gave a shake of her head. 'I don't leave the twins with complete strangers.'

'And if I vouch for both Marie and Pierre's trustworthiness?'

Eva gave a humourless smile. 'Believe it or not, I still consider you a stranger as far as the twins are concerned!'

His brows rose almost to his hairline. 'Isn't that a little... short-sighted of you, in the circumstances?'

Eva knew exactly what circumstances Michael was referring to, and she refused, absolutely, to talk about what had happened between the two of them last night. Bad enough it had happened at all, without having a damned post-mortem about it! 'I'm big enough to look after myself. And take the consequences,' she added coolly. 'But I'm much more circumspect when it comes to the welfare of the twins.'

'I wouldn't harm a hair on either of their heads!' He frowned darkly.

'Perhaps.' Eva calmly took a bite of her honey-coated croissant.

'Damn it—'

'Language, Michael,' she reminded him dryly.

He stood up abruptly and began pacing the room, shooting Eva thunderously frowning glances every now and then as he did so, as she calmly finished eating her croissant before attempting to clean away the worst of the debris of the twins' meal.

All the time totally aware of Michael as he prowled restlessly up and down the kitchen.

As far as Eva was concerned last night had been completely out of character for her, and the sooner they both forgot about it, the better she would like it.

And she was still angry with Michael for cancelling

her airline tickets without even consulting her. The least he deserved was a little payback for that!

The fact that he looked almost edible this morning wasn't helping her to maintain this distance between them. His hair was slightly tousled from his walk to the bakery, stubble darkening the square thrust of his chin where he hadn't shaved yet this morning, and the white T-shirt and faded denims clearly showed the whipcord strength of that lean and muscled body.

At this rate Eva was going to need another shower— cold this time!—once Michael had left for the gallery!

Just looking at him, her gaze drawn to those sculptured lips that had pleasured her so thoroughly the night before, was enough to make her feel hot and trembling inside. And the throbbing reaction of her breasts and between her thighs, just from looking at him, should be made illegal. As it was, Eva's only defence against that physical attraction was to attempt to keep Michael at a verbal distance. By whatever means.

Besides, it was rather fun winding up the coldly aloof Michael D'Angelo. And goodness knew Eva felt in need of a diversion from the embarrassment she was feeling this morning!

She stood up. 'I have to bath and dress the twins now, and isn't it time you were leaving for the gallery?'

His mouth thinned. 'Don't try to dismiss me, Eva, because it won't work.'

She quirked one dark brow. 'I have no idea what you mean.' She gathered up both Sophie and Sam before turning to face him, a baby held defensively in each arm.

'Archangel,' Michael bit out through clenched teeth. 'Twelve o'clock.'

'I told you—'

'It wasn't a request, Eva,' he assured grimly.

'And I don't react well to orders, so it looks as if we're once again at an impasse…'

Michael held back his temper with effort. A temper that no one else in his acquaintance had ever been able to rouse as easily as Eva now did; even his brother Rafe had to work a little harder at it nowadays! But it seemed that Eva, with just a lift of her eyebrow and a challenge in her voice, was instantly able to annoy the hell out of him.

He drew in a long controlling breath. 'Fine. I'll leave twelve o'clock today free in my diary for you, if you find you can spare the time. How's that?'

Her lips twitched, as if she was holding back a smile. 'I'll see how the morning goes, but I'm not promising anything.'

Michael's tension eased and he held back an answering smile as he saw the satisfied glint in those violet-coloured eyes, and realised the little minx was enjoying this battle of wills between them. 'Good enough.' He nodded. 'Bye, Sophie. Bye, Sam.' He bent down to let the babies kiss him on the cheek in parting as they reached their arms up to him, but made no move to leave as he instead looked down at a suddenly watchful Eva. 'This is all very domesticated. Do I get a goodbye kiss from you too…?'

Her cheeks instantly blazed with colour. 'In your dreams!'

Michael bared his teeth in a smile. 'Believe me, Eva, in my dreams last night you did so much more than just kiss me on the cheek.'

That colour deepened in her cheeks. 'I— You—'

'Yes?' It was Michael's turn to quirk a mocking brow.

'No!' Eva snapped, very aware of the two babies she held in her arms even if Michael wasn't. Although their age obviously ensured there was absolutely no possibility that the twins could understand a word they were saying to each other. That wasn't the point—

Then what was the point?

Eva was too flustered to remember what they had been talking about before, let alone know what the point of *this* conversation was!

She did know that Michael had very neatly turned her little rebellion around on her, and was obviously now enjoying himself at her expense. As she had enjoyed herself at his just minutes earlier!

Ah, yes, now she remembered… 'Have a good day at the office, dear,' she taunted with saccharin sweetness.

Obsidian-black eyes glittered down at her appreciatively. 'Don't work too hard yourself…sweetness,' Michael came back dryly. 'Or forget our date at twelve,' he added challengingly.

'I haven't said I'll be there yet.' Eva frowned. 'And it certainly isn't a date!'

He arched one dark brow. 'We could make it one…'

No, they really couldn't!

Eva might have briefly lost sight last night of her reason for being in Paris, but she would not allow herself to become distracted by this attraction for Michael by doing so again. She certainly didn't want to start thinking of Michael D'Angelo in a romantic way, let alone go out on a *date* with him…

'I don't think so, thank you,' she refused with cool dismissal.

'Pity,' Michael murmured.

Eva gave him a sharp glance, but was totally unable to read anything from the coolness of Michael's expression as he steadily returned that gaze with cool black eyes.

She gave a shake of her head. 'I don't happen to think so.'

Michael gave Eva another searching glance, once again

noting the dark shadows beneath her eyes in her too-thin face; Eva really did have the look of a woman this morning whose emotions were delicately balanced on a knife-edge.

Was that so surprising when in the last eighteen months she had lost both her parents and her younger sister, put her career on hold when she had taken over custody and care of her sister's twin babies, and now had the added distress of seeking out the newly married father and asking for his help?

Michael making love to her last night certainly couldn't have helped Eva's already tautly strung emotions!

'I know you were up with the twins a couple of times during the night, so try to get some rest today too, when the twins take their nap, hmm, Eva?' Michael reached up with the intention of gently brushing those shadows beneath her eyes, only for his hand to drop slowly back to his side as Eva flinched back and away from his touch.

Her chin rose challengingly. 'Is that an order or a request?'

'It's a suggestion,' he corrected harshly.

She smiled slightly. 'In that case, I'll take your suggestion under advisement.'

Michael bit back his frustration with her reply, knowing Eva well enough now to realise that if he continued to push the point she would do exactly the opposite. 'You do that,' he bit out tersely, glancing at his watch before looking up at her again. 'I have to go and take a shower now.' He turned sharply on his heel and left the kitchen.

Eva gave a groan as she knew she would carry that image—of Michael's lean and muscled nakedness as he stood beneath the cascade of the hot shower water—around in her head with her all morning!

CHAPTER EIGHT

'I TRUST I'M not…interrupting anything, because by my calculations Eva and I had an appointment ten minutes ago…?'

Eva gave the handsome Pierre an apologetic smile before turning to face the owner of that coldly sarcastic voice. Michael looked every inch the dark and compelling archangel he was named for as he bore down on where she and Pierre were standing talking together in the reception area of the gallery.

And Michael was right—Eva should have been in his office on the third floor ten minutes ago for that twelve o'clock appointment he had suggested over breakfast this morning. She just hadn't been able to resist stopping and talking to his assistant manager, when the charmingly flirtatious Pierre had approached and spoken to her as she entered the gallery.

Or trying to pump him for information on Rachel and Rafe while she was about it!

And she hadn't got very far in that endeavour, had only just got around to casually mentioning her sister's visit to Paris last year, when Michael so rudely interrupted them.

A Michael, eyes glittering like black onyx, nostrils flared, skin taut over the sharpness of his cheekbones, sculptured lips thinned, jaw tensed, who looked absolutely nothing like the sexily tousled, stubble-jawed man she'd had breakfast with this morning, let alone the sensual and sensitive man who had made such exquisite love to her the evening before...

Michael continued to look down coldly at Eva for several more seconds before turning those glacial black eyes on Pierre. 'Shouldn't you have gone to lunch by now?'

Eva drew in a sharp breath at Michael's coldly cutting tone, pretty sure she was responsible. Michael certainly hadn't liked her attempt to question his assistant manager three days ago about whether or not he had remembered Rachel from the previous year, or known anything about Rafe's relationship with her!

'If you remember, you asked that I take care of Miss Foster's children during your appointment with her...?' Pierre now reminded his employer politely.

A nerve pulsed in Michael's tightly clenched jaw. 'Then perhaps you should have offered to do that rather than delay Miss Foster arriving promptly for that appointment.'

Eva had heard quite enough—more than enough, when Pierre's comment made it obvious that Michael was allowing his assistant manager to believe that Sophie and Sam were her children, rather than Rachel and Rafe's!

'It's very kind of you to offer, Pierre.' She turned to give the Frenchman a warm smile as she touched his arm lightly in thanks. 'As you can see, my niece and nephew are both fast asleep at the moment.' She glanced down to where Sophie and Sam slept in the pushchair, their angelic faces revealing none of the mayhem they had caused in Michael's apartment since their arrival.

The playpen and high chairs Michael had ordered to be delivered had helped to ease some of the strain they had suffered that first evening, when she and Michael had needed to chase the twins all over the sitting room in an effort to prevent them from breaking anything. Michael might have admitted to having no previous experience with babies, but he certainly seemed to know what was needed to make life easier for coping with them.

Or, more likely, he was just trying to protect the priceless artefacts and statuary in his apartment!

Whatever his reasoning, Eva had made good use of the high chairs and the playpen, most especially this morning when, after tidying the apartment, she had been able to put the twins safely in the playpen while she changed to go to her twelve o'clock appointment with Michael.

Which she now wished she hadn't bothered to keep, when she could literally *feel* Michael's brooding disapproval of having found her in conversation with the handsome Pierre. A conversation which, frustratingly, hadn't as yet yielded any new information on Rachel and Rafe's relationship...

She ignored Michael's disapproval as she gave Pierre another warm smile. 'You know where I am if you should need me.'

'Of course.' He returned Eva's smile with a charming one of his own, at the same time as he seemed to be keeping one wary eye on his employer.

Eva's smile noticeably disappeared as she turned to look coldly at Michael. 'Shall we go?' she prompted tersely, not waiting for his reply as she turned and walked off down the marble hallway towards the stairs that would take them to the upper floors.

Michael managed to catch up with Eva enough in three lengthy strides to be able to take a light grasp of her elbow. 'Not here,' he rasped grimly between gritted teeth as she instantly tried to pull away from that hold, his fingers tightening enough to prevent her from doing that without actually bruising her.

Daggers shot out of those violet-coloured eyes as she gave him an angry glance. 'You behaved like an arrogant boor just now to Pierre!'

Yes, he had, Michael accepted, knowing he had been both rude and overly curt towards the younger man. Although he found his reasons for doing so were a little harder to explain...

His morning at the gallery hadn't exactly been his finest hour either, as he had snapped and snarled at everyone he spoke to, almost reducing Marie to tears at one stage with his bad temper. Which had only succeeded in making him feel more annoyed, even as he offered Marie his apologies.

Consequently he had been restlessly pacing his office as he waited for Eva to arrive at twelve o'clock, the minutes ticking by slowly once the clock on his desk reached the noonday hour. By eight minutes past twelve Michael had decided to call his apartment, and when he received no answer to that call had hoped it indicated Eva was on her way here, which was when he had decided to go downstairs and wait for her in Reception.

Reaching the bottom of the marble staircase, and seeing Eva in obviously easy conversation with his charming assistant manager, the two of them then laughing together over one of Pierre's remarks, had made Michael see red.

Or, rather, black...

Because a black tide of displeasure had seemed to sweep over him as he strode purposefully towards the two of them, blocking out all rational or logical thought.

And Michael had absolutely no idea why it was he had reacted in that way...

Except to know he hadn't liked seeing Eva so relaxed and comfortable in another man's company. That same ease of companionship Michael had thought he and Eva had uniquely shared together over these past few days.

Until last night…

Last night had changed everything between them, and Michael hadn't been at all sure that Eva would keep the appointment.

To realise that she had come to the gallery after all, but had delayed going up to his office because she was downstairs in conversation with the too-handsome and too-charming Pierre, had tipped Michael's already precarious mood over into burning displeasure.

He wasn't angry…he was jealous!

Michael drew in a sharp, hissing breath at the thought of what that might mean.

Because he knew, despite the circumstances under which they had met and his initial assumption she was a gold-digger, that he liked Eva… Not only was she beautiful, but she was also intelligent. Her conversation was astute and thought-provoking, and her exquisite photographs, most especially 'Harmony', proved she was also a gifted photographer.

And, after last night, it would be ridiculous of Michael to even attempt to deny he also *desired* her.

Added to which, he also admired her for her emotional resilience, after losing both her parents and her sister in so short a time. And he had no doubt about the deep love she felt for the twins—that love perhaps all the more intense *because* of those other recent family losses?

But to imagine, to think, that he might be starting to have any deeper feelings for Eva was totally unacceptable to him.

It was unacceptable to him to realise he had actually liked, *enjoyed*, these evenings he and Eva had spent together, playing with the twins before feeding and bathing them and then putting them to bed, before the two of them then sat down to enjoy a leisurely dinner together, along with scintillating and intelligent conversation.

So much so that Michael was aware the apartment was going to feel empty, lonely, once Eva and the twins had returned to England...

That last realisation was especially unacceptable to him!

Michael was never lonely—the opposite, in fact. He had always enjoyed his own company, and valued his solitude. As well as the fact that he was answerable to no one in his private life. Business was a different matter, of course, because there he had a responsibility to Gabriel and Rafe, but in his private life he did exactly as he pleased.

And for the past three evenings it had pleased him to be with Eva and the twins...

'Take a seat,' he ground out in invitation once he and Eva had entered his office, closing the door behind them before crossing the room to resume his seat behind the marble desk.

Which was when Michael realised Eva had made no move to do as he asked, his eyes narrowing as he realised how seasonably bright and lovely she looked standing across the room in a sundress of pale lilac, her complexion creamy and smooth, just a pale lip gloss on the full pout of her lips. Her hair was that silky, ebony curtain against the bareness of her lightly tanned shoulders, her legs slender beneath the dress's just-above-the-knee length, flat white sandals on her feet.

His mouth tightened as he felt his shaft throb in recognition of all that unaffected loveliness. 'Eva?'

She still didn't move. 'You really were incredibly rude to Pierre just now—'

'I believe you can safely leave my dealings with my staff to me!' Michael dismissed unyieldingly.

Eva's eyes widened at the unmistakeable coldness in

his tone. Could this man, who looked at her with such cool indifference, really be the same one who had made such exquisite love to her last night? Whose hands and lips had touched her everywhere? Who had *tasted* her so intimately?

The answer to those questions was no, of course this wasn't the same man...

This man was every inch the one she had first met, the unapproachable and suspicious Michael D'Angelo, wealthy part-owner of the Archangel galleries, rather than the man who last night had revealed a sensitivity Eva had only guessed might exist.

'You do know that Pierre is married...?'

She frowned across at Michael, not liking the scorn she detected in his expression. 'I had assumed so,' she answered slowly, 'after you told me he has two children of his own...'

Michael nodded abruptly. 'I just thought I would make sure you're aware of that fact.'

'Michael—'

'Eva.'

She gave a shake of her head at the hardness of his tone. 'I don't think I like what you're implying.'

'I'm not implying anything—'

'Oh, I believe that you are!' she said with certainty, sure now more than ever that Michael's obvious distrust of women lay somewhere in his past...

'Won't you please sit down, Eva?' Once again Michael indicated the chair across the desk from his own.

Eva supposed she should be grateful that at least he had said please this time...

She moved slowly forward before perching on the edge of the chair facing Michael across that marble desk, instantly regretting it as she became aware of the way in which it seemed to put more than just the distance of the width of that desk between them, turning this meeting businesslike rather than personal.

As it was meant to?

Of course it was meant to do that, Eva ruefully answered her own question; no doubt Michael was as eager as she was to put their relationship back on an impersonal footing.

She sat up straighter in her chair. 'I assure you, I have absolutely no personal interest in Pierre.'

'And I apologise if you thought I was implying anything else.' Michael nodded brusquely, only too well aware that he *had* been implying something else, that he had totally overreacted to seeing Eva talking with Pierre.

As aware as he was that he refused to acknowledge the reason for that overreaction...

'So, what was it you wanted to discuss with me?' Eva prompted just as briskly.

Michael's brows rose. 'I take it you're not in the mood to exchange pleasantries first?' he drawled dryly. 'Polite enquiries as to whether or not we've both had an enjoyable, or in my case profitable, morning?'

'No,' she dismissed hardly. 'Could we just get this conversation over with?' she added impatiently as Michael continued to look at her steadily. 'It's getting late, and I want to take the twins to the Eiffel Tower today.'

Michael had been aware that Eva had filled her days by taking the babies around Paris. Where the three of them had been, and the things they had seen, had been part of their conversations over dinner in the evenings.

What surprised him now was the tug he felt to accompany the three of them on this afternoon's excursion...

The Paris Archangel had been open for eight years now, and Michael had spent at least three years of those eight in the French capital in two-to-three-month periods, and he had long grown accustomed to seeing the historical sights of Paris. In fact, he could see the Eiffel Tower from his apartment.

Which would seem to indicate that his interest wasn't in visiting the Eiffel Tower at all but in spending time with Eva and the twins...

His mouth tightened at that realisation. 'I wanted this meeting to take place here at the gallery because I have a business proposition I'd like to discuss with you.'

Eva instantly grew wary as she could think of only one business proposition Michael could possibly have in mind. And after their lapse last night she shouldn't really be surprised. No doubt, having had the morning to think about it, Michael was now eager for her to leave his apartment.

She gave a shake of her head. 'I don't believe you should think about paying me off until after we've spoken to your brother—'

'We aren't speaking to Rafe, Eva, I am,' Michael corrected harshly as he straightened abruptly. 'And I have no intention of paying you off, as you put it, when we haven't yet established that Rafe is the father of your sister's children!'

Eva felt the flush of anger in her cheeks at his continued doubting of her claim; Rachel might have been many things, immature and irresponsible being two of them, but she certainly hadn't been a liar, and before she died she had clearly told Eva that Rafe D'Angelo was the father of the twins. 'I will speak to your brother myself—'

'That's not going to happen,' Michael assured her grimly.

Eva's eyes widened at the certainty in his voice. 'You may be a rich and powerful man, Michael, but you can't prevent me from seeing and talking to Rafe if I want to. And I do,' she added determinedly.

'This has nothing to do with how rich or how powerful I may or may not be.' He sighed heavily. 'Eva, don't you think it would be…kinder to Nina, Rafe's wife, if I were the one to talk to him? Privately,' he added softly.

The blush deepened in Eva's cheeks at the quiet rebuke she could hear in Michael's voice. 'If I had wanted to make things unpleasant for Rafe's wife then I would already have done so. Instead I agreed to wait until they return from their honeymoon before talking to him.'

She had, Michael accepted. Because he had asked her to do so.

'All I want to do is get to the truth,' Eva added softly.

'As do I.' Michael nodded tersely. 'And I believe we will achieve that more…discreetly, if I'm the one who talks to Rafe.'

Although how the hell Michael was even going to begin to broach the subject of Rachel Foster to his newly married brother, let alone whether or not Rafe could be the father of her twin babies, he had no idea!

Even if Rafe denied it, as Michael seriously expected him to do—his brother might have been something of a playboy before he met and fell in love with Nina, but he certainly hadn't been irresponsible enough not to have used contraception in all of his previous relationships—then he had no doubt that Eva would demand blood tests in order to prove that denial, further complicating an already delicate situation.

Michael had never seen Rafe as happy as he had been since he fell in love with Nina, and the thought of Eva's accusations of Rafe's paternity and the damage it might cause to his brother's relationship with Nina, made Michael feel physically ill.

But at the same time he felt empathy for Eva's situation.

He had come to know Eva well enough to know she wasn't doing any of this out of spite or malice, or any sense of revenge, or with the intention of blackmailing Rafe for money, that she truly was just finding it impossible to financially care for Sophie and Sam, and needed their father's help to continue doing so. Understandably so, when caring for the twins meant Eva could no longer work at her chosen profession, and the day-to-day care of two babies was an expensive business.

Which left Michael feeling damned if he did and damned if he didn't.

And the stiffness of Eva's pride told him she would never accept financial help from him, no matter what the outcome of his conversation with Rafe.

'I really didn't ask you here to talk about any of that,' he dismissed evenly.

Eva sighed. 'Then why did you ask me here?'

His mouth thinned at the weariness of her tone. 'As I said, I have a business proposition to put to you—it doesn't involve paying anyone off!' he bit out as he saw she was about to refuse a second time.

Eva looked at him searchingly for several long tense seconds, but as usual she could read none of Michael's thoughts from his closed expression. 'Then what does it involve...?' she finally prompted slowly, suspiciously.

'Your Tibetan photographs.'

She blinked her surprise at his answer. 'Sorry?'

Michael shrugged. 'You mentioned you had brought back enough photographs of Tibet from your visit there last year for a second exhibition?'

'Yes...'

'And you already know that I'm a great admirer of E J Foster's work,' he drawled ruefully.

'Yes...' Eva felt the warmth enter her cheeks at the memory of exactly how she knew that. Of exactly where she had been, where they had both been, when she had discovered that. And the intimacies that had followed...

Michael nodded. 'I'm also—conveniently,' he added dryly, 'one of the owners of a collection of international art galleries and auction houses.'

'Yes...'

He eyed her impatiently. 'Is that "yes" spoken in that less than trusting way going to be your only contribution to this conversation?'

'That depends...'

Those onyx-black eyes narrowed guardedly. 'On what?'

'On exactly where this conversation is going!' Eva wasn't sure what else she could say, when she had no idea yet what Michael was leading up to with this conversation. An idea had occurred to her, certainly, but it was such a fantastically unrealistic one it couldn't possibly be right.

No way Michael would ever want, ever think of suggesting, that she—that E J Foster—consider having an exhibition of her Tibetan photographs in one of the three prestigious Archangel galleries!

No, of course Michael wasn't suggesting that. It would be madness on Eva's part to even think that he might—

'What I'm proposing, Eva,' Michael bit out evenly, 'is that you consider exhibiting a selection of E J Foster's Tibetan photographs in the Archangel gallery of your choice.'

CHAPTER NINE

EVA'S EYES WENT wide with disbelief as she continued to stare across the desk at Michael for several long seconds, before another emotion took its place, her eyes glittering with anger as she stood up abruptly, a flush to her cheeks now. 'How could you?' she accused emotionally, trembling hands clenching into fists at her sides, angry tears blurring her vision. 'I knew from the moment I met you that you were a hard, cold man—'

'Eva—'

'—who didn't believe a word I was saying to you—'

'Eva!'

'—but even knowing that,' she continued as those tears began to fall hotly down her cheeks, 'I didn't think even you would ever be so deliberately cruel.'

'Damn it, don't cry…!' Michael stood up to move quickly out from behind his desk before reaching out for her.

'Don't touch me,' Eva warned through numbed lips even as she stepped away to evade his grasp. 'How could you, Michael? How could you *be* so cruel? How could you…?' she choked again as she raised her hands to bury her face in them, the scalding-hot tears falling between her fingers.

'Damn it, Eva…!'

Eva had no fight left inside her to be able to pull away

a second time as Michael drew her firmly into his arms, her salty tears instantly dampening the pristine whiteness of his silk shirt as one of his hands cupped the back of her head and held her gently to his chest.

She *knew* none of this could be easy for Michael—any easier than it had all been for her when she first learnt of Rachel's pregnancy and illness—and she empathised with the shock he must have felt when she had turned up at the gallery with the twins.

Yes, Eva could sympathise, but this—this was uncalled for. Cruel, as she had already said, when Eva ached inside, longed for nothing more than to be able to continue with her career, and to exhibit more of her photographs.

The very carrot Michael was now dangling so temptingly in front of her nose...

But she would never, could never take that carrot, when the price might endanger the twins' future!

Michael was at a complete loss to know what to do with the silently sobbing Eva as he continued to hold her in his arms.

Not sure whether he felt angry or hurt at Eva's accusation of 'I didn't think even you would ever be so deliberately cruel...'

Even him?

What did that mean? That Eva believed him to be cold and hard obviously, but that she also hadn't believed that coldness and hardness to be deep enough, ingrained enough, for him to treat her cruelly?

Bad enough in itself, but Michael had no idea what cruelty Eva was referring to.

He had thought she would be pleased with his proposition.

What the hell sort of cruelty could there possibly be in

his having invited her to exhibit her latest photographs in one of the Archangel galleries—?

Michael tensed as the answer hit him squarely between the eyes. 'Eva, do you think my offer of the exhibition is another way of me paying you off…?' he grated slowly. 'As in, your silence about Rafe in exchange for exhibiting your photographs at Archangel?'

'What else could it be?' She sniffled miserably as she attempted to mop up some of the tears dampening Michael's chest.

What else indeed…?

Michael now knew exactly what emotion he was feeling! 'You know, Eva,' he bit out with steely calm, 'I knew, from the moment I met *you*, that you could be impetuous and outspoken, but I hadn't realised until now that you could also be so damned insulting as to accuse me of blackmailing you into silence!'

'You don't like the accusation any more than I did…'

No, he didn't. Because he had believed, after last night, that Eva was learning to trust him. As much as he now trusted her…?

Whatever he had believed he had been wrong, damn it!

He reached up to grasp her arms and hold her away from him as he looked down at her with glittering black eyes. 'Look at me, Eva,' he instructed harshly as she continued to look down at that damp patch on his shirt. 'I said, look at me, damn it!' he repeated hardly.

She raised wet dark lashes to look up at him with eyes of a deep and bruised purple, her face deathly pale. 'I never—I didn't use the word blackmail…'

'You didn't need to!' A nerve pulsed in Michael's tightly clenched jaw. 'It was right there alongside your other accusations…coldness and cruelty.' He released her arms to walk across to stand in front of the floor-to-ceiling windows looking out onto the Champs Élysées, not seeing any of the grandness of the wide avenue. 'I thought you had come to know me better than that, Eva. Believed we had reached an understanding— Oh, to hell with what I believed; why should you be any different from every other bloody woman?' he added bleakly. 'I think you should leave now, before one or both of us says something else we're going to regret.'

Eva stared across at Michael, the rigidity of his stance unmistakeable: tensed shoulders, back stiff and straight, hands thrust into the pockets of his tailored trousers, feet slightly parted.

He looked...chillingly unapproachable. Because of the things she had said? Because she had assumed that his offer was an attempt on his part to blackmail her into silence—?

When she put it as bluntly as that it did sound pretty awful, Eva realised with a pained wince. Especially when she now realised Michael hadn't actually said that...

What had he said, exactly?

That he wanted to offer her, as E J Foster, the opportunity to exhibit her Tibetan photographs at the Archangel gallery of her choice.

There had been no mention in that offer of anything to do with the twins, or Rafe, or anything else to do with that situation, only that it was a business proposition.

Did that mean Michael really had just been offering her the chance to exhibit her photographs with no strings or conditions attached?

Eva moistened her lips with the tip of her tongue before speaking again, her voice gruff from the tears she had shed. 'If I was mistaken—'

'Oh, you were!' he assured grimly.

Eva wasn't in the least encouraged by the coldness of

Michael's voice or the way he kept his back turned towards her as he continued to look out onto the busy Champs Élysées. 'Then I apologise,' she finished lamely.

'Big of you!' Michael did turn around now, his expression as coldly scathing as his tone as those black eyes raked over her with merciless intensity. 'I don't believe I can talk about this any more just now, Eva,' he finally bit out with cold dismissal.

'You have another appointment…?'

'No, I just can't—I think it best if we don't discuss this any further right now,' he answered uncompromisingly.

Eva winced as she heard the cold implacability in Michael's tone.

He really was icily, chillingly, furious. Rightly so, if her accusation really had been so far off the mark! 'Then later? At ho—er—at your apartment?' She grimaced, her cheeks blazing hotly at the slip of having almost called Michael's apartment 'home'.

Its luxurious impersonality barely rendered it as being Michael's Parisian home, let alone her own!

His mouth twisted derisively as he obviously realised the reason for her embarrassed blush. 'Yes, perhaps we'll talk about this again later at the apartment.'

Eva frowned. 'Perhaps…?'

He drew in a deep and even breath, as if fighting to maintain control of his temper. 'At this point in time I'm not sure there's anything left for us to discuss.' He shrugged. 'There's always a chance I might feel differently about it later on today.'

And that, Eva acknowledged heavily, was the end of the subject for now, as far as Michael was concerned. And, if his offer really had just been the business proposition he'd said it was, then she couldn't exactly blame him for feeling that way!

She had, Eva realised, with a few choice words and her accusing tears, succeeded in totally destroying the shaky truce that had slowly been growing between the two of them, but had already been so severely tested by the intimacies they had shared the night before.

'I'll go now,' she said abruptly. 'I— What time should I expect you back for dinner?'

Michael's mouth twisted with derision as he realised Eva had carefully avoided referring to his apartment as 'home' a second time.

'I have absolutely no idea,' he dismissed flatly, not sure it was a good idea for him to join Eva at the apartment for dinner this evening at all.

Hadn't he decided earlier that having Eva and the twins at the apartment was becoming just a little too cosy, too domesticated for comfort? *His* comfort?

A cosiness and domesticity Michael realised he was in no mood for this evening, after Eva's distrust of him. 'I could be late, so just order something in for yourself,' he added coolly as he resumed his seat behind his desk. 'Could you please send Marie in on your way out...?' he added distractedly as he pulled the proofs for the next Parisian Archangel catalogue towards him and began to read through them.

Eva took one last lingering look at Michael, as he bent over some papers lying on the top of his desk, before leaving, knowing herself well and truly dismissed...

The digital clock on Eva's bedside table read eleven fifty-one in the darkness of the bedroom when she heard Michael use his key to enter the otherwise silent apartment. Listening intently, she heard him drop his key into the glass bowl on the table in the hallway alongside the spare key he had given her some days ago, followed by the soft thud of his briefcase as he placed it beneath that table, before moving quietly to the kitchen.

And Eva was aware of him making every single one of those soft movements—because she had left her bedroom door slightly open for just that purpose when she crawled miserably into bed a couple of hours ago!

After what had been a long and awful afternoon and evening as far as Eva was concerned. The twins, having predictably picked up on her tension when she had returned downstairs to collect them from Pierre, had then proceeded to be cranky and fretful all afternoon. And they hadn't improved when they all returned to the apartment, throwing food at each other when Eva fed them their tea, and splashing water over each other when she bathed them.

Eva had given a sigh of relief when it came time to put them in their separate cots for the night!

Only to then find she had the rest of the long and lonely evening stretching out in front of her...

Michael hadn't returned by nine o'clock, and Eva had felt too despondent to order any food in for her own dinner, deciding to settle for making some toast instead, and ending up feeling quite sorry for herself as she sat down alone in the quiet of the kitchen to eat it.

She had never been a particularly social person, had shared accommodation at university, but had preferred the privacy of her own space after she moved to London. The twins had shattered that privacy three months ago, of course, but even so Eva had never felt lonely, just exhausted, once she had put the babies to bed for the night.

She had been very aware of feeling lonely this evening...

Because, in just a very short space of time, Eva knew she had become accustomed to spending her evenings with Michael. Had come to appreciate, to enjoy, their quiet dinners together, their conversation, and even their silences had seemed companionable rather than awkward.

This evening there had just been a yawning great hole of loneliness where Michael should have been.

Leaving Eva with hours and hours to wonder where he was and what he was doing...

She very much doubted he had been at a business meeting all these hours, so he had probably spent the evening socially. With another woman.

Another woman...?

That would seem to imply that Eva thought of herself as being a woman Michael was involved with. Which she didn't—did she...?

Of course she didn't! That would just be asking for trouble.

She'd never thought to ask, and Michael hadn't volunteered the information either, as to whether or not he had a woman currently in his life.

But of course there would be!

How could Eva have been stupid enough not to have realised that earlier? Michael was a darkly gorgeous and complex man, and an experienced and exquisite lover, added to which he was seriously wealthy, and Eva had no doubt there was sure to be some other woman currently appreciating all three of those highly attractive qualities.

Had that other woman been appreciating those qualities this evening?

It really was none of her business, Eva accepted heavily. Just because Michael had made love to her last night didn't give her any right to feel hurt, or jealous, because he was spending the evening with another woman.

Except Eva knew that she did...

She felt incredibly hurt just thinking about it. And she felt jealous because—because Eva had realised, as she sat alone in Michael's apartment this evening, waiting for him to come home, that she had been falling in love with him!

He was totally the wrong man, and it was totally the wrong time for her to fall in love with anyone, and yet Eva knew that was exactly what she had done. She was in love with Michael D'Angelo, the very last man who would ever allow himself to fall in love with her, the woman accusing his brother of fathering her niece and nephew.

And quite how she was going to continue staying on at this apartment with Michael, until Rafe returned from his honeymoon, knowing that she was in love with him, Eva had absolutely no idea. She—

'Eva…?'

Every part of Eva froze as she realised that, while she had been lying here agonising over the fact that she had fallen in love with Michael—a man she could never have, and who would never allow himself to feel the same way about her—he had obviously left the kitchen and walked down the hallway, seen her bedroom door was slightly ajar, and decided to see if she was still awake.

'It's no use pretending to be asleep, Eva, because I could actually feel your recriminating thoughts pounding at me just now through the bedroom wall.'

'Recriminating?' Eva repeated challengingly as she gave up all pretence of being asleep. She sat up abruptly in the bed, uncaring that she was only wearing a soft white cotton camisole top and loose boxers, as she frowned across at Michael's silhouette in her now fully open bedroom doorway. 'I don't have the right to feel that way,' she continued sharply, 'when I'm so obviously an unwanted guest in your apartment!'

'I think what happened between us last night totally disproves part of that statement,' Michael came back wearily, at the same time as he ran a distracted hand through his thick hair, his head pounding painfully with the headache he'd suffered for the past two hours.

A headache certainly not helped by the sight of Eva wearing a barely there top, her hair a glossy ebony tangle about her bare shoulders, as the blood pounded hotly through his veins in response to her.

'You—'

'Have you eaten?'

'I— No, not really.' Eva was taken aback by the abrupt change of subject. 'Just a piece of toast,' she added softly.

Michael nodded abruptly. 'I'm about to go back to the kitchen and make myself an omelette, if you would care to join me?'

'You haven't eaten this evening either?'

'No,' he sighed.

'I assumed you would have been out for dinner...?'

He shook his head. 'I've been working in my office all evening.'

Eva fought to hold back the elation she felt at hearing this. 'I thought you couldn't cook.'

'An omelette isn't cooking,' he assured dryly. 'And I didn't say I couldn't cook, only that I don't.'

'Semantics.' Eva nodded ruefully, feeling more light-hearted than she had all evening. Because she now knew that Michael hadn't been out with another woman this evening, after all...

'Yes or no to the omelette, Eva?' Michael was hoping that food might help relieve some of his pounding headache. Although, with Eva looking so sexily tousled, he doubted it very much as his shaft now pounded, thickened and hardened, to the same rhythm of that pulsing headache...!

'Yes.' She threw back the bedclothes with the obvious intention of getting out of bed.

Giving Michael a clear view of the silky bare legs she swung to the carpeted floor before she stood up to pick up her robe from the chair, that short walk revealing that she wore a loose pair of black boxers to sleep in along with that barely there white top.

Michael turned away abruptly as his hardened shaft pulsed eagerly in response. 'I'll see you in the kitchen in a few minutes.'

'I'm just—'

Michael didn't linger in the doorway to hear what else Eva was going to say as he turned sharply on his heel and returned to the kitchen, just that brief glimpse of her in that sexy top and boxers enough to set his blood pounding even harder. He moved grim-faced about the kitchen collecting up the ingredients for their omelettes.

'Did you have an enjoyable evening working?' Eva prompted huskily as she quietly entered the kitchen to stand near the door watching as Michael whisked the eggs in a bowl.

'No.' He kept his back towards her. 'You?'

'No.'

'Why not? Were the twins difficult?' Michael didn't need to glance away from tipping the egg mixture into the pan to be achingly aware of Eva's every move as she crossed the kitchen to sit down on one of the chairs about the table in the centre of the room.

He could smell her, that perfume that was uniquely Eva: a mixture of citrus and hot earthy woman.

'A little. But that wasn't it. I—I've been…unhappy, about the way we parted earlier,' she admitted huskily.

Michael continued to keep his back to her as he closed his eyes, counting slowly to ten as he willed himself not to respond to that admission. If their argument this afternoon, the things Eva had said to him, had shown him nothing else, then it had convinced Michael that it was in the best interest of both of them if he avoided Eva's company in future.

And so he had stayed away from the apartment this evening, filling those hours with work, uninterested in eating dinner as he kept himself busy, and resulting in his now having this blinding headache.

He faltered slightly as he carried the first laden plate over to the table as he saw Eva looked more luscious than ever. 'Eat,' he instructed tersely as he placed the plate of hot food on the table in front of her, before turning sharply away to return to the hob to cook his own omelette.

'Mmm, this is really good,' she murmured appreciatively seconds later.

Michael made a gruff noise of acknowledgement, having no appetite for his own omelette now but tipping it out of the pan and onto the plate anyway before walking over to sit opposite Eva at the wooden table.

If anything Eva felt more miserable now than she had earlier this evening.

She had felt briefly happy at knowing he had spent the evening at his office rather than going out, but that had now been replaced by the fact that at least before she had only been able to guess at the anger Michael felt towards her. Being here with him now, able to see and feel that displeasure firsthand, was unbearable!

So much so that Eva could only push the rest of her omelette uninterestedly about her plate, Michael appearing to do the same with his as the minutes slowly passed with the marked ticking of the kitchen clock. They brooded in silence, Eva because she simply couldn't think of anything to say, and Michael because he obviously just didn't have anything he wanted to say to her...

Eva lowered her lashes and looked down at the table

as she heard Michael's chair scrape on the tiled floor, so miserable now she was totally unable to prevent the tears from falling softly down her cheeks; damn it, she had cried more in the last few days than she had for months!

'Eva…?' Michael's legs appeared beside her first, and then his chest and face as he came down onto his haunches to look up at her bowed head. 'Why are you crying…?' he prompted softly as one of his hands moved up and his fingertips gently smoothed those tears from her cheeks.

'This time?' Eva asked.

He gave a rueful smile. 'My offer of an exhibition of your work at one of the Archangel galleries still stands, Eva.'

Her gaze flicked up to his in surprise. 'It does?'

Michael nodded. 'No conditions. Absolutely no strings attached,' he added grimly.

Eva ran her tongue over her lips. 'I— That's very generous of you after the things I said to you earlier.'

'You think?' He arched dark and mocking brows. 'I'm sure my brothers would both assure you that I'm just using good business sense by securing the next E J Foster photographic exhibition for our galleries.'

Eva's heart plummeted. Because she had wanted, hoped, that Michael having repeated his earlier offer meant he had forgiven her for the things she had said. 'I see.'

'Somehow I doubt that.' Michael's dark gaze roamed freely over her make-up-free face as he gently smoothed the hair back from her temple. 'I've been fighting coming home and doing this all evening, Eva,' he groaned huskily, 'but now that I'm here with you again, I can't fight it any longer!'

She swallowed. 'This…?'

'This!' One of his hands captured both of hers before he straightened abruptly, taking Eva with him. 'I want to make love to you,' he grated huskily. 'Do you want me in the same way?'

The best thing to do, the sensible thing to do, would be for Eva to say no, to just walk away and go back to her bedroom and close the door behind her; she had absolutely no doubt that Michael would accept the closing of that door as her final answer.

That was the sensible thing to do.

'Yes.' Eva didn't even attempt to qualify that one-word answer by adding anything else.

She did want Michael. Madly. Passionately.

And if tonight was all she was going to have of him then she was going to take it!

CHAPTER TEN

MICHAEL DREW IN a harshly ragged breath at hearing Eva answer him with her usual straightforwardness. He should have expected it of her, of course, but he had hardly dared to hope that might be her answer...

'My bedroom or yours?' he prompted gruffly as his arms moved possessively about her waist, the headache that had been plaguing him all evening having miraculously disappeared.

'Does it matter?' Her hands slid slowly up his waistcoat and shirt-covered chest to his shoulders, before her fingers moved to become entangled in the hair at his nape.

No, it didn't matter where, Michael accepted, all that mattered at this moment was making love with Eva, a need that he was only too well aware had consumed his every waking moment since last night.

'Whichever bedroom it is I think you're a little over-dressed for what we have in mind!' Eva teased huskily.

The two of them must look slightly ludicrous, Michael accepted ruefully; Eva was dressed in her nightclothes, and he was still wearing the white silk shirt, waistcoat and trousers of the formal three-piece suit he had worn to work that morning, his jacket draped over the back of one of the kitchen chairs.

'Shower first,' he announced firmly. 'Some of us have

been working all day and all evening!' He swung Eva easily up into his arms.

'Whoa!' She laughed, her arms moving about his neck so that she could hold on tightly as Michael walked out of the kitchen with her in his arms and then down the hallway to his bedroom.

He didn't so much as hesitate outside the door but instead just kicked it open and strode inside the darkened room and straight through to the adjoining bathroom.

Eva's eyes widened. 'I get to watch you shower?'

'You get to join me in the shower,' Michael corrected gruffly.

'I've already taken a shower this evening,' Eva protested laughingly as Michael sat her down on top of the vanity unit before moving to switch on the light and turn on the water, the smoky glass-sided shower so large it took up almost half of the spacious and opulently appointed bathroom. The tiles on the walls and floor were terracotta and cream, with gold fittings in the shower and double sink, with half a dozen fluffy gold-coloured towels on the warmer.

'Not with me you haven't,' Michael said with satisfaction as he turned, his dark gaze holding hers captive as he took off his tie before unbuttoning his waistcoat and taking that off too. He threw both items onto the narrow marble bench running along one of the walls.

Eva was fascinated, watching Michael as he slowly unfastened his shirt before slipping that off his shoulders and down his arms. Muscles rippled in his tanned chest and back as the shirt joined the rapidly growing pile of his clothes. She couldn't think as far ahead as the shower he was obviously suggesting they take together.

His torso was…magnificent. Olive skinned, silky dark

hair down the centre of his chest, lean and muscled, with not an ounce of superfluous flesh anywhere, and—

Eva's breath caught in her throat as Michael's hands moved to the fastening on his trousers before lowering the zip, the colour burning her cheeks as her gaze moved quickly back up to his face.

'Doesn't this seem fair to you after last night...?' he prompted gruffly.

When Eva had been completely naked and Michael had remained fully dressed...

'Yes,' she confirmed huskily, grateful for what he was doing, and determined not to avert her gaze as Michael first dispensed with his shoes and socks before removing his trousers too Now he wore only a pair of black boxers that hugged his sculpted hips and thighs above long and muscled legs.

Black hip-hugging boxers that also did very little to hide the lengthy bulge of his arousal!

And then it wasn't hidden any more as Michael stood completely naked in front of her, his arousal surging up towards his taut abdomen.

Michael was gorgeous in his nakedness.

Unashamedly, blatantly, beautifully gorgeous!

Eva was completely unaware that she was running her tongue slowly over her lips as the heat of her gaze feasted on all that blatant olive-skinned maleness. His thick and pulsing shaft seeming to lengthen and thicken even more as she gazed her fill.

'God, Eva...!'

Her gaze flickered up to Michael's face as she heard the husky longing in his voice at his reaction to having the heat of her gaze on him. He breathed shallowly, his whole body tense, hands clenched into fists at his sides, as if he was waiting to see what she would do next.

Eva knew what she wanted to do—

What she was going to do!

Last night she had longed to touch and taste Michael in the same intimate way he had touched and tasted her. In the way his aroused nakedness now invited her to touch and taste him...

Eva's gaze held Michael's as she slowly slid down from her seat on top of the vanity unit before walking barefoot across the heated tiles towards him. Her gaze lowered as she came to a halt just inches away from him and she ran the fingertips of both hands lightly across his chest and stomach, before curling them about the long and silken length of his shaft.

'Eva...!' He gave a strangulated groan, hands clenching into fists at his sides even as his hips thrust up instinctively forward into those encircling fingers.

She dropped gently to her knees in front of him onto the heated tiles, once again running her tongue across her lips. She brushed the soft pad of her thumb over his moistened tip and, holding his gaze with hers, she brought her thumb to her mouth.

He tasted delicious, slightly salty, with an underlying addictive sweetness that she suspected was uniquely Michael.

Whatever it was she wanted to taste more of him, breathing softly against that sensitive head as she moved closer before parting her lips and taking him completely into her mouth.

'Eva, I'm not sure I can— Dear sweet heaven!' Michael groaned in ecstasy as Eva took even more of him inside the heat of her mouth, her tongue an erotic rasp as it flattened over the sensitive head.

She repeated the same caress over and over again, licking, lapping, even as she sucked him deeper and then deeper still, and all the time her fingers clasped tightly about the inches she couldn't manage, pumping in the same rhythm, taking the fullness of him a little further each time until he felt the back of her throat caressing, stroking that sensitive tip.

'No more, Eva…!' Michael's hands moved out to grasp her shoulders, his eyes burning down into hers as she looked up at him without releasing him, her eyes deep purple between silky dark lashes. 'I'm not going to last if you don't stop now.' He drew in a deep and ragged breath as he once again felt the caressing sweep of her tongue. 'I want to be inside you when I come,' he bit out between gritted teeth, his control now balanced on a knife's edge as he felt himself torn between the longing to allow Eva to continue, to just give in to the pleasure of her caressing mouth and hands until he came, exploding into that welcoming heat, and the desire he also felt to be buried deep inside her when that happened. 'Please, Eva…!' he groaned achingly.

Her shoulders relaxed beneath his hands as she sat back slightly on her haunches, lips sliding slowly, reluctantly, back along the length of his shaft until she released him, eyes dark and sultry as she looked up at him, her full lips red and slightly pouting.

Michael chuckled huskily at the reproachful look in Eva's eyes as his hands moved beneath her elbows and drew her up slowly until she stood in front of him. 'I assure you, stopping you hurt me a lot more than it did you!' He tapped her playfully on the end of her nose, groaning softly as he watched her run her tongue slowly over her lips as she enjoyed the lingering taste of him, first the top one, then the lower one, humming softly in her throat as she did so, her eyes half closed in pleasure.

Eva hadn't wanted to stop, had felt totally aroused just

from kissing and tasting Michael, her breasts aching with that arousal, between her thighs hot and moist, the lips there swollen with her need, her hunger to take him deep inside her.

And if she had ever had any doubts about Michael 'melting' during lovemaking then she didn't now—he was as on fire for her as she was for him!

She trembled slightly as Michael now slipped the robe from her shoulders and let it fall to the tiled floor before gazing down at her round breasts as they thrust against the thin material of her camisole. Eva had no need to look down to know that her tingling nipples were aroused to the size of plump berries. Just as her core was also plump and wet. So very wet, and even hotter with need…

Michael didn't think he'd ever seen anything as sexy as Eva looked right now in the simple white camisole top and those black boxer shorts! More sexy, more desirable, than any female model ever could have done displaying the skimpiest of satin and lace underwear!

There was just something so damned beautiful, so utterly feminine in the way the male boxers sat low on her slim hips, and her thin camisole revealed her peaked nipples.

He held her gaze with his as he reached down and lifted that top up and over her head, dropping it to the tiled floor with her robe as he proceeded to drink his fill of those perfect and naked breasts. Full and sloping globes that he already knew fitted perfectly into his hands, tipped with ripe nipples he couldn't wait to taste again.

He lowered his head slowly to lingeringly kiss each one as he hooked his fingers into the top of her boxers and slid them down her hips and thighs, able to smell the sweet lure of Eva's arousal as he dropped to his knees in front of her and buried his face in her ebony curls.

'No fair!' Eva protested huskily even as she stepped away from him. 'If you won't then neither will I,' she explained huskily as Michael looked up at her with hot, questioning eyes. 'Besides, the room is filling up with steam from the shower running, and think of all the water we're wasting!'

'This isn't a time for practicality, Eva!' Michael chuckled indulgently even as he picked her up in his arms and carried her over to the glass-sided shower.

'You like doing that, don't you—? Michael!' Eva gasped in protest as he stepped beneath the hot spray of the shower with her still in his arms, soaking them both in seconds.

Michael looked down at her, rivulets of water cascading over his dark, silky hair and down his body. 'I like doing this even more,' he assured huskily, kissing her hungrily as he allowed her body to slide down the length of his.

Eva felt completely dazed with pleasure by the time Michael broke the kiss and reached for the shower gel, his gaze holding hers as he began to wash and caress every inch of her, not a single part of her left untouched by the sureness of those arousing hands. 'My turn,' she murmured softly as she proceeded to wash him in the same intimate way.

Michael withstood those deliberately arousing caresses for as long as he could before finally wresting the shower gel from Eva's hands and placing it back on the shelf, turning off the cascading water before picking Eva up in his arms once again and striding out of the shower unit, across the heated tiles, and into his adjoining bedroom, all without collecting any of the fluffy gold towels on the warmer.

'We'll make the bed all wet!' Eva's protest was only half-hearted as Michael placed her down on top of the bedcovers before quickly joining her.

'Who cares?' Michael grated as he kissed the long

column of her silky throat before turning his attention to those full and tempting breasts, the slope of her abdomen, and then lower still.

'I need you inside me now, Michael,' Eva groaned achingly just minutes later, her face flushed with arousal, those purple eyes dark with longing. 'Please!' She looked down at him pleadingly.

Michael could still taste Eva as he slowly moved to lie between her parted thighs before positioning himself at her entrance, his hands on her hips, his gaze holding her fevered one as he forced himself to enter her slowly, inch by silken inch.

He gritted his teeth in an effort to maintain control as the heat of her channel surrounded him, claimed him, drawing him in deeper, and then deeper still as her legs moved up about his thighs, her feet touching his lower back as she arched up and into him, taking him deeper, deeper and deeper until Michael knew he touched the very heart of her.

Eva groaned with pleasure as Michael's mouth claimed hers even as his shaft filled her completely, stretching her as he began to slowly thrust in and out. Her hands clung to his shoulders as her thighs lifted to meet each of those thrusts, even as Eva lost herself in the wonder of the possession of his tongue thrusting into the heat of her mouth in the same erotic rhythm, taking her pleasure higher, wilder, as she met and matched each of those firm thrusts.

Her groans grew more fevered as Michael broke the kiss to claim one of her nipples, suckling deeply, his tongue an arousing rasp against that sensitive flesh, teeth biting as Eva's groans grew throatily breathier.

'Michael…!' she finally cried out, pleading, as the pleasure grew to an almost unbearable intensity as his thrusts grew fiercer, wilder still, faster, her nails digging into his flesh as the pleasure took her higher, and then higher, until it seemed that Michael held her suspended on that plateau of wild pleasure.

Her head thrashed from side to side on the pillows, her breath a broken sob before she cried out, screamed, as the dam broke inside her and the pleasure coursed hotly into and through every inch of her at the same time as Michael cried out, back arching, head thrown back, and she felt the heat of his hot release pumping into her again and again as she continued to climax.

Minutes, hours later, the last of the pleasure finally spent, only the lingering sensitivity and warmth of feeling remained. The sound of their ragged breathing filled the still, heavy air that now surrounded them.

Eva had never known anything—had never experienced anything so—had never realised that anything could be so—

'Dear God, what have I done...?' Michael suddenly groaned, taking his full weight on his elbows as he raised his head from her throat to look down at her. 'I'm so sorry, Eva. I didn't—I never meant things to go as far as this!'

Eva looked up at him blankly, too befuddled still, too satiated, from the intensity of their lovemaking, to be able to make sense of what he was saying.

Michael's expression was grim, a bleakness in the darkness of his eyes as he looked down at her searchingly for several long seconds before shaking his head. 'I'm really sorry, Eva,' he bit out gruffly. 'That was—'

'Another mistake?' Eva had recovered enough now to see how grim he looked. And the bleakness in his face wasn't the expression of the replete and happy lover she so wished for him to be!

His mouth thinned. 'I didn't say that—'

'You didn't have to!' Tears of humiliation and hurt

burned and blurred Eva's vision as she turned away. 'I think you need to get off me,' she instructed flatly as she kept her face averted from looking directly at Michael, unable to believe that just minutes ago, seconds ago, the two of them had been— That they had been—

Whatever Eva had thought was happening between the two of them she had been wrong. *She* might know herself to be in love with Michael, but his behaviour now, the things he had just said, showed that he had only desired her, and that he now considered even that as having been a mistake.

'I said get off me, Michael!' she repeated forcefully at the same time as she pushed against his chest above her.

'You don't understand—'

'Oh, I understand perfectly, Michael,' she assured him as she stared up at him, using scorn to hide the depth of the hurt she was feeling. 'Now, get off me—'

'I didn't use contraception, Eva!' Michael interrupted harshly as he slowly eased out of her before rolling onto the bed to lie beside her, disgusted with himself for having been so lost in the pleasure of making love with Eva that he hadn't thought to protect her. 'I didn't use contraception...'

This hadn't happened to him since the situation with Emma fourteen years ago, and it shouldn't have happened now either. The last thing— The very last thing that Eva needed in her life right now was an unexpected pregnancy of her own, when she was already exhausted, completely tied, by having to care for her sister's six-month-old twins. It was too soon—would be utterly disastrous if Eva were to have a baby of her own now.

'Eva—'

'Don't!' she warned as she moved sharply away from the hand he had reached out to touch her, her face deathly pale as she sat up on the side of the bed before turning to look back at him scathingly. 'You're in luck, Michael,' she continued scornfully. 'Because, not only am I disease free, but I'm also, for health reasons, currently on the pill.'

Eva could see the relief her assurances had given Michael as he closed his eyes briefly at the same time as he released his breath in a long, satisfied sigh.

She turned away sharply in order to hide the stinging tears that once again blurred her vision. Tears of pain this time. She loved this man, and he— Michael— This was— 'This is even more humiliating than last night.' Eva flatly spoke her thoughts out loud.

'What "health reasons"…?' Michael questioned slowly.

'Nothing serious, just erratic and painful periods,' Eva dismissed unconcernedly. Discussing the intimate workings of her body seemed to be the least of her worries after the intimacies she and Michael had just shared. 'Lucky for you, huh?' she derided dismissively.

'Lucky for both of us,' he corrected softly. 'Eva—'

'I don't intend having a post-mortem about tonight either, Michael!' Eva stood up abruptly before going into the adjoining bathroom, pulling on and fastening her robe over her nakedness before collecting up the rest of her clothes, determined that she wouldn't cry—couldn't allow herself to cry, until she was back in the privacy of her own bedroom.

Thank goodness they hadn't gone to her bedroom in the first place, otherwise she would have the further humiliation of having to sleep in the bed she had briefly shared with Michael, surrounded by the sheets that bore the signs and the intimacy of the scents of their lovemaking.

As it was, no doubt Michael would strip those damp sheets from his own bed, and so eliminate all evidence of this night. Eliminating all evidence that Eva had been in his bed at all...

'Eva—'

'Will you just leave it, Michael?' Eva turned on him fiercely as he tried to talk to her when she re-entered his bedroom, sitting up on the side of the bed now looking across at her with unreadable obsidian eyes. Eva turned away again. 'This was a mistake. My being here at all is a mistake,' she added bleakly. 'And whether you like it or not, I'm booking a flight tomorrow for myself and the twins to return to England.'

He frowned darkly. 'You're right, I don't like it—'

'Tough!' Eva came back unsympathetically. 'Because I assure you that's exactly what's going to happen.'

'You—'

'The subject isn't up for discussion, Michael.' Her eyes flashed briefly in warning before she strode determinedly out of his bedroom and down the hallway to her own room, Michael able to hear the door closing softly behind her just seconds later.

He groaned as he fell back on the bed, knowing he had handled this badly.

That he had handled this whole situation with Eva badly, from start to finish.

And he didn't even try to kid himself that this wasn't the finish for them...

Maybe if he tried to explain about Emma, told Eva what had happened to him in the past, she might understand his distrust of women, this obsession he had for contraception—

No, he answered his own question flatly. If he had tried to talk to Eva about that now she would only have misunderstood him even further, and the gulf stretching between them would only have widened. If he was going to explain about Emma, and his sordid past, the reason he was always so careful to use contraception—a caution that simply hadn't existed tonight with Eva!—and that his concern tonight had been for her and not him, then he would have to wait until Eva had calmed down.

If she ever did…

CHAPTER ELEVEN

EVA KNEW SHE was just going through the motions the following morning, automatically waking as she responded to hearing the twins calling out to her, before getting up to pull on her robe and going through to the adjoining bedroom, carrying them both through to the kitchen and putting them in their high chairs as she prepared their food, talking to them encouragingly in between bites of their breakfast.

And all the time she did so Eva was totally aware of Michael as he sat broodingly across the kitchen table from her drinking a cup of coffee from the pot he had obviously made earlier, already showered and dressed for work in his dark three-piece business suit and pale blue silk shirt and tie.

As aware as she was that she felt completely numb inside…

Last night had been…beautiful, incredible, pleasure unlike anything else Eva had ever experienced.

It had also ultimately been more painful than anything she had ever experienced…

Because Michael had made it clear he hadn't made love to her because he was falling in love with her. No, Michael had desired her, and it was a desire he had more than satisfied last night. To the point that his only response afterwards had been to worry about whether or not he might have accidentally made her pregnant by not using contraception!

Well, thank goodness that wasn't even a possibility, because there was no way, after the things Michael had said to her last night, that Eva would ever have told him of that pregnancy even if it had occurred.

As it was, the only thing that interested Eva this morning was booking a flight home for herself and the twins.

'I have no choice but to go into the office for a while this morning.' Michael's voice was huskily low. 'But only long enough to make the arrangements for Pierre to take over my appointments for today, and I would appreciate it if you didn't leave before the two of us have had a chance to speak again.'

Eva raised eyes of dull violet as she looked across the table at him. 'We have nothing left to say to each other.'

'I disagree,' Michael bit out tersely, able to feel the nerve pulsing in his clenched jaw, and knowing, from looking in the mirror as he shaved earlier, that his face was pale and grim this morning.

Not surprising, when he had barely slept all night as he replayed in his mind, over and over again, that last disastrous conversation with Eva.

She shook her head. 'I realised long ago that the only reason you insisted on my staying here with you in the first place was because you wanted to avoid the possibility of my repeating any of my accusations regarding the twins' paternity to anyone else. Don't even try to deny it, Michael, because you and I both know it's the truth,' she warned sharply as he would have spoken.

'Yes,' he sighed in acknowledgement. 'But we've both moved on from there—'

'I haven't,' she assured him flatly. 'And I give you my

word that I won't do or say anything more about it until after I hear from either you again or your brother Rafe. But I am leaving today, Michael. Whether you like it or not,' she added firmly, uncompromisingly.

Michael didn't like it, knew there was so much more he and Eva had to say to each other before he could even think of letting her go. Before he could bear to think of her leaving him.

But they were things he needed to say that the determined expression on Eva's face, as she looked across at him so coldly, said that she didn't want to hear from him. Which was a pity, because Michael was just as determined that she would hear him out.

He stood up abruptly. 'I will be back later this morning, Eva, and I would deem it a courtesy to me if you didn't leave until after we've spoken again.'

'A courtesy to you...?' She looked up at him.

'Yes,' he bit out grimly.

That derision now curled the fullness of Eva's lips. Lips that Michael had kissed and enjoyed last night, as he had kissed and enjoyed all of her...!

'Isn't it a little late for formal politeness between the two of us?' she taunted as her thoughts obviously ran along similar lines to his.

Michael's mouth tightened. 'Possibly,' he conceded. 'But I'm asking anyway.'

Eva looked up at him for several more seconds before releasing her breath on a long sigh. 'Okay.' She nodded wearily. 'But that's all I'm agreeing to,' she added sharply. 'I fully intend to book those flights today.'

'The D'Angelo jet—'

'Has absolutely no place in my own or the twins' immediate plans,' Eva assured him sharply, just wishing Michael would go and leave her to suffer her misery in peace; quiet would just be asking too much when in the company of the boisterous twins! 'The sooner you go, Michael, the sooner you'll be back, and then I'll be able to leave,' she added pointedly.

Michael bit back his own sharp reply, knowing now, in the presence of the twins, wasn't the time or the place to have the conversation he and Eva needed to have. 'I should be back in an hour or so.' He nodded tersely.

'Don't rush back on my account,' Eva dismissed.

How, Michael wondered, had the two of them gone from that incredible lovemaking last night to such cold and clipped politeness this morning?

Because he had behaved like an idiot, came the immediate reply. Because he hadn't explained himself to Eva properly last night. Because he should have insisted then that she listen to what he had to say. But hadn't.

And he had no idea whether or not Eva would even allow him to attempt to correct that omission later this morning...

It was almost an hour to the minute later that the doorbell to the apartment rang, Eva placing the twins in the playpen before going to answer it. 'Did you forget your keys—?' She broke off with a frown as she saw that it wasn't Michael standing outside in the hallway.

'Pierre...?' she questioned uncertainly. 'Has something happened to Michael?' she added sharply. She might be angry with him, disappointed in him, but she still loved him, and would be devastated if anything happened to him.

'Mr D'Angelo...?' Pierre repeated with a puzzled frown. 'No, I—I haven't seen him this morning.'

Eva's eyes widened. 'But he was coming in to the gallery to speak with you...'

Pierre Dupont grimaced. 'I haven't been to the gallery yet this morning either.'

Eva gave a dazed shake of her head. 'Then I don't understand...?'

'No, of course you do not.' The Frenchman sighed heavily as he ran a hand through his already tousled dark hair. 'It is you with whom I wish to speak,' he added grimly.

'Me?' Eva looked at Pierre more closely, realising his appearance was dishevelled. He had a pale face, and a dark growth of unshaven stubble on the squareness of his jaw, and a suit that looked as if he might have slept in it. And his perfect English was no longer as perfect... 'What's this all about, Pierre...?' Eva prompted warily.

'I would rather not discuss it outside in the hallway... May I come in, please?' he prompted huskily. 'I promise I will not take up too much of your time.'

Eva wasn't sure inviting Pierre into Michael's apartment was a good idea, considering the way Michael had reacted the last time he had caught Eva talking privately with his assistant manager. But as she was still angry with Michael, and leaving Paris later today—she had managed to get three seats on the afternoon flight to England—she didn't particularly care what Michael thought if he should arrive home and find her talking privately with Pierre!

'By all means, come in.' She stepped back to open the door wider, leaving Pierre to enter the apartment and close the door behind him as she hurried back to the sitting room to check on the twins; they had been suspiciously quiet for the past few minutes.

Although what Pierre Dupont could possibly want to discuss with her she had no idea...

Michael was in a foul temper by the time he let himself back into his apartment two hours later, his morning not having gone in the least the way he'd wanted it to. First that stilted conversation with Eva, and her insistence that she was leaving today. Then Pierre hadn't turned up for work, resulting in his having to call Pierre's wife, who had informed him that Pierre wasn't at home, either, so must be on his way to the gallery.

Michael had stayed at the gallery for another half an hour expecting Pierre to arrive with an explanation for his tardiness, aware with every second that ticked by that Eva could even now be on her way to the airport and her flight back to London; he had absolutely no doubt that if there was a flight available Eva would take it, and to hell with his wanting to speak with her before she left!

In the end Michael had just walked out, leaving a slightly perplexed Marie in charge at the gallery while he hurried back to his apartment. And Eva, he hoped.

It was extremely quiet in the apartment as he stepped into the hallway, the sort of empty silence that would once have filled him with satisfaction but today only succeeded in filling him with trepidation. He was too late, Eva had already gone, and the twins with her!

His shoulders dropped in defeat as he entered the sitting room, for a moment not sure he was seeing what he thought he was as he looked at the twins sleeping peacefully in their pushchair, two packed suitcases beside them, and Eva sitting silently in one of the armchairs, as pale and beautiful as a Bellini statue. 'Eva…?' Michael questioned softly.

She turned to look at him, her eyes deep purple wells in the pale alabaster of her face. 'It's all over, Michael.' She spoke flatly, unemotionally.

His heart seemed to somersault in his chest. 'At least give me the chance to explain—'

'There's absolutely nothing for you to explain, Michael,'

she assured him in that same unemotional voice. 'Not any more.' She turned away. 'My taxi should be here in a few minutes, but—I'm glad I've had this chance to talk to you before I leave. To apologise.' She drew in a ragged breath. 'You were right, Michael—it wasn't Rafe.'

He looked at her blankly. 'What wasn't Rafe?'

She still didn't look at him as she gave a humourless smile. 'He isn't the twins' father.'

'He isn't?'

'No,' she confirmed tightly.

'How can you possibly know that?'

'Possibly because I had a visit this morning from the man who is!'

Michael gave a dazed shake of his head. 'What? Who? How would he know to come here?' he questioned sharply. 'No one else even knew you were staying here!'

Eva still couldn't look at Michael but she could hear the confusion in his voice. 'Did you see Pierre at the gallery this morning?' she prompted huskily.

Michael gave a start. 'No, he didn't turn up for work today—Pierre?' he echoed sharply. 'Are you telling me that Pierre is the twins' father?' His eyes were wide with shock.

That was exactly what Eva was telling him!

Pierre Dupont. Married Pierre Dupont. Married and father of two Pierre Dupont. And now—now, it seemed, the father of four!

Eva stood up restlessly. 'Apparently he hadn't realised, had no idea of my connection to Rachel until I mentioned her name yesterday morning. When he looked after the twins for me he noticed—' She breathed deeply. 'He realised then that, apart from the colour of their eyes, Sam and Sophie look very much like his other two children. Which was when he did the maths, and came up with the correct answer that he's the twins' father. He was the one involved with Rachel when she came to Paris last year, Michael,' she explained as he still looked stunned. 'The two of them met right here in the gallery, and, because Pierre is married, he gave her a false name—'

'Rafe D'Angelo...'

'Yes,' Eva confirmed dully. 'In the certainty, he said, that there would never be any reason for her to realise he had lied,' she added bitterly. 'Apparently he's done it before, several times in fact, and after that first day he always arranges to meet those women for lunch or dinner well away from the gallery.' Eva still felt deeply shocked by Pierre's confession this morning, hadn't so much as thought of him as a possibility for being the twins' father. How could she have when Rachel had told her quite clearly that the father of the twins was Rafe D'Angelo?

But Eva could visualise it all now, Rachel and Pierre's initial meeting, the mutual attraction, the married Pierre giving Rachel a false name so that he might carry out his illicit affair with the fun-loving Englishwoman. Now that Eva knew the truth, the handsome and charming Pierre was exactly the sort of man Rachel would have been attracted to!

Which explained why, when Eva had thought Michael was Rafe that first day, she'd had such difficulty imagining Rachel and Michael together; Michael was far too complex a character for Rachel's tastes.

But, unfortunately, not Eva's...

She loved Michael with all of those complexities. Maybe because of those complexities; he certainly wasn't a man who would ever bore her, as she had so often been bored by men in the past. As for their lovemaking...! Michael was as complex in that as he was in everything else, which deepened the connection to far beyond the physical. To a degree that Eva knew no other man would ever measure up to the depth of passion and pleasure she had shared with Michael last night.

None of which altered the fact that she had been wrong. That Rafe D'Angelo wasn't the twins' father after all.

That she and the twins had been staying at Michael's apartment under false pretences...

And she couldn't stay here a moment longer, had to leave, before she broke down completely. 'So I was wrong all along, Michael, and you were right; Rafe isn't the twins' father,' she repeated evenly. 'And I apologise for—for any distress I may have caused you and your family.'

'Eva—'

'The twins and I are booked on the afternoon flight back to England—' she bent to collect her shoulder bag from beside the chair where she had been sitting moments ago '—and the taxi will be arriving any minute to take us to the airport, so—'

'Eva, I'm sorry!'

She did look at him now, not feeling in the least encouraged by the grimness of Michael's expression as he looked across at her with those unreadable black eyes. 'You have nothing to apologise for, Michael.' She gave a weary shake of her head. 'I made a mistake—God, when I think of the even worse mistake I could have made if you hadn't stopped me!' She groaned achingly. 'I could have just barged into Rafe's life with my accusations and ruined his marriage before it had even begun!'

Michael was very aware of that, had always been aware of that, which was why he had behaved in the way that he had. But that wasn't what concerned him now... 'What is Pierre going to do about this situation?'

Eva closed her eyes, willing the tears not to fall as she caught her bottom lip briefly between her teeth. 'I— He has to talk to his wife. Confess all, I suppose—no hiding the fact that he's a serial adulterer with the evidence of Sam and Sophie to prove it!—and see how she reacts to the news of the twins' existence.'

'How does he think she'll react?'

Eva's smile was bitter as she opened her eyes again. 'He has absolutely no idea, has apparently been up all night going over and over in his mind what he should do. He finally decided to come to me this morning and confess all.' She grimaced. 'Confessing his infidelities to his wife may be a little more difficult.'

'Deservedly so,' Michael bit out grimly, disgusted by his assistant manager's behaviour, in not only using Archangel to meet these other women, but using his brother's name to do so.

The latter Michael believed the three brothers should perhaps take some of the blame for; none of them had ever been at any of the Archangel galleries long enough to have realised Pierre's duplicity. Something Michael intended dealing with when he spoke to his two brothers next, although the fact that they were now all based at a single gallery, Gabriel in London with Bryn, Rafe in New York with Nina, and Michael in Paris, would go a long way to ensure that nothing like this ever happened again.

At the moment it was Eva and the twins who were of prime importance to him. 'What are the options?'

She swallowed again. 'She divorces him, taking his other two children with her. She stays with him, and the two of them continue on as before. Or—or she stays with him and—and agrees to accept the twins into their own family—'

'Over my dead body!' Michael exploded as he crossed the room to lightly grasp the tops of Eva's arms. 'That isn't going to happen, Eva,' he bit out determinedly. 'I simply won't let it.'

She gave a shake of her head. 'Isn't it exactly what you warned me might happen if Rafe was their father?'

'That was before I knew you.' He scowled. 'Before I realised how devoted you are to Sam and Sophie, the sacrifices you've made to keep them.' His expression softened as he looked down at the two sleeping babies. 'You love them as if they were your own.'

'Yes. Well.' Eva cleared her throat as her voice broke emotionally. 'The thing is, they aren't mine.' She sighed. 'And Pierre and his wife have a ready-made family to offer them—'

'A family that consists of a womanising father and a long-suffering wife!'

She gave a stiff shrug of her shoulders. 'And a judge would probably still consider that a better option for the twins' future than a woman on her own.'

'It isn't going to happen, Eva,' Michael bit out grimly.

She looked up at him ruefully. 'I realise you're a powerful man, Michael, but I don't see how even you can stop it if that's what Pierre and his wife decide to do.'

'I'll find a way. No one is taking the twins from you,' Michael assured grimly. 'You love them. They're your children now. They belong with you.'

She smiled sadly. 'It's kind of you to say so after what you initially thought of me—'

'I was wrong, damn it!'

'But it doesn't change the fact that Pierre is their biological father,' Eva continued firmly.

'That has yet to be proven. Maybe—'

'Careful, Michael,' she warned tautly. 'My sister may have been many things—too trusting obviously being one of them, considering the way she fell for Pierre's practised lies—but taking two lovers at the same time was not something she would ever have done. Pierre *is* the twins' father.'

And Michael couldn't accept that Sam and Sophie might be taken away from Eva. Having come to know the three of them, having witnessed Eva's love and devotion to her dead sister's twin babies, and their contentment with her, it was cruel in the extreme to think of them ever being taken away from her.

His mouth tightened. 'How did you leave things with Pierre?'

Eva sighed heavily as she gave a shake of her head. 'I told him that I have every intention of leaving Paris today, and gave him my address in England where he can contact me once he knows what his intentions are.' Tears once again blurred her vision. 'I need to go home to England, Michael. I feel— I feel, probably mistakenly, that there's a sense of safety there for the twins and me.' She was also, Eva knew, hoping that once she was back in her flat in London with the twins she might be able to think of this time spent in Paris as having merely been a bad dream.

A bad dream she had brought completely on herself, Eva accepted, by seeking out the twins' father in the first place...

But she hadn't expected to discover that Rafe D'Angelo wasn't the twins' father, after all.

Any more than she had expected to meet Michael D'Angelo and fall in love with him...

Or to be made to realise quite so painfully, after they had made love last night, that it was a love he would never return.

She blinked back the tears and straightened determinedly as the doorbell to the apartment rang. 'That will be my taxi.'

Michael scowled darkly. 'I'll drive you to the airport—'

'I would rather you didn't,' Eva cut in stiltedly. 'Far better we say our goodbyes here, Michael.' She couldn't quite meet the darkness of his gaze—couldn't look at Michael at all without breaking down completely—so instead gazed sightlessly over his left shoulder. 'You've been very kind—'

'I'm not kind—'

'Yes, you are,' Eva contradicted ruefully. 'Beneath that armour of cold aloofness you're one of the kindest people I've ever known. The twins adore you,' she added, as if that settled the matter. 'I really do have to go now,' she insisted as the doorbell rang for a second time.

Michael felt totally helpless to stop her as he looked at the determination in Eva's expression. 'What about the E J Foster exhibition—?' He broke off with a wince as Eva gave a rueful laugh. 'I can't believe I just said that!'

'You're a businessman first and foremost.' She shrugged as she walked over to take charge of the pushchair. 'If you're still serious about that—'

'I am.'

She nodded. 'Then I'll be in touch.'

'When?' Michael prompted as he carried the two suitcases over to the door for her, knowing his question about the exhibition had nothing to do with business and everything to do with his seeing Eva again.

'I really don't know.' She sighed. 'Everything is so up in the air at the moment—I'll call you,' she said again as she opened the door to greet the taxi driver.

'I'll bring the cases down—'

'I really would rather you didn't, Michael.' Eva turned to look at him, tears shimmering in those violet-coloured eyes as she reached up on tiptoe and kissed him lightly on the cheek. 'I hate protracted goodbyes, don't you?' she murmured before she followed the taxi driver down the hallway to the lift without so much as a glance back at Michael.

Michael had never really thought about it before now,

but he did know, as Eva and the twins got into the lift, that he hated *this* goodbye, at least. That he didn't want to say goodbye to Eva at all!

Or the twins...

He had grown fond of the little rascals over the past few days of helping care for them, knew his apartment was going to have the oppressive silence of a morgue once they, and Eva, had gone.

Most especially Eva...

With this need for a hurried departure to the airport, Michael hadn't so much as had chance to talk to Eva about the misunderstandings of last night, and he certainly couldn't talk about it now she had left!

Besides which, Michael fully intended to sort out this situation with Pierre before talking to Eva again...

CHAPTER TWELVE

'MICHAEL...?' EVA'S EYES opened wide as she didn't even attempt to hide her surprise, after opening the door to her flat to find him standing outside in the hallway of the slightly shabby Victorian building she had lived in for the past three years.

It had been four days since she had left Paris—and Michael—and flown back to England with the twins. Four very long and oppressive days, when she had missed Michael as much, if not more, than she had dreaded hearing from Pierre Dupont again, in regard to the twins' future.

So far there had been complete silence from Pierre, lulling Eva into—what she was sure was a false hope!—thinking that maybe he had decided not to do anything about them, that things could just continue the way they had been, and the twins would stay with her. Ridiculous, perhaps, but even so it was all that had kept Eva from going quietly insane.

Seeing Michael again—literally visually eating up his casual appearance in a pale blue shirt unfastened at the throat and worn beneath a black soft suede jacket, and faded denims—was more wonderful than she could ever have imagined. And she had imagined seeing Michael again a lot!

Had missed being with him beyond that imagining.

Loved him beyond imagining too…

'Are you going to invite me inside…?' he prompted gruffly.

'Of course.' Eva stepped back in order to open the door wider so that he could step into the hallway before she closed the door behind him, instantly aware of how tall and wide-shouldered—and immediate—he appeared in the narrow confines of the hallway. 'Come through to the sitting room,' she invited as she stepped past him to lead the way.

'Have I arrived at nap time…?' Michael prompted ruefully as he looked around the deserted and silent sitting room. A room that so obviously reflected the warmth of Eva's personality, the colours an amalgam of warm russets to cream, with multicoloured cushions on the sofa and chairs, several of her own framed photographs adorning the walls.

'How did you guess?' She chuckled softly as she indicated he should sit down in one of those armchairs.

Michael remained standing as he turned from looking at those photographs in order to study Eva more closely, noting the deepened shadows beneath her eyes, and the fact that her face seemed thinner than ever, no doubt a sign that worry over the twins' future had caused her to lose weight since he had last seen her. Unless… 'Are the twins both well?' he prompted concernedly.

'Very much so.' Eva lightly dispelled that worry.

'Good.' He nodded his satisfaction. 'And you?'

She grimaced. 'I'm as well as can be expected when I still haven't heard anything from Pierre.'

Michael straightened. 'That's one of the reasons I'm here.'

She tensed warily. 'It is?'

He nodded grimly. 'Pierre has decided to give up any and all rights to the twins and allow you to formally adopt them, if that's agreeable to you?'

Relief washed over Eva, hot tears welling in her eyes and spilling unchecked down her cheeks, her knees feeling suddenly weak and causing her to stagger blindly over to drop down heavily into one of the armchairs before she buried her face in her hands and began to sob in earnest.

'Eva…?'

'I'm okay.' She waved away Michael's concern even as she tried to mop up the worst of the tears. 'I just— You didn't coerce him or force him in any way, did you?' she prompted suspiciously as she realised that maybe this solution to the problem that had kept her awake for so many nights was perhaps just too good to be true.

Michael gave a humourless smile. 'I would have done everything in my power to do exactly that if Pierre hadn't come to me yesterday and told me that he and his wife have spoken at length on the subject, for the last three days apparently, and that the two of them have decided to give their obviously rocky marriage another go. But not with the twins as a constant reminder of Pierre's infidelity. Something I could have—should have—telephoned and told you yesterday,' he added, 'rather than wait until today so that I could come here and tell you in person.'

Eva was just too relieved at the news to care when she was told. 'He won't change his mind…?' she prompted uncertainly.

'He assures me that he won't,' Michael said hardly. 'And, as I no longer require his services at any of the Archangel galleries, I've arranged a…change of employment for him, as another incentive for him to keep to that decision.'

'What sort of change of employment?' Eva prompted uncertainly.

Michael shrugged. 'Believe it or not the world of art galleries and auction houses is a relatively small one, and Pierre is intelligent enough to know that if I chose to do so then I could ensure that he never works in another gallery again. Anywhere,' he added grimly.

'And that isn't coercion?'

'Not in the least, when I didn't make the arrangements until after he had told me his decision regarding Sam and Sophie,' Michael dismissed. 'Which was when I told him that my own decision is that he will never work in an Archangel gallery ever again.' He grimaced with distaste. 'He saw the…practicality of my suggestion, once I'd told him that I would arrange for him to work in another gallery elsewhere. Apparently he's always wanted to work and live in Rome, and feels that it would be better for his marriage if he and his wife were to start somewhere completely afresh. Whether that's true or not remains to be seen, but in the meantime I have no intention of allowing him the time to change his mind where the twins are concerned.'

'How do you intend stopping him?' Eva looked up at him slightly dazed, thrilled at the idea of the twins being completely hers, and so grateful to Michael for what he had done for her. For them, she reminded herself, because Michael had done this for the twins as much as for her.

'Immediately after Pierre told me of his decision I contacted the lawyers who act for our galleries in Paris and London, instructing them to liaise on the application for the formal adoption of the twins,' Michael revealed huskily. 'Those papers are now waiting at the lawyers' office in London to be signed and formally submitted.'

Eva could barely breathe, had no idea what to think, knowing that, despite all her false accusations of paternity the previous week, Michael had still done this for her and the twins.

Tears once again blurred her vision, but they were happy tears this time. The twins were going to be truly hers, so that no one, and nothing, could ever take them away from her again.

'And you said you aren't kind!' she reminded teasingly through the falling of those happy tears.

'I'm truly not,' he denied ruefully.

'You truly are!'

He looked at her intently. 'And if I were to tell you that my reasons for doing any and all of those things, even being here today, are completely selfish ones...?'

Eva gave a puzzled shake of her head. 'What could you possibly hope to gain by helping me to adopt the twins?'

The moment of truth, Michael realised. The reason he was here today. The reason he hadn't been able to stay away a moment longer...

His Parisian apartment had been every bit as much like a morgue as Michael had expected it would be after Eva's departure: silent, cold, and empty. So empty.

He had filled his days with work at the gallery, of course, but each evening he had returned to his apartment, knowing that Eva wouldn't be there, that the twins wouldn't be there. And he had hated it. Every damned moment of it.

He had felt as if he were truly damned and bereft without Eva's sunny personality and warmth to come home to, without the twins' antics to laugh about with her.

And he couldn't stand the distance yawning between them another moment longer, so moved down on his haunches beside Eva's chair before taking one of her hands in his. 'Eva—' He broke off, his voice very hoarse as his fingers lightly caressed hers. 'There's one detail on the adoption application that hasn't been filled in yet.'

'Oh?' Her expression became wary again.

'Nothing for you to worry about,' he assured firmly. 'I just—I wanted—Eva, you misunderstood me the other evening!'

And warier still... 'About what?' she prompted distantly.

Michael released her hand to stand up restlessly. 'I didn't—I wasn't—' Damn it, this indecisiveness wasn't like him! 'The reason for my concern, about our not having used contraception that night, was for your benefit, not mine,' he bit out forcefully. 'You already have the twins, and they're so young still, and I thought an unexpected pregnancy of your own would be a very bad idea right now.'

Her cheeks were flushed a fiery red, her gaze no longer meeting his. 'You're right, a very bad idea. For you as well as me. Which is why—why I quickly assured you that you had no need to worry about it—'

'I told you, I'm not worried on my own account, Eva,' he insisted fiercely. 'We could have another set of twins immediately for all I care. Three sets! We would cope. I just—' He thrust his hands into the pockets of his denims. 'I didn't—I don't want it to happen like that for you. For us,' he added huskily.

Questioningly, it seemed to Eva, almost afraid to hope, and yet knowing that hope was growing, building inside her, nonetheless.

She swallowed before speaking. 'I don't understand...'

Michael drew in a harsh breath. 'There's something I need to tell you, and ask you in a moment, but first I want to explain about something that happened to me fourteen years ago—'

'You don't owe me any explanations—'

'I was twenty-one at the time,' he continued determinedly. 'One of the three eligible D'Angelo brothers, slightly wild, slightly naïve, and no doubt more than slightly full of myself— Oh, yes, Eva,' he drawled as she gave a disbelieving snort, 'I think I was probably all of those things then.' He grimaced. 'Anyway, I became involved with someone while at university. Her name was Emma. We had a good time together, and I thought I was in love. And when she came to me one day and told me that she was pregnant, I— No, this isn't a pretty story, Eva,' he acknowledged grimly as she gasped.

Not pretty, no, but Eva was starting to suspect it might be the reason for Michael's distrust of women, and surely responsible for his instant and assured denial of her initial claim as to his being the twins' father, when she had mistakenly thought he was Rafe D'Angelo. It had already happened to Michael once, and it wasn't something he would ever risk happening again.

Except he had...

With her.

Oh, she might not be pregnant, her pill having ensured that she wasn't, but Michael hadn't known that at the time...

'Go on,' she encouraged softly.

He nodded. 'I asked her to marry me. We were making plans for the wedding when she met someone else, someone wealthier, older, and decided that he was a much better prospect as a husband. The—the baby miraculously disappeared overnight.'

'God...!' Eva breathed softly.

'I told you it wasn't a particularly pretty story.' Michael sighed at his naiveté all those years ago. 'It's the oldest trick in the book, I'm told.'

'She was lying the whole time...'

'Yes,' he acknowledged grimly. 'She tried the same trick on the new man she'd met, and was furious when I warned him what she was up to. None of which is important now—' he straightened dismissively '—except I hope it might explain some of my behaviour this past week?' He looked at her searchingly. 'I was distrustful when you arrived with the twins, first claiming they were mine and then that they were Rafe's, and I made accusations that I'm sincerely ashamed of—'

'I understand the reason for that now.' Eva understood so much of Michael's previous behaviour now; was it any wonder he had been so suspicious of her motives after this girl Emma had tried to trick him into marriage with a false pregnancy all those years ago?

'Yes. But I want you to know that has nothing to do with my worry over our not having used contraception the night we made love together,' he continued decisively. 'As I told you just now, we can have half a dozen sets of twins as far as I'm concerned. I just don't want that for you right now.'

'You said you had something else to tell me and something to ask me…?' she reminded huskily, still too afraid to truly hope.

'Yes.'

'And?' she prompted tensely when he remained silent.

'And I've fallen in love with you!' The words burst out of him, as if from lack of use. 'I love you, Eva.' It seemed easier for him to say the second time, the darkness of his eyes glowing with the emotion. 'The last four days without you have been—they've been hell on earth!' He gave a shake of his head, his expression bleak. 'I can't think, can't sleep for thinking of you, wanting to be with you. As for the apartment—! I couldn't stand spending another single day or night there when everywhere I look, every room I go into, reminds me of you, and your being there with the twins. With me.'

The hope Eva had been holding in check now blossomed, burst free, and she rose quickly to her feet to go to Michael, hating that look of desolation on his dear beloved face. 'I love you too, Michael.' She raised a tentative hand to his cheek. 'I love you so much, and it hurts so much not being with you!'

'Eva...!' His eyes glowed down into hers like black onyx as he swept her up into his arms and kissed her.

Eva had no idea how much later it was when they finally surfaced long enough to be able to talk again, having been too lost in the wonder of loving Michael and knowing that he loved her in return to notice the passing of time.

'Will you marry me, Eva?'

She looked up at Michael uncertainly as they lay together on the sofa. 'The twins—'

'Will be ours,' Michael assured firmly.

Eva gave a pained frown. 'Are you sure? It's an awfully big responsibility to take on someone else's children—'

'As you should know, but they'll be our children, Eva. That's if you'll agree to marry me...?' he prompted uncertainly. 'I don't want some brief relationship with you, Eva, I want to know that you'll be mine. For always.'

'I am yours, for always.' Eva had no doubt that the love she had for Michael, that he had for her, was a tried and tested love, the sort of love that would last and endure.

'Then marry me,' he urged huskily. 'Eva, the only detail missing from the adoption papers is the names of the adoptive parents, and I would deem it a great privilege if you would allow my name to appear next to yours...'

'Oh, Michael!' Eva choked back the tears. 'Yes,' she cried. 'Yes, yes, yes.' She covered his face with happy kisses.

'Is that a yes to marrying me or a yes to my adopting the twins with you?'

'Both!' She beamed up at him.

'I was hoping you would say that!' Michael's arms tightened about her possessively. 'I promise to love you for the rest of our lifetime, Eva Foster,' he vowed fiercely.

'And I promise to love you for the same lifetime, Michael D'Angelo—' She broke off as one of the twins let out a cry. 'Oops.' Eva chuckled ruefully as she sat up. 'This could be the story of our life, you know, baby *interruptus*!'

'I'm looking forward to every moment of it!' he assured as he stood up with her to go to Sam and Sophie.

So was Eva.

So was Eva...

EPILOGUE

Four weeks later, St Mary's Church, London.

'IT REALLY IS a case of how the mighty have fallen this time, isn't it?' Rafe remarked lightly to Gabriel as the two men sat beside each other on the front pew of the church.

'More like the felling of a giant oak tree that's been standing strong and unmoving for hundreds of years,' Gabriel came back dryly. 'Who would ever have thought that Michael would not only fall in love but also become the father of twins in just a few short weeks? And now he's getting married too!'

'And after mocking our own recent demise.' Rafe nodded.

'I'm not taking any notice of either of you,' Michael drawled unconcernedly as he sat closest to the aisle waiting for Eva to appear in the church, his two brothers beside him acting as his best men. 'As long as I have Eva as my wife and the twins as our children I'm going to remain totally immune to your teasing in future!' The three brothers were all settled into their respective galleries now, Gabriel in London, Rafe in New York, Michael in Paris, all of them determined that nothing like the Pierre episode should ever happen again in their name.

'We aren't teasing, Michael, not really. We're just happy for you,' Gabriel assured sincerely.

'We truly are,' Rafe echoed just as sincerely. 'Eva is beautiful. And the two of you are perfect for each other.'

'Thank you,' Michael accepted softly.

'And we aren't just saying that because you managed to secure the second E J Foster exhibition as well as a wife!' Rafe couldn't resist adding teasingly.

'Enjoy it while you can, Rafe, but I'm going to have the last laugh…' Michael assured dryly.

'How so?' Gabriel prompted cautiously.

Michael grinned unabashedly. 'It was my suggestion that Eva have Bryn and Nina as her bridesmaids, and it was a stroke of genius on her part to have Bryn carry Sophie as the third bridesmaid, and Nina carry Sam as the ring-bearer. The two of them fell instantly in love with the little darlings, and I have no doubt that the two of you are going to be in for some serious wheedling about having children of your own later this evening!'

'Fine with me,' Rafe murmured smugly.

'Me too.' Gabriel nodded happily.

'God, we're a sappy lot, aren't we?' Michael murmured ruefully. He thought about the house they were in the process of buying in Paris, with a garden for the twins to play in.

'And happy to be so——' Rafe broke off what he had been about to say as the organist began to play the wedding march, the three brothers rising quickly to their feet.

Michael turned proudly to watch as his bride, as his beloved Eva, walked down the aisle towards him, a vision in white satin and lace, their love shining brightly as they gazed into each other's eyes.

The love of a lifetime.

And a lifetime to love…

* * * * *

Join Britain's BIGGEST Romance Book Club

50% OFF your first parcel

- **EXCLUSIVE offers every month**
- **FREE delivery direct to your door**
- **NEVER MISS a title**
- **EARN Bonus Book points**

Call Customer Services
0844 844 1358*

or visit
millsandboon.co.uk/subscriptions

* This call will cost you 7 pence per minute plus your phone company's price per minute access charge.